PRAISE FOR
SEARCH FOR THE GOLDEN SERPENT

'One of the things I absolutely loved is that Luciana Cavallaro has
clearly done her research. She so vividly describes past cultures that
we very rarely read about in historical fiction that you feel like
you're really there.'
Carrie Slager—The Mad Reviewer

'This novel not only whisks you away into adventure, but it also
vividly shows the mystique of ancient civilisations and religions. It
is a true delight, particularly for those who love mythology and the
hero's adventure.'
Linnea Tanner—Author of *Apollo's Raven*

SEARCH FOR THE GOLDEN SERPENT

SERVANT OF THE GODS: BOOK ONE

Also by Luciana Cavallaro

Accursed Women: A Collection of Short
Stories

SEARCH FOR THE GOLDEN SERPENT

SERVANT OF THE GODS: BOOK ONE

Luciana Cavallaro

Mythos Publications
PERTH, AUSTRALIA

Mythos Publications
PO Box 7120
Perth, WA, 6152
Australia
www.luccav.com

Publisher's Note: This is a work of fiction. Names, characters, places, and incidents are a product of the author's imagination. Locales and public names are sometimes used for atmospheric purposes. Any resemblance to actual people, living or dead, or to businesses, companies, events, institutions, or locales is completely coincidental.

Book Layout ©2013 BookDesignTemplates.com

Cover designed by Scarlett Rugers Design www.scarlettrugers.com

Ordering Information:
Quantity sales. Special discounts are available on quantity purchases by corporations, associations, and others. For details, contact the "Special Sales Department" at the address above.

Search for the Golden Serpent/ Luciana Cavallaro. -- 1st ed.
ISBN 978-0-9874737-6-9

Acknowledgements

Writing is a solitary profession yet the creation of a book takes many people. This story has had many transformations and its final rendition would not have made it without the help of wonderful and giving individuals. First, thank you Michael Albany, who was kind enough to give up his precious time, even during the serious illness of his lovely wife Inta, to read, edit and give feedback. Second, my amazing beta-readers, each with a different approach to the story, provided constructive comments which helped so much in the final composition. Thank you Anne Frandi-Coory, Rosary McQuestion, fellow independent authors and, Craig Pendlebury, historical reader aficionado.

I'm also grateful to Sally Odgers, Australian writer and editor of Affordable Manuscript Assessments for her unfailing ability to pick out and improve my manuscripts.

This past year has been a difficult one, as I struggled with professional and personal issues. If it wasn't for my life coach, Bronwen Kerr of InspiredtoB, keeping me on the "train track", I'd still be veering in different directions. Her unending compassion and astute ability to keep me focussed has enabled me to reach my goal and keep moving forward. Thank you Bron, you are amazing and inspiring.

To my family, who are always there and supportive. I would like to thank my parents, Lucia and Frank, and sister Flavia, brother-in-law Gavin, nephew Brandon and niece Imogen. And to my sister Vivian a big thank you, for her reassurance and encouragement and the occasional kick in the butt when I needed it. By the way, I'm just getting started.

Great deeds are usually wrought at great risks.

—HERODOTUS, *THE HISTORIES*

PROLOGUE

He's been having these strange dreams. Could they be messages or lost memories?

In one, Evan carried a sword and shield, in another he was in a building made from stone. It looked familiar yet not. There were other people in his dreams. They were wearing clothes from another time. He chatted to them as if he knew them. In another he was drawn to a woman. She had long dark curly hair, an oval face and light blue eyes. Tall and statuesque, she reminded him of the marble statues from Greek and Roman times. There was something else; the way others spoke to her indicated she was a leader.

At first, the dreams were snippets of images, like the shorts from a film, but none of it made sense. He ignored them for after all, what are dreams? Just your subconscious talking to you, bits of information picked up during the day. Well, that's what he thought. Now he was not so sure. It was similar to déjà vu. As though he'd seen it before or had experienced it already.

He did not believe in the strange and supernatural but this latest experience was too bizarre. Something unusual happened to him last night while sleeping. Thinking about it made him uneasy. Most people said he was reliable, honest and a realist. Given the events of the last few days along with the nocturnal jaunt, he admitted to being rattled.

It prompted him to research.

He found nothing useful.

He looked up dreams on the internet and it spat out a plethora of listings for dream dictionaries. The word "sword" related to strength, ambition, and competitiveness; a "shield" referred to protection—emotional, physical and spiritual; a "building" represented the self and body. None of it explained the purpose of his dreams.

Last night's nightmare fell into the category of "Nutsville". He fell asleep without a hitch and then found himself drowning, being sucked into a vortex. He knew people dreamed of drowning but in his case, it happened!

Dragged into the watery depths, he watched as the light from the surface of the sea faded and darkness swelled. He tried to swim but arms and legs floundered as a baby's did when immersed in a tub. Water gurgled in his ears, loud yet muffled, as though wool wrapped his head. Water bored into his nose, searing a trail to his brain. His lungs burned and still he kept sinking, as something dragged him in deeper. An experience like this cannot be imagined, he thought as sea water licked his tongue.

His eyes fluttered and he tried to wake up.

His fingers grazed something. He shuddered. It was viscous and limp. An object floated into view. He screamed. A horrific creature came at him, mouth open and dark eyes staring. Water flooded into his mouth, but he was unable to stop screaming. He tried to get away. Arms propelled him backwards as fast as possible until he ploughed into something flaccid. His heart raced like a galloping horse as he pushed it away. Then his fingers got caught in its twisting coils.

This cannot be happening. It's not real!

He tried to pull free from the ever-clutching tendrils when the face of death swam into view. *Wake up! Wake up!* His brain recoiled, and he began to hyperventilate. In gushed more water. He spun one way then the other to get away, yet a mob of bodies surrounded him, faces distorted and bloated. Their expressions were frozen, a grim parody of the living. They reached out to him, as if to embrace him in their eternal fate. They floated closer. His brain shouted to escape but he could not move.

The sun emerged from behind a cloud, and light sliced through the depths. It beckoned him. He kicked hard. Desperate hands grappled at his feet, fingertips grazed his skin. He had eyes only for that shimmering glow. A surge of adrenaline jolted his body, and he swam towards that beacon.

His head broke through the water's surface, mouth open wide to draw in his first breath. He heaved and seawater spewed forth like a geyser. He laboured to draw air. His lungs seared. Tears ran down his face. He struggled to inhale and exhale, the sound loud and harsh as it echoed over the expanse of the sea. The lungs began to work, and he closed his eyes. He wondered how this could be happening.

The splash of water forced him to open his eyes. *What the heck?* Strewn around him was floating debris: broken oars, splintered timber, thick ropes and pieces of torn sail. With clumsy strokes and heavy limbs, he swam to a plank of wood, grabbed it and hauled himself out of the water. *What on earth happened?*

He lay flat on his stomach, enjoying the warmth of the sun and relieved to be out of the cavernous clutches of the sea. He shook his head and swallowed a yawn. He tried to turn and lie on his back but something heavy prevented him from moving. He glanced over his shoulder.

'What is that?'

He reached behind his back. It felt cold and metallic, round, with the surface embossed. He couldn't see the image. Then he became aware of another item. It ran from his left shoulder to his right hip. He turned his head to the left. His eyes widened. It was the hilt of a sword. The other had to be a shield.

'What in the name of the gods?'

What DID I say? This is not real. I am at home, in bed, asleep. This is a nightmare.

He lay on top of broken timber, a solitary soul amidst the vastness of the sea, surrounded by the scattered wreckage. He squeezed his eyes shut.

'I am at home in bed and not adrift in the sea. This is not real. I am having a vivid dream that is in colour, my version of the Holodeck from the *Star Trek* series. A virtual experience is what I'm having.'

When he did wake, he was home, but there was an unexplained detail. He lay in bed drenched, not from night sweats, but soaked. There was a scent too, as if he had spent the day swimming in the ocean. His skin had a residue of salt grains. He lived thirty minutes from the closest beach and there was no way he drove there and back as he slept. It happened, though he didn't know how it was possible. How could a dream become real? Maybe he had a brain tumour? He shook his head. That didn't explain the drenching or the smell.

CHAPTER ONE

The words on the paper blurred, and his head fell forward, eyes closing. He jerked his head back and stifled a yawn. He jiggled from side to side to wake up and thought an infusion of caffeine might do a better job. He suppressed a groan as he got up from the desk and headed over to the coffee machine.

Evan emptied and cleaned the basket, refilled the cradle, slotted it back in place, slipped a cup underneath and pressed the button. While it processed the coffee, he leaned against the bench, pinched the bridge of his nose and yawned again.

'Did you have a big night?' a colleague asked.

'You could say that,' he said, glancing over bleary-eyed.

'Where did you go?' His co-worker looked at him with an eager expression. Because he was the only single guy in the office the others often asked what he did on the weekends and who he dated. They'd go out for drinks on Friday nights after work but after a few rounds the others left to go home to their wives and children. He stayed on till late.

He gave his workmate a wry grin. 'Nowhere exciting.'

'Aww... come on, you must have. Look at you, can't even stay awake.'

'Let's say this place is way beyond the normal haunts.'

The man's eyes sparkled. He leaned closer and said in a quiet voice, 'Who was she?'

'Nothing like that,' he said. The machine finished and the smell of rich caramel filtered upwards. He grabbed the cup and took a sip. 'Ahhhh... nectar of the gods.'

'What did you say?' his associate said with a laugh.

'Well, if they had known about coffee perhaps they'd still be around,' he said, trying to cover up the faux pas. His mobile started to ring. He pulled it out of his pocket and checked to see who was calling.

'Sure,' his colleague said, shaking his head and smiling. 'Next time you see Aphrodite, tell her to work a little of her magic on the missus.' He walked away, grinning.

What made me say that? Crazy enough with the dreams but now I'm saying weird phrases too? Maybe I need to see a shrink. He headed back to his desk, coffee cup in hand, sat and answered the phone.

'Hi Max... yep, I have the plans drawn up, proofed and ready for presentation on Thursday. I'll be at your office at 10am. I think you'll like our proposal. The specs meet your requirements and will add value to the building... Okay, see you later.'

He swivelled in his chair. 'Jerry, is the PowerPoint presentation ready?'

'Almost, I just have a few extra points and images to add.'

'Make sure it's error free too,' he said. 'Alex, are the big plans printed?'

'One left to complete. I'm still waiting for electrics and plumbing for the library wing to be finalised.'

'Follow it up and get it sorted. I want the plans completed by ten o'clock.'

Alex picked up the office phone and nodded.

Evan turned back to the stack of papers and began the arduous task of filtering requests for the next architectural job. Their reputation for delivering on time and on budget was one of the reasons companies requested their service. It was that, and the unusual designs. Inspired by the engineers of the ancient past, he wanted to emulate many of the buildings that stood the test of time. Their current project was the biggest, one that reflected the grandeur of an organisation responsible for gathering knowledge from the greatest thinkers of the time. Drawings of the Alexandria Library no longer exist, apart from artists' representations. Inspired by those works, he created a unique version of the library. He hoped this project put the company on the world's radar.

It took many years, a lot of late hours and hard work to build the business but it was worth the sacrifices made along the way. To be the best in this industry it took dedication and in the early stages of establishing his business, he had worked alone. Now he had twenty employees and a portfolio other architectural firms envied.

'Boss... there's a man wanting to speak with you regarding a job in Greece,' Jerry said, his eyes wide.

'Greece? What have you been smoking, Jerry?' He snorted.

Jerry waved the phone at him, hand over the mouthpiece. 'His name is Zeus um... his last name is unpronounceable.'

'Zeus? His name is Zeus?' He looked at Jerry, brow raised. This had to be a joke.

Jerry nodded and thrust the receiver at him. His expression was serious.

Evan took the phone from him. 'Hello, Evan Chronis of EC Architectural Services, how may I help you sir?'

'Hello Evan, my name is Zeus Pantokratora.' His English was perfect, with a hint of an accent. There was something familiar too. 'I have a job that requires your expertise. My family's home needs help and you are the person who can protect it from further ruin.'

While Zeus spoke, Evan had the oddest sensation. He was not sure how to explain it but it reminded him of being light-headed after a hard game of basketball or a tough workout at the gym. Then you felt great, those endorphins having spread their magic through your body. That's what he was getting from Zeus.

'Mr Pantokratora, what you need is a structural engineer,' Evan said. 'I could recommend a company that can address your concerns.'

'No Evan, I need the services of an architect,' he said.

The hair on his nape tingled. Zeus, it seemed, did not get rejected often.

'We're rather busy and my calendar doesn't free up until six months from now,' Evan said, flicking through his diary.

'That will not do. My home doesn't have long,' he said.

'Mr Pantokratora, what is the nature of the problem?'

'The foundations are weakening and if not attended to right away, it will cease to exist.' From the tone of his voice it was evident the condition of the dwelling was dire.

'From what you have just told me sir, a structural engineer is your answer. I have a contact in Athens I can refer you to, to assess the damage.'

'Evandros,' Zeus said. A chill went up Evan's spine. 'I am calling upon you.'

Nothing he said changed Zeus' mind. A dull ache started at the base of his skull. *Great, a headache is not what I need right now.*

'Where is the building, Mr Pantokratora?'

'On Mount Olympos.'

Evan's mouth fell open. 'Did you say "Mount Olympos"?'

He sensed Jerry and Alex had stopped working, their attention now focussed in his direction.

'Yes.'

'Right.' *I'm dealing with someone who needs to be hospitalised.*

'Evandros, the Family needs you, time to come home.'

***

Evan was no longer sitting at his desk with the phone in hand. Seated before him, on a purple-lined massive throne, was a towering figure of a man. He had long, wavy blonde hair and a beard. His eyes were blue and so pale they were disconcerting. He wore a silver dress, leaving one muscular shoulder bared and on the other, a gold pin held the material together.

On a throne next to him was a gorgeous woman, with long golden hair and the same coloured eyes. She exuded power and the way she stared at Evan made his skin crawl. She wore a similar outfit though the bodice displayed a generous figure.

It was then he became aware of the others. They too were sitting on thrones, flanking the man and woman, all twelve looking at him. Evan's stomach churned. Bile rose and his mouth watered. He took a step back.

'He looks unwell,' the woman said with a slight smirk on her face.

A man, trident in hand, sat perched on the edge of his seat. He too was fair haired. His hair was short and he had a beard. His outfit was as blue as the sky on a clear sunny day, and he shared the eye colour of the two seated on the central thrones.

Evan squirmed. Their attention was intense and unnerved him.

'Does he remember?' the trident-bearer asked.

The man next to him shook his head. 'Not yet.'

'Should we help him recover his memory?' the woman said, standing up.

'That could prove problematic,' another said.

Evan spun on his heel and came face to face with a younger man. He hadn't heard or noticed him move.

'Why so?' asked the woman.

'If we speed up his consciousness, it may cause irreparable damage to his brain.'

'Hold on here,' Evan said, managing to find his voice and backing away. 'No one is laying a hand on me. Who are you? Where am I? And how the hell did I get here?'

'At least we know he can speak and think,' the woman said, her tone wry.

'You are on Mount Olympos.'

He blinked, and the cogs in his brain clicked. 'You're Mr Pantokratora?'

The man on the largest throne stood. 'I am. This is the Family.'

Evan swallowed. 'What in the name of the...' He blinked, unable to complete the sentence.

Zeus grinned and finished, '...*gods*, I believe you were going to say.'

His legs wobbled. 'I need to sit.' Evan's knees folded beneath him and he collapsed to the floor.

***

Someone was shaking him. A voice, though faint, beckoned. He thought he knew it and tried to remember the person's name. An image of a stunning woman with straw-coloured hair and grey eyes smiled and held out her hand to him. He sensed from her warmth, the comfort of homecoming. In spite of this, her clothing jarred him; that and the entourage of the twelve imposing figures. The one who called himself Zeus walked towards him.

'Boss... boss...'

Evan clutched his head as a sharp pain pierced behind his left eye and spread to the forehead. He was lying on the floor near his desk. As the throbbing subsided he looked up at the concerned faces of his colleagues.

'Evan, are you okay?' Alex asked as he crouched beside him.

'Wh... what happened?'

'One minute you were on the phone talking to that dude from Greece and then you passed out,' Jerry said from behind Alex.

'Passed out,' Evan repeated.

Jerry nodded while Alex continued to study him as if he were an exotic specimen. He pushed himself upright.

'Steady on; you may have hit your head,' Alex said, grabbing his arm. He helped Evan to stand. A little woozy, he swayed from side to side. 'Jerry, get a chair.'

Once seated, the faint-headedness faded, and he began to feel a semblance of normality.

'We should take you to a doctor,' Alex said, his brow furrowed in deep creases.

'I'm fine, first time it's happened and won't again,' Evan said with a careless shrug.

'Still, you should have it checked out.'

'Nah, it's just the lack of sleep.'

'Then one of the guys can take you home and you sleep it off,' Alex said.

'I can't go. We have this job to finish and—'

'Jerry and I will attend to it.'

'There's too much to do,' Evan said shaking his head. 'No, I am staying here.'

Alex crossed his arms against his chest and frowned.

'It was nothing, I'm fine. As I said, all I need is sleep.'

'Fine.' Alex pointed at him. 'But when the clock chimes five, you're out of here.'

'Okay, okay.' Evan raised his hands in mock surrender and nodded.

Alex walked back to his desk, hands in his pockets.

Jerry turned to Evan with a questioning look. 'Are we taking that job in Greece?'

'No.'

'A pity, I was hoping we were.' Jerry smiled and returned to his work.

Was what he experienced a figment of his overwrought mind, a serious health concern or was it real? Either way, the answer was something he might not want to know. A good night of undisturbed sleep would sort it out, but stopping by the chemist to pick up sleeping tablets might be a good idea.

CHAPTER TWO

Evan did not look forward to going to bed that night. He needed a prescription for sleeping tablets so opted for a natural remedy. He grabbed the bottle of Valerian, recommended by the pharmacist, and read the instructions.

'Take one capsule with milk or herbal tea—yeah, right—thirty minutes before bed.' He twisted the cap, broke the seal and took one out. A warning caught his eye. "Do not drive or operate heavy machinery or combine it with alcohol once taken." *A bit of cognac won't hurt.* He did as instructed, went into the lounge and sat on the sofa with a finger's worth of liquid amber while he watched the latest episode of *The Following*.

Halfway through the programme his eyelids began to flutter and droop. Dozing on and off, he captured snippets of Kevin Bacon's FBI character who ditched his partner to find his paramour to save her from the clutches of her serial killer husband. The Valerian was working its magic.

***

'I've been here before.' Barefooted, Evan padded across the marble floor looking from side to side. 'Extraordinary flutes on the col-

13

umns, the walls painted in gold and silver. The detail is exquisite and...' He stared at the ceiling, mouth opening and closing like a fish's. It resembled the sky. 'What the...' It changed from daylight to night, and glimmering stars dotted the celestial dome. There was a constant drone coming from behind him and it got louder and louder. He turned to see where it was coming from and froze.

'SILENCE!'

It was that guy Zeus, and he stood hand outstretched clutching a... Evan rubbed his eyes... a thunderbolt! He knew then and there, that something was not right in his head. Despite the misgivings and what he was seeing, it was hard to ignore. He watched Zeus eyeball everyone before descending the multihued steps. The others fell silent and moved aside as he walked amongst them.

'The Moirai have spoken. They've seen the end of our existence. We must devise a plan to stop it from happening,' he said, voice steady and authoritative.

'Are they positive?' It was the same man who had sneaked up behind him in his earlier blackout. Evan detected a sneer in his tone.

'You understand better than I, Apollo, the truth of their predictions,' Zeus said. 'The Moirai saw our future in a tapestry woven by their hands.'

'How is this possible?' said a woman. She was gorgeous and the way the dress draped over her body didn't leave much to the imagination. Evan refocussed as she pointed to the other women. 'We are immortal! We cannot die.'

'Our fate is not death but worse,' Zeus said. 'Our power will diminish and in time the human race will no longer worship us. We will be cast aside and forgotten.'

Their fear was palpable. The tension in the room was thick and an underlying threat of violence was building.

'This is crazy. I've got to wake up.' Evan banged the side of his head with the palm of his hand.

'So what can we do?' another of the men asked. He was grasping a sword, knuckles taut and white. 'I will visit the Moirai and demand their deaths.'

Zeus spun and glowered. 'Ares, you will not go anywhere near them.' He turned his rapier gaze on the others. 'If one of the Moirai dies, we seal our fate. Nonetheless, there's a way to save ourselves.'

He strode back to his throne and sat. The Family followed him and hovered at the foot of the steps. Zeus leaned forward, and stared at the one who clutched a trident.

'There is one who is able to help,' Zeus said.

This other man shook his head. 'What if he's not ready?'

'He will learn to be,' Zeus said.

A chill went up Evan's spine. Fine tendrils of alarm spread from the base of his skull and bored into his brain. Why did he get a sense they were talking about him?

'This is ridiculous. Just another nightmare,' he said out loud. 'Time to stop dreaming.' He turned to avoid looking at the scene but his head was wrenched back, his heart beating like a rabbit's. 'Jesus!'

Zeus frowned. He did not look at all pleased.

'This is why I've brought you here and to this time,' he said, his brow still furrowed. 'I wanted to show you the beginning of the demise of our Family.'

'Listen Mr Pantokratora, I don't know what you're up to or what drug or combination of drugs you are taking but this has got to stop,'

Evan said, backing away. 'I don't care who you think you are or what your problem is. It has nothing to do with me.'

'But it does,' Zeus said, eyes narrowed. 'You are experiencing a series of visions of an age long gone, of people and unusual places. Images you cannot explain yet which provide familiarity, a sense of belonging.'

Evan gaped at him. 'How could you know this?'

'I put them there,' he said.

It took Evan a few seconds to comprehend what he had heard and to decide what to say, and then it all tumbled out. Words were jettisoned from his mouth, machine gun fire, rapid and sharp. 'What nonsense is this? Have you drugged me? I will call the police and see to it you are charged with kidnapping and abuse! Then I will sue you for all you've got and not only that, I will come after your "Family"!' He could not stop shaking, as hot blood stirred and pounded in his veins.

Zeus gazed at him with an amused expression. 'Are you finished?'

Evan gawped at him and began to splutter, spit flying everywhere. 'You son of a—'

'That is more than enough.' Zeus' light steel blue eyes hardened. Evan flinched as the older man reached out and squeezed his shoulder. His knees buckled. 'I brought you here to show you the calamity that befalls our Family and to witness what none of the other gods have seen.' He lowered his face within millimetres of Evan's. 'Do I have your attention?'

The young man grimaced and tried to dislodge Zeus' hand but he clamped even tighter.

'Fine,' he said through clenched teeth. Zeus released the pressure and Evan sighed in relief, but Zeus did not remove his hand.

'Good. Now watch and listen,' he said. With his free hand, he turned to the now still images of his Family. The figures wavered and disappeared as did the building they were in. They stood atop a mountain surrounded by a huge expanse of desert and craggy outcrops.

'Where are we?'

'On Mount Sinai.'

'We're in Egypt?'

Zeus nodded and pointed. 'Now just watch.'

Evan turned. He saw a man, staff in hand, climb an unwieldy path, a steep incline, and head in their direction. In the plains below hordes of people gathered, and the hum of their voices carried to where they stood. Goose bumps formed on his arms and the hair on his neck prickled.

'Who is that?' His voice was so soft he didn't expect Zeus to answer the question.

'That is Moses.'

He blinked. 'Moses! The man given the Ten Commandments and rules for the Jewish religion?'

Zeus nodded, his jaw tight. 'The one and the same.'

Evan choked back a snort. 'This is crazy. I'm not really here. Now I am sure I have a tumour, it's the only explanation.'

'You do not have a tumour,' Zeus said.

'Well that's a relief, I guess. Then I must be crazy, it's the most reasonable explanation for what is happening.'

'No, you are not crazy.' Zeus sighed. 'I brought you here to witness the event that was the onset of our Family's downfall. About three thousand five hundred years ago, I observed unrest in the city of Thebes and decided to investigate. The Aegyptian Pharaoh

Neferhotep the First did not like, nor did he allow the teachings of this new sect, and forced them to leave his city. Moses spoke of a new god and of his benevolence. His name was Yahweh. He offered to lead them to a new home where they could worship this god without persecution or oppression. They say they honour one god for no other exists.'

'And what does this have to do with me?'

'You and your people can stop it.'

'Hate to be the bearer of bad tidings, but it has happened. People believe in one god,' Evan said, brows arched. 'Well, a majority do.'

Zeus smiled and tapped the side of his nose. 'Your reality is not what it seems.'

'Huh? What do you mean?'

'Your current position, or rather life, is one I created.'

'That is not possible.' Evan shook his head and took a step back. 'My life is not real? This is not real.' He pointed at the ground. 'You don't exist, none of this does. It's a stupid dream.' He took a step, ready to walk away but then a chime caught his ear. The ringing grew louder and persistent. 'What is that?' A cacophony of voices and background music permeated the air.

***

'Good morning viewers and welcome to Tuesday's morning show. Before we get into the great stories we have for you, what is the news for today, Anne?'

Groggy, mind numb with fatigue, Evan stared at the television. He struggled to sit up and grimaced, neck stiff from falling asleep on the sofa. There was that ringing again. With a groan, he pulled himself upright and reached for the mobile.

'Hello?'

'It was not a dream,' the voice said. It was as if the line crossed and linked with another person's conversation.

'Hello? Hello! Boss, it's me, Jerry.'

'What?' His head was throbbing and his back resisted attempts at straightening. 'What do you mean it wasn't a dream?'

'It was not a dream,' the voice repeated. This time it was clearer, just like one of those party lines, though he knew for certain he did not subscribe to such a service.

'Man, I can't do this.'

'Hey boss, what are you talking about?' Jerry sounded confused.

'Did you hear another voice on the line?'

'What voice?'

'Never mind.' Evan dropped his head into his hand, and clutched his forehead, pressing thumb and index finger into his temple. 'Why are you calling so early?'

'It's eight o'clock, boss,' Jerry said with a hint of humour.

'Oh, right. Are you at the office?'

'Yeah, thought I'd get an early start and finish up those plans so when you come in they're ready, but that's not why I rang.'

'Something wrong?'

'No,' then Jerry paused. 'That guy Zeus rang.' Evan's head jerked upright. 'He offered to cover all expenses for travel and accommodation, plus a generous fee for your services, on top of the usual charges.' Jerry went quiet. 'Boss... this job could put the company on the global map.'

Evan didn't answer straight away. His head swam with last night's latest venture plus he wasn't feeling well. It was possible the Valerian had side effects and he should have heeded the warning not to drink alcohol.

'What do you want to do, boss?'

He sighed, leaned back and stared up at the ceiling. 'Let me think on it and we'll have a meeting to discuss it.'

'Okay, see you later.' Jerry hung up.

There were no other voices on the line but he waited to make sure, then pressed the button to end the call. It was time to make an appointment to see the doctor. While he was at it, he'd do a bit of research into the Greek gods and the history of Greece. He'd refresh his knowledge and perhaps learn something new.

CHAPTER THREE

It turned out there was nothing wrong with him. The doctor ordered CT scans and if an anomaly was present in the image, then it was off to see a neurosurgeon. He was relieved the tests were clear, but it didn't explain the odd nocturnal experiences. The GP suggested attending a sleep clinic where they could record his brain patterns. It might provide answers and track the activity of his mind as he slept.

The clinic was situated in a private hospital and from the number of patients sleep disorder was a common problem with more men than women seeking help. Evan sat in a comfortable chair in the waiting room, paperwork signed and payment for admission completed. A nurse with a clipboard called his name a few minutes later. She led him into a room where she recorded his blood pressure, weight and medical history. He asked her what the most common sleeping problem was. She told him most patients had issues with snoring and sleep apnoea.

Later he was shown to a room where a bed was attached to a few monitors and a multitude of cables. The array of technology did little to lessen his nerves. Once changed into shorts and a t-shirt, he got into bed and waited. He'd brought a book with him and picked it up to read. Just as he flipped to the first page, a man dressed in black trousers and a cream shirt entered the room. Evan placed the book on his lap.

'Hello Evan, my names is James. I will be your doctor while you're here.' He was an older man, nearing sixty, with grey hair and brown eyes. He had a skinny frame, standing a few inches shy of six feet, and looked as if he kept fit. He smiled, eyes crinkling at the corners. 'You've been experiencing sleeplessness.' He glanced at the documents on the clipboard he held.

'That and vivid dreams,' Evan said.

'We'll find out what is going on,' the doctor said with confidence. 'What we hope to determine is what happens when you sleep. We measure the brain waves and the frequency of animation. The cables each record different elements: Delta waves, Theta, Alpha and Beta. But we also check Gamma brain waves and the sensory motor rhythm. The measurement is categorised in Hertz; the slower the action the slower the rate. If more active, there's an increase in frequency.'

'And how will that help me?'

'Once we identify the problem, we devise a plan to help you get a better night's sleep.'

'That would be great.'

'I will place these patches across your temples. You won't hear a sound as the volume is turned off on the monitors. I and two nurses will be checking on you during the night. Would you like a cup of hot milk to help you relax?'

Evan shrugged. 'Why not.'

'I'll let one of the ward nurses know.'

'Thank you.'

'Don't worry Evan, the solution is at hand.'

He smiled though in the pit of his stomach the acids stirred. After the doctor left, he tried to get comfortable on the bed, the mattress firm and unforgiving. He chuckled to himself. The leads snaked over his head and reminded him of Doctor Frankenstein with his monster in the Gothic style laboratory. He grabbed the book and started to read Stephen King's latest story. Someone recommended it; said the story was about JF Kennedy's assassination.

He was at the scene where the main protagonist agreed to meet the owner of a local diner, when a middle-aged woman entered his room carrying a cup of hot milk on a tray. The smile on his face stiffened as he watched her.

'Here you are, a nice cup of warm milk to help you sleep,' she said, placing the tray on the table and rolling it alongside the bed.

'Have we met before?' Evan said, the muscles in his neck tightening.

'I don't believe so. How could I forget meeting such a handsome man?' she said with a grin.

He gave her a small tense smile. She nodded and turned to leave.

'Good night, sweet dreams.'

'Night.' He couldn't shake the feeling he'd seen her someplace but where? She was an attractive woman, with long wavy brown hair tied up in a ponytail and light blue eyes. She had a full figure, but from that brief interlude, it was obvious she took pride in her physical appearance and worked out.

Evan tried to resume reading but was too distracted. So much for getting to sleep! He took a sip of milk and hoped it worked. After finishing the drink, he reached for the remote for the bed, and pressed the button to lower the mattress. He closed his eyes and counted backwards from one hundred, a self-imposed strategy to help him get to sleep.

***

A tall striking woman stood in silence, framed by the doorway, and watched a man as he worked at a desk. Her face glowed with love and lit up when she smiled. Evan followed her gaze as she looked around the room. The wooden shelves brimmed with rolled parchments and the walls were covered in charts. They contained detailed nautical maps of the world and geographic sketches of islands and continents hand-drawn by skilled cartographers. The latter depicted the location of rivers, mountains, harbours and settlements.

The largest map was different. Drawn by an artist, it illustrated three concentric circles of water surrounding two rings of land. The more he stared at the map, the more it resonated. Why? A niggling thought tugged at the edges of his brain. It showed large plains and mountain ranges but the mapmaker had included houses, an agora, civic buildings and park land. Bridges and canals linked the terrain, allowing inhabitants ease of mobility. He could tell from the isle's unique topography it was rich in minerals and agriculture, and no doubt a source of wealth for the people who lived there.

He turned his attention back to the woman in the doorway. Though it was difficult to comprehend, and yes she was an exceptional beauty, he felt warmth and stirrings of desire. *Great, now the nurses will witness more than they bargained for on their shift.* He squirmed and tried to ignore the throbbing as it increased. A hint of mischief lurked in her eyes as she walked into the room.

'Evandros,' she said in a soft musical voice.

Evan stiffened. 'What did she say?'

The man at the desk jumped in fright and knocked over a small pot filled with ink.

'Oh Zeus!' he said.

Evan jerked back as if punched in the face.

The man called Evandros blotted the spilled ink with quick movements and pushed the documents to the side at the same time. 'Sibyl, please don't do that again! You scared me!'

'I am sorry my love,' she said with a laugh, bending and putting her arms about his shoulders, and kissed him on the cheek. 'I am off to the market and wondered if you wanted to join me?'

The man turned to look up at his wife and stood, taking a moment to wipe his ink stained fingers. Evan's heart thudded; it felt as if a bass drummer pounded out a solo encore performance in his chest. And if his eyes could grow any wider, he'd swear they'd pop out of their sockets.

'That man has my face, my body,' he said in a high pitched voice. 'Time to wake up!' He slapped his face. When that didn't work, he pinched himself. 'Ouch!'

'That man is you,' said a familiar voice.

'Not you again,' he said as Zeus came to stand next to him. 'I have had enough! This has got to stop. I want you gone.' He spun on his heel and walked away but Zeus blocked him. 'How did you...'

'Enough of this foolishness, Evandros!'

His eyes flashed and his jaw clenched. 'Stop calling me that!'

Zeus continued as if he didn't hear Evan's outburst. 'I have brought you back twenty-five-hundred years to observe what occurred in the hope it will help you remember.'

'You don't get it!' Evan said, pointing to his head, face reddening and voice rising. 'There is nothing to remember! I'm from the twenty-first century, born in a world with every possible convenience. That's it! Nothing else.' His chest heaved and blood pulsed fast through his veins as he tried to keep control of his emotions. He did not want to go into one of his rages. In these, he lost all sense of self and the bloodlust took control. Worse still there had been times when he blacked out and had no idea what he had done until someone told him.

'No one has been able to explain why you experience these inexplicable bouts of fury,' Zeus said, tone even. 'Perhaps what you see next will clarify the reason.' He grasped Evan's shoulders and turned him around. The room was still there but empty. 'The woman was your wife Sibyl, a priestess to the Mother Goddess. You loved her very much.' Zeus waved his hand and the couple appeared.

Evan flinched at seeing a replica of himself and stepped back but the man behind him held him fast. He was unable to move and forced to watch.

'I'd love to come with you,' Evandros said. The next bit made Evan cringe as the man chased the woman called Sibyl, caught her, daubed ink on her nose and then kissed her. 'Shall we go... to the bedroom?'

She laughed and pushed him away.

'Later, but first the market.'

The scene changed as Zeus and Evan stood in the same place. It was like a 3D movie, except they were in the vision. The heat of the sun on his head and the hard uneven surface of the cobbled pavement under his feet felt real. The couple strolled along the street hand in hand. A waft of the heady perfume of apple blossoms hung in the air. They were now walking past a gymnasium. It reminded him of the ruins he saw at Olympia except this one was intact and still in use. An image of throwing a javelin, and practising with a sword and shield came to mind.

Evan shook his head but was soon distracted by the cheerful sounds of people talking and laughing. Behind the chatting and laughter hawkers bartered. He choked back a chuckle. *Nothing's changed; it must be in the merchants' DNA to try to make a sale.*

A noisy and carefree game of chase was in progress as children played on the grass in front of the stalls.

Sibyl and Evandros neared the markets, passed civic buildings, altars, a fountain house and temples. Evan was grateful to have the knowledge of ancient architecture and seeing these buildings intact was inspiring. When he woke up, he would start on new design concepts. His head brimmed with new ideas from seeing the ancient city. He almost rubbed his hands together in anticipation but the looming presence of Zeus stopped any such movement.

The temple disappeared from sight and straight ahead was a stoa, a covered portico, where vendors set up stalls between the columns. In one section, stacked in neat rows, were large urns of olive oil, while next-door in a butcher's section hung slaughtered livestock. A few columns along, benches with piles of leavened bread and bowls of pitted dates enticed a few customers. In other bowls dried apricots soaked in honey and goat's cheese were on the menu for interested buyers.

Evan's attention was drawn to the women, who were the most stunning he'd ever seen assembled in one place. A majority wore a national dress; bright coloured full skirts and bodices. A few ladies were dressed in similar attire to Sibyl, in a khiton. The men's clothes too were vibrant, in either loincloths or a shorter version of a khiton.

Sibyl and her husband knew several people, stopping many times to chat as they ambled from stall to stall. He carried the basket as she stocked it with juicy tomatoes, apples, bread, wine, olives, cheese and spinach.

Evan's heart lurched when he saw Sibyl frown as a woman approached her. *Odd; why did that matter?* The expression on her face didn't go after they finished chatting. His stomach clenched as she turned to re-join her husband. It was as if the glow of her happiness had been extinguished.

'Is everything all right?' Evandros said.

She gave him a quick smile of reassurance and nodded. 'It is nothing. Come, let's finish shopping.' She took his hand and led the way to another stall.

The ground trembled just as Sibyl reached out to pick up an orange. Evan pitched forward, and Zeus grabbed him, and prevented him falling to the ground. Pots teetered and crashed, splintered into hundreds of pieces, the contents spilled onto the marble floor. The children screamed and ran, going one way then the other, looking for their parents. The fear was tangible; he could taste it as the people panicked and lurched from side to side, while the earth shuddered. Then it was still.

'You brought me here to witness an earthquake!' Evan flung Zeus' hands off his shoulders and stepped away. 'What a sick joke!'

'No joke,' he said shaking his head. 'The people are experiencing the same consequences as their ancient ancestors, and face destruction if these events continue.'

'Oh yeah, so what? The history of the world has a long list of natural disasters. What makes this one so important?'

He jabbed Evan in the chest with a finger. 'You can prevent their demise.'

He looked at Zeus, brows arched so high, his hairline moved. 'It's official, you are insane.'

He had the grace to smile. 'I have more for you to see.'

CHAPTER FOUR

'Your wife Sibyl…' he was saying.

'She's not my wife,' Evan said crossing his arms. They were back at the couple's house.

'Your wife Sibyl has left for the Temple of the Mother Goddess.' Zeus carried on as if he hadn't interrupted. 'While she was away you received a visitor. I must add at this point you are a historian, an expert on the study of your ancestors.'

'Who's this Mother Goddess?'

'I am certain you will remember the Mother Goddess and every-thing else soon,' he said, unsmiling.

'I doubt it,' Evan said under his breath.

They watched as Evandros stomped to the front door and wrenched the door open. He faltered on seeing a man who wore a long white khiton trimmed in royal blue. Without a word, he stepped aside for the newcomer to enter.

'Evandros, son of Hermia and Antipater?'

He nodded.

'I am Ikaros. By the order of the Senate I must escort you to the House of Elders.' Ikaros withdrew a rolled parchment from the sleeve of his khiton.

Evandros hesitantly took the parchment, unrolled it and read the contents.

'I don't understand. This doesn't explain why I am summoned.' He pressed his lips together, brow furrowed.

Ikaros gazed back, expression bland. 'I am not privy to the reasons why the Senate sent for you. My job is to ensure the message is delivered and carried out.'

'And we need to leave now?'

Ikaros nodded.

They didn't talk much as the two paced towards the House of Elders. Their walk gave Evan an opportunity to study the metropolis. The place was nothing short of impressive. The architects and engineers must have been exceptional. To replicate just one of these buildings would be a mammoth task. The two and three-storey structures reminded him of New York before the advent of skyscrapers. These buildings, he surmised, would be residential and from the sheer number it seemed there was a large population.

The men headed up a slight incline to a large temple on the summit. Its position signified the importance to the people. On the slopes of the hill below stood a series of buildings, unique in style and reminiscent of smaller ones he saw at Knossos. His heart beat faster the closer the two men got to these. Faces flashed in his mind. Who were they?

They entered the House of Elders and followed a short passage into a chamber. A huge mural of a city covered the breadth of the wall. He had seen it before somewhere, except that one had been chipped and old, with pieces missing. That wall frieze had been incredible, but this was extraordinary. The ancient painting he saw represented a mythical place destroyed by a volcanic eruption. His tongue went dry.

'Is that...'

'Atlantis,' Zeus said.

'Holy smoke!'

This image was fresh, the colours brilliant and luxurious: people on boats, on land, heads peeking out from the balconies of those same style buildings he just saw moments earlier. His head whirled.

Five chairs were positioned in front of the mural, one larger and carved out of white marble. The arms and legs were etched with dolphins and various sea creatures. Both Evandros and Ikaros moved, breaking Evan's stunned stupor.

'You are to sit and wait,' Ikaros told Evandros.

Evan saw three other men in the room.

'Who... who are they?'

'They are your travelling companions. Why?'

'I... ah... I saw their faces... earlier.' He didn't say how.

Zeus smiled. The Cheshire cat could learn a few tricks from this guy. Evan raised a hand to his brow, horrified how it trembled, and dropped it out of sight, clenching it tight. Three people, two men and a woman entered the room, re-directing his attention. They stood in front of the three smaller chairs. The four men knelt straight away and bowed their heads.

'Where's the fourth person?'

'The High Priestess to the Mother Goddess is attending to the needs of Mother,' Zeus said. Evan squirmed at the intensity with which he stared. Few people could make him uncomfortable; the exception was his mother when she was on a tirade about marriage and grandchildren. Zeus made him wary. Each time he has one of these dreams, a sense of foreboding cloaked him. It was not unlike stepping into a condemned building with the coldness seeping into your bones.

One of the newcomers began to speak, the man's tone deep and sombre. It reminded him of the few times as a child going to church and listening to the priest as he launched into a sermon.

'Poseidon, our glorious god, we await you.'

No one moved or spoke. Evan tugged his ear and shuffled his feet. They were protesting at the length of time standing idle. *If this was a dream, should my feet hurt?* He pondered this new development as the atmosphere in the room grew heavy and then his ears popped.

'Rise sons of Atlantis.'

Evan's head jolted upright. 'No... is that...?'

'My brother Poseidon,' Zeus said. 'You may recall seeing him on your visit to Mount Olympos.'

The God of the Sea sat in the ornate chair, grasping a silver trident in his hand. He had the same short white blonde hair and beard. Here he wore an ankle-length blue khiton, clasped at the shoulder by a golden shell. A smile played on his face and his eyes twinkled as he gazed at the men's stunned expressions.

'Come now, gather your wits,' he said.

The men still looked dazed. Evan could relate to how they felt.

'I come at the request of my divine brothers and sisters. We have learnt the rule of the gods is coming to an end and have been prevented from acting. If we interfere, it will precipitate our fall.' He paused to eyeball each of the men. 'You are chosen to recover the sacred relics of the Mother Goddess and restore them to the idol that is here on Atlantis. With your particular skills, success is possible. The lost objects, a golden double-headed axe and a golden serpent, are hidden somewhere in the lands your ancestors once travelled. A word of caution: only the High Priestess to the Mother Goddess can handle these items. If touched by another they will bring about a horrible death.'

Evan's arms broke out in goose bumps. He didn't know whether it was the words or Poseidon's tone and he was not keen on learning where it was heading.

'Oh Zeus!' he heard Evandros mutter. The man had paled three shades lighter than his golden tan and the sheen of perspiration covered his forehead. Evan's heart skipped a beat. He clenched his hands. *Why am I affected?* He shook his head and told himself to stop being inane.

'Though your talents will help on this journey, they are not enough.' Poseidon stood up, a towering and powerful figure. 'Leander, come forth.' The man standing next to Evandros drew in a shaky breath and tottered to the front. Poseidon lowered his trident until the pointed tips touched the man's chest. Poseidon closed his eyes. A bolt of lightning struck Leander and forced him to his knees.

'What the!' Evan hopped back and covered his eyes.

'Rise, Leander,' Poseidon said. Leander faltered as he stood, then stilled. Poseidon placed a hand on his shoulder and smiled at him. 'You have made me proud, Leander.'

The man's face shone with joy. From out of nowhere, Poseidon plucked a bow and a quiver full of arrows. From where he stood, Evan saw the container had unusual pictographs etched into the surface.

'You will never run out of arrows,' Poseidon told Leander, handing him the weapons.

'My thanks, Divine Poseidon.' Leander bowed his head and then stepped back in line.

Poseidon called for a man named Homer; a huge man, not overweight but all muscle, like a bull.

'He's not the same Homer who gave us the story of the *Iliad*?' Evan said to Zeus.

'No, that Homer has been dead for centuries.'

The Sea God gave Homer a sword. Its sheath had the same imprints as the quiver. Next was a man called Hektor who lumbered forward, a bearlike hulk. His gift was a formidable looking weapon; a double-headed axe. The head was silver and gleamed under the wavering light. It was finally Evandros' turn. Evan's knees wobbled as he watched Evandros walk towards Poseidon. The god placed the tips of the trident against the man's chest. Evan covered his with a hand. His breathing quickened as he watched.

Boom!

Evandros fell to his knees; head thrown back, as the veins in his neck bulged.

Blood coursed through Evan's veins, a torrent of molten fluid. His head twitched. Everything slowed, as if time stopped. Twirling lights filled his vision. He opened his mouth to speak but was unable. Powerless, he watched as an incorporeal part of himself drew away and intertwined with another form.

'Done.' It was Zeus who spoke. His voice sounded distant but pleased at the same time.

Feeling as weak as a baby, Evan struggled to stay upright. *What just happened?* Zeus tapped him on the shoulder. He looked at him, mind fuzzy and vision blurred. Zeus pointed to the scene.

'You will keep record of what happens on the expedition,' Poseidon was saying. A silver quill and a black writing tablet appeared. 'Your writing tool will never run dry and your tome will always have paper.' Poseidon stared at Evandros with such intensity, Evan's hands tightened into fists and then loosened. Two more items materialised.

'No, no, no,' Evan said, backing away.

'These gifts are from my brothers. Hades gives you this sword and Zeus the aegis.' The shield, made from layered bronze, had a silver embossed thunderbolt at the centre. Poseidon's face was grim as he clasped Evandros' shoulder. 'Furthermore, you are charged with the protection of the High Priestess.'

'No...' Evan whispered as a shroud of darkness enveloped his eyes.

'It shall be as you have decreed,' Evandros said.

It was the last thing Evan heard.

CHAPTER FIVE

'Mr Chronis! Mr Chronis, wake up!'

'No. No. No.' Evan's head thrashed from side to side.

'Mr Chronis, can you hear me?'

The image of Poseidon handing the sword and shield to Evandros burned in Evan's mind. Zeus' last word, "Done", kept repeating over and over in his head. *What's done? What does it mean?* He moaned and tried to move. Trapped! He couldn't. His limbs were held tight by an unseen assailant. The regulation hospital white cotton blanket was coiled around his body, just as a mental patient is trussed in a straitjacket. Hands took him by the shoulders and gave him a gentle shake. Evan stirred. His eyelids fluttered.

'Mr Chronis!' The voice was insistent.

Jarred awake, he saw a nurse with a concerned expression leaning over him. She helped to untangle the blanket, a feat that took time. Once he was free she took his wrist in one hand and in the other lifted the small fob watch pinned to her uniform on the left of her chest.

'Your pulse is racing,' she said after a minute. A frown marred her manicured brow. 'Must have been an intense dream. How long has this been occurring?'

Evan rubbed his eyes. 'Of late, it's happening more often than I prefer.'

She walked to the foot of the bed, grabbed the clipboard and wrote notes. She then scanned the monitors. The nurse blinked. When she turned to Evan, her face was plastered with a practised smile. He knew what that meant. It was the same expression the nurses used on the day he and his parents learnt his sister had terminal cancer. Her clinical demeanour was meant to be non-threatening and reassuring, but did little to allay his fears.

'You may get dressed. The doctor will be in to sign the discharge papers.'

After she left, he sat there and stared at the bland cream wall. What did the readings show? It's obvious something is not right. *Zeus said I didn't have a tumour, so what could it be?*

Idiot, Zeus doesn't exist. He is a colourful figure manifested in a dream. Besides, the GP ruled out cancer.

Evan flung the blanket off and swung his legs over the edge of the bed, annoyed for thinking that way. The grey linoleum floor was cool under his feet as he stood. He pulled open the cupboard door and grabbed his overnight bag. He dropped it on the bed, opened it and yanked out his clothes. It didn't take long to dress and by the time he ran a comb through his short blue black hair, the doctor had arrived.

'Morning, Evan.'

'Morning, Doc. So... what's the diagnosis?'

'I've looked at the readings and while the brain activity is normal there was an anomaly,' James said.

'O... kay. Good, bad...?'

'I want to study the readings more and with your permission show them to a colleague. We may be able to figure out the cause for the interruption in the brain waves.'

'Right... what interruption?'

The doctor scratched his chin. 'That's what I intend to research and discuss with another physician. There are two types of sleep, REM, rapid-eye-movement and NREM, non-rapid-eye-movement. Last evening I explained how the frequency of brain waves function.' Evan nodded and James continued. 'REM is more obvious in higher activity in sleep patterns and NREM is lower. When in this state, it's difficult to wake a person as their brain is less responsive to external stimuli. In a normal healthy sleep pattern, both types cycle during the night. The NREM sleep occurs in the first part of the night, the REM follows and the phase repeats. In your case the REM was off the charts, not odd in hyperactive brains, but what occurred next is baffling.'

'What happened?' Evan's heart hammered against his chest.

James stared at him, flummoxed. 'While in your second cycle of sleep, the monitors did not record any data. The screens were blank from 12 am until 4 am this morning.'

'Huh? What does that mean?'

'I am not sure,' the doctor said with a shrug. 'It was as if you weren't in the room.'

Evan caught his breath.

'We don't have cameras in the room, the monitors are enough,' James said, 'and the nurses check the rooms. With our patients it's not necessary to check every hour. From the notes on your chart, it looks like the nurse on duty was diligent. It rules out sleepwalking but not the absence of those hours.'

'Could the monitors be faulty?' Evan needed an explanation.

'It is possible,' the doctor said, nodding, 'and I will have our technicians examine them. As I mentioned earlier, I plan to investigate further and find the cause of your disorder.'

'I too, want to find out what's happening,' Evan said. 'What can I do in the meantime?'

'I'm going to prescribe a sleeping pill. The dosage is high so I recommend you take a tablet at 8 or 9 pm. No alcohol and no driving while you take these.'

'Will it affect me during the day?'

'The effects are different for each person. I suggest for the first few days at least have a friend or family member drive you to and from work. If you do have side effects such as burning or tingling in the hands, arms, feet, legs, change in appetite, dizziness, constipation or the opposite, unable to keep balance, stomach pain, weakness, or uncontrollable shakes, stop taking them and call my office.'

'More information than I wanted to know.'

'Important to know,' the doctor said. 'You may not experience any effects but there is a small chance of being affected.'

'Can you tell me why the dreams are occurring so regularly?'

'We still have a lot to learn regarding the brain. While there have been exceptional achievements, a significant proportion remains a mystery. Some people remember their dreams while many do not, and those such as you have vivid ones. While we can measure the activity of a brain we cannot always determine the stimulus. An image, an experience or reading may trigger the dreams. In the same way as a fingerprint is unique to each person, so are our thoughts and what we dream.'

'These... dreams I'm having seem real. I can feel the grains of dirt under my feet, the coldness of a marble floor, even the breeze on my skin. That doesn't seem right.' Evan's shoulders slumped.

'Dreams do give a person the impression they are experiencing whatever the mind has conjured; it's clever that way. In a sense, the subconscious takes over and projects subliminal messages. They are easy to relate to; people know the touch of a breeze on their skin and walking on dirt, toes digging into the earth. The brain retains this information in the long-term memory. When we're awake, our consciousness takes over and what we see, hear, touch, taste is stored in the best computer in the world. Our conscious state allows us to establish reality from fantasy. The brain is at work while we are asleep and unconscious. It processes the information and projects it in a form that is not easy to cognize.'

'So in essence my mind is creating graphic imaginings?'

The doctor nodded. 'Your brain is very active. Except for those hours we cannot account for, it is normal.' He paused. 'What do you do for a living?'

'I'm an architect.'

'You create and envision the appearance of building, from the exterior to the interior,' he said. 'Then follow through from the concept, to the drawing to its physical stage, yes?'

'In a sense, it depends on what the client wants.'

The doctor smiled. 'Your brain thinks through possible problems and comes up with solutions. Makes changes and amendments according to the client's specifications.'

Evan agreed.

'I surmise you are one of those individuals who doesn't stop ruminating.'

Evan gave a slow nod. 'You could say that.'

'It may be an idea to take up meditation, a way to relax. I can suggest a couple of different techniques to do this. One is to sit with a candle and stare at the flame. Your focus is on the flame and nothing else. Another suggestion is to concentrate on the rhythm of your heartbeat. With this exercise, it works best when you close your eyes to minimise distractions. If it helps, place a hand over your heart to feel it beat. Start with five minutes each day and increase the length of time when you've met the goal.'

The doctor then told Evan to ring his office to make an appointment in six weeks' time. By then he hoped to have answers to the missing time frame. The doctor signed the papers, gave them to him and departed. Evan sat for a few minutes thinking of the lost hours and the dream.

I hope the doctor finds something to explain this.

Then, with a sigh, he left the room and headed for the elevator. Once on the ground floor, Evan handed the discharge papers to the women at reception and left the hospital. He paused on the footpath and stared at the passing traffic, his mind elsewhere. He pondered what the doctor said. It made sense but a part of him was saying otherwise. He drew in a deep breath and exhaled through his nose.

An hour at the gym will do me good and then I'll try meditation, he told himself. I'll try whatever strategy I can to stop the dreams.

He walked over to the car park.

CHAPTER SIX

Later that night, after Evan had taken a sleeping tablet, he sat in the lounge room reading the book he'd started in the hospital. Between the tablet and the book, he hoped a dreamless sleep would follow. The main character in the book, Jake Epping, stepped through a portal in the diner's storeroom and arrived in 1958. Evan turned the page and heard a popping sound. He lowered the book to his lap and looked around the room. He resumed reading when he heard no other noise.

Snap! Crackle!

What was that?

Evan set the book aside, stood and left the room. He first searched the bedrooms, checked the bathrooms and went into the kitchen. Convinced there was nothing amiss, he turned the light on to the outdoor living area. He unlocked the multi-folded glass door and slid it open. He stepped out on the terraced patio, and walked around before heading to the sunken garden. The backyard was lit up with solar lights placed in the garden beds. Just as he was to step onto the sandstone paver, his foot hovered. He set his foot on the floor and squatted to inspect it more closely.

'That can't be...?'

He reached out to touch it. His hand wavered over the dark pool. He swallowed and pulled his hand back. The viscous liquid ran down the steps in rivulets, the blood red substance a stark contrast against the pale stone. It formed a puddle at the foot of the pavers and spread across the path. His mouth went dry and his temperature dropped a few degrees. He looked over the garden and peered into the gloom. He jumped, avoiding the steps, and began to search the backyard. As he reached the rear, he glanced back at the well-lit patio. Blood drained from his face. A chill seeped into his bones.

When I came out that was not there.

The vision became clearer the longer he stared. Hesitant, he took a step, wanting to go but at the same time not. Before he could take another, he rocketed backwards. His arms and legs flung out, swept into a maelstrom, engulfed in white light.

***

'Leave me alone!' Evan twisted one way and then the other, trying to dislodge the hands anchored on his shoulders.

'You will watch,' Zeus said, tone implacable.

'I have had enough of this! You are ruining my life. I want it back as it used to be!' Evan feinted a shrug, felt the hands lift, spun away and threw a punch at his abductor's face. Zeus' eyes flashed, and he grabbed Evan's fist with one hand and squeezed hard. Evan grimaced. The pressure was excruciating and he expected broken bones but dared not show how much pain he felt. With his free hand, Zeus gripped Evan's head, the palm and fingers enclosing the back of his head. The thumb and pinkie finger pressed into the corner of his eyes. Evan thought his eyes would pop out, so great was the force.

Zeus leaned in, voice harsh as he whispered into Evan's ear. 'This is your life. The sooner you accept it, the sooner the transition will be seamless. Your current existence in the twenty-first century is not where you were born. I put you there.'

'I thought you said you created it for me.' Evan closed his eyes and willed the agony to ease.

'I did. I placed you in that world. You are a man out of time.' Zeus wrenched Evan's head back and forced him to look at the chiselled features of his captor wrong way up. Cold steel blue eyes with dilated pupils bored into his. 'You will view a series of events until the day you and your companions depart Atlantis.'

Evan tried to pull away but Zeus held his head in a vice-like grip. 'Then what?' he said, vocal cords straining against his arched throat.

Zeus yanked his head back further. Evan's larynx clicked open and closed as he struggled to breathe. 'Then it is time you take your rightful place here, in this world.'

'Not... my... world...' he said in bouts of breathless spurts.

Zeus growled and thrust his head forward but did not let go of his iron hold. Evan saw the air before him shimmer and a blue spinning orb materialised. In the image he saw Zeus, with the orb between his hands. It swelled to the width of his shoulders then an image appeared within the sphere. It showed young women, dressed in full-length peplos; an elegant sleeveless tunic pinned at the shoulders and cinched at the waist. They were silent as they walked in pairs along a causeway towards a temple, golden thighs flashing with every step. Evan's eyes flickered to the side as a newcomer entered the scene.

'So it has begun,' the woman said as she stood alongside Zeus. 'A pity. She is very beautiful, for a mortal.'

'That is Hera, my wife.'

Evan jumped. He didn't expect Zeus to speak any more, not after his rant.

'Must it be her? Couldn't another be selected for the sacrifice?' another stunning woman said with a sad sigh. 'This will change him.'

Zeus gave her name as Demeter and then went on to point out the others. Their names Evan knew; everyone knew of the Olympian Gods but not their appearance.

'This must happen,' Zeus in the vision said, tone blunt.

The women carried various items to the temple and followed a circuitous path into the sacred precinct.

'This is an extraordinary turn of events.' It was Ares who spoke. 'Instead of fighting the Christians ourselves, as we did the Titans, we sacrifice this human to secure our imperium. She's an interesting choice.'

'Is she the right one?' Hestia said. The procession of women entered the sacred enclosure of the temple. 'A youth or child would have been more than adequate for our needs.'

'No, it must be her,' Zeus said.

'Why must it be her?' the Goddess of the Hearth persisted.

'She is pure of heart, an innocent and incapable of wrongful doing. Besides, she is the wife of Evandros. In order for him to do what he must, her death will ensure success.'

Evan recoiled. 'You killed her? You brought me here to witness a person die? Was that her body on my patio? What a cruel b—'

'The High Priestess is your sister.'

Evan fell silent. His sister died a few years ago.

'Are you not concerned he may defy us once he learns the truth behind his beloved's death?' said Apollo.

'No, he is a faithful servant and will not spurn us.'

'If he does rebel, we eliminate him,' Hera said in a dispassionate voice.

'We will soon see how he will react,' said Ares with a nod at the scene.

The woman, guided by two others, walked up the steps to the waiting High Priestess. Evan frowned. She looked familiar. He had seen her before, but where? Though there was familiarity, the woman did not in any way resemble his younger sibling. Dressed in a red peplos, with her hair tied back, the High Priestess gripped a dagger. Sibyl knelt at her feet and lifted her head. She stared at the other woman.

'Dear Mother, here we stand,' the High Priestess said voice faltering, 'with an offering of greatest virtue. We ask, with this woman's gift of life, grant our warriors victory in the gods' quest.'

She bent and kissed Sibyl.

'I wish it were not so,' Evan heard her whisper. His heart raced.

Sibyl smiled, her face filled with radiance and expectation. 'I am chosen and know my death serves in the success of the journey.' She paused and added in a soft voice, 'Please look after my dearest.'

The High Priestess nodded and blinked back tears.

Evan strained and tried to free himself from Zeus' clutches.

'NO!' he shouted.

The woman plunged the knife into Sibyl's heart. A keen mournful wail filled the temple grounds as the young priestess crumpled to the floor. A pool of blood formed around her body. Fine rivers of red trickled over the steps towards the keening women. The High Priestess fell to her knees and gathered the dead priestess into her arms. She rocked back and forth hugging the woman to her chest.

'That is most unfitting behaviour for a High Priestess,' Hera said, lip curled.

'Oh Hera, must you be so unsympathetic?' Aphrodite said, clucking her tongue. 'She has just killed her brother's wife.'

'Little wonder she feels wretched,' said Athene with a sad sigh.

'It is done. Now it is time for the Atlanteans to leave.' Zeus gathered the orb, the image of the two women disappearing. 'We know the relics are in the land of our devotees, but not the locations.'

'Have you thought how to divulge the information to them, Father?' Athene asked. 'Given what the Moirai said we are not to interfere.'

'I am considering several avenues.'

Evan again tried to move but Zeus did not relinquish his hold. 'Watch.'

CHAPTER SEVEN

The setting changed, and they were back at the Senate House. From the preoccupied expression on Evandros' face, it seemed he did not take any notice of the Elders' attendants who left the room. Evan saw him blink and lift his head when an Elder began to speak.

'Your success in finding the relics is essential,' she said in a solemn tone, studying each of the men. She turned to her colleagues as if seeking permission. They nodded. 'There is something you must be aware of but neither of you may speak of it. No one, not even your family, can learn of what you are told.'

No one spoke. Tension and fear filled the air. Evan swallowed back the rising bile in his mouth as the man with his face and body stepped forward. His stomach clenched as he watched. Why did it affect him so much?

Evandros bowed his head. 'Honoured Elder, I pledge my life to you and Divine Poseidon, and will not repeat what I have learned here today.'

Evan bit his lip and sensed unpleasant news was to follow. The other three men stood alongside this man and echoed the same words. Evan heard a door slam shut in his head, as if the fate of the men was signed and sealed with no chance of turning back. Why then did he think this portent included him?

The Elder pursed her lips, as if to determine the best way to disclose the information. 'As Divine Poseidon stated, the future of the gods is in peril but they are not the only ones whose lives depend on the triumphant outcome of the quest. When the Sea God saved our ancient ancestors and led them to this land, a union formed. Our numbers were low and to help populate the place, the gods visited. For centuries this practice continued and to this day, the immortals still come. The plight of the gods is linked to our destiny. Many of us are their descendants, others much closer still, for their divine blood flows in us. As such, if they cease to exist then so do we.'

Evan's breathing quickened, his knees weakened. The four men looked as he felt—dumbstruck. Silence flooded the room. No one moved, but their eyes shifted restlessly, as if looking at the Elders or each other might affirm what they learnt.

One of the men cleared his throat. 'Why us?'

'I believe you already have the answer to your question,' she said.

'Every Atlantean will die?' Leander said, horrified. 'How? Our people's divine lineage is old. Won't that preclude us from death?'

The Elder sighed. 'I wish it were so but this land and people the gods created. Their demise will destroy our home and everyone.'

'What if we leave and live elsewhere?' Homer said, his jaw tightening.

She shook her head and gave him a sombre smile. 'Our unique bond ties our fate with theirs. We can migrate to the southernmost point on this Earth and it will not matter.'

'Then we find the sacred relics,' said Hektor with grim determination.

The Elder rose, and the others followed her. 'Assemble here in two days, at the tenth hour.'

They filed out of the room, leaving the men alone. Leander moved out from the line and turned to the other men.

'I am Leander,' he said, sticking his arm out in greeting to Homer. The other grasped his arm and nodded.

'Homer.'

One by one they introduced themselves. Hektor suggested they leave as it wasn't proper to linger in a building where the Elders convened. They left the room, made their way to the akropolis and into the city's centre. Evan took note of the many trees planted; lush cypress intermingled with palms and firs, which created an ambiance of peace and harmony. Verdant terraces juxtaposed walkways and courtyards where flowers flourished. Crimson poppies, the feathery purple foliage of larkspurs and violets grew in abundance. The myriad of colours was mirrored in the fresco Evan saw in the Senate House.

'What do you think of our impending expedition?' Leander asked.

'I'd say it was madness if I hadn't heard it with my own ears,' Homer said.

'It is a great honour the gods have bestowed on us,' Hektor said.

'What of you, Evandros?' Leander said, peering over at him.

'It will be fraught with danger and we don't have any idea where to begin,' Evandros said.

'Well, I think it is exciting!' Leander said, his eyes twinkling with boyish enthusiasm. He pointed at the ocean, the great expanse of water that sparkled under the sun. 'You do realise we will be the first

Atlanteans since the ancients to leave our home. Don't you wish to
see the places and people we've studied since childhood?'

'I have always wanted to meet the Aegyptians and the seafaring
Mesopotamians,' Evandros said with a grin.

Leander slapped him on the shoulder and beamed. 'There we go.
We have a great adventure ahead of us and wondrous things to see.'

'Mind, Evandros is right,' Homer said, tone as serious as the expression on his face. 'We don't have any clue on what perils we face
nor where to look. I, for one, want to know more. And as you said
Leander, no Atlantean has ever left the island since its foundation
and we know why. We must be careful not to repeat the transgressions of our ancestors or the hunt for the relics will be for naught.'

'I don't believe that is of concern,' Leander said jutting out his
chin. 'In any case, the past is long gone and now we can show how
we've changed. Besides, Evandros knows better than most the truth
of what happened and no doubt will remind us to desist if we go
astray.'

'The High Priestess is more suitable than I to make sure we
don't,' said Evandros.

'You are right,' Hektor nodded. 'She is the one we must listen to
and follow.'

Homer agreed. 'She is the mouthpiece of our goddess and can
communicate as needed.' He paused. 'I, for one am grateful the High
Priestess is coming with us.'

***

'What are we doing back here?' Evan asked as the scene switched
back to the house. 'You know I've had enough. I want to go home.'

'This is your home,' Zeus said.

Evan went to shake his head but Zeus still held it fast.

'There's a meeting I need to attend in the morning and I want to get in at least a few hours of sleep. It is a big contract and if I'm not lucid during the presentation, we can kiss it goodbye. My team has spent months on this project and I won't allow this sojourn of yours to ruin our chances.' Evan felt Zeus' fingers tighten on his scalp. His breath quickened as the pressure intensified.

'You will not be returning,' Zeus said through clenched teeth.

'This... is... not... my... life!' Evan managed to say. He jerked his head, loosening Zeus' grip. Eyes squeezed shut, Evan focussed on the image of his backyard. Bit by bit the weight and unyielding grasp on his head eased. The surrounding air was cool and the blades of grass prickled under his feet. He opened his eyes and exhaled in relief, glad to see the outdoor entertainment area flooded by fluorescent light instead of flickering flames of torches.

His eyes widened and cheeks billowed as if he had the wind punched out of him.

'Nooooooo.....'

CHAPTER EIGHT

'Hephaistos, I want the fine netting you used to trap Aphrodite and Ares,' Evan heard Zeus say. His voice sounded far away. Evan clutched his head to stop it from lolling from side to side. He was too groggy to move. *What the hell happened?* He retched but nothing came up. The sensation of nausea didn't go away. A face loomed close. Evan blinked.

'You've upset me, my boy,' Zeus said, the hard chiselled lines on his face as pronounced as the undertone of his anger. 'You will pay attention to what I show you and will remain silent until I declare otherwise.'

From behind, a white strip of cloth dropped over Evan's head and pulled taut between his lips. The material was tied so tight, it bit into his cheeks. His hands were bound behind his back. He was hauled from the floor and onto a stool. Just as he turned to see his assailant, a fine golden mesh wrapped his body, the weight of the unusual metal feathery. He kicked at it but the netting immobilised his legs. He tried to stand but was unable.

'No matter how much you try, you cannot and will not be able to escape,' Zeus said. 'Hephaistos is a master blacksmith when it comes to forging metal and created this fine cloth of lattice. It is imbued with magic and imprisons whoever it covers.'

Evan turned his attention to Hephaistos, who was a head shorter than Zeus. He had dark thick hair, and a close cropped beard. Ice blue eyes gazed back in sympathy as the smith clasped his big hands behind his back. Scorch marks on his leather apron showed evidence of his trade. His upper arms were thick and muscular as was his torso. Strong trunk-like legs poked from beneath the short khiton, calf length leather sandals protected shins and feet. Evan saw one turned inwards at an awkward angle. The men stood on either side of him.

'Now to watch the rest,' Zeus said, paused and then added with a hint of sarcasm, 'Pretend you are at the cinema.'

Evan scrunched up his nose and sniffed. The gag in his mouth was already damp with saliva. An image began to form. He dropped his chin. They were back at the house. Evandros sat at his desk, moving so much Evan wanted to scream at him to sit still. He turned with an air of expectation and happiness, and a smile lit up his face. Evandros brushed back the hair from his forehead and stood up.

'Evandros! Are you home?'

'These are your real parents,' Zeus said as he left the room. The older couple waited in the foyer of the house. The maturity on their faces hinted at their true age, but their bodies were still firm and supple. The way they stared at Evandros made Evan's chest tighten and a feeling of dread crawl up his spine.

'Morning Mother, Father. What brings you here so early?'

'We bring you tidings from the High Priestess,' his mother said, voice breaking, eyes welling with tears.

His father placed an arm around his shoulders. Evan's stomach quivered. He watched with a sense of foreboding as the parents moved closer, the mother clutching Evandros' hand.

The older man cleared his throat. 'Son... Sibyl...' he lowered his gaze and hugged his son closer, 'will not be coming home.'

Evan's cheeks were wet, his eyes glazed with tears. He swallowed back the lump in his throat. He couldn't understand why he felt wretched and swore to strangle Zeus as soon as he was released. Before he had a chance to compose himself, the image was replaced with another event. This time Evandros, accompanied by his parents, set out for the akropolis. Evan surmised it was the day the four men had to return to meet with the Elders.

The man called Leander greeted them, and his cheerful disposition and chatter made them smile. The tension on Evandros' face eased as they spoke. The other two men had brought their families with them and were soon chatting and learning about each other.

The door to the House of Elders opened, and the men were summoned. One by one they entered, leaving their families outside to wait. Evandros turned to his parents, gave them a cheerless smile, and with slumped shoulders followed the others. Evan's heart lurched as the door shut with a resounding click. He recalled a saying by Alexander Graham Bell: "as one door closes another opens; we regretfully look back to the closed instead of to what the new door has opened". In this case, Evan didn't believe what lay ahead for these men was positive; instead it had the hallmarks of unforeseeable trouble.

The door to the antechamber opened, diverting his attention, and out filed the Elders and their attendants laden with rucksacks. One by one, the aides placed a bag at the men's feet.

His mouth fell open as he stared at the Elders. The woman with the long dark curly hair and light blue eyes stood alongside the Elders. His heart thumped like a jumping jack rabbit. Why didn't he see it before? How could he have missed it? The High Priestess was the same woman in his dreams. What did Zeus say about her? It took him a few moments to remember, as he'd seen so much and been overwhelmed by it all. His sister, that's right, she was supposed to be a sibling. Dazed by the revelation, it took him a few minutes to realise someone was talking.

'Each bag has a blanket, a hooded woollen cloak and a water skin. Take along extra items of clothing, and depending on how long you will be away, you may be required to purchase food and garments on your journey. Interact with the local inhabitants as they may have information on the relics,' said one of the Elders.

'I have a concern,' said Homer, raising a hand. The Elders turned to him. 'Our education of these people is limited to ancient texts and a long time has passed since we've had any contact with them. No doubt they are not the same people our ancestors once traded with. We are leaving with no foreknowledge of these places or the people.'

An Elder nodded. 'Your concern is well justified, Homer. We do know of the developments of the outside world, and not much has changed. After the destruction of our ancestral home progress remained static. The cataclysm affected a majority of places, and skilled artisans, discoveries and the written language vanished. In recent times, they have begun to relearn that knowledge.' The Elder nodded at Evandros. 'Evandros has studied the ancient texts and his familiarity with the cultures can guide you.'

'No offence, Evandros,' Homer said, glancing at him, 'but that information is dated. How can we use it?'

'It will be useful,' the Elder said in a firm tone.

Hektor cleared his throat and everyone turned to him. 'Honoured Elder, where do we start? We have no clue where to begin or how to find these relics. The world is a vast place.'

'One of the items is secreted in the lands of Aegyptos,' said the High Priestess. Evan noticed Evandros did not look at her when she spoke. He did everything to avoid looking at her.

'Is it too presumptuous to ask how you know this High Priestess?' asked Hektor.

'The last of the High Priestesses to the Mother Goddess, along with a small group of Atlanteans, was shipwrecked on the shores of Aegyptos. She hid the item before they left.'

'Why did she do that? Why not bring it here?' Leander said.

'The relics are powerful and together can change the fate of lives but also destroy. The ancestors having been punished for their iniquity, she decided they must be hidden.'

'Why not just smash them?' Homer said.

'One cannot break the magic they hold.'

'What did she do with the other sacred object?' Evandros asked in a quiet voice, head bowed.

The High Priestess paused, and a flicker of sadness shone in her eyes, but had gone in an instant. 'She entrusted the item with another priestess. Their location is unknown as the ship bearing the other priestesses vanished at sea.'

'How long will we be away?' Leander asked.

'Until you recover the sacred items,' the Elder said.

'It could take years, even decades,' Homer said, his tone flat.

The Elders did not respond but the expression on their faces was enough.

'Evandros, the charts chronicled by the ancient cartographers will be useful though you will need to amend the information,' the Elder said.

He nodded, though it was an automatic gesture other than one of acknowledgement.

'When do we leave?' asked Leander.

'You are to return here on the seventh day at the fifth hour.'

CHAPTER NINE

Evan blinked. His mind reeled at the new setting. He didn't have time to digest what he had just learned before he saw Poseidon stomping into the throne room on Mount Olympos. From his dark, thunderous appearance, it didn't take a genius to work out he was angry. Evan hated to admit that he was curious to learn what irritated the God of the Sea. Evan smirked, entertained by the reaction of the others in the room.

Apollo's fingers halted and the last melodic note hung in the air discordant and adrift. The Graces and Muses stopped singing as everyone became aware of Poseidon's march across the marble floor. His eyes flashed like the turbulent Aegean Sea during a storm.

'It is done,' he said between gritted teeth.

'We knew one day this would happen,' Zeus in the image said.

'Why must it be them?' Poseidon said, chest heaving.

Zeus frowned at him. 'Why do you ask when the answer is obvious?'

'They are not wise of this world,' Poseidon said.

'They will adapt or will die.'

Poseidon's nostrils flared. Zeus leaned back on his throne, and stroked the head of his eagle perched beside him while Hera, sitting to his left, was amused.

'Oh do sit, Poseidon, and stop these theatrics,' she said with a careless flick of a hand.

Poseidon's face turned mottled red. He took a step towards her. Apollo and Ares leapt across the floor and grabbed his powerful arms. He strained forward as they struggled to hold him. Zeus sprang to his feet and gave his wife a warning glance.

'Have you forgotten our blood runs through their veins?' he said, spitting. 'We are sending them to their death!'

'And have you forgotten they too will die if this threat is not stopped?' Hestia said, her brow creased.

'We understand your trepidation, Poseidon,' said Demeter, walking over and laying a hand on his arm. 'Each of us wants to preserve the welfare of the Atlanteans, but they are the only ones who can stop this. Our inability to stop the onset of the new god has crippled us, and now we must rely on them. Did we not do the same when the Achaeans fought the Trojans? Each of us had children who were in the war and provided aid as needed. No one wanted to see their offspring die but their fate was set.'

'That conflict divided us,' he said, shoulders sagging.

She nodded and then prodded his chest with an elegant finger. 'This time we are united, and that makes us stronger, just as when we battled the Titans. We will prevail.'

Flick. Evan blinked.

'Wisth yoush stopth do'n thath,' he said mumbling through his gag. 'It'th an'oyin' and g'vin' mesh headath.'

'We have a lot to get through,' Zeus said, tone unsympathetic. 'Do you remember how you got that scar on your hand?'

Evan arched a brow at him. Zeus removed the sodden cloth. Whenever he caught sight of the markings he tried hard to recall what had happened. It ran from the mound of his pointer finger to the outer edge of his palm. He clenched his left hand and fingered the jagged lines. Even now the memory eluded him.

Zeus snapped his fingers. Evan's gaze tracked Evandros who wandered the city. His walk covered all four points of the compass, traversing the bridges to cross from one place to the next. He went from urbanised settlements to agricultural and pastoral lands. He stopped to look at the deer, goats, sheep, bulls, cows and geese that roamed or grazed on the abundant feed.

'What's he doing?' Evan said.

'He's taking a last walk around his home before departure,' Zeus said.

'I wish he'd get on with it,' Evan said, shifting on the stool. His backside was numb and wished he could stand to ease the discomfort. 'Oh great, now we get to watch him sleep.'

Evandros woke with a start, reached out and grabbed emptiness. His face fell, eyes watered, and a mournful air hung over him like an oppressive fog. He punched the mattress a few times, then threw off the blanket and got out of bed. He grabbed the sword and shield and left the house. It was pitch black, and he waited on the doorstep for a few minutes before leaving.

'This is more interesting,' Evan said.

Hephaistos' mouth quirked. Zeus' face darkened like a stormy cloud.

Evandros arrived at a gymnasium much like the one Evan saw in Olympia. But this was no ruin. It had pillars and shelter around the large rectangular grassed area. He knew this was where the athletes trained for the events and had space to exercise. Evandros strapped on the large heavy shield and picked up the sword. He swung the weapon from side to side and rotated his wrist.

'Who does he think he is? A gladiator?' Evan stifled a laugh. Next, he was flung forward, the back of his head smarting. 'Ouch! What was that for?'

'Watching is what you need to do, not give a commentary,' Zeus said.

Evan bit back a retort. Strangling will not be enough, he thought, a scowl deepening on his face.

They watched Evandros stop to admire the workmanship of the sword and shield. Next he did an experimental twist of the hand, the blade a blur. He followed it with a lunge and thrust, pivoted, slashed, stabbed and spun again on his heel. With controlled strokes and using the shield to protect his body from an unseen assailant, he kept moving and swinging. The drills went on for a while until his arm shook and couldn't hold the sword any longer.

He dropped the sword and unstrapped the shield. As soon as the shield hit the ground, he sprinted to the end of the gymnasium. Back and forth he went until an hour later he fell to his knees and hung his head. He lay back on the grass panting and stared up at the stars in the night sky, glimmering like jewels on a necklace.

'Sibyl...' he whispered as his eyes fluttered and he fell asleep.

The beginning of a new day announced itself with the golden glow on the horizon. Evandros stirred and as he rolled over, the hilt of the sword jabbed his side. Eyes still closed, he pushed it away. He flinched and sat up with a start.

'OUCH!'

Evan sucked in a quick breath.

Blood gushed from his left hand. He clenched it to stem the flow, but ruby liquid dripped onto the grass. He stood cursing at his stupidity and bent to pick up the shield. His bloodied hand made the leather straps slippery and difficult to tie. When he did manage it, he grabbed his sword and left.

Evandros arrived home to find his parents waiting for him. His mother, seeing the injury, attended to the wound without saying a word. His father helped undo the straps on the shield. Neither asked what happened. He sat in mute silence as his mother bandaged the hand. There was a knock at the door.

'I will answer it,' his father said. He left for a few seconds and when he returned his face was drawn. Evandros stood at once and eyes widened for an instant.

'Alexina,' he said in whispered surprise. 'Forgive me, High Priestess.'

'Evandros, Mother, Father,' she said.

'Please sit.' He pointed to a long bench with orange, blue and yellow cushions. 'You honour my home with your presence.'

The High Priestess sat opposite the others. She clasped her hands on her lap and gazed at them. Evandros' knee bounced up and down as they eyed each other. His mother took his hand and gave it a gentle squeeze.

'I am here on our Mother Goddess' wishes,' she said breaking the uneasy silence. His knee bounced faster. As Evan watched, his chest grew tight, as if someone was squeezing his heart. Evandros jumped to his feet, forcing his mother to let go of his hand. His left eye twitched.

'I am honoured to live and serve our Mother Goddess,' he said then spun on his heel and ran out of the room.

The High Priestess called out to him but he was out the front door and running. He ran and ran, past houses and veered away from the centre of the city. Evan could hear the sound of his harsh breathing. Evandros at last came to a stop, unable to go any farther. He bent over gasping, hands on knees, hair damp with perspiration. After a while he straightened and stared at the dark blue ocean, the water lapping over his sandaled feet. Evan couldn't begin to understand how the man felt or what he was thinking. The idea of the High Priestess being your sister and the one to kill your wife must be difficult to reconcile.

To Evan it seemed like hours had passed before Evandros left the beach and returned home. He wanted to get up and stretch and besides he needed to relieve himself but it didn't look like Zeus was ready to release him. He stretched his head from side to side and closed his eyes, grateful for the successful crunch. Evan swung his head in a circle, one way then the other. He supressed a yawn. What he'd give to be in bed right now.

Evandros' parents and sister hadn't left during his absence. He stormed past them, and went straight into the bedroom. He stood at the foot of the bed, hands curling into fists, and took a moment before glancing around the room. Evandros seized the rucksack, dropped it onto the bed and shoved inside a few items of clothing and an extra pair of sandals. He then picked up the writing tablet and was about to put it in the bag when he hesitated. He lifted it closer, peered at the cover and ran his fingers over it.

Evan's fingers tingled and images of pictograms came unbidden. 'From the beginning.' His voice echoed what Evandros said. Zeus smiled. Evan felt the blood drain from his face. 'How did I know he was going to say those exact words?'

'Now it is the end,' Evandros concluded.

'That is not true.'

Evandros whirled around and came face to face with the High Priestess. He turned away and thrust the tablet into the bag.

'Did you know Sibyl was to be sacrificed?' he said, the words heated and rapid. 'On the day the Elders summoned me?'

'Yes,' she said. 'It was not my decision. The gods ordered it so and we must obey. Even I cannot go against their wishes.'

'But why Sibyl? There hasn't been a human sacrifice since the destruction of our ancestral home. Wouldn't an animal been enough?'

'I do not know,' she said, tone solemn. 'The gods required the life of a human for the first phase of the quest, and to fulfil a prophecy.'

Evandros sank onto the bed and covered his face with his hands. The High Priestess sat next to him and put an arm around him.

'I am sorry. I wished it wasn't Sibyl,' she said in a soft voice. 'We need to honour her death and find the sacred relics.'

Evandros looked at her, grief etched into his face which then hardened. 'The gods will not be taking any more lives.'

CHAPTER TEN

'Can I go home now?' Evan said in a tired voice.

'This is your home,' Zeus said.

'My home has a queen-size bed and is where I want to be right now.' Evan waggled his head at Evandros who was asleep. 'That is NOT a bed, more like a cot. How can two people sleep on it? From the way he is tossing and turning, it doesn't give the impression of being comfortable either. What is it filled with? Straw?'

Hephaistos scratched his head, bemused. 'This doesn't appear to be working, Zeus. He is not remembering his life. Perhaps we should bring in the boy. He may stir recollections of the times they shared.'

'Boy? What boy? Hey, I don't dance with dudes. Women are more my taste. Ask the guys at work,' Evan said raising his voice.

'Dudes? What are dudes?' Hephaistos said as he glanced at Evan still ensnared in his trap.

'Men, males, gentlemen, boys,' Evan said rolling his eyes. 'Where have you been?'

'Who don't you dance with?' said the God of the Forge.

Evan drew in a deep breath. 'I am not gay.'

The god's eyebrows squished together.

'Jeez... Listen as I say... I do not have sex with men or boys for that matter.'

'Oh...' Hephaistos said his face brightened. He chuckled. 'The boy I was referring to, you befriended, more a father figure, not for intercourse.'

'That's a relief,' Evan said. 'Why, I don't know since this whole bizarre situation isn't real.'

The way Zeus studied him would have made Evan squirm if he could. The fine gossamer net wrapped around him prevented any movement.

'This whole thing could go faster if you made a movie, and there'd be no need to do this,' he said.

'Movie? What is he talking about?' Hephaistos said.

'Evandros is referring to a form of entertainment akin to the theatre except the actors are not performing in person. It is captured by a recording device,' Zeus said.

Hephaistos tilted his head to the side. 'A machine that records movement... interesting.'

'How is it you know what a camera is and your pal here doesn't?' Evan said to Zeus.

'I am the one who hid you in the future,' Zeus said. 'It was decided I alone knew where you were to protect you and your location.'

'You hid me? Oh man, this dream is getting nuttier by the minute,' Evan said, shaking his head. He bit the inside of his cheek. 'Okay, I'll bite, why?'

'You were not ready to confront the individual we are at war with and if you had, you would have died.'

Evan blinked. 'And I am ready now?'

'Compared to the person you were, yes,' Zeus said. He glanced at the man in bed. 'Your knowledge of antiquity and the experiences learnt in the new world will be beneficial to our quest.'

'You see, the thing is... I am NOT that man!' Evan's voice rose with anger, face flushed. 'How many times do I need to tell you!'

'Can you explain how you're experiencing the same feelings as him?' Zeus pointed to the slumbering body.

'Easy,' Evan said eyes flashing. 'I am not a cold-hearted bastard like you and understand how it feels to lose someone you love.'

'Of course, your sister,' Zeus said as he rocked back and forth on his feet. 'Be grateful you had a family, I didn't have to give you one. Nonetheless, that is not what I am referring to, which you well realise. Whatever emotions he experienced, you did too.' He leaned down, his face inches from Evan's. 'That, you cannot deny.'

Evan gulped. 'It is not possible. It defies the laws of physics.'

Zeus smiled, though it did not reach his eyes. 'Divine nature controls the law of physics. 'Our Family,' he said as he pointed to Hephaistos and himself, 'holds that power.'

'So, you are saying...' Evan tried to order his thoughts, 'you can manipulate time?'

'To use a term you are familiar with, I can engineer events.'

'In that case, why can't you influence the timeline and get rid of this threat?'

'Did you not listen or see what I have shown you?' Zeus said nostrils flaring.

'Of course, I'm not stupid,' Evan said snapping back. 'If you tamper with the outcome you guarantee your demise, but you're holding something back. Information you haven't shared with those people.' He stopped, the realisation hit like a light bulb aglow in a unlit room.

'You can't change it because someone else has interfered and now controls that period. Another with the same ability as you.'

Zeus remained silent.

'You aren't supposed to be aware of ...' Hephaistos said but Zeus raised a hand.

'This is why you placed this Evandros... me into the future, to learn the past.' Evan paused, and his mind raced with various scenarios. 'Somebody with the knowledge of the future can end what is happening. Why aren't you looking for this other person?' Evan pursed his lips, eyes narrowed. 'You know who but can't find them, can you? They're a ghost.'

This time when Zeus smiled, his face lit up.

'Why are they doing this?' Evan said.

'I believe you are able to answer that question,' Zeus said.

'Stop being so cryptic...' His mouth formed an O. 'How did they escape? From the stories I've read, the place was impregnable.'

'Hades is investigating how it happened,' Zeus said. 'Now you have made the connections, shall we continue?'

Evan tried to shrug. 'Can you remove this net?

Zeus gazed at length at him. 'No.'

Evan muttered under his breath and then saw another image unfold. Evandros marched along the same white marble avenue to the House of Elders. He had the pack over his shoulder and it bumped against the shield as he walked. The hilt of the sword was visible over his left. It was quiet. The absence of birds singing or the chatter of people was odd and eerie. Even stranger, he was the only pedestrian on the promenade.

A dull drone vibrated and grew louder. He reached the corner, turned and halted. A large crowd gathered outside and stared. No

one spoke. He moved forward with slow steps, and the throng parted in silence and let him pass. When he reached the entrance, he
looked back at the sea of faces and nodded. He placed a shaking hand
on the door and pushed it open. The chamber was gloomy as the
flickering glow of the torches provided little in the way of light.
Evandros jumped as the door swung shut behind him.

'Ah, Evandros, at long last you have arrived,' said a tired voice.
He bowed to the Elders, then joined the other men and gave them a
brief smile of acknowledgement.

'We arrived just moments ago,' Leander said in a low voice as he
leaned towards him. 'Did you see the people?' Evandros nodded and
brushed his brow with a trembling hand. 'I think all of Atlantis is out
there!' Leander added in a hushed but excited voice.

The High Priestess moved from where she stood with the Elders
and took her place alongside the men. She was attired in an aquama-
rine khiton, white sparkling stones adorned the neckline, and reflected the colour of her eyes. She and her brother looked at each
other for a few seconds and then turned to the front.

'I don't have to remind you how important it is to succeed,' said
an Elder. 'The fate of the gods and our people is in your hands. We
cannot help once you leave, and your knowledge and skills will be
tested. Do what you have to ensure the recovery of the relics.'

The Elders stepped towards them. The five Atlanteans knelt.

In one voice they said, 'Mother Goddess and Divine Poseidon,
we ask you to watch and protect our people as they embark on this
journey.' The Elders, one by one, placed a hand on their heads, a
feather-like touch. Afterwards the Elders ordered them to rise and
follow.

The Elders walked to a heavy metal door on the opposite side of the room and formed a semi-circle in front of it. Each raised a hand, palms faced towards the door. A low melodious sound filled the room, and the door swung outwards. The doorway was pitch-black but as an Elder crossed over the threshold, yellow light flooded the corridor. When the Elders had gone through, the men entered in a single file. Homer was the last to pass through and as he cleared the doorsill, the door swung shut. The torches fluttered. They continued along the passageway in a silent procession. A slight breeze ruffled their hair and the hems of their khitons.

'What is happening?' Homer said with a bellow. He bumped into Hektor who came to a standstill after he knocked into Leander, who in turn collided into Evandros. 'Keep moving...' Homer's eyes widened.

To their right loomed a wall, the length of which ran until it disappeared over the horizon. A fresco painted in bright colours adorned a section, the figures so detailed they gave the impression they were alive. In the centre sat Poseidon with his wife Amphitrite, and they watched and smiled as mermen and mermaids frolicked.

'Remarkable,' Leander said in wonder. The Elders urged them on but Evandros' mouth fell open.

'By the Gods!'

'By Triton!' Hektor said as he stumbled out from behind Leander.

'Who are they?' Evan said as he watched the men crane their necks and stare at the colossal statues.

'You should recognise who they are,' Zeus said, his brow creased.

'Well, I don't.'

'They were once kings of Ancient Atlantis, and the one nearest the pier is King Minos.'

Evan nodded. 'His wife gave birth to the Minotaur, right?'

'That's right,' Zeus acknowledged with a nod. 'Important you remember the legend.'

'Huh? Why?'

'You will need the information.'

'I wish you'd stop being so cryptic,' Evan said with a glower. 'Say it rather than dance around the issue.'

'I am showing what you need to remember,' Zeus said. 'What transpires afterwards when you resume this life is still not determined.'

'What I need is sleep!'

'Soon, a little more to see,' Zeus said.

'Thank God!'

Zeus' jaw tightened. 'Refrain from using that word.'

Evan gave him a questioning look. 'What? "Thank God"? It's an expression.'

'Nevertheless, stop using it and other similar phrases.'

'Talk about over reacting,' Evan said under his breath.

'Enough! Focus your attention on what I am showing you,' Zeus said, face dark.

Evan rolled his eyes. 'Fine.'

CHAPTER ELEVEN

Evan drew in a deep breath, exhaled and took note where the Elders waited. He squinted and saw a name plaque by the foot of the statue: King Atlas.

'Did these people really exist? King Atlas, King Minos, Theseus, Akhilleus, Homer?' he said.

Hephaistos choked back a laugh as Zeus stared at Evan with a pained look on his face.

'I am asking because historians and archaeologists haven't found evidence to confirm their existence. Apart from the mythologies, there's not much else.'

'They lived, thrived and breathed,' Zeus said and he ground his teeth together.

Evan tilted his head to the side. 'Why isn't there any proof to show they existed?'

'The stories confirm they were alive.'

Evan's nose wrinkled. 'Still, there isn't evidence of artefacts to suggest—'

'Evan, I will bind your mouth again if you do not stop talking and it will not be a pleasant experience,' Zeus said, nostrils flaring. 'And I do not mean to use a cloth.'

Evan opened his mouth to respond, but no words came out. He shouted and screamed until his throat ached.

'Now to continue,' Zeus said with a satisfied smile, and ignored Evan's silent curses. 'The Elders are going to introduce the captain of the ship to you and your companions.'

An enormous wooden ship swayed from side to side and bumped against the pier. The four men stared in wonder at a black painted hulk. It appeared to be alive the way it rose and fell with the gentle swell of the ocean. The hull, aligned with the jetty, had fifteen oars tiered on three levels. Oars protruded along the length of the ship from uniformly spaced holes, except on the deck, where they threaded through the wooden rail. The stern was narrow and curved high above the water. Two massive steering paddles sat motionless in the water, connected by a horizontal beam.

The bow was wider and had a beak sheathed in metal. An eye was painted on either side, the irises the brightest of blues, like a sapphire gemstone. At the centre was the mast, the sail not yet unfurled.

'What type of boat is this?' Homer said as he ambled closer. 'I've never seen one of this class. It is different to the vessels the ancestors built.'

'The *ship* is a trireme,' said a gruff voice from behind. A well-built man, with dark wavy hair and a trimmed beard, gazed at them. Intelligence shone in his green eyes, further emphasised by a weathered face and skin bronzed by the sun. 'The design developed from what we saw during our voyages.'

'This is Captain Sostrate. He will take you through the Pillars of Herakles and beyond,' said the Elder.

'What are the Pillars of Herakles?' Evandros asked.

Evan groaned and dropped his chin to his chest.

'Herakles was the mortal son of Zeus,' Sostrate said. 'He had the strength of the gods and was a hero to the people. The pillars are great rock cliffs he split to create a narrow passage between the ocean and the sea.'

'Why do that?' Leander asked.

'To separate the two lands and commemorate his journey,' the captain said.

'What an odd thing to do,' Leander said.

'Not when you understand the nature of the man and his purpose it isn't,' Sostrate said. He then turned to the Elders and bowed. 'We must set out while the winds are favourable.'

They nodded, the captain gave a brief bow, turned on his heels and sauntered over to the ship. Homer and Hektor were quick to follow, with Leander and the High Priestess a few paces behind. Evandros hung back, and appeared unwilling to board the wooden vessel. The captain made his way to the stern and watched, a wry grin spread across his face, as Evandros placed a tentative foot on the gangplank. Evandros scurried aboard. He gripped the railing and with faltering steps made his way to the prow to stand alongside the others.

'Oars ready!' Sostrate shouted.

The ninety man crew hefted long and heavy oars and thrust them out of portholes to hover above the water. The captain hollered, and the oars plunged into the ocean and were held at arm's length. With another command, the crew pulled the oars towards their bodies and the ship shuddered into movement. Evandros lurched against the timber railing.

Evan couldn't help but grin as he watched them struggle with the rocking and rolling of the ship. He loved sailing and spent as much time as possible on the water, but this ship was different to the sail-boats he sailed.

'Gods!' Evandros said, eyes wide in surprise.

Evan gawped.

The wall was larger than it first appeared and ran the entire length of the east side of the island. Then something unusual began to happen. The farther the ship sailed, the smaller the island became and a heavy mist descended and consumed the isle. The horizon blurred and in its place was the blue of the ocean and the clouds. The island vanished.

'Where is Atlantis?' Evandros said, astonished.

'It's under the protection of the gods,' Sostrate said, raising his voice an octave over the splashing of oars.

'Does this happen each time you leave home?' Hektor asked.

'It does.' The captain then turned to his first mate preventing further discussion.

'Why was the wall built?' Evandros said, turning to the High Priestess. 'I don't recall any mention of such a structure in the histories.'

'In the early years of settlement, the eastern quarter was battered by strong winds and increasing tides. The wall was constructed to protect the land from further erosion.'

'And the statues? Why were they placed outside the walls?'

'The figures were put up before the construction of the wall, and the ancestors believed they'd be enough to safeguard the land, but they weren't.'

'Why not move them?'

'It was a mammoth task to create and position the sculptures. They decided to leave and preserve them.'

The companions stared as the distance grew. The disappearance of their home was a chilling reminder of the danger of what may come to pass. Evan shuddered. He couldn't begin to fathom how it must feel not to have a home or a country of birth. It must have been a frightening prospect of not knowing and being responsible for the fate of your people.

The ship, built for speed, glided with ease. Evan smirked as the companions spent many days seasick. His amusement however, was short-lived as he became light-headed and bilious. His stomach lurched and mouth watered as the bile rose. He choked back a burp, pitched forward and dry retched. Perspiration filmed his forehead as he fought back another attack, and swung from side to side.

Zeus watched on with a thoughtful mien.

'What are you going to do?' Hephaistos said. 'He doesn't seem to re-member anything.'

'Perhaps it's time to thrust him back into his life.'

Hephaistos frowned. 'Won't that endanger him and the outcome of the quest? Apollo said if sent too soon, it could cause him irreparable damage. I am concerned with his lack of recall.'

Zeus rubbed his brow. 'His refusal to acknowledge this life is blocking any recollection. I fear he will not and does not want to remember.'

'Did we leave him there too long?'

'It was a risk but the longer he stayed away the more the chance of discovering his whereabouts lessened. If we recovered him earlier, he wouldn't have the knowledge and skills needed to succeed.'

'But now we face the possibility he won't be able to accomplish his directives,' Hephaistos pointed out. 'Should we call Mnemosyne and have her induce his memories?'

'No.'

'Why not?'

'Evandros not remembering could work in our favour,' Zeus said. He crossed his arms and tapped a finger against his lips.

'How so? Not recalling his past puts the companions at a disadvantage and at risk.'

'His refusal to accept the truth will make him unpredictable and stronger.'

'But what if the opposite happens? That he is unable to comprehend and cope with his new environment?'

'He did it once before and can again.'

'He is not the same person we sent away,' Hephaistos said, unconvinced.

'That was the intention,' Zeus said. 'We needed him to be different.'

'Yes, but what if he's changed too much?'

'We'll have to wait and see how he behaves.' Zeus turned back to Evan.

'When do you intend to place him back with us?'

'Soon, very soon.'

CHAPTER TWELVE

Before long, Evan felt better, observed the Atlanteans had regained their colour and moved around the ship without difficulty. He saw a pod of dolphins racing alongside. He admired the majesty of these mammals, and when out sailing he'd jump into the water to swim with them. Distracted by movement on board, Evan watched Evandros reach into his bag and pull out the black tome. With quick strokes, he drew the dolphins as they cavorted and kept up with the ship.

He then drew his companions. His first subject was Homer, whose face showed strength and a strong resolve. His brown-black hair was short, showing the squareness of his jaw-line. He had a high forehead, deep-set eyes, a long pointed nose and thin lips. His powerful physique topped by broad shoulders strained the fabric of his khiton. At seven feet tall, he towered over everyone.

Evandros moved on to Hektor, built like a bull and a head shorter than the others. From the way he moved, he was light and nimble on his feet. He had a flat face, full lips, short brown hair, and a crooked nose that looked as if he'd had it broken in a fight. His eyes shone with intelligence but there was a hard glint to them.

Leander was likeable and outgoing, got on with the crew as if they were old acquaintances, and was quick to make friends. He was the same height as Evandros, over six feet tall but wirier and appeared to be more agile. His hair was fair, while Evandros' was black. Leander's face was lean with a high forehead, a long straight nose, a generous mouth and a ready smile.

The High Priestess stood at six feet, and had long ebony curly hair which she tied back with ribbons woven through the tresses. She had an oval-shaped face, a refined nose and full lips. The High Priestess wore a long khiton showing her slender, yet voluptuous, body. She was striking and had the full attention of every man on the ship. She commanded the men's respect.

'Greetings, Evandros.' Leander sat next to him.

'Greetings, Leander.' He was shading definition to the High Priestess' hair. Leander leaned over to sneak a glimpse.

'You have captured our likenesses very well... and more,' he said in a thoughtful tone as he studied the drawings. 'When we return home perhaps they will paint frescoes of our quest.'

Evandros smiled. 'That would be a great honour.' He smudged the High Priestess' cheekbone with a thumb and held it at arm's length to examine the artwork. Satisfied, he closed the flap of the tome and put it away. 'How goes the sailing?'

'The captain is happy with our progress and grateful the winds have been good. He said we should see the Pillars of Herakles in a few days.'

'Poseidon has favoured us.'

Leander nodded. 'The gods are with us.'

***

Evan wanted to drive a nail through his eye. The captain and his crew did not stop talking of the different places, people and the sea monsters they encountered. For one, it was tedious to listen let alone to watch; and two, their captive audience, enthralled by the tales, asked many questions, making it more torturous. Evan had studied the places the captain and crew spoke of, many of which no longer existed, either conquered and re-named or vacated due to natural disasters.

'What of the people?' Leander said.

'Each is different, speaking in various languages, with diverse beliefs and practices. Yet what is common is the exchange of goods,' the captain said. 'Be prepared for possible hostilities, for not everyone welcomes outsiders.' He paused. 'And the treatment of women is not the same as the way we honour them.'

'What do you mean?' asked Hektor.

'Our womenfolk are respected for their connection with the Mother Goddess, the giver of life, and bind their importance in our society. In your travels, you will come across those who do not see women in the same way as we do. Their status no better than an animal's and they have little or no say in their home or as a member of society,' Sostrate said.

'Why are they treated this way? Will this affect our quest?' Homer said.

The captain shrugged. 'I don't know why. I don't believe it will affect your search but, with the High Priestess in your midst, I suggest you be vigilant.'

Hektor snorted and shook his head. 'Have they lost their senses?'

'How can they ignore the wisdom of women?' Leander said, baffled.

'We should not judge these people or their values. It's not our place to cast aspersion on what we don't understand,' the High Priestess said. 'Our main concern is to locate and recover the sacred relics, return home and save the gods and our people. Don't forget we are their guests and will respect their laws.'

'Of course, High Priestess,' said Leander and bowed his head. The others followed his example.

'Captain, tell us how the Pillars of Herakles earned its name,' the High Priestess said as she clasped her hands behind her back.

'Of course, High Priestess. Herakles committed a terrible crime and to atone for his actions, the Oracle told him to visit the King of Tiryns. The king set him twelve tasks of strength and courage. If he completed all twelve, he would become immortal and his past deeds would be forgiven,' Sostrate said. 'The separation of the two lands commemorated his tenth task.'

'What did he do?' asked Homer.

'He murdered his wife and children.'

'Why didn't they punish him with death?' Hektor said, arms crossed.

'To better understand the story, let me start from the beginning. Herakles was the son of Zeus and the mortal Alkmene. The goddess Hera, angry at his infidelity, did what she could to get rid of this child. What they did not expect was his remarkable strength making it difficult to kill him. Herakles killed a lion with his bare hands.' Sostrate lifted his hands. 'As she could not destroy him, Hera caused Herakles to go mad and while in this fugue, he slaughtered his family.

'At the conclusion of the twelve tasks, he remarried and had a son. Life was good for a while until a centaur attempted to rape his wife. Herakles shot the centaur with a poisoned arrow and, as it lay dying, the beast instructed his wife to collect his blood. He told her it might be used as a love potion if her husband strayed. Afraid of his wayward affections, she smeared the blood on Herakles' clothes. When he put on the tunic, his skin burned as if consumed by fire. Distraught by her stupidity, she committed suicide. Knowing death was near, Herakles, with his son's help, built a pyre. He lay on the wood and ordered his son to light it. A crowd gathered to mourn a great hero, but when the smoke cleared, there was no body. It's believed Athene and Hermes took him and he now lives on Mount Olympos.'

'What a tragic story!' Leander said.

'A man of honour,' Hektor said with a crisp nod. 'He realised he had to atone for his wrongdoings.'

'The tasks he faced were legendary and I will tell them another time but for now admire the pillars he made.' Sostrate pointed.

Their gasps were audible and Evan admitted the pillars were impressive. He was more familiar with their modern name, the Straits of Gibraltar. The sun hit the rock face and reflected their brilliant whiteness. The Atlanteans shielded their eyes as the ship sailed closer, the harsh glare from the pillars blinding.

'By Triton!' Leander said as he craned his neck to take in the sheer size.

The captain bellowed orders as he steered towards the gap between the great rocks. The ship rose and fell with a heavy splash. Seawater showered the deck. The currents in the passage were strong as the crew fought to keep the large vessel on its path. As they drew nearer to the mouth, the tip of the craggy cliff face was swallowed by the clouds. The sheerness of the precipices became clearer, both sides looming and dwarfing the ship as they entered the pass. Evan leaned forward as much as he could and stared at the three dark shapes marring the blue sky. They moved with speed and appeared to be heading for the ship. Evan frowned. His scalp prickled. Why did he get an overwhelming sense that something terrible may happen?

'This strait takes us into the Mediterranean Sea and once cleared, we'll set course for Carthage,' the captain said. 'It's a major seaport and a good place to begin your search.'

'If you think that is best,' Evandros said. He turned to gaze up at the sky.

'Here, take hold of this and keep it straight,' Sostrate said, the muscles in his arms bulging as he gripped the two helms. 'The currents are strong and with each of us controlling a rudder, there's less chance of capsizing.'

Evandros grasped the one closest and was yanked off his feet. He clenched his hands around the wooden handle until his knuckles turned white. He pulled himself upright and planted his feet on the slippery deck. The captain grinned at him and he beamed back. He strained to keep control of the rudder, the muscles on his face and body as taut as a stringed bow. Saltwater drizzled over them as the ship splashed into the waves. Both men were sodden from head to toe. Water dripped from Evandros' hair and into his eyes. He shook his head.

In time, the choppy waves subsided, and the spray lessened. The waters became calmer and gentler as the ship sailed beyond the pillars. A dazzling turquoise sea lay ahead for as far as the eye could see. Situated north was the European continent and to the south, separated by the sea, lay the North African lands. Evan had been to Europe a number of times but never to the exotic cities of North Africa. He'd planned to go a year ago but the growing clientele of his business made it difficult to book vacation time.

'What you see ahead is the Mediterranean!' the captain said in a loud voice as he shifted to take control of both helms.

'How did it get its name?' Evandros asked as he relinquished the rudder and stepped aside.

'It comes from a Latin word meaning "middle earth".'

'Latin?'

The captain nodded. 'The word comes from a small colony, a new civilisation from the Italics.'

CHAPTER THIRTEEN

'Why is the captain sailing towards the coastline?' Hektor asked, noticing the undulating landscape.

'It is common practice to sail within reach of land,' Evandros said, 'in case of storms or some other calamity. However, they must sail far enough not to hit coral reefs or sand banks.'

'Treacherous business this sailing,' Hektor said. He turned away from the vista and leaned back, elbows resting on the railing.

'In most circumstances it's safe,' Evandros said with a shrug.

'Not very comforting Evandros,' Hektor said with a shake of his head.

Evandros smiled and patted him on the shoulder. 'Captain Sostrate is a seasoned sailor as is his crew. We've nothing to worry about.' He slid down, leaned against the hull and closed his eyes.

'If you are that confident,' Hektor said and sat as well.

The two men slumbered away while the crew with steady and even strokes moved the ship further away from the strait and deeper into the sea. The constant hum of voices and splash of oars dipping into the water was rhythmic and soothing. Occasional laughter and banter interrupted the cadence, creating a happy and relaxed atmosphere.

Then the ship rocked from side to side and water splashed across the deck. Evandros slammed into Hektor and flung forward.

'What in the name of the gods!' Hektor said, startled. He scrambled to his feet, and lurched one way then the other as the ship swayed. 'The High Priestess!' Picking up his gear, Hektor stumbled away.

Evandros grabbed the railing and turned to catch sight of his bag and weapons sliding away. He hurled himself forward and seized them before they plunged into the sea. Sprays of seawater sprinkled across the deck as the ship rose and heaved onto the waves. He fell against the railing. Evandros scrambled to his knees, ignoring the smarting pain. He swung the bag over his shoulder and strapped on the weapons with multiple knots. The ship teetered from side to side; he was unable to grab hold of the railing. He rolled and watched with wide eyes the dark turbulent sea as it captured the ship.

The water frothed around the hull. The ship took flight and crashed hard. Water spurted into the sky like a geyser and pelted down until the deck swam. Evandros clutched the rail and peered over the side. A shadowy mass spread beneath the ship.

'Can you see what hit us?' a bedraggled oarsman shouted.

'Not a thing!' he hollered. Evandros turned, half ran and half slipped his way across to the other side to take a look. He scuttled further along and three entities caught his attention. 'What are those?' he yelled, pointing to the sky.

'By the gods!' an oarsman said, his face paling. 'Soul-eaters!'

'What?' Evandros said brushing wet hair from his eyes. 'Soul-eaters? Where are they?'

The ship struck a hard object. It listed high above the water, the hull exposed. People screamed. Oarsmen fell against each other, pinned down and powerless to move. The deck was in chaos. Evandros fell and slid across the deck. He wrapped his arms around the railing. Water lapped at his head.

'Did we hit something?' he called out.

The captain shook his head. 'We'd be sinking if we had!'

'Perhaps something hit us!'

'By The Titans!' a crewman said with a shriek. 'What in the name of Poseidon is that?'

A long, black sleek tentacle burst from the choppy sea. One side was smooth and the opposite dotted with holes big enough to swallow a man whole. The tip was small, the size of a man's thigh, and grew larger. The rest disappeared into the sea.

Evan's heart thudded. He knew what it was and hadn't thought such a large sea creature existed.

'There's another!'

'And there! Another one!'

'Oh gods!'

Several black menacing limbs metamorphosed from the water and encircled the ship. A tentacle strayed over the deck, picked up a sailor and lifted him into the sky. He twisted and kicked, legs thrashing, but the limb curled tighter around the mariner. The sound of bones breaking filled the air. The sailor's horrific screams were cut short.

Evan's blood pulsated, his heart racing as an inexplicable sensation of rage took hold. He spotted Evandros running forward, sword in hand, swinging and cutting off a large part of the tentacle. Evan wanted to yell out encouragement but had to settle for a silent cry of praise. Inky viscous blood spurted over Evandros. The tentacle slithered off the deck. Before it slunk back into the sea, it coiled around three men and took them.

Water churned around the ship. Black sinuous tentacles erupted from the depths of the sea, wrapped thick limbs around the vessel and lifted it out of the water. Wood splintered. Everyone on board tumbled, as if struck by a ten-pin bowling ball, bodies smashing. Evan winced as Evandros rolled like tumbleweed and crashed into the wooden wall of the stern. Blood dripped from his brow. Evan's head ached. Evandros started to yell. Evan glanced over.

'Oh my God,' he whispered, face ashen.

The sea monster rent the ship in two. The bulk of the crew fell into the roiling sea. Evandros hurtled towards the churning water. More tentacles grew out from the large sinister shadow. Unable to tear his eyes away, Evan watched in horror as the creature opened its cavernous mouth, and in flowed water and men. Several sailors were impaled on its jagged teeth.

'Jump!' Evandros hollered. He twisted onto his stomach, reached out and dug his fingernails into the wooden planks, leaving deep gouge marks. His feet hit the ledge. His toes clutched onto a small crevice. He stretched and latched onto a small section of the deck. He looked over his shoulder, and glimpsed the monster lurking and waiting beneath the churning waves. Evandros closed his eyes and inch by inch, crawled to the other side. He clung to the wooden ledge, and pulled himself upright.

The sea monster tossed out more limbs. Evandros jumped into the swirling water just as the creature flung one half of the ship away, and pushed the rest into its gaping mouth. Evandros began to sink amid the terrible screams of the crew.

Evan stared at the now silent scene. There was nothing but the blue sea for miles, except the floating debris, to show a gruesome tragedy had occurred. All those lives lost for what? The picture vanished and Zeus stood in front of him.

'Time to finish what you have started,' he said.

Evan gazed up at him, puzzled. Then Zeus and Hephaistos were gone, and he no longer sat wrapped in the unyielding mesh. He was again drowning, experiencing the same dream that started this craziness. The weight of the weapons and bag pulled at him. He did not want to revisit those awful images from last time and hoped he'd wake up soon. Mindful of the fact if he drowned here in the dream, he would be dead back home, Evan kicked hard and swam towards the surface. His chest and lungs hurt as in the dream. *How can this be happening?*

His head broke the surface, and he drew in a deep breath. Wooden debris floated everywhere. Evan rotated one way and then the other, grabbed a piece of wood and clung to it.

'Time to wake up,' he said. He closed his eyes and waited to wake up safe and sound at home. The splash of the waves, the salty smell and the constant bobbing of wreckage surrounded him. Evan's skin prickled and his breathing quickened, just as it had the time a huge German Shepherd chased him when he was six years old. He didn't want to open his eyes. His eyelids flew open. Something solid brushed against the soles of his feet. This was not where he belonged. An object grazed his legs. He leapt out of the water and onto a wooden plank. Evan scoured the water but couldn't see what touched him. He clenched his hands and gritted his teeth.

'Zeus, you sadistic bastard! Get me out of here right now!' Evan yelled. 'You will put me back where I belong!' Chest heaving, Evan pounded on the plank. 'Do you hear me? I want to go home!'

'You are home,' said Zeus' familiar voice, though Evan could not see him. 'It is time to accept this is where you are meant to be.'

'No! My place is back with my parents, friends and running a business!' Evan hollered. 'Send me home, now!'

'This is quite enough, Evandros!' Zeus said, and the sky darkened. 'You will do as you're told.'

'That is not my name!' Evan shook his head. 'If you don't send me home, I will jump into the water and let nature finish what it started.'

'Don't be a fool.'

'Fine.' Evan dived into the water and let the burden of his load drag him deeper. His chest compressed as the sea enveloped him in its embrace. He smiled, knowing it soon would be over and opened his mouth to quicken his death.

'Noooooooooooooo!' Evan screamed. He was whisked out of the watery tomb and flung onto a larger piece of wood. 'Why can't you leave me alone?'

'You will not dishonour me,' Zeus said in an icy tone. He stood over Evan, who lay curled at Zeus' feet. 'No son of mine will put his own impudence before the needs of others and his Family. This self-indulgence of yours is pitiful and I will no longer tolerate it.'

'Son?' Evan blinked, looked up at Zeus and flinched. Zeus' eyes changed from ice blue to black.

'Recover the sacred objects and then you can go home,' Zeus said.

'Son?' Evan repeated dazed and gave himself a mental shake. 'What did you say? I can go home?'

'Do you think I would entrust an important task such as this to anyone? Only my son can lead and find these items.'

'Home...' Evan said lying back on the plank. 'Herakles was your son, so was Perseus, Theseus...'

'Sleep now, Evandros,' Zeus said in a soft voice as he laid a hand on his head.

CHAPTER FOURTEEN

'Captain! Man overboard!'

Two men dived into the water. Between them, they tied a rope around the man's torso.

'The sword and shield should fetch a good price at the markets,' one said. He reached out to undo the leather straps, but they had swelled and were difficult to untie.

'Leave it. We'll take it once he's on board the ship.' The second man swam around to face the deck and shouted, 'Pull him up!'

Sailors grunted and the muscles in their arms and legs strained as they laboured to pull up the dead weight. Half way up, the body bumped against the wooden hull. The head flopped from side to side, like a puppet's, with each tug. When the body reached the top, many men had to lift it over the railing. They groaned and grumbled as the extra burden of the weapons caused a few men's knees to buckle. The captain and crew gathered around the man. The two men who rescued him clambered aboard and thrust their way forward, ready to lay claim.

'How, in the name of Baal, did this man survive the wreckage of his ship?' the captain said, hands on hips. He bent over to peer closer at the man's features. 'Most unusual.'

The man's angular features were distinctive under the shadow of a beard. His nose was long and straight, and he had a high forehead and short black hair.

'How tall do you think he is?' the captain said.

'I reckon he stands near four to five cubits,' his bosun said.

'Hmm...' The captain clasped his chin with thumb and finger. 'To be in possession of quality weapons as these, he'd have to be an elite warrior or at least a mercenary for hire. Bosun, check to see if his heart still beats.'

The short, squat bearded man knelt on one knee and placed his ear on the man's chest.

'It beats, though slowly, Captain.'

'Take him down below and have the boy administer to him. He'll fetch a good price at the slave market.'

The two men who had dived into the sea and who still stood nearby, rushed forward and worked on loosening the straps of the shield and sword.

'Bring those weapons to me when you're done,' the captain said over his shoulder.

The sailors froze. One pressed his lips together while the other clenched a hand as they watched the retreating back of the captain.

'I *told* you! We should've taken them while we had the chance!' one said with a hiss.

The other scowled and wrenched at the man's arm to pass it through the strap. He moaned. The two sailors lost their footing and fell on their backsides, their eyes wide as they stared. The man's eyelids fluttered, his head slumped to the side. He opened and closed his mouth like a fish.

'Do we give him water?' one said as they kept their distance.

The other shrugged. 'I guess so.' The man moved again. 'Well, go get a cup of water!'

The sailor ran to a large clay pot lodged into the neck of the prow and filled an earthenware cup with drinking water. He returned, brown liquid spilling over the rim, handed it to his mate and took a step back.

'What do you think he's going to do? Hit you! In his state?' his mate said with a disgusted snort. He shook his head, lifted the man's head and tipped the cup against his lips. Water ran down the man's chin before his mouth began to work.

The man sputtered and coughed, and pushed the sailor's hand away as he leaned on an elbow and spat out the water. He wiped his mouth with the back of his hand and looked up at them.

'By the god Moloch!'

The man sat upright. The sailor, taken aback by the colour of his eyes, stared, mouth hanging open for a few seconds before words came tumbling out.

'Where have you come from?'

The man spoke, his voice hoarse. The deckhand and his mate stared at him, and then they looked to each other. What did they do now? The man pointed to the cup.

'Water? You want more water?' The sailor picked up the cup and raised his brows. The man nodded. 'Go get water.' He thrust the cup at his mate. While he waited, he studied the foreigner. The blue-eyed man, oblivious to the other's curiosity, stared at the sea for a time before turning his piercing gaze on him. The sailor blinked. His eyes were unusual and bright, almost like ice. Then he said something. The sailor shook his head and held out his hands, palms faced upwards. Before long, his mate returned and handed him the cup. The man lifted the cup and peered, his nose wrinkling. He took a sip, shuddered and spat the water out.

'I told the captain he's wakened. He wants to speak with him.'

'He won't understand.'

'Captain's orders.'

They helped him up and one tried to take the sword and shield. The man spoke, tone brisk and clipped, and pushed the sailor's hands away. The sailor lunged at him but fell face first onto the deck. He sprang to his feet and spun on his heel. The man sidestepped to dodge a flying fist. Face red and chest heaving, the sailor clenched his hands and took a step.

'That's enough! Bring him here.'

The sailors grabbed the tall man and pushed him across the deck to the captain. It was a strange sight, as the man towered over every man on the ship. The burly captain glowered up at the man, who gazed back, head cocked to the side.

'What is your name?' the captain asked.

The man shook his head and did not respond.

'Why doesn't he answer? Is he dim-witted?'

'I don't think so, Captain. He doesn't speak our language.'

The captain scowled. 'He recovered fast. He'll sell well. Take him below, and give him a little of the rations. I don't want him undernourished when we arrive at port.' The captain turned away, eager to get away from the man's unrelenting stare. 'And take those weapons from him.'

The sailor who had tried earlier to take the weapons sniggered. He seized the stranger's arm, fingers digging into the sinewy flesh, and attempted to wrest the shield away. The man captured his hand, gave it a slight squeeze and flicked it away. Eyes narrowed, he shook his head at the sailor. The deckhand's nostrils flared, his ears turned red and he punched the man in the stomach. The foreigner doubled over and clutched his middle. His head flew back, and blood spurted from his nose. He staggered before regaining his balance. He straightened and stared at the sailor. The crew began to jeer and throw insults.

Amid the din the sailor screamed, 'You motherless dog!'

He rushed forward, hands clenched, and threw a flurry of punches into the man's stomach. The man did not try and protect himself and the sailor continued his furious assault. Blow after blow, the man stood without flinching and not making a sound. The deckhand soon tired, and let his hands drop to his sides, chest heaving. His quarry drew back a balled hand, knuckles white. The sailor flew into the air and landed with a thud mid deck. He did not move.

The few men standing closest took a step back and gawked. Blood streamed from his nose, over his mouth and dripped from his chin, drops splattering the deck. He touched his torso, a bright angry red, and winced. He stared at the prone sailor and frowned. He then took a few faltering steps and turned. Those nearest jumped away. His searching eyes fell on the deckhand who'd given him water and he beckoned him. The sailor, uncertain, turned to his captain with a questioning look. He pursed his lips and then gave a curt nod.

The sailor swallowed, took a few hesitant steps and stopped an arm's length away from the stranger. His head lowered, the man winced as he touched his nose, and muttered a few inaudible words.

He looked over at the deckhand who stood waiting and trembling. The sailor flinched as the man raised a hand, and then relaxed as he lifted it to his mouth. He nodded and hastened to fulfil the request but as he neared the fallen mate, he slowed to look. He was still not moving. One punch. With that in mind, he quickened his pace.

'Man your oars! And clear Akbar off the deck!' the captain ordered.

The crew cleared, leaving the man standing on his own.

Within minutes the sailor returned and handed the cup over, water spilling over the side. The man gave him a nod, poured water onto his hand and washed the blood from his face. He pointed into the cup. The sailor gestured for him to follow. He led him to the water urn where the man filled the cup and finished cleaning his face. He handed the cup back to the deckhand, wandered to the starboard side of the ship and gripped the railing. The sailor watched him for a few minutes, took a deep breath, and murmured a small appeal to the sea god before moving. The man looked at him, startled.

'Pha... Phameas,' he said pointing to himself, voice shaking.

'Phameas...' the man repeated with a frown. Phameas nodded and pointed to the man.

'Evan... dros.'

'Evandros?' Phameas said pronouncing the name "ee-van-dros".

CHAPTER FIFTEEN

'If this is a joke, it's not funny,' Evan said as he stood alone at the bow of the ship. The mild wind ruffled his hair, the sea air bracing, a hint of a change in the weather. He leaned into the railing, the wood smooth and solid under his hands. 'Come on! I've had enough! You didn't need that jerk sailor to pummel me.' Evan placed a hand against his chest and pulled a face. Though there was no bruising it hurt to touch. 'What do you want from me?' he shouted, then he gripped the rail and lowered his head onto his hands. 'God damn it!'

His eyes narrowed. 'Where the hell are my clothes? And shoes?' Evan began to breathe faster and he clenched a hand.

'Ee-van-dros?'

Evan whipped his head around, teeth bared, about to tell whoever it was to go away.

Phameas jumped back, the concern on his face mixed with fear. Evan felt the anger ebb, raised a hand with the palm facing out and straightened.

'My apologies, Phameas,' he said annoyed with himself for frightening the one person who spoke to him kindly. The language with which the crew conversed sounded similar to Hebrew and yet not; there were variations in tone and words. From a young age, Evan had showed a flair for foreign languages and now spoke seven of them. He'd considered applying for work at the United Nations but when his sister became sick he decided to stay home.

'You... sad?' Phameas asked, pointing at Evan. He made fists and rotated them in front of his eyes. Evan smiled. He remembered doing the same thing when he used to tease his sister when he wanted to make her cry.

Evan shook his head. 'No, I am angry.'

'For the loss of your ship and crew?'

How do you tell someone you weren't on the ship when it went down, let alone say this is not where you belong? Instead Evan nodded. He rubbed his brow and pressed his lips together. He removed the sword and shield, rotated his shoulders and stretched his neck from side to side. The weight of the weapons was heavier than expected. With his back against the wall of the ship, he levered himself down and sat. He pulled the aegis towards him and studied the embossing. In spite of his circumstance, Evan could not help admiring the craftsmanship of the shield. At the centre was a lightning bolt and starting from the rim were complex motifs. The first was an artistic form of a wave, followed by swirls. The sword was double-edged, with a leaf shaped blade, the length close to seventy centimetres. The hilt was forged in black metal and etched with the images of hoplite soldiers fighting and with glyphs. Evan scratched the back of his head. He'd seen those symbols somewhere before and no matter how hard he tried, he could not remember what they were or where.

Phameas sat next to him, leaned over and studied the weapons. He pointed and asked to hold them. His face lit up as he smiled; eyes sincere. Evan nodded. Phameas tried to lift the sword but struggled. Evan picked it up and handed it to him.

'Moloch!' he said, eyes wide. The sword lay across his lap and pressed into his flesh. He peered at the etchings on the scabbard which depicted scenes of the Olympian Gods fighting the Titans. He gazed at Evan in wonder. 'This,' he said, hand pumping the air above the sword, 'is magnificent.'

Phameas returned the sword, arms quaking. He then put a hand out to touch the shield. His fingers hovered for a second before he ran them over the bronze plating. Phameas snatched his hand back, just as his fingertips grazed the lightning bolt.

'What is it?' Evan asked with a frown. 'Are you hurt?'

Phameas stared at the shield for a long while then looked to Evan, his expression indecipherable. He pointed at the weapons, pointed at Evan and then to the sky. Evan shook his head, perplexed.

Phameas leaned towards the scabbard and pointed at one of the images.

Evan barked out a laugh. 'You've got it wrong my friend.'

Phameas nodded, head bobbing up and down with long sweeps. He patted the image and then Evan's shoulder.

'Not me, I'm just a man, out of time and place.'

Phameas beamed, got to his feet and returned to his duties. The smile on Evan's face faded. The deckhand's idea of him being a god was laughable but his current predicament wasn't. He pulled his knees up, wrapped his arms around them and rested his head. The sun warmed his back and as he sat there, the sound of water splashing against the hull and men chatting lulled him into a slumber.

'Evandros?'

He whisked his head up and looked around. No one was anywhere near him. Evan dismissed it as a trick of the wind and went back to sleep.

***

To pass the time, Phameas began to teach Evan words and phrases during his breaks. On occasion, his attention strayed and focussed on the images on the weapons.

When alone, Evan examined the ship, the equipment and style of dress. While at university, he'd studied Ancient History, one of his favourite subjects besides his chosen field of architecture. He tried to determine what period he was in, but as there were no significant markers he couldn't.

One afternoon, while Phameas was instructing him, Evan posed his question.

'Phameas, can you tell me what year this is?'

The deckhand shrugged. 'It's like every year, one passes onto the next no different to the cycle of days.'

'Of course,' Evan nodded, 'but do you know what year it is?'

Phameas' brow creased. 'Why? Is it important?'

Evan clasped the back of his neck with a hand and then let it fall by his side. 'I guess not.' He gazed out onto the endless Mediterranean blue sea, the hint of land beyond the horizon a tantalising gift of hope. 'Where are we heading?'

'We're a day out from Rusaddir. There we'll stop and collect supplies then to Hippo Regius to drop off goods before sailing to Carthage.'

'Carthage?' Evan said, ears pricking. The name of that city came up in one of the visions Zeus forced on him. He searched his memory for information he'd learnt on the history of Carthage and its people. One point he did recall, the Carthaginians descended from the Phoenicians and were great seafarers. In the Middle Ages, the Arabs conquered the region and it had remained in their jurisdiction since that time. 'Do you think the captain will take me with you?'

'Can't say,' Phameas said. 'He intends selling you at the slave markets but given your physical prowess and weapons he may turn you over to the army.'

'I am not a soldier, nor do I fight,' Evan said. 'I design buildings.'

'Then why do you carry such expensive and well-made weapons?' Phameas said, pointing to the arms.

'Still figuring that out myself,' he said with mutter. 'Come on, let's go see the captain,' he added out loud.

The ship was different to the Atlantean vessel. The stern curved, rising high above the water, and provided shade over where the steersman stood. At the opposite end, the prow was reinforced with iron and sat low in the water. The main sail was square, had four ropes and could be dropped or hoisted at a moment's notice on the captain's orders. There was a foresail as well and when both sails were up, the ship glided in double time. Below deck in the hull, part of the space was used to store water and food, and there was a small area for men to sleep. On the deck, merchandise was kept secreted under a tent-like structure, with the overflow stowed beneath. The captain also used it as his quarters. A heavy cloth, like the sail, was pulled forward to create a shelter.

In spite of the benevolent nature of the voyage, the crew was well armed. At the stern, the captain handled one of the two large steering oars while his bosun controlled the other. With the sail up and billowing, oarsmen were free to complete maintenance, mend sails and ropes, and attend to other small jobs.

'Captain, I've told Evandros we are sailing for Carthage and he wants to come with us,' Phameas said.

The captain looked from Phameas to the tall hulk standing by his side. 'I plan on presenting him to General Mago, who may take him on as a mercenary.'

'As I told Phameas, I'm not a soldier,' Evan said, 'but if I could join you on the journey to Carthage, I'd be grateful.'

The captain gave him a startled look but covered it up quickly. 'It appears Phameas' lessons have progressed further than I expected.'

'He is a good instructor,' Evan said, patting the shorter man on the shoulder.

Phameas glowed under the praise.

'You could make good money as a soldier,' the captain said, 'and General Mago is a fair and generous officer. You will do well under his command.'

'Not interested,' he said, shaking his head. 'I prefer to go to Carthage with you.'

'Why?' The captain gave him a flinty look. 'What's in Carthage?'

'It... it was where the... my ship was heading,' Evan said.

'I am sorry your ship was destroyed and everyone killed by the Kraken, but my mind is made up.'

'I am willing to work as a crew member. I have worked on boats before, not one such as this, but I am a quick learner, as Phameas can confirm.'

'How well can you row?'

Evan glanced over at the long wooden oars. 'I've rowed canoes and been part of an eight-man scull; the principle is the same.'

The captain narrowed his eyes and compressed his lips. He said, 'All right. If you prove to be as good as your word, I will take you. Phameas, you will be responsible for him and if he doesn't perform, I will dock your pay. He'll sit in front of you, that way you can keep an eye on him.' With a sharp flick of his head, he added, 'Go and get organised.'

As the two men walked away, Phameas glanced up at his companion. 'What is a canoe and a scull?'

'Small rowing boats.'

'How small?'

'One holds eight rowers and the other a single oarsman.'

Phameas shook his head, dismayed. 'You will find this different and harder.'

'I realise that Phameas, for one this is a big wooden ship and heavy.'

'What is the purpose for such small boats? They wouldn't be good for transportation or for long distances.'

'You'd be surprised, Phameas. They are very good for manoeuvring in narrow or tight spaces and carrying modest loads. And,' Evan stopped walking and wagged a finger, 'excellent for racing competitions.'

'Racing?'

Evan nodded and resumed walking. 'Great test of endurance.'

'Where do you come from that has races in small boats?'

'That, my friend, is a story for another time.' Evan then added under his breath, 'One that I hope not to explain.'

Phameas spent the next few hours instructing Evan on the finer points of being a deckhand and oarsman. Afterwards, he led the tall man to his sitting position.

'Melqart, sit in your seat and let's show Evan what he has to do,' Phameas said. The swarthy man slipped onto the crude wooden block and hefted the long oar with practiced sureness. 'We start rowing at a signal.' Phameas pointed to the drum stationed at the stern on the next level and beneath where the captain stood. 'If one man is out of rhythm it causes problems for all of us. So it's important to keep in time with the beat and watch the man in front of you.' He told Evan to sit behind Melqart. 'Pick up your oar.'

Evan leaned forward and grabbed the oar. The handle was smooth to the touch and stained from the sweat of many hands. Evan lifted it and was surprised by how well balanced it kept in spite of the length.

'I don't want you to dip the oar in the water but to move it around in the air, get a feel for the weight and size,' Phameas said.

Evan moved it up and down and in circles. Before long, beads of sweat formed on his brow and the muscles in his arms tightened.

'Now I want you to follow what Melqart does, mimic his actions.'

Melqart leaned forward, his knees drawing up, the oar out in front of him, and then pulled it back towards his body as he moved backwards. A frown formed on Evan's brow and he bit his lip as he tried to keep up. When Phameas called them to stop, Evan was panting, his chest rising and falling as he struggled to catch his breath.

'When you put the oar in the water, it will be different,' Phameas said with a grin as he clasped Evan's shoulder.

'If only the seat moved on rollers,' he said between gasps. 'And here I assumed the eight-man scull was hard!'

'Come, let's get you a drink.'

Evan's legs shook when he stood and the muscles in his arms and back protested. He stifled a groan and plodded with heavy steps after Phameas.

After having a drink, Evan sat at the bow and leaned back. His gaze fell on the bag. Since his rescue, he hadn't bothered to check inside, as he did not want to acknowledge this existence. He presumed he'd be home soon, dealing with contractors.

With a sigh, he lifted it onto his lap and flipped open the flap. A few rolled parchments and a cylinder lay on top which he pulled out. He reached inside and grabbed a black object that looked like a clipboard and placed it next to the parchments. Next, he took out a woollen blanket, until it came apart and realised it was a hooded cloak. Finally, he pulled out extra tunics. That was it. He rolled the cloak and shoved it back into the bag and turned his attention to the black book. It was the same one he saw in the visions.

He took the corner of the cover and lifted it. There he saw the pictures of the companions as well as dolphins and crew members at work. Evan flicked through the pages, seeing the indecipherable script interspersed with images. He snapped it shut and dropped it into the bag. Next he picked up one of the scrolls and removed the cord. His eyes grew wider as he unrolled it. Thicker than paper, it stretched to a metre in length but that's not what caught his attention.

It was a map of the world, detailed with names of places and outlines of the geography of the land. From what Evan could tell there were discrepancies but despite those, it was an excellent depiction. He put it aside and grabbed another. It too was a map except this featured the Mediterranean and the surrounding land. He grabbed the last one and when he unrolled it, smaller inserts fell out. The hair on the back of his neck stood on end.

'Cripes.'

The map illustrated the region known as Greece with the islands and settlements in Turkey and Sicily. But it was the other parchments that caught his eye. Evan straightened one out and studied the image.

'I know a professor who'd love to examine this,' he murmured to himself. 'Heck, the entire ancient historical community would want these.' Evan licked his lips. One outlined the island of Krete and the Minoan settlements and included images of palaces and people; the other was of Thira, a smaller version of the one he saw on the wall of Evandros' house. He rolled them up except one.

'Now where did Phameas say we're heading?' He scanned the map and the coastline of North Africa. Evan pressed his lips together. There was something about the pictograms. He had seen them before, just needed to remember where. 'That's it! Linear A, the Minoan script.' The professor of ancient cultures had brought samples of artefacts when he was at university. If he could read the indecipherable text, their current location and names of places would be easy to identify.

A shadow blocked the sunlight on the map. Evan looked up. The sailor who attacked him a few days earlier stood over him. Evan got to his feet. The two stared at each other for a long few minutes. The other man thrust out a hand. Evan searched his face, saw there was no ill intent and reached out to shake hands. Instead, the sailor grabbed his wrist with a firm clasp, gave a curt nod, let go and walked away without saying a word.

'That, I believe was an apology,' said Phameas as he came up from behind Evan. The two watched the sailor as he ambled back along the length of the deck and disappeared into the hold.

Evan scratched his head and then shrugged. 'Can you show me where Rusaddir is?' He held out the map to Phameas, who leaned over and squinted.

'That is Rusaddir.'

'Hmm... that is in Morocco,' he said in a mutter. He ignored Phameas' questioning look and asked, 'Can you read what is written here?'

Phameas shook his head. 'I can't read.'

'Really? You knew where Rusaddir is.'

'Maps are easy to follow. I learned how to identify familiar landmarks and memorised the shape of the coastline,' he said.

'Impressive,' Evan said, brows arched. 'Can someone else read it to me?'

'The captain can help,' Phameas said with a slight shrug.

'I'll ask him once we arrive.' Evan rolled up the map. 'Did you get the opportunity to learn how to read and write?'

'Men like me don't need to know such things,' he said and then looked away, 'besides, it's the wealthy and aristocrats who are taught.'

The two men stared over the vast blue sea. 'I can teach you if you want.'

Phameas turned to him and gave a small smile. 'Thank you but for a man in my position, there's no point in learning.'

'You never know Phameas, one day it could come in handy,' Evan said. 'The ability to read and write is a powerful tool.'

'Yes, and that is why nobles rule.'

'My offer still stands if you change your mind.'

'You must come from a highborn family to be educated,' Phameas said, tilting his head to the side.

Evan laughed. 'My friend, I come from a line of ancestors who toiled the land.'

'How is it you...'

'Can read and write?' Evan finished for him. Phameas nodded. 'Where I come from, everyone goes to school.'

Phameas' gaped at him. 'What a fortunate and wondrous place to live! Where are you from?'

The humour in Evan's face faded. 'Too far from here.' The question was how did he get back home? His ears began to prickle and his shoulders tingled.

'Evandros.'

'Evandros, help us.'

He spun around, eyes flicking from side to side. 'Did you hear that?'

Phameas gave him an odd look. 'Hear what?'

Evan turned back and scanned the ship. No one was anywhere near them. 'I thought...'

'Thought what?'

Evan clasped the back of his neck and squeezed. 'Don't worry about it.' He gave a wry smile. 'Just a little tired after the practice session you put me through.'

Phameas grinned. 'With more training, you will be a first-class oarsman.'

Evan dropped his chin to his chest and groaned.

'Speaking of which, break time is over, back to practice.'

'What? Now?'

'Of course,' Phameas said. 'This breeze won't last.' He wet his finger on his tongue and raised it. 'Its strength is weakening. The captain will soon want us at the oars. Come along.' He beckoned with the same finger.

With an inward sigh, Evan picked up his gear and followed.

CHAPTER SIXTEEN

A weary Evan struggled to keep upright as he and Phameas gazed over the dazzling turquoise waters. He squinted at the horizon, the seascape murky. The haze began to clear as the ship sailed closer to the land. Evan leaned on the railing and shaded his eyes against the glare of the sun. Even from this distance he saw the peaks of mountains as they touched the sky and where the plains dipped low. It gave the impression the horizon was rising and falling.

'We'll arrive early in the morn,' Phameas said, breaking the silence. 'The captain will give us a few days rest before we set out for Hippo Regius.'

'What is it like?' Evan asked.

'It's no different to other ports, lots of noise, busy with traders and dangerous.'

'Dangerous? How?'

'There are pickpockets, cutthroats and thieves but the Carthaginians have soldiers stationed at the ports who deal with the criminals. In any case, it is always wise to keep alert.'

'Right.' Evan's stomach fluttered. This feeling of not knowing what to expect reminded him of his trip to South America. That was

exciting but scary at the same time, in particular when he heard stories of people disappearing or dying while travelling in and around
the continent. He had no intention of perishing here even if it was
an elaborate dream he was having.

As the sky darkened, the men settled down to sleep and except
for the occasional snort, burp and fart, the ship was quiet. Water
splashed against the hull as the ship rode the swells. Evan tossed and
turned, unable to get comfortable. In the end he gave in and got up.
On light feet, he stepped over Phameas and a few others and clambered the steps onto the deck. It was pitch black, with the only light
from the smoking oil lamps. He glanced across the inky landscape,
the difference between the beginning and end of the sea and sky
difficult to distinguish. The two blended. Evan hadn't experienced
sailing of this kind. The use of computers and satellite navigation
provided guidance and information on weather patterns in his
world. Here, the captain had a small rectangular wooden tool with
string knotted at regular intervals that he held up against the stars.
Each knot represented latitudinal points. Evan surmised it must take
years to learn how to read the constellations. He admired these ancient mariners, who dared to brave the unpredictable seas and
weather using their wits, intelligence and courage.

Evan propped his elbows on the rail, the wind ruffling his hair as
he stared across the impenetrable surface of the sea. He wished he
had a magic wand and poof... he'd be back at home. With what he'd
seen, he could write a book or even a script for a movie. He lowered
his head onto the beam.

'If only I could get back home.'

The surrounding air changed. A stillness came upon him, as if he
was in a void where sound and breeze ceased. Evan straightened, the

hair on his arms tingling. Something caught his eye; he leaned over the railing to take a closer look. He did a double take, rubbed his eyes and shook his head.

'What on earth?'

The white caps of the waves stopped in mid-action. The break of the water against the hull no longer moved. He checked along the length of the ship and saw it was the same. As he turned his head for a better look, his mouth fell open. The sail on the masts, pregnant with air, looked as if dipped in starch. Evan took a tentative step. One side of him wanted to investigate but part of him didn't want to concede it was happening. It was too surreal and none of it made sense.

A blue circle of light pierced the black night sky and descended with lightning speed. Evan's lips parted and he backed away as fast as he could, the nimbus hurtling towards him. He tripped over his feet and fell sprawled on his back. It floated within a hairsbreadth of his face for a few seconds and then moved aside. Evan's heart thumped against his ribcage as he watched the ball of light change.

'What are you trying to do? Give me a heart attack?' Evan said, glaring. He struggled to his feet.

'Quite,' said Zeus with a small smile. 'I needed to get your attention.'

'I think you achieved that,' Evan bit back.

'Now that I have it,' Zeus said in a mild tone, 'you need to rescue your sister, the High Priestess, and your companions.'

'Who?' Evan said. 'What are you talking about? Didn't everyone on that ill-fated ship die?'

'That would be counterproductive to our purposes,' Zeus said. 'A ship found and saved them.'

'Then how am I not with them? If we were together, why didn't we get picked up at the same time?'

'Your journey is not complete,' Zeus said.

'Huh? What is that supposed to mean?'

'There are experiences you've yet to face.'

'That is not even an answer!' Evan said, getting angry. 'Tell me, without your usual fluff, what you're trying to say.'

Zeus tilted his head. 'One should not know too much about one's future.' Zeus held up his hand as Evan opened his mouth to retort. 'Your sister and fellow Atlanteans are held captive at the palace in Kyrene. You need them to complete the quest.'

'You're supposed to be a powerful god, so why don't you go and rescue them? In fact, why don't you find those relics and get this over with, then I can go home.'

'Stop being obstinate,' Zeus said, his eyes flashing. 'Save your fellow Atlanteans and find the relics.'

'And how do you propose I do that? I am just one person.'

'You are intelligent, find a way.'

'And if there is resistance, what am I supposed to do?'

'Use the sword and shield; it's what you've trained for these past years.' Zeus turned away from him.

'Wait a minute... I haven't...'

Zeus was gone.

'Goddammit!' Evan slammed a fist onto the railing. The wooden beam splintered. 'You're despicable Zeus and I don't care who you think you are!' he shouted into the night sky.

Evan staggered forward. The ship shifted, the sail billowed, and the waves splashed against the hull. Evan gripped the rail and gritted his teeth; the knuckles on his hands turned white. His life was spinning out of control and for what? To fulfil a delusion that had no bearing on his life?

'Grrrrrr...'

The tendons in his neck bulged and the muscles on his arms stuck out as he clenched the railing tighter. He was stuck in a place with no way to get back home! Never before had he felt so helpless and he did not like how he was being manipulated. But what could he do? There must be a way to get back to his reality... After a while his anger began to ebb and the longer he thought about it, the more elusive seemed the solution.

'An answer will come to me and when it does, I'm gone,' he murmured. Evan relinquished his hold on the railing, the muscles groaning in relief. He noticed the night sky had lightened and turned eastwards. On the horizon a rosy glimmer emerged and stretched its arms to embrace the earth. It was the most beautiful sunrise he'd seen and he wished he had a camera to take a picture. Flawless and pristine, there was none of the grime and pollutants of modern days in the air to mar the scene. He watched the sun make its glowing ascent and marvelled at the myriad of colours as it changed from the reddish tinges to a golden glow.

'That was worth seeing.'

Evan turned and saw the makings of a settlement not too far from the coastline. As the sun soared higher, the outline of the buildings became clearer. The crew stirred, and the boards creaked as a few of them started moving. Harsh, gravelled voices rose from the belly of the ship and got louder as the men ascended to the deck. Evan watched as the seafront and settlement loomed closer. His mouth went dry. Here he was, about to step foot into a world far removed from his own. What would he see? What would the people be like? His study of ancient civilisation might come in handy but he did not think it would prepare him for the real thing.

'Ahoy, Evandros.' He looked over his shoulder and saw Phameas walking towards him. 'Did you stay out here all night?'

He nodded. 'Couldn't sleep. Thought the fresh air might help.'

They gazed at the scenery; ridges of the mountain cliffs and beaches home to low shrubs where bushes grew in abundance. A scattering of houses and cleared land was dominated by the natural environment. In Evan's time, this land encompassed vast cities and urban scaping.

'Come Evandros, we need to prepare the ship for docking,' Phameas said.

Evan tried to quell the fluttery feeling in his stomach. This was one adventure he did not volunteer for. He pushed away from the railing and followed Phameas, focussing his energies on the task ahead.

CHAPTER SEVENTEEN

'Evandros is alive!' Alexina said, bursting into their chamber. She stumbled to a stop, spotting Leander and Hektor treating Homer's most recent injuries at the hands of the king's guards.

'Are you sure?' Leander gave her look of disbelief.

'How could you know this?' Hektor said as a deep line creased his forehead. 'Only the gods are privy to such information.'

'Mother Goddess,' Alexina whispered, her face paling as she stared at Homer. One eye was swollen shut, his nose broken and lips split and bleeding. His breathing was laboured and noisy, and he winced when she laid a hand on his arm. 'What have they done to you?'

'The king wasn't happy when I refused to answer him and injured a few of his guards,' he said, through impaired lips.

'This madness cannot continue Homer. The king will kill you.' She stood, her eyes flinty and jaw rigid. 'I'll go to the king and demand he stops.'

'No High Priestess!' Homer's face contorted as he reached out to clasp her hand. 'You mustn't! The king can inflict whatever horrors he wishes on me but we're sworn to protect you.'

Alexina sank to her knees, tears welling. 'Dearest Homer...'

'He must not touch you,' he insisted and looked at her with feverish eyes. She nodded with reluctance, her cheeks wet with tears. He sighed, relaxed his grip on her hand and lay back. 'You said Evandros is alive.'

'Yes.' A small smile crept across her face. 'He's on a merchant ship bound for a place called Rusaddir.'

'How is that possible?' Hektor said, hands on hips.

'Zeus came and told me he was alive' she said.

'Is he aware we survived? Where we are?' Leander said, eyes sparkling.

Alexina nodded. 'Divine Zeus told him where to find us and he is on his way. We have to wait. It may take him a while to get here.' She paused. Her forehead wrinkled and marred her beautiful face. 'There's something else.'

Leander frowned. He and the other two men exchanged wary glances.

'What is it?' Hektor asked, breaking the uneasy silence.

'There is a possibility Evandros doesn't remember the purpose of our journey...' she said and then faltered.

Homer stared at her and the sheen of sweat on his face intensified.

'What else is there?' Hektor said, his voice clipped and lips pressed into a thin line.

'It... he...' More tears sprang to her eyes. Leander took her hands in his and gave a reassuring squeeze and a tentative smile. 'Evandros has no memory of his life or of us.' Alexina said in a whisper, her head bowed.

The slack-jawed expression of astonishment on Leander's face mirrored Hektor's and Homer's. Hektor opened and closed his mouth, the words not forthcoming. The pallor on Homer's face grew pastier and he looked as if he might pass out.

'Was he injured when the monster destroyed our ship?' Leander asked in a quiet voice.

Alexina shook her head and lifted her tear stained face. 'Divine Zeus did not say, except... except not to expect him to be the same man we knew.'

Homer turned away and stared up at the ceiling. Leander gathered the High Priestess into his arms as new tears welled in her eyes. Hektor ran a hand through his hair.

'Gods! What a mess,' he said in a despondent tone. 'Evandros was supposed to guide us. His knowledge of the histories and of the people and places was the reason the gods chose him. How are we to navigate our way through these lands?'

'Divine Zeus said in time he will remember and once he re-joins us, it may stir what he has forgotten,' Alexina said. She patted her eyes and face dry with the corner of her khiton.

'May? That does not sound promising,' Hektor said, mouth down-turned.

'And if he doesn't, what then?' Leander said, looking at the High Priestess.

Alexina did not answer straight away, although from the expression on her face, the same question crossed her mind. When she did respond, a steely resolve replaced any sense of disquiet she felt.

'It is my understanding Evandros can still give us the necessary information to do what we must.'

'Yet he cannot remember his life and us?' Hektor said, eyes narrowing. 'Doesn't that strike you as odd?'

'I'm not schooled in the complexities of the mind,' Alexina said in a firm tone. 'I, for one, am grateful he is alive. No doubt we will learn more when he arrives.'

Hektor acknowledged this with a bow of his head. 'Of course, High Priestess, I did not mean to be disrespectful. I anticipate his arrival with eagerness.'

Alexina gave him a small smile. 'We are all anxious, Hektor. It's natural to voice doubts and concerns. Our current dilemma has accentuated our fears but we must remain strong and not allow them to take control. More than ever, we need to stand together and deliver a united front. We do not want the king to sense any weakness.'

'Of that you can be assured,' he said, eyes glowering and jaw tightening.

'Good,' she said, her smile fading.

CHAPTER EIGHTEEN

Evan did not have time to dwell on the impending arrival as he was too busy securing goods in the hold and on deck. The captain made it clear if any item broke or was damaged during the docking, the men did not get paid. It did cross his mind how risky it was going to be but he was summoned to man the oar. He wanted to see how the ship was docked. Apart from educated guesses taken from stories by the ancient historians and playwrights, the method had not been determined.

The ship drew closer, and the captain ordered the oars raised and withdrawn. Evan, eager to watch, dashed up onto the deck. He sucked in a breath as the ship coasted towards a man-made trench where on one side a wooden walkway led from the beach into the water. The wide keel made contact with the beach. Evan, not prepared for the impact, lost his balance, and his hip hit the railing. He grimaced and rubbed his side. Men on the walkway caught thick ropes and looped them around sturdy posts. Heavy stone anchors were dropped from the bow and stern. The captain called the crew to attention once satisfied the ship was fastened and secured. Phameas grabbed Evan by the arm and pulled him into line with the other crewmen.

'Tomorrow at daybreak, everyone must return to unload the goods. May Baal forsake those who fail to appear!'

'Aye, Captain!' The crew scurried, as rats do scavenging for food, and collected their meagre belongings before they quickly disembarked.

'Come, Evandros,' said Phameas, 'let's go find a taverna and drink.'

Evan joined him and a few others he'd befriended. He took a step onto a wooden plank, and his legs shook so much he walked like a drunkard. Evan forced himself to concentrate and was grateful it was a handful of steps to the beach. He followed Phameas, careful not to fall into the water. The jetty was wide enough to walk in a single file.

As soon as they reached the shore, people swarmed and surrounded Evan, in the same way honey attracts bees. He stood head and shoulders taller than them but it did not deter or frighten the crowd. They held out their hands with pleading voices and desperate eyes. Their clothes were torn and dirty and hair matted. An odour wafted up and Evan gagged. He covered his nose with his hand and the stench faded but when he lifted it away, the smell returned in an instant. Women pawed at his arms. Someone pulled at his clothing. Evan tried to jerk away, twisted one way then the other, but they pressed in closer. The tugging was relentless and persistent. He whipped his head from side to side to look for a familiar face, and then a small voice caught his attention. He glanced down. A thin boy stared up at him, eyes dull, hands outstretched.

'Off with you! Bloody parasites!' Phameas barged his way through with three other sailors alongside, and shoved the beggars out of the way. 'Bugger off!' Phameas took Evan's elbow and ushered him through the throng. 'What happened? Thought you were right behind me?'

'I was!' Evan said with a shudder. 'I need a shower.'

'A what?'

'You know... a bath.'

Phameas chuckled. 'A few drinks at the taverna and it will be forgotten.'

'Those people...' He glanced back. His eyes happened to meet those of the boy.

'They are vermin, scum who beg for money and food,' Phameas said with a sneer. 'Such filth, they should be condemned to death for harassing honest folk.'

'They can't help their circumstances,' Evan said, the memory of the stench and desperation still strong.

Phameas snorted. 'Of course they can. Everyone has the potential to find work. It's a matter of whether they want to earn an honest living or not. Forget about them, time to celebrate your good fortune at being alive.'

Evan followed Phameas, the three sailors at his back, and strolled through the crowd. Colourful tents of various sizes and shapes adorned the stretch of beach. Several sold hot food and others, different wares. As they moved from the seaside and onto firmer ground, Evan caught sight of a group of people as dark as night shoved into an enclosure. The men wore loincloths and the women skirts. He knew straight away who they were: Afrikaans. They shuffled against one after the other, shoulders wilted and heads bowed except one. A teenage boy, defiance and hatred oozing, glared as they walked past. The boy's back was flayed, the bloody flesh beneath exposed. Evan stumbled, and fell to his knees, bile rose and his mouth watered.

'Evandros!' Phameas rushed to his side and with another helped him to his feet.

'Can't we help them?' he said, swallowing back the bitterness in his mouth.

'Who?' Phameas looked around, bewildered.

'Those people.' Evan pointed.

Phameas turned to see, mystified by his question. 'They're the spoils of war and to be sold as slaves.'

'No person should be a slave,' Evan said. He started towards the cage.

Phameas, quick as a snake, stepped out in front of him. 'You do not oppose the Carthaginian Empire,' he said in a low voice.

'But...'

Phameas stood his ground. 'A wise man knows which fights can be won and those that cannot.'

'It has always been this way, and besides it is the law of nature,' one of the sailors said. 'These people are inferior, so who cares what happens to them.'

'Their differences do not make their lives lesser than anyone else's. Humans, regardless of their stature, should be treated with respect,' Evan said.

'That may be the case where you are from but here it is life. Now, let's move on before we draw attention. I, for one, do not want to be interrogated by soldiers.' Phameas gave Evan a gentle shove, and he moved on with reluctance.

They traversed a maze of streets, turned one way then another. It reminded Evan of the narrow and older streets of Rome. The frequent changes of direction made his head spin and if he was to head back to the docks there was no way he'd remember which way they came.

'Here we are.' Phameas stopped outside a closed door, the timber slats hewn with shoddy workmanship. A slight hum came from the other side. 'This place is favoured by sailors; the captains tend to go elsewhere though on occasion a few do come here.'

Phameas pushed the door open and stepped into an open-aired courtyard. Trees lined the walls, creating an arbour. Wooden tables and benches were arranged in the centre. Seated at the tables were the toughest looking men Evan had ever seen. Many of them shouted greetings to Phameas and the others. The expressions on their faces changed and fell quiet. Heads turned and eyes stared. The faces were weathered and hardened from time spent on the sea.

Evan fidgeted, uncomfortable by the attention. He leaned to Phameas and said in a low voice, 'Are they always this hostile?'

'Don't worry,' Phameas said, smiling and slapping him on the shoulder. 'Foreigners are treated with suspicion until they get used to you. Come along, let's get something to eat and drink.'

They neared a table of three men, each with long dark hair, elaborate curled beards, and conical hats. They dressed in fitted tunics that exposed their left shoulders and wore wide, coloured sashes around their waists which emphasised powerful torsos.

'Greetings, honoured Captains,' Phameas said with a nod.

'Stop there!' one of the captains demanded as the group passed by and approached the taverna.

'Captain?' Phameas said as Evan and the others stopped behind him.

The captain stood and pointed. 'Him. What is his story?'

'He's a member of our crew. We docked a short time ago and have come for food and drink,' said Phameas, unperturbed.

'Where does he hail from?' the captain said, taking a step closer.

'A man's origin is not important as long as he can wield an oar,' Phameas said, his gaze flicking to his mates.

The captain looked from Evan to Phameas. 'You don't know where he's from, do you? And what of the weapons he carries? Can he use those weapons as well as an oar?'

'Is there a point to this line of questioning?' Evan said to the captain, eyes hard as granite.

The captain's head jerked and he took a few seconds to respond, eyes narrowed. 'Your stature and bearing speaks of nobility, so how is it you have come to this place and with these men?'

'I am not a noble and am fortunate to be in the company of these honourable men. Now if you excuse us, we are going to order our food and drink,' Evan said, then turned to move away.

'I am a captain, and you do not take leave without permission!'

Evan stopped, his shoulders rigid.

'Evandros, it will not do to punch a captain,' Phameas said in a frantic whisper.

'I don't intend to,' he said. He spun on his heels, took a few steps towards the captain and leant forward, his face in the other man's. 'One, you earn respect and not through ultimatums; two, you are not my captain and therefore I don't heed any command other than his; and three, it's none of your business where I come from or why I am here.'

The captain swallowed.

Evan straightened, the hard glare of his gaze relentless. 'Now, my friends and I are going to enjoy our meal, in peace.'

Without another word he returned to his companions. Phameas tried to hide a smile while the other three gawked at him, but they did not hesitate to follow as he ducked to enter the poorly lit taverna. The courtyard was silent for a few minutes and then it erupted as the patrons' animated voices flooded the courtyard.

'No one has ever stood up to a captain before,' said one of the sailors in awe.

'I'm not a fan of bullies,' Evan said, sitting at one of the empty tables.

'Fan? Bullies?' the sailor repeated in a puzzled tone.

'People who use their position or size to push others around, demean and threaten.'

'That's what people in power do,' another said as he sat next to Evan.

'I know, but it doesn't give them right to abuse others.'

'You are an unusual man,' the third one said. 'Not many men with your standing would stick up for the likes of us or want to help slaves.'

Evan shrugged. 'I am no different than you. Let's talk about something else. Enlighten me on Hippo Regius. What should I expect when we get there?'

CHAPTER NINETEEN

The following day Phameas and Evan strolled along the water's edge, where the beach teemed with large and small ships. Many had arrived the day before, after they departed for the town. Evan slowed his pace and stopped in front of a large and formidable vessel. It had three tiers of oars. The prow was shaped in the form of a bird's beak, and jutted out on the beach. The wooden beak was encased in metal, and the stern had an ornate reproduction of fern fronds. It curled over the steering platform. The ship had two masts, the smaller closest to the prow and a larger one in the centre.

Evan recognised the vessel. It was a war ship, sleek and built for speed. He'd seen pictures in books and on the internet.

'What a majestic ship!' he said, unable to contain the excitement from his voice. 'It is Phoenician, isn't it?'

Phameas quirked a brow and gave him an odd look. 'It's one of our war ships.'

Evan reached out and touched the beak, the metal warm and smooth. 'How on earth did they do it?' He wandered closer and stared at the hull, the planks of wood fitted so tightly, even a piece of paper could not pass through. 'Remarkable. Wish I had my camera with me.'

'Camera?' Phameas scratched his head and looked from Evan to the ship and back.

Evan turned to his companion. 'Do you think we'd be allowed to go aboard? I'd like to take a look around.'

'The captains of these ships tend not to allow strangers and in particular, outsiders, on board.'

'That's a shame.' Evan studied the length of the ship to where the stern sat in the water.

'If only you had paper and something to draw with,' Phameas said.

'Phameas, old boy, you are a genius!' Evan beamed, eyes shining. He reached for the bag slung over his shoulder, rummaged inside and pulled out the obsidian book, ink and stylus. 'Forgot these were in here.'

He flipped it to a blank page and began to sketch. Phameas stood by his shoulder and watched. It didn't take long for Evan to draw an outline of the ship and then fill in the details. A few strokes later he stepped back to get a better view of the deck. When he'd finished, Evan walked to the starboard side and drew that as well. He completed his set of drawings with a view of the prow.

'They are very good,' Phameas said.

'Thank you. My job is to draw and construct buildings,' Evan said.

'You must be exceptional at what you do.'

The smile on Evan's face vanished. 'It is something I enjoy and hope to resume.' He took hold of the cover to close the tome but a gentle breeze flipped the pages.

Phameas stuck out his hand.

'You have the gift of the gods!' he said in awe, staring at the pictures. 'Who are these people? And this woman, she is an extraordinary beauty.'

'They were companions on the ship,' Evan said, staring at the unfamiliar faces. 'The woman is my sister. She is a High Priestess.' He gazed at the images; they were strangers to him. He turned his attention to the young woman and agreed with his friend, she was stunning. These were the people Zeus wanted him to rescue, by himself no less. He could hold his own in a fight, which he had done after a night out on the town, but this was different. He carried weapons he had no idea how to use. At the bottom of the bag he discovered a dagger. The previous owner must have put it there sometime before the gigantic octopus destroyed the ship. Now he supposed it was his, along with the other stuff. Evan scowled. He did not enjoy being manipulated.

'Are you hungry?' Phameas asked, breaking his musings. 'There's a good selection of food over at the stalls.' Not too far from where they stood, colourful tents dotted the shoreline, each hawking various wares and refreshments.

'What I'd give for a cup of coffee,' he said.

'What is coffee?'

'It is a hot, black, bitter tasting beverage that gives you a boost in the morning,' Evan said slipping the tome and stylus into his bag.

'Doesn't sound pleasant to drink,' Phameas said, unconvinced.

'It's a matter of the quality of the beans, how they are roasted and brewed,' Evan said.

Phameas shook his head. 'You have strange ways about you, Evandros.'

'Come on, let's go and see what they're selling.'

After last night's meal, Evan was not sure what to expect. The dish had been drowned in brown slop, with pieces of tough gristly meat. He thought it was mutton but did not want to ask. Some things should not be known. A side dish was a bowl of overcooked lentils. The wine, rough and unrefined, gave him heartburn. His father's homemade wine which he had thought was crude, tasted better.

The two wandered through the busy makeshift market. Owners bartered with customers over goods. They spoke fast and used local phrases, which Evan did not understand until Phameas explained.

Drawn by a strong aroma, Evan approached a stall and began to sneeze. Bags packed with coloured powder and seeds were arranged three rows deep on a wooden table. He ducked his head under the canopy and started sneezing again.

'Shoo! Shoo!' A stooped old woman, her face lined with age, shuffled towards them waving her arms. 'Shoo!'

'I just want to check what spices you have,' Evan said stepping back to avoid her propelling arms.

'Go. You scare away customers.'

Evan glanced around and quirked an eyebrow at her. 'How do you know we're not customers?'

'Are you going to buy?'

'Well... no... but...'

'Go away. You waste my time.' The old woman scowled and turned her back on him.

'She is not going to make any sales with an unpleasant attitude,' Evan said in a huff as they moved away. 'What was the harm in checking the goods?' He stopped and turned back to the stall, and the old woman glared at him. 'I don't get it! Mature women love me.'

Phameas chuckled. 'Not this one.' He strolled towards another stall.

Evan took a backward step and collided with someone.

'Pardon me. I didn't stop to look where I was going. My apologies.'

'No apologies necessary,' said a seductive voice.

'My, aren't you a big one,' said a second female.

Two attractive women dressed in sheer clothing stood on either side of Evan. Their hands stroked and played a sensual game on his arms. They smiled up at him. Their lips were painted ruby red and black kohl enhanced the hue of their eyes. They moved closer until their bodies pressed against his. One ran her tongue over her lips. Evan coughed, his face turning pink. He looked over his shoulder to Phameas, but he was faced the other way and busy purchasing food. Before he could call out to his friend, Evan was dragged away. The women stood side by side, and glared, hands on hips. Then one shook a fist.

'Sicilia! You rotten boy!'

'Come with me. Come, come,' said a small insistent voice. It was the young beggar boy.

'Wait a minute, my friend is back there.'

'I find you a safe place. Those women are no good,' the boy said.

'I am aware of what those women wanted, and had no intention of playing their game,' Evan said with a frown. He stopped. 'My friend will be wondering where I am. Thank you for your help but I'll be leaving.' He sidestepped the dirty beggar boy and started back to the market.

'You come from a faraway world. You do not belong here,' the boy said.

Evan halted mid-step and then spun around as the words sank in.

'Say that again.'

'You're from another world.'

'What the...' Evan said, drawing out the words. 'My home is a long way.' He stared at the boy.

The boy cocked his head to the side. 'Your home is in a different place and time.'

Evan felt his mouth fall open. He clamped it shut. 'What makes you say that?'

'You don't fit in here.' The boy took a step towards Evan and pointed to the weapons. 'They belong to another man. You may be identical in appearance but not the same. You are not safe here, danger is all around you. People will die.'

Evan swallowed. 'How do you know I'm not from here?'

'I did not say that. Once, this was your home, now you are no longer in accord with this place. You have seen and experienced a life that has changed you.'

Evan's mouth went dry. He swallowed a hard lump and then said, 'How can you have any idea of where I lived?'

'I see things others cannot.'

'Such as the future?'

The boy gave a slight nod. 'That and a person's destiny and when time has changed.'

'How am I in danger?'

The boy frowned in concentration. 'There are those who will try to stop you from completing the task. Your father will protect you as much as he can, but even he cannot stop fate.'

Evan felt a chill snake across his back. 'Are you saying I will die? Here in this god-forsaken period?'

The boy shrugged. 'A person's journey is never certain, this is just one path, and we have many.'

Evan sank to the ground, his mind reeling. He did not know what to think. It was too much. The boy sat next to him and they stared out over the azure sea.

'I thought clairvoyants were only supposed to give good news,' he said after a while.

'I don't understand what you mean,' the boy said.

'Never mind. So I am really from here.'

The boy nodded. Evan fell silent. The voices of the stall owners and customers washed over him. Their garbled bartering reminded him of the times when he went to the local farmers' market to buy fruit and vegetables. It was comforting to hear recognisable sounds in a foreign world.

'Why can't I remember the life I had here? Nothing about this place is familiar.'

'Perhaps you don't want to.'

Evan leant forward and rested his arms on his knees. 'How old are you?'

'One and ten annuals.'

'Where are your parents?' Evan took in his grubby face, black stained feet and the holes in his tunic, the dye long gone. A sense of world-weariness exuded from his being but his eyes told another story. Courage, cunning and intellect gleamed there, as did sadness.

'Dead. Killed trying to protect me from the master.'

'I see. Those women called you "Sicilia", is that where you are from?'

The boy nodded. 'The Phoenicians raided our village and killed many people. My parents and I and others who did not resist were spared and taken as slaves.'

'Are you still with this master?'

The boy shook his head. 'I slit his throat while he slept and came here.'

'How long have you been on your own?'

'Three annuals.'

'What is your name?'

'Dexion.'

'Well Dexion, you are a very brave and wise young man. Glad to meet you. My name is Evan. Evandros.' He stuck out his hand. Dexion looked at it and then to Evan, bewildered.

'Where I come from, well the place I remember living,' he said with a wry smile, 'we shake hands when we greet another.'

Dexion, hesitant, put out his hand, Evan grasped it and shook it up and down, then let the boy's hand go. Dexion's face lit up with understanding.

'Why have you been brought back?' Dexion asked.

'I thought you'd have that information.'

'What I see is that you must stop a man who challenges the way we live and our beliefs. You have a difficult path ahead. The images I receive are not always well-defined, yet in spite of this I'm never wrong,' Dexion said.

'According to Zeus, or Jupiter as you call him, I and others need to find ancient artefacts of the Mother Goddess. Once we have them, their power can prevent the birth of Christianity.'

Dexion frowned. 'Christianity...' His eyes then glazed over and voice changed. 'This man is a shepherd, one who gathers and protects his flock. His heart is pure but those who follow in his stead change his teachings. Greed, fear and power drives their desires and many will die by their hand.' The boy turned to Evan, his eyes large and filled with dread. He bit his lip and when he spoke his voice shook. 'The world will see turmoil for thousands of years and there is no end to the horrors.'

Evan shuddered. What Dexion didn't realise was his prophetic declaration had come to fruition. War peppered the world's historical timeline. It was the nature of man to fight for a cause, good or bad. Was it possible to change the course of events through the actions of a small group? Even if it meant the prevention of one man's destiny?

CHAPTER TWENTY

The next day as the sun peeked over the horizon Phameas and Evan made their way back to the ship. They raised a hand in greeting when they saw other members of the crew. They converged on the ship. There was the buzz of excitement as the men waited and chatted. The captain arrived and within minutes half the crew boarded while the others remained on the shore.

'Why aren't we going on board?' Evan asked.

'We have to push the ship into the water,' Phameas said.

'And how do we get on?'

'Ropes.' Phameas beckoned him. 'Come this way.'

Evan followed Phameas along with the other men, half on one side of the prow and half on the opposite side. There was a shout from the deck and within seconds, the ground crew began to push the large, heavy wooden ship. The men grunted and breathed heavily, muscles in their arms and legs strained as they worked to move the ship. After a few days of sitting idle on the banks of the shore, sand had built up around the hull. Evan gritted his teeth and bent his head. His feet dug deep into the sand, his arms stretched and his hands pressed against the hull. There was a slight movement. With renewed vigour, the men kept going until the sand gave way and they entered the water.

The crew on board thrust out the oars and began to row when most of the stern was immersed.

'Quick Evandros, catch hold of a rope,' Phameas said as he grabbed one next to him.

Evan splashed his way over to the hull and reached for a swinging rope. His foot slipped against the ship, and he lost his grip on the rope. He tried again and hauled himself up the side of the ship. Once on deck he sank down with a grateful groan, legs splayed out. He hung his head, a hand on his heaving chest.

'It gets easier,' Phameas said, with a small grin as he squatted next to him. 'Next time it may be a good idea to put your gear on board beforehand.'

Evan lifted his head and glared at Phameas. 'If I had known, there was no way I'd have lugged this equipment.'

Phameas' grin broadened and he clapped a hand on Evan's shoulder. 'Come along, we need to take our places at the oars.'

Evan grunted, he got to his feet, limbs protesting, and trailed behind Phameas. He placed his gear beneath his seat and glanced around as he waited. Where each oarsman sat, two planks of wood jutted out from the hull of the ship, one to sit on and a smaller piece for the feet.

'Oars ready!' the bosun bellowed.

Evan grabbed the oar and leaned forward. Loud splashes resonated as the long wooden oars plunged into the water. With another shout from the bosun, the oarsmen pulled back. It did not take long for the crew to find their rhythm and the ship left the port, the coast a mere speck in the distance.

Evan was soon covered in sweat. Salty rivulets trickled down his forehead and into his eyes. His hands slipped on the oar. He clutched tighter. His nose began to twitch. The smell of body odour grew stronger. Evan tried not to retch. It made his head swim. Then, there was silence.

'Oars up!'

He pulled in the oar, wiped his brow, collected his equipment and headed for the prow. Once there, he drew in a deep breath and tried to cleanse the stench from his senses. He could not remember the last time he smelt this awful. What he wished for was a long hot shower and soap. He gazed with longing at the deep Mediterranean blue water.

'What are the chances of the captain anchoring the ship so we can go for a swim?' he said to Phameas who arrived at his side with a cup of water.

'Why?'

'To refresh the body and feel clean.'

Phameas shook his head, amused, and passed the cup. 'You say the most peculiar things, Evandros.'

'How long will it take to get to Hippo Regius?' Evan said, sighing.

'If Baal grants us favourable winds, it should take two days.'

'What happens once there?'

'The captain has to pick up extra goods and then we sail for Carthage.'

'How many...'

'Catch him!'

'The little bastard, grab him!'

Evan and Phameas looked at each other as feet thundered below deck followed by further angry shouts. A group had gathered around the hatch and hunched over the opening. Those standing behind craned their necks to see what was happening. Hurtling out of the hold a boy jumped and bolted, weaving from one side of the ship to the other. One of the crew members burst out from below and gave chase. Another tumbled out and joined the other.

'Master! Please! Help me!'

One of the men, a few steps away from the boy, reached out and caught him by the scruff of the neck. The sailor lifted a hand.

'Stop! I know this boy!'

His hand wavered as he and the others turned. Evan hurried towards them, Phameas right on his heels.

'How is it you know this bag of filth?' the crewman said, lip curled.

'I met the boy at the markets. He is harmless.'

'He is a stowaway and must be punished!'

The man raised his hand again.

'Wait!' Evan said. He stepped closer to Dexion. 'That's not a good reason to hit him.'

'Filthy little creatures such as him are thieves and rob people for a living.'

'That may be the case if he was on the streets but we're on a ship. A bit difficult to escape don't you think?' Evan then turned to Dexion. 'Did you steal from anyone here?'

He shook his head. 'No!'

'The question is, why is he here?' Phameas said, staring at the boy.

'I followed Master Evandros. I wanted to go with him. He needs me.'

'Ah... now I understand.' The sailor laughed and nodded to the others. 'This miserable beggar *wants* to be with his *master*.'

The others joined in with a snigger.

Evan narrowed his eyes and with jaw clenched thrust his face into the other man's.

'What's going on here?'

The laughing stopped and the humour in their eyes and faces evaporated as the captain threaded his way through the cluster.

'We have a stowaway, Captain.'

The captain glared at Dexion who cowered and tried to twist his way out of the man's grasp.

'The boy wanted to be with *his* master.'

'Right, I have had enough of these disgusting inferences.' Evan's hands tightened into fists.

The sailor leered at him and then turned to grin at his audience. Evan's face darkened, and the blood flowed through his veins like a fast flowing river. He squared up to the sailor and drew back a balled hand.

'Desist!' the captain barked.

Phameas grabbed Evan's arm and pulled him back.

'Well boy, what are you doing here?'

'I did not follow Master Evandros to give sexual favours,' Dexion said, eyes flashing. 'He treated me with respect and gave me a coin for food. I came to assist him on his journey.'

Evan stared at Dexion, not sure what to think. There must be more the boy had not told him.

The captain was pensive as he looked from the dirty beggar to the stranger and then he flicked his fingers at the sailor. 'Release the boy.'

'What?' the man said, eyes bulging.

'Now!' barked the captain.

The sailor glared at Evan and with reluctance let go of Dexion. The captain then ordered him to take first oar at the stern. He turned to Dexion, eyes hard and unflinching. 'You'll earn your keep while on this ship. Give the men water until I order you to stop. Understood?'

Dexion nodded.

'As for the rest of you flea-bitten dogs, get back to your seats and ready your oars!'

The crew scrambled in different directions, eager to be out of the captain's wrath.

'We need to talk,' Evan said to Dexion, 'but for now you'd better follow the captain's orders.'

'What is going on, Evandros? Is there something I should know?' Phameas said as they watched Dexion scurry away towards the urn.

'I'm not sure of anything Phameas, not since you found me.'

CHAPTER TWENTY-ONE

It wasn't until later in the day, when the crew took a break for a meal, that Evan was able to talk with Dexion. With bread and a bowl of spiced lentils stewed with lamb in hand, Evan and Phameas sat with their backs against the bulwark of the ship. Dexion sat cross-legged with his own bowl, mesmerised by what he held.

'Tell the truth now,' Evan said around a mouthful of bread and stew, 'why did you follow?'

The gaunt boy looked up from his bowl to Evan and then to Phameas.

'Whatever you have to say, Phameas can be trusted.'

The Phoenician sat up straighter and puffed out his chest at Evan's words. Dexion placed his bowl on the deck by his side and leaned forward.

'I had... another vision,' he said in a tentative voice, glancing at Phameas.

Phameas did an about take. 'Wha—?'

'Dexion is able to foresee the future,' Evan said. 'What has it got to do with me?'

'You are not the only one seeking the treasure,' he said. 'Another is trying to find them and he will have help from one whom the gods insulted. Together they will be formidable and difficult to beat.' Dexion's voice dropped to a whisper. 'They have the power of the gods and cannot be killed. If they recover the items, nothing can stop him from destroying those who ruined his family and their followers. The one I told you of back in Rusaddir, the shepherd?'

Evan nodded and stiffened.

'This other I speak of intends to guide the shepherd and make sure he is favoured by the people. If he wins, this man will be revered for eternity.'

Evan had a bitter taste in his mouth. The food he just ate curdled in his stomach. 'I am familiar with the individual you described,' he said in a flat voice. 'Nothing can prevent it from happening. It's what the people want.'

'There is something else,' Dexion said, face tight.

'Of course there is,' Evan said, trying to make light of the conversation.

'He will kill your children.'

'Children? What are you talking about? I don't have any.' Evan snorted and moved to stand.

'A woman you love will give birth to twins, a girl and a boy,' Dexion said. 'You'll have more children but you must defeat this one who threatens to change the world.'

'Dexion, I appreciate you coming to tell me this but what can I do? I am an ordinary man with little to offer. I just want to go home, back to the twenty-first century.' Evan got onto a knee, ready to stand. Dexion clamped a hand over his, the grip strong for a malnourished boy of eleven years.

'You are not ordinary,' Dexion said, 'that much I have seen. You were chosen for this and must complete your journey. This is why I am here, to aid you.'

'What journey?' Phameas, mystified, looked from Dexion to Evan. 'Twenty-first century? What is it? A place?'

'You should tell Phameas what's going on, as he's coming with us.' Dexion picked up his bowl and bread and began to eat.

'Wait a minute.' Evan sat back on his haunches with a thump. 'You didn't want to say anything with him here earlier, so what's changed?'

Dexion swallowed, scooped up more stew and added, 'We need him, and besides he has made up his mind.' Dexion then stuffed bread and stew into his mouth.

'What is the boy babbling about?' Phameas asked when it became clear Dexion wasn't going to speak any more.

'I'm still figuring that out myself,' Evan said, staring at Dexion's bowed head as he continued to eat with relish.

'What is this journey he mentioned?'

Evan scratched his head. 'I and four others, from the destroyed ship, were selected to find particular items. When the pieces are united they have the power to vanquish the one who threatens the gods' sovereignty. The combination of the objects reinstates their supremacy.'

'Where are these... items?'

Evan shrugged. 'Somewhere in Egypt or Carthage. They were mentioned as possible locations from which to start the search. Don't ask me why, I haven't any answers.'

'That's where we get our first lead to find one of the treasures,' Dexion said. His attention was still focussed on the now near empty bowl.

'What if I don't want to go?' Phameas said.

Dexion lifted his head up and gave the Phoenician a small smile. 'You have decided. You were going to leave with Master Evandros when the ship docks at Carthage.'

Phameas   gaped. 'How, in the name of Baal, could you know?'

'You made yourself responsible for him,' Dexion waved his bowl at him. 'And when I mentioned "treasure" your eyes sparkled. This is not like one of your voyages on the sea, Phameas, danger follows Master Evandros. Are you prepared to give your life for his and this quest? Your beliefs will be tested by what you see. Are you ready to be a witness to what cannot be explained?'

The Phoenician put a hand over his mouth and pressed his fingers into his cheeks. His eyes flickered from Dexion to Evan and back.

'Phameas, you do not...' Evan said.

He dragged his hand over his bearded chin. He turned to Evan with a look of determination and gave a curt nod. 'I will go with you.'

Evan was relieved Phameas decided to come along, for he didn't have a plan or any idea what to do once in Carthage. Travelling alone in a strange country and era was something he did not relish either. Despite Dexion confirming this was the period he was from, this world was alien to him. Nothing stirred a memory, not even the outfit he wore: a colourful linen skirt, with an apron at the front and rear and underneath a codpiece. Phameas' attire differed. He wore a knee length close-fitting brown tunic, as did the rest of the crew except for the captain's more elaborate clothing. Each man wore a conical hat and had groomed beards, curled into one, two or more rows.

Evan longed for a pair of sneakers, shorts and a t-shirt or a singlet. But until he found a way back he'd have to wear what he'd got.

'When are you going to tell the captain?' he said to Phameas.

Phameas bit his lip. 'There is no good time to approach him. He will see it as an act of betrayal and disloyalty.'

'Maybe tell him when he is in an agreeable mood,' Evan said with a slight grimace.

'Those occasions are rare,' the Phoenician said with a long face.

'Then wait until we get to Carthage; that way he can't throw us off the ship or leave us stranded on some island,' Evan said.

Phameas gave a slow nod. 'Either way my life at sea is over and I will no longer work on another merchant vessel.'

'Perhaps not on one that is Phoenician but you can get work on others.'

Phameas shrugged and gave Evan a bright smile. 'It doesn't matter. This adventure will offer many opportunities. Once completed, we may have more.'

'Let's resolve this first,' Evan said. Once they recovered these mysterious objects, he intended to get back home and to his job.

'That will not be so easy,' Dexion said looking at him, his dark eyes boring into Evan's light blue ones.

'Huh? I don't know what you are talking about.' Evan turned away, uncomfortable at Dexion's uncanny insight.

'When the time comes, the decision to leave here may not be as easy as you'd expect,' the boy said. The expression on his face was as bland and innocuous as a blank piece of paper.

The hair on the back of Evan's neck prickled. 'This is not where I belong, you said so yourself.'

Dexion stood and put a hand on Evan's shoulder. 'Are you sure?'

'What is it you are not telling me?' Evan's forehead creased in deep furrows.

'Be prepared for the unexpected.' He picked up his bowl. 'Better get moving. The bosun is going to call you back to work.'

'What did he mean?' Phameas said. 'And what is this twenty-first century? Is it part of the journey?'

'You could say that,' Evan said. 'A very long one.'

CHAPTER TWENTY-TWO

After two days at sea, they arrived in Hippo Regius. From the large number of people gathered around the port, it seemed the city was bigger than Rusaddir. Evan wanted to disembark and explore the vibrant city, but they stopped for a short period to pick up merchandise. In spite of his situation, Evan was excited and curious. He hankered to walk around the city, study the buildings, the layout and the people. Unlike the ruins in his time which were Roman, this Hippo Regius was a living and breathing Phoenician city.

Evan didn't have any time to dwell on the missed opportunity, for the captain had the crew busy hauling the goods from the dock to the ship. Once the items were on board, they were soon heading out to sea. Evan never shied away from hard work or getting his hands dirty and had a newfound respect for how tough a life it must have been. He imagined it must be much more demanding than what he experienced and knew it was worse for women and slaves. Even the experts in the field of archaeology couldn't envisage what he'd seen so far.

Evan, Phameas and Dexion gathered during one of their breaks. They discussed how to approach the captain with regards to leaving on arrival in Carthage. Each idea was explored in full but deemed flawed in view of the captain's volatile nature. They concluded there was no easy way to inform him of their intentions.

'It's pointless,' said Phameas, mouth down-turned and face glum. 'He'll never let me leave the ship, he'll hand you over to the general and Baal knows what will happen to young Dexion.'

'I still think our option to take whatever we can and jump ship as soon as it docks is a good one,' Evan said.

Phameas shook his head. 'It won't work. There are guards posted along the wharf and when the captain raises the alarm, we're as good as dead.'

'What about the maps?' Dexion said, looking at Evan.

'Maps?' Evan frowned.

'The parchments in your knapsack,' Dexion said. 'What if you offer the captain one for our freedom? They are old and no doubt he will see the value of them.'

'No way,' Evan said shaking his head. 'One, they are not mine to give away and two, they are valuable. When this is over I plan on taking them back home.'

'What if you don't give him an original one,' said Phameas, narrowing his eyes.

Dexion's face lit up. 'That is an excellent idea.'

Phameas grinned and nodded at Dexion. He turned to Evan. 'You can draw, copy one, and give that to the captain.'

'You don't think the captain won't realise it's not genuine?' Evan said. 'He's not a stupid man.'

'Of course he isn't. If it is made to give the impression it's old, he will believe it's authentic.'

'I don't know...' Evan said.

'It will work,' Dexion said with confidence.

Evan looked at him and Phameas, whose smile was as vast as the sea they sailed on, gave an assured nod.

'Well, I guess it's decided then,' he said.

***

Eris, the Goddess of Discord, drummed her long elegant fingers on the arm of her throne. The seat was hewn out of the black coarse stone found everywhere in Tartaros. She scowled, leant her head against the crested bar and gazed up at the interminable blackness of her home. Not for the first time, she cursed Zeus for incarcerating her in this dreary and miserable place. A smile tweaked at the corner of her mouth as she recalled the reason. She chuckled and then her face darkened.

'If they had invited me to the wedding I wouldn't have had to resort to turning up unannounced. At least I brought a gift.' Her lips curved into a wicked smile. 'It was so much fun to witness Hera, Athene and Aphrodite argue over a silly golden apple. Not my fault each thought she was the most beautiful and wanted to possess it.' She tilted her head to the side and gazed at the impenetrable sky. Eris sat up and stared. 'What is that?' She stood, not taking her eyes off the flickering light in the distance. She snapped her fingers. 'See that? I want you to investigate and return with information on what is happening up there.'

The three harpies turned their heads in unison to where the goddess pointed and as quick as the wind, took flight. Eris kept an eye on them until they disappeared into the fathomless sky. She sat back down, perched on the edge of her throne. While she waited, she heard the familiar sounds of the thief and murderer Sisyphos making another attempt to escape by rolling a boulder up the steep hill. Then there was the howling of Ixion, doomed for eternity to remain tied to a flaming wheel for throwing his father-in-law into a pit of fire.

Not to mention the Titans imprisoned here after losing the war with the Olympian gods. She came across the old gods in the early days of her incarceration; isolated from everyone else and guarded by the Hekatonkhires, giants with fifty heads and one hundred arms each. Zeus was not taking chances on any of the Titans escaping. She almost felt sorry for them.

Almost.

She detected movement and stood as two of the harpies came into view.

'Where is Aëllo?' she said as soon as they landed.

One pointed while the other answered in short barks.

'Why, that is very interesting,' Eris said, 'a small fissure. Can anyone fit through it?'

The harpies shook their heads.

'How did Aëllo pass through the void?' Eris waited as Okypete explained. 'I see, so there is a gap in the shield yet filaments stretching across it can cause harm.' She paused and tapped her lips with a finger. 'Go join her and learn what the gods are doing.'

The harpies grinned, their razor-sharp teeth gleamed and their eyes sparkled in anticipation. It had been a long time since they tasted the flesh of mortals. They hungered to devour their meat. The two took a few steps, stretched their wings, and lifted themselves into the air, and melted into the jet-black sky.

For the first time in a long while, Eris began to make plans.

CHAPTER TWENTY-THREE

Carthage lay on the north coast of Africa, a city built on a peninsula that jutted into the Mediterranean Sea. Evan had read about the famous ports of Carthage but in no way did it prepare him for what he saw when they neared the site. The captain navigated the ship around the heads and into the bay. Evan's hands slipped and stopped rowing.

'Oh my God!'

'What is wrong with you? Keep rowing. Your oar is in the way,' said the oarsman sitting behind him.

'But look!' Evan said, pointing.

'I've seen it before,' the man said with a grunt as he pulled on his oar. 'Now pick up the oar!'

Evan waited for the next stroke and resumed rowing. His attention kept being drawn to the great walls that lined the coast right up to the cliff face. Farther along and from the varying heights, he discerned the walls were still under construction. Every kilometre or so were defensive outposts and from the figures standing on the wall, it seemed wide and stable.

Evan sucked in a quick breath as the ship drew closer. Where the walls were yet to be built another major structure was underway. He identified the familiar scaffolding, though cruder than he was accustomed to, set up to mirror a circle. In the centre sat a building near completion and warships were moored in the outer ring.

'Oh... my... God,' he said again.

The ship cruised past, sailed around a rocky outcrop and turned into a bay. A huge square pillared gate was held fast with massive chains that dematerialised into the sea. The merchant ship coasted into the rectangular harbour and on either side were ships, each moored to its own pier. The captain ordered the oarsmen to half speed, and the sails dropped.

Guided to a mooring place by a man waving a red flag, the captain with skill and years of seafaring steered the ship. Not long after, the captain commanded the rowers to stop and stow their oars. Even though eager to take a better peek at the legendary ports, Evan made sure he secured the oar. At this point he did not want to anger the captain. It would not work in their favour if he made a mistake by ruining equipment. He dashed out towards the bow of the ship after double checking the oar.

'This is incredible!'

Lining the dockyards stood brick buildings used for storage and administration. They would fit in any modern port. On the other side of the quay, facing the sea, it was the same, with fewer buildings.

'This is magnificent! What an amazing feat of engineering,' he said, waving his arms at the vista. He turned and his heart skipped a beat. 'Now that is outstanding.'

The entrance to the outer circular harbour was complete and several of the docking berths were in use. Evan wanted to examine the interior of the mooring stations. He had seen pictures of stone platforms on which the ships were built and stored during the seasons when too dangerous to sail. The naval headquarters erected in the middle of the harbour stowed more ships raised on wooden beds.

'Evandros! Shall we go and talk to the captain?' Phameas walked over to Evan who nodded, still enthralled. 'What is it?'

'Now isn't that fantastic?' Evan said flinging a hand out. He turned to Phameas, eyes gleaming. 'What a masterpiece!'

Phameas scratched his chin and looked at the massive wooden frame. 'If you think so. Evandros, we should go see the captain.'

'No time like the present,' he said.

'Huh?' Phameas' face drew a blank.

'It's an expression from back home.'

'Oh... then now is a good time.'

'Let's go.'

Evan grabbed the copy of the map he'd drawn from his bag and the two headed for the stern.

'What are you going to say to the captain?' Phameas said in a low voice.

'Me? He's your captain.'

Phameas gave a nervous chuckle. 'Since the map is yours it's better if you speak.'

'It was your idea Phameas,' Evan pointed out. 'I've dealt with tough customers before and won them over. I hope he's in an amenable mood.'

The captain was conversing with the bosun, who nodded and said a word here and there. As they approached, Evan, with a slight turn of his head, said from the corner of his mouth, 'Remember, this was your plan if this goes sideways.'

Phameas threw him another baffled look but Evan ignored it. He didn't have time to explain what he meant.

'Captain, may we have a moment of your time?' he said as the bosun walked away.

The captain looked up at him, his face stern and eyes flicking from Phameas to Evan.

'What is it you want?'

'Have you made a decision as to what you intend to do with me and young Dexion?'

'Why?' the captain said, tone sharp.

'I have a proposal that may change your mind.'

The captain clasped his hands behind his back and gazed at Evan, eyes unblinking and as hard as steel.

'On with it,' he said after a long few moments.

'In exchange for letting me and Dexion go,' Evan began, ignoring the astonishment on Phameas' face, 'I offer this map to you. It is old, and was charted by my people as they sailed these seas and much further.' He unrolled the map. 'You will be familiar with many of these landmarks. Plus it has places you may not yet have journeyed to.'

The captain poked his head at the map Evan held, his eyes darting one way then the other.

'No other person has seen this.'

'What are these?' The captain pointed to the symbols.

'The script of my people. I can write the names out so you can read it.'

'No, not necessary. How old is it?'

'Not sure, but at least a hundred years old.'

'How has it not perished?' The captain looked up at Evan, brow creased.

Evan held up the cylinder that contained the original map. 'Our documents are stored in air-tight containers, reducing exposure to air and contaminants. Not everyone is allowed access to these ancient texts.'

'How is it you have it?'

'The Elders, leaders of my home, entrusted me with it.'

Evan fell silent to allow the captain to continue studying the map. After a while he dropped the map, handed the cylinder to Phameas and began to roll up the map. The captain reached out, his hand hanging in the empty space.

'There is one other condition,' Evan said. The captain looked up at him. 'I am not familiar with these lands and while Dexion is very astute and clever, he is a boy. I need someone to guide me.'

The captain pursed his lips. 'Phameas.'

Evan nodded. 'Phameas, yes.'

The captain drew in a deep breath, clenched his teeth but could not take his sight off the section of the map not yet rolled. He exhaled through his nostrils.

'Fine, his service on my ship is terminated.'

'Thank you Captain.' Evan finished rolling up the chart and slid it into the container. 'Now, to the business of wages.'

CHAPTER TWENTY-FOUR

Evan threw a khiton over his head, a bit self-conscious at wearing a skirt. Although in the context of where he was the outfit wasn't out of place. It was weird and uncomfortable and he was not used to such attire. He shook his head. He'd have to put up with the clothes until he got home. He strapped on the sword and shield, picked up the bag and joined Phameas and Dexion who waited nearby.

He looked at them, and his stomach fluttered as they gazed back with serious expressions. Evan enjoyed the security and safety while on the ship and he knew what role was expected from him. As he was now to embark on a new stage of the voyage and enter a world very different from his own, his mouth went dry. He hoped the knowledge he gained at university proved to be useful. He took a deep breath and squared his shoulders.

'Ready?'

'Ready,' Dexion said with a nod.

'Phameas?'

The sailor's face was grim and he nodded. 'Aye.'

'Time to go.'

Members of the crew gathered near the ramp secured between the ship and the pier. The atmosphere was sombre and the men quiet. Evan shook hands with those he befriended and said goodbye. He and Dexion then stepped onto the ramp and walked across to the jetty. They waited as Phameas said his farewells to the men he'd sailed alongside with many years. When he did join them, his eyes were sad and filled with unshed tears. Evan squeezed his shoulder and gave a reassuring smile.

'You don't have to come with us,' Evan said. 'We'll be fine.'

'My life on the sea has been good and served me well. This is a start to a new life and an exciting journey I am looking forward to sharing with you,' Phameas said, voice quavering.

'Which way shall we go?'

'To the market to buy food and afterwards we'll decide what to do next,' Phameas said.

'Lead on.'

Phameas lifted his chin and walked towards the waterfront. He stopped, turned and waved to the crew, then continued along the path in front of the warehouses, setting a fast pace.

Evan was astonished by the size of the warehouses and the sophisticated construction. They were much bigger up close and better built than he anticipated. Even though he'd read how skilled the Carthaginians were, he did not expect this level of excellence or quality. Evan, distracted by his surroundings, almost bumped into Phameas, who halted by a smaller building.

'This will take us into the streets of the lower city,' he said in a quiet voice.

Evan stepped around Phameas, patted him on the shoulder and walked on with Dexion by his side. When they moved out of the shadow of the building and out into the street, Evan came to a stand-still. A number of trees stood at the crossroads but that was not why he ceased walking. The city was erected on the side of a hill and the residences and housing blocks were built on terraces. A great many were two storeys and others were larger, up to six storeys.

'This is incredible,' he said, staring. 'I did not expect it to be so well organised nor this big. Nor did I imagine the buildings to be this extensive.' He stood there star-struck, scanning everything his eyes and brain were able to digest. His professional instincts took over as he scrutinised the design of the city.

Evan's brain was in overdrive. He tried to work out how the ar-chitects and engineers planned it but then he caught sight of the hilltop overlooking the city. 'It appears something is on fire.'

'That is Byrsa Hill where the sacred fire is kept burning,' Pha-meas said from behind them.

'What is that over there?' Evan said, pointing further down the street.

'That altar is sacred to sailors and sacrifices are made to ensure safe voyages.'

'What animals are sacrificed?'

'Sheep and cattle but during terrible times children are used.'

Evan's blood chilled. He glanced at Dexion. 'Why children? Isn't it a bit... extreme?' He didn't want to offend Phameas by saying it was wrong. He'd read various texts and articles on this practice but the experts were unable to explain the purpose. The explanations given were educated guesses rather than based on evidence.

'Children are pure, their hearts and spirits not tainted by experi-ences of life. Their deaths appease the gods and stop the calamity that befouled our home.'

'Does it work?'

Phameas tilted his head to the side. 'The gods must be satisfied as a child hasn't been sacrificed in a long time.'

'How can you be sure?'

'Our people are growing in strength and wealth, and control much of this coastline and to the east. It could not happen without the support of the gods.'

'Do you believe they are benevolent?'

Phameas shook his head with such vigour his curled beard jiggled. 'Goodness no, a majority are harsh in their punishments and unyielding. That is why it's important to honour the gods with rituals and sacrifices. What of your gods? Do they expect much from your people?'

'Too much,' Evan said and glanced back at the site of the smoke, thinking of his interactions with Zeus. 'You know what I want to do?' he added, turning to Phameas and Dexion. 'Wash. Is there a bathhouse in town?'

Phameas blinked. Dexion shrugged.

'There's one on the west side of Byrsa Hill,' the Phoenician said.

'Great. Do they wash clothes?' Evan said, rubbing his hands.

'It will cost extra.'

'I don't care,' Evan said. 'Which way do we go?'

'We follow this street to the end and go left, then turn left again when we come to the new naval harbour. From there we head towards the hill and—'

'That's fine Phameas, you don't need to give us directions all at once,' Evan said, laying a hand on his shoulder.

'Oh... well, right.'

The early morning sun warmed their backs as they strode out onto the street. Three large evergreen oak trees, planted at the junctures that resembled the points of a triangle, cast long silhouettes. The multi-storeyed buildings were constructed from sun-dried bricks and stone with flat roofs. They reminded Evan of dwellings from the Middle Eastern countries. They soon came to an intersection. On a plot of land set between the two streets hundreds of stone steles clustered close together, standing like silent sentinels.

'Is this a cemetery?' Evan asked. Several were engraved with an image of a man holding a child with the left hand and right one extended. Above the etching were three flowerets encased in a circle. Others were more elaborate: a relief of a child carved within a rectangular shape; the more popular motif had a stick-shape outline of a girl. The steles were tall, short, rectangular, and square or finished with a triangular peak.

'I am not familiar with that term,' Phameas said. 'This is the Tophet, where the ashes of sacrificed children are buried.'

'So many...' Evan said in a quiet voice. To see proof of the ritual made it more real and difficult for his twenty-first century mentality to understand.

'We want to get to the baths before midday,' Phameas said, disrupting Evan's melancholy thoughts. 'The service is better, and it's much quieter. Once there's a crowd, it's harder to get the attendants' attention.'

They veered left, the site of the children's graveyard soon behind them. The sounds of clanging metal hitting stone and sawing of wood got louder as they neared the perimeter of the naval harbour. The voices of many men carried over the din as artisans strove to talk to each other while they worked. Evan itched to stop and talk with the stone masons and carpenters but there was always another day. He didn't know how long they would stay in Carthage or even where to begin searching for the information he needed.

He closed his eyes for a moment, wanting to shut out the panorama. The blood in his veins began to throb. He clenched his teeth, trying to stem his rapid breathing. Evan cursed Zeus. It was his fault he was here. It took his entire resolve to stop himself from shouting out obscenities.

'Master Evandros, what is the matter?' Dexion said, brows drawn together.

'Give... me... a... minute,' he said through gritted teeth.

He squatted and dropped his head, chin touching his chest. Evan closed his eyes and clenched his hands so tight the knuckles turned white. He took in a deep breath through his nostrils and with slow controlled breaths, exhaled through his mouth. Evan, focussed on breathing, did not see the look exchanged between Phameas and Dexion.

Five minutes passed and then another five before Evan lifted his head. His companions stared at him. Dexion bit his lip and Phameas rubbed his forehead.

'What is it? Are you in pain?' Phameas said. He took a step towards Evan and then hesitated. The expression on the other man's face stopped him.

'Pain, no,' Evan said, straightening.

'Perhaps if you tell us what is troubling you, we may be able to help,' said the Phoenician.

'I appreciate your offer; you are a good friend,' said Evan. 'But no one can help me with this particular problem except the person who did this to me. And he has no intention of doing so.'

Phameas stood quiet for a few moments, his eyes squinting as he contemplated his friend's comment. 'This venture, is it his plan?'

'He's the one in charge so I guess it was his idea.'

'Is he a powerful man?'

'You could say that.'

'Did he choose you?'

'More accurate to say I was selected by default.'

'By default? What do you mean?'

'I am filling in for someone else. According to... let's call him "my patron", the other man lacked specific skills required for this mission. And here I am in his stead.' Evan couldn't bring himself to say Zeus' name out loud. To hear the words spoken would be like admitting or acknowledging the truth and he wasn't ready for that. If this was a dream, it was incredible and very real.

'Let's go to the bathhouse,' he said, changing the topic. 'We should get moving if we want to get there before the crowd.'

CHAPTER TWENTY-FIVE

They walked in silence. Evan's anger ebbed with each turn of the street, his attention diverted by the layout of the well-ordered city. In front of many buildings were deep plaster-lined cisterns filled with water. The closer they got to the hill and bathhouse, the more the quality of the houses changed. They were bigger and the brick work refined. A few had storefronts that opened onto the street. The main entrance to these multi-storey homes was at the rear via a laneway.

'Here we are,' Phameas said.

The bathhouse spread the length of the street and had two huge entrances. It resembled the dwellings in Carthage, but it was bigger and on a single level. Phameas walked through one of the doorways. A man emerged from the dark recesses without making a sound, much like a spectre. He wore a tan coloured close-fitting cotton tunic that reached to his knees. His beard was long and curled with meticulous care. He bowed his head.

'Welcome to the House of Ea.'

'We've come to bathe and have our clothes washed,' Phameas said.

'Of course.' The man bowed his head again. 'Please come this way,' he said, indicating towards the passage.

He led them down a wide hallway, the floor tiled and decorated in geometric patterns. Each tessellation contained a sphere within a series of smaller interlocking circles. The images were set in a square and repeated. Vibrant colours of blue, yellow, red and green painted in abstract shapes and motifs adorned the walls. The three were escorted into a room where a stone bench ran the length on one side. Phameas placed his belongings on it. Evan and Dexion did the same.

'Please disrobe and hand me your clothes. I will see to it they are laundered,' the man said. The manner in which he spoke reminded Evan of a cleric, calm, even toned and a little too polite.

'Wait!' Evan said to the attendant who turned with a questioning look. He dashed to his bag and pulled out more items. 'I want these washed too.'

'As you wish.' The attendant took the proffered garments and left.

Three young men entered, carrying large cylindrical brass bowls. Phameas moved to the centre of the room and knelt. He turned and beckoned Evan and Dexion to join him. The floor had a slight slope where Phameas waited and nearby was a hole, the size of a child's fist. Evan knelt, not sure what to expect.

He gasped.

Cold water doused his head and sluiced over his body. Given a bar of soap, Evan turned the grey block over in his hands, lifted it to his nose and sniffed. It became slippery in his hand. He shrugged and began to lather his body. Next, Evan washed his hair and baulked as his fingers got caught in the knots. His hair must be longer than he thought. When he finished, Evan stiffened in readiness for a bowl of water to rinse off the soapy residue. The dirt and grime eddied down the hole. He stood and the attendant handed him a coarse towel. After Evan dried himself, he wrapped the towel around his waist. He clasped his jaw and grimaced.

'Do they shave and cut hair?' he said to Phameas.

'We don't shave our beards,' the sailor said, alarmed. 'It's part of our manhood.'

'That's fine, I'll do it myself. What about a haircut?'

'I'll ask one of the attendants,' Phameas said.

'Can you also ask for a bowl of warm water?' Evan said. 'And a mirror... something with a reflective surface?'

When Phameas returned, a short rotund man accompanied him. The barber carried a bowl and a pair of scissors which reminded Evan of shears. The shears had two bronze blades as big as daggers, the handles fixed by a thin, flexible strip of curved metal. He placed the bowl and scissors on the stone bench.

'Who wishes to have his hair cut?' he asked.

'That would be me,' said Evan.

'Moloch! You are tall!' the barber said, eyes blinking as Evan stood. 'Where do you come from?'

Evan almost said Australia, but the country was not discovered yet let alone anyone from this era sailing that far south. 'I come from an island beyond the mouth of the Mediterranean Sea.'

'Are your people as big as you?'

Evan thought back to the dream sequences. 'They are,' he said with a nod.

'Moloch!' the man repeated. 'Your kind must be descended from the gods.'

'No more than you,' Evan said, face hardening. 'How much to cut my hair short and trim the beard?'

'Two copper shekels.'

Evan sat on the bench. The barber picked up the scissors and squeezed the blades together, making a swishing sound. 'So how much do you want cut off?'

'Do you have a mirror?'

He plucked out a mirror from the folds of his outfit and handed it to Evan. He recoiled when he saw his reflection. The image was wavy, similar to theme park mirrors but it wasn't the distortion that made him react. The person who stared back looked like a stranger.

'I will tell you when to stop,' he said.

The barber pulled out a comb and hair pin from his tunic. He gathered and pinned the hair on both sides, leaving what remained underneath. He trimmed the section and continued to cut away until the floor and Evan were covered with hair. The man stepped away and Evan checked his handiwork with the mirror.

'More,' he said.

Other than clucking his tongue, the barber did not speak and did as instructed. After fifteen minutes, he stepped back. Evan ran his hand over his hair, the length no longer than the first knuckle on his little finger.

'Perfect, now clip away at the beard.'

The barber pursed his lips and trimmed the beard.

'Dexion, come here and hold the mirror for me,' Evan said when the barber finished and moved away. He handed the mirror to Dexion, wet his face and lathered it. He shaved the remaining stubble with the dagger. When he finished, he washed his face and took the mirror from Dexion. Evan smiled.

'You looked more handsome with long hair and beard,' said the barber as he collected the mirror from Evan.

Evan ran a hand over his face and head, grinning. Not the closest shave or the best haircut he'd had, but he felt a semblance of normality.

CHAPTER TWENTY-SIX

The harpies soared over the watery depths of Poseidon's home. Their wings spanned over ten metres and cast a long profile on the glassy surface of the Aegean Sea. As they reached the lands of the Olympian Gods, one broke formation. It swooped towards the grassy knoll, gathering speed, and seized a young shepherd.

The herdsman tried to break free, and his arms and legs flailed. His hat plummeted to the ground as they soared higher and higher into the air. He screamed as the talons tightened around his body. His shrieks were lost amongst the peaks of the mountains. The harpy's knife-like claws pierced his flesh. His screams stopped.

The harpy circled a mountain, spotted a small clearing and began her descent. She released the shepherd, the body hitting the ground with a dull thud. The harpy landed and straddled the dead boy. She bent over him and with razor-sharp teeth, tore off his head. Splattered blood turned the ground a crimson red.

Her sisters flew in and landed close by. The harpy lifted her human face at them and grinned, eyes gleaming. Her teeth dripped with blood. Gore covered her breasts. One of her sisters shuffled nearer to take a bite but the blood-covered harpy squealed. She bared her teeth and, with a talon, moved the remains out of reach. They shrieked at each other. The inhuman sound incited living creatures within the surrounding countryside to flee and seek haven.

The harpy relented and allowed her sisters to eat the legs. After her fill, she stepped aside and watched as her sisters devoured the rest as she preened and cleaned herself. When they finished the harpies took to the skies and headed for Mount Olympos.

They flew over the mountainous regions of the Peloponnese and Aetolia to reach Thessaly. The harpies veered north east and soared for the ridged peaks of Mount Olympos. They came upon the enormous gates of the clouds. Coming to a halt, the three lingered for a minute. The gates were left ajar, the gap big enough to slip through one at a time. They took their time and inspected the perimeter.

The three goddesses of the Seasons, whose job was to stand guarding the gateway, were absent. The harpies grinned at their good fortune and zoomed through the entrance. They sped past the stables unnoticed. The divine canines rushed out of their kennels barking, their growls deep and loud. Servants ran out to investigate.

The cacophony soon reached the gods' court. Apollo put his lyre to one side. The bestial sounds intensified, drowning out the gods' conversation.

'I will go and see what has disturbed the animals,' said Hephaistos. He left the court as fast as his lame leg allowed him.

While incarcerated in the tenebrous realm of Tartaros, Eris cast a spell over the harpies. The incantation made them invisible. The harpies giggled when their bodies blurred and blended in with their surroundings. They coasted into the royal court, where the Olympian gods gathered, and perched on a golden beam.

'Did you make any progress with Evandros?' Poseidon said as the gods stood before Zeus and Hera.

The King of the Gods did not answer straight away. He pressed his lips together in a thin line before saying, 'He has disembarked in Carthage.'

'That's not what I asked,' Poseidon said with a frown. 'We know where he is. The question remains as to whether your experiment was successful. Will he be able to perform and complete the task required of him?'

'When you consider how long he's been away, I doubt he will be able to fight, let alone kill,' Ares said with a sniff. 'He'll turn and run at the first sign of a battle.'

'He will succeed,' Zeus said, nostrils flaring.

'Ares makes a point. Your son has resisted every overture made by you. Don't you think he would have remembered his life by now? He doesn't even recognise his wife!' Apollo said, thrusting his chin into the air.

'He is my son and when the time comes, he will prove his ability to fight, recover the relics and stop this new god from taking our place,' Zeus said.

The gods became quiet.

'What can we do to help?' Athene said, her strong unwavering voice cutting through the silence.

'The Moirai said we cannot interfere,' Ares said. 'If we do, all is lost.'

Athene turned to him, her beautiful face hard. 'I am referring to providing assistance and did not mention intervening. Two very different concepts if you stopped to reflect on what I said.' Her lip curled, baring her teeth at him. She turned her back on him. 'There must be a way we can offer guidance to our champion and his companions.'

Zeus smiled at Athene with pride. He gave a nod. 'Information; we can offer pertinent advice and directions. Excellent, Athene.'

Hephaistos returned, looking bewildered.

'I could not find or see what caused the animals to behave in a strange manner. Perhaps a bird from the mortal realm strayed onto the grounds.'

'Perhaps,' said Zeus frowning, not convinced a mere bird had upset the sacred animals.

**

In the confines of Tartaros, the harpies sat with Eris. The winged creatures relayed the details of the discussion between the gods.

'Did they explain in detail the experiment Zeus conducted on his son?'

The harpies shook their heads.

Eris tapped her lips with a finger. 'Mmm...' The goddess stood and stared across the endless expanse of her desolate realm in deep thought. 'Go to Carthage and follow this Evandros. Learn as much as you can in connection to him, where he goes and what he does. I must know what Zeus has done to his son.'

CHAPTER TWENTY-SEVEN

'Where to now?' Phameas said as they left the bathhouse.

'Do we have enough money for accommodation and food?' Evan said.

The captain had paid Phameas his remaining wages and given Evan a small amount for his service. He did not want to take advantage of his friend.

'I can get us money,' Dexion said. He was looking at his hands and arms, turning them one way then the other. He brushed unseen lint from his clean tunic. The young boy hadn't stopped smiling since leaving the baths.

'We want to earn the money in an honest way,' said Evan.

'The money will get us through for a month, although it depends on how long we stay in Carthage,' Phameas said.

'There is information I haven't told you...' Evan said and then stopped.

'What is it?' Phameas said.

Evan took a deep breath. 'There were more survivors from the ill-fated ship. They are held captive by the king of Kyrene and I've been instructed to rescue them.'

'Who told you? When did you learn this?'

Evan shifted from one foot to the other. He clasped the back of his neck. 'You wouldn't believe me.'

Phameas stared at Evan. 'The quickest route to Kyrene is by ship. Finding a captain going to Apollonia, the city's port, may be difficult. Many merchant ships avoid the place. They say the king is a tyrant and charges hefty taxes. We'll need more money to pay a handsome fee to convince a captain to take us.'

'What about by land?'

Phameas pursed his lips. 'It will take months and it's dangerous. There is a vast desert to cross.'

'What if we travel on horses or camels?'

'They will save time but we'll need to carry extra water and food for the animals. Besides, only nobles can afford horses.'

'We may need to consider the possibility of travelling over land,' Evan said. 'We should start making enquiries and petition a few captains at the harbour and look for work.' He resumed walking. 'Is there a place where information is stored in a building, like a library?'

Phameas nodded. 'There is, why?'

'Something else I need to do while we're here, but let's get food. I'm hungry.'

The streets were quiet as they headed seawards. The small number of people who were out and about went in different directions, turned and stared as the trio passed them. That changed as the din of voices increased nearer the marketplace. The market was a large square open space. Shops lined the perimeter with colourful makeshift tents filling the centre. Evan was amazed by the huge number of people and the different products available.

They wandered past stores. Evan paused to examine the more unusual items. He drew the attention of the store-owner who was quick to try to sell something. He declined many times and did his best to avoid being lured into bartering. The vendors shook their fists and shouted as they hastened away.

'Good grief!' Evan said as one shopkeeper tried to sell sweets by trailing and talking at them. 'Astonishing how some things never change!'

Stray dogs were kicked and shouted at by irate store-owners as the animals skulked in and out of stores. One short shopkeeper lashed out at a dog and waved a stick. He missed it only by a hair's breadth, yelling expletives as the animal scampered away.

Evan sniffed the air. 'Hmm... what is that smell?' He let his nose guide the way and came to a food stall. Evan licked his lips as he gazed with longing at the contents in the cauldron. 'How much for three pieces of flat bread and the stew?'

'One copper shekel,' said a thickset man, face shining with sweat, squinting up at Evan.

With bread filled with stew in hand, they wandered the markets. Evan asked Phameas to explain certain objects that caught his attention, careful not to take too keen an interest in the wares after the earlier experiences. A number of women helped their male counterparts in the stores. They wore full length dresses and sashes wrapped around their waists in elaborate knots. Many women covered their hair with a cap, others with a hood, their long, curled tresses draping over their shoulders. Many wore bracelets, headbands, necklaces and rings. Each time they moved, their bodies sang, accompanied by tinkling music.

'Where's Dexion?' Evan said, stopping in front of a large tent and scanning for the boy.

'He was here a minute ago,' Phameas said, looking back at where they had come from.

Evan spotted him sauntering towards them with a vacuous expression. Evan crossed his arms and waited until Dexion re-joined them.

'How much did you take?'

Dexion shrugged. 'Enough for food and board, besides I only took from those who are wealthy; they don't need all that money.'

'Regardless how rich someone is, we don't steal,' said Evan. 'I know you had to while living on the streets but now there's no need.'

'If we are unable to get work then we are going to require money,' Dexion said.

'He has a point,' Phameas said.

'Let's try to find work first and later decide what to do next if we don't,' Evan said. He was about to move on when he spotted a skinny bald man inside a stall struggle to lift a pithoi. 'Would you like help?'

The man stopped and turned. From beneath bushy eyebrows, his dark eyes took in the newcomers.

He stepped back and pointed. 'It needs to go there.'

Evan handed his bag to Phameas and leant his sword and shield against the table. He ducked under the low hanging tent, lifted the large urn and relocated it.

'That was full of olive oil!' the man said eyes bulging. 'How in the name of the gods did you lift it?'

'I've carried heavier objects,' Evan said backing out of the stall.

'You must be a descendant of Herakles,' the man said, agog. 'Only one with his gifts can pick up weighty items. You're big and strong like him too.'

Evan gave a wry grin which was more of a pained grimace. 'No relation.'

'You have heard of the great Herakles?'

Evan nodded. 'Of course, his twelve tasks are legendary tales.'

'You're a Hellene?'

'Could say that,' he said with a slight shrug. 'My family's heritage is Grecian.'

'Greetings, fellow kinsman. I am Gelon, son of Sophos and citizen of Patrae,' Gelon said, eyes sparkling.

'This is Phameas and Dexion and I am Evan... dros.'

'I don't suppose you'd be willing to move a few other urns for me?'

'If you are offering paid work, then yes, if not...' Evan raised his brows. He waited a couple of minutes, and when Gelon didn't respond, he collected his gear. 'Let's go,' he said, and walked away.

They had passed a few stalls when Gelon called out. 'Wait! Please wait!' He hurried towards them. 'Come, come, we shall talk.' He walked back to his store, his short legs moving quick stirring puffs of dust in his wake. They did not move. Gelon looked back and with a sharp flick of the hand beckoned them to follow.

Gelon's mood was buoyant as he led them into the tent. He directed them to the rear where there was a small table and two wooden stools. He lit a lamp and placed it on the table alongside a small brass statue.

'I'm sorry,' he said throwing out his arms. 'Not much of a place for guests. I use it twice a year for trading, and when I'm not here I let other vendors use it.'

'That's fine,' Evan said.

'Please sit.' He pulled over a squat urn and sat. Dexion sat on the dirt floor next to Evan, legs crossed and arms resting on his knees. 'How is it you are here in Carthage?'

'We arrived on a merchant ship,' Evan said. 'We are looking for work before moving on.'

'I can offer you men work but the boy...'

'He is very good at running errands,' said Evan, 'and reliable.'

'How long will you be staying?'

'Until we've earned enough money.'

Gelon clasped his bearded chin, gaze fixed on Evan. 'As you are a fellow countryman I will offer you and your friend three copper shekels a week and the boy half a copper shekel.'

Evan looked at Phameas who gave an imperceptible nod.

'You have a deal. When do you want us to start work?'

'I have a few more urns filled with oil that need moving, and then I will take you to my ship.'

CHAPTER TWENTY-EIGHT

Gelon kept Evan and Phameas busy moving urns filled with oil from his homeland. Meanwhile Dexion ran back and forth giving instructions on how many to load onto carts. The three had free time on the days they had to wait for shipments, and spent hours at the market. There were stalls that sold brooches and amulets to ward off malevolent spells, death masks and pottery.

Evan used this opportunity to talk with the locals and asked if they knew or had heard of the Mother Goddess. He was not surprised when the responses were negative though he could not help but feel disappointed. The gods they worshipped were different. Despite their goddesses having a high status in the society, there was no recollection or resemblance to the one he sought. He'd hoped due to the cosmopolitan nature of the city, someone may have heard of the Mother Goddess.

Carthage attracted peoples from various parts of the world. The mix of languages spoken in the market and at the waterfront fascinated Evan. He sat and listened, eager to learn where individuals came from and to pick up their vernacular. He was grateful for the knowledge he had; it gave him a sense of reassurance to recognise the various cultures. The Numidians were easy to distinguish, their skin as dark as his was light. According to Gelon they formed much of the Carthaginian cavalry due to their prowess as accomplished horsemen. Greeks, Egyptians, Persians and Afrikaans visited and traded here. It was a polyglot of nations.

'Phameas, Dexion, time to visit that library,' Evan said after a particularly depressing outing. 'That's where we should have gone in the first place instead of asking people.'

'I'll find out where it is,' Phameas said.

While Evan and Dexion waited for Phameas to return, they ambled over to a tree and stood under the shade. As Evan stared across the busy market square, his mind wandered, and he thought about his parents and how his business was going.

'You should stop doing that,' Dexion said out of the blue.

'What?' Evan said, startled.

'It's not good to keep thinking where you came from,' Dexion said. 'You need to keep your mind in the present. If you are to find these objects you must disregard the time in which you lived.'

Evan shook his head. 'How can I ignore what I know is to be true? It is who I am and where I grew up.'

'Yes, it was your life,' Dexion agreed. 'But so is this one. You must make an effort to try to remember for your sake as well as ours.'

Evan frowned. 'Why? What do you mean? Have you had a vision?'

'It's a bit jumbled. What I am sensing is the importance for you to accept where you are or deal with consequences.'

'That could be difficult as I don't believe this era,' Evan pointed to the ground with sharp jabs, 'is where I belong.'

'The time will come when you must choose between the life you know or the one you want,' said Dexion.

'That won't be difficult,' Evan said. 'I know which I prefer.'

When Phameas returned, he noted Evan's sullen expression in contrast to Dexion's calm demeanour.

'What happened?' he said looking from one to the other.

'Nothing,' said Evan. 'Did you find out where the library is?'

Phameas nodded. 'It's next to the senate chambers down by the military harbour.'

'Great. Let's go.' Evan turned on his heel, and within a few quick strides entered a side street.

Phameas and Dexion ran to catch up and the trio made their way to the senate district. They walked in silence. Evan's dour mood set the tone and neither Phameas nor Dexion felt compelled to talk. They followed the road until it opened onto a large open spaced quadrangle, surrounded by a series of buildings varying in size and configuration. To the east and backing onto the unfinished military harbour, were four buildings. Two were rectangular; one was long and thin, the other wider and two storeys, and both had columns in the front. The remaining two were square, one a small shrine and next to it a larger edifice with an open foyer. On the north side two buildings sat side by side. One was four-sided and unique, with a courtyard in the middle; alongside was an L-shaped rectangular construction, a shrine, trees, and two more structures.

'Is this it?' Dexion said, breaking the silence.

Evan dragged his attention from the remarkable and complex constructions to where Dexion pointed. He gaped at the sight of the u-shaped building, the courtyard filled with palm and oak trees.

Large columns painted in bright yellow bordered the paved court-yard.

'This is the library,' said Phameas. 'I was told we will have to pay the custodian for the information we seek.'

'Let's go and see if the librarian can help,' said Evan. He led the way to the library, the others right behind him. They walked across the shaded courtyard and entered the cool entryway. Evan stopped on the threshold and blinked. The interior was dim, a stark contrast to the brightness outside, and it took a few seconds for his eyes to adjust. He wrinkled his nose and tried to detect what he smelt. He glanced around and smiled. The walls were lined with wooden nich-es made from cedar.

'What brings you to the House of Thamugadi?'

Evan turned and saw an overweight man who sat behind a long quadrangular table. He looked at Phameas who gave an encouraging nod and walked towards the curator. Nearing the table he saw un-rolled parchments of differing lengths concealing the surface.

'I am hoping you may have information we seek,' Evan said.

'Well, what is it that you need?'

'Facts or material relating to the Mother Goddess.'

'Mother Goddess...' The librarian pursed his thick lips. 'I haven't heard of such a goddess. Is she called by another name?'

Evan nodded. 'Yes. She's also known as Gaia or Ge.' He spelt the names.

The man frowned and tapped his lips with a finger, then his eyes brightened. 'Oh yes! There's a scroll which mentions this Ge. Wait here, I'll go and get it.'

The librarian struggled to his feet, waddled around the table and trudged towards a unlit corner of the room. While they waited,

Evan took the opportunity to inspect the interior of the building. The few lit torches added little lighting. The room needed light-wells along the top of the walls. A library should be bright and welcoming, which this wasn't. The alcoves contained rolled parchments and metal objects, many cylindrical in shape while the rest were flat, similar to the one he carried in his pack. He wondered what they held; the scholar and history buff side of him wanted to read them.

'Ho there! I need you to come here!' the librarian called.

Phameas picked up the sputtering oil lamp from the table and they went to join him.

He pointed to a shelf. 'I cannot reach that scroll.'

'Which one?' Evan said. There were many scrolls on the shelf. In fact, every single niche was filled, many stuffed to the brim with manuscripts, the contents ready to spill out onto the floor.

'The scroll is darker than the others and sealed with black wax.'

Evan scanned the shelf and spotted the document. It hid in the shadows, tucked in the top corner. He reached for it, and his finger-tips began to tingle and then to go numb. Evan flexed his fingers and ignored the sensation. He grabbed the parchment and at the same time felt something wrap his head and squeeze. The pressure grew and he thought it may crack his skull. Evan remembered the time a nail gun had misfired and pierced his hand. This was worse. He yanked his hand away, and the pain disappeared.

'What's wrong with you, boy? Can't you reach it?'

'Huh?' he said, dazed.

'Evandros?' Phameas touched him on the arm.

'I'll get it. Just give me a minute.'

Face set in grim determination, Evan seized the scroll. A sudden gust of wind swirled around him, buffeting his clothes and hair.

'Most glorious and greatest of all mortals, great trouble awaits thee; bring to bear spirit and purity of heart, for these strengths will undo the evil that grows.'

'Well, hand it over boy,' the librarian said in a clipped tone.

'Did you hear that?' Evan said, his heart hammering.

'Hear what? Have the gods addled your brains? You've been standing there holding the document and I've been trying to get your attention!'

Evan looked to a concerned Phameas who nodded and then to Dexion who stood with his head tilted to the side, staring at him.

'Come on, come on! Give me the scroll.' The librarian flapped his fingers back and forth in quick succession.

Evan held out the parchment. The terse custodian snatched it from him and walked back to the table as fast as his bulk allowed.

'What happened?' Phameas said in a low voice as they trailed behind the librarian.

'Not sure,' Evan said, shrugging. 'I'll tell you once we leave.'

'Are there any other references I can use to narrow my search for this Mother Goddess of yours?' The librarian broke the seal and placed lead weights on the corners as he unrolled the scroll.

'There may be a connection to Egypt,' said Evan. He leaned closer, curious to see the form of script used. The lettering was distinctive and he saw its relationship to ancient Greek and Aramaic characters.

'The land of the pharaohs, hmmm...' The librarian, with a chubby finger as a guide, followed the text from right to left, went onto the next line, scanning left to right. He muttered to himself as he read.

While they waited for the librarian to finish, Evan could not help dwelling over the incident. Who was it that spoke? Where did it come from and why did no one else hear it? What did it mean?

'Ah ha! I've found it!' The librarian pointed to the text. Evan leaned in and came close to butting Phameas' head. 'It says,

"A serpent of gold longs for his Mother.
It lies in wait invisible to the Age of Amun.
Beware! Only the True One may touch the golden serpent.
A death most horrible will befall the one who claims it as their own."'

'So we need to recover a golden serpent.' Evan drew in a deep breath and shook his head. 'How much more cryptic does this need to be?'

'It doesn't give the location of the serpent?' Phameas said, grumbling.

'It indeed does,' the librarian gloated. 'The "Age of Amun" refers to the City of Thebes. Thebes has a temple dedicated to this god, and that's the site of the golden serpent.'

Evan thanked and paid the librarian for his services. Once outside, he paused and stared at the lush courtyard.

'What is it?' said Phameas, looking up at him.

'I've always wanted to go to Egypt,' he said. 'Didn't think it'd happen this way.'

'Don't forget you need to rescue your companions,' Dexion said.

Evan let out a loud sigh. 'Will it be easy to find a captain to take us to Kyrene, take on extra passengers and then sail to Egypt?'

'There are captains who will take passengers but it will be expensive,' said Phameas.

'Let's hope Gelon is generous and gives us bonuses,' said Evan. 'In the meantime, we scout and find a captain willing to take us.'

CHAPTER TWENTY-NINE

'Zeus! What have you done?'

'Divine Mother!' Zeus bowed his head.

A white light flooded the court of the Olympian Gods and encircled the gods, their heads too lowered in obeisance. As the bright light faded, the Mother Goddess stood in the centre of the throne room.

'You have endangered the future of the world and the children of Atlantis.'

'Divine Mother, we had no choice...' said Hera.

'Silence!' The Mother Goddess' eyes glinted.

Hera cringed and averted her face.

'My innocent daughter, her life taken to ensure the quest is a success as well as your wellbeing.' She shook her head in disgust. 'Her sacrifice was not necessary.'

'It was a difficult decision, one that was essential to our future,' Zeus said, stiffening. 'There was no other recourse.'

'Enough!' The Mother Goddess paced from one side of the throne room to the other, her long golden tresses streaming in her wake. She spun and pointed at Zeus. 'If only you had left well alone!'

'But the Moirai...' said Poseidon.

She turned her cold gaze on the Sea God who cowered. 'They saw a fu-
ture that terrified them and turned to you to alter the path. In doing so you
precipitated a series of events and the outcome will be much worse than you
intended. It may not be possible to stop any of it from happening.' She
paused and did a slow turn and eye-balled each immortal until she came
back to Zeus. 'You will do everything in your power to protect and make
sure the Atlanteans' are kept out of harm's way. And yes, they can stop
your demise, but their re-introduction to the mortal realm was premature.'

'What of Evandros? He can prevent what is destined with his
knowledge of the future,' Zeus said.

The Mother Goddess' face softened at the mention of Evan's name. 'He'll
prove to be valuable but I don't know if his expertise is enough. We expect
mortals to behave in a particular manner but they are unpredictable. Even
the most loyal follower may turn against us if promised untold gains.'

'But if we did nothing, we'd be cast out, forever,' said Demeter, wring-
ing her hands.

'We had to make sure it did not happen!' Ares said with a growl. 'We
beat the Titans, we can defeat this new upstart.'

'As I said, it is possible to stop this new god from rising but the loss will
be great. Are you prepared to make personal sacrifices to win?' she said.

Ares opened his mouth, eyes glittering. The Mother Goddess held up a
hand.

'I suggest you think hard before you answer for victory may be bitter-
sweet.' She lowered her hand. 'This new path you created will not be without
perils. The time will come when you must make a choice between stopping
the new god or the death of your chosen.'

The Gods of Olympos stood in silence, her words ringing in their ears.

'Divine Mother, are you able to alter the threads woven?' said Athene.

The Mother Goddess pressed her lips together for a moment. She said, 'There has been too much interference with the timeline. To tamper with it any further could cause catastrophic upheaval of the planet.'

'So we wait and see what happens?' said Ares with a snarl. 'Perhaps we should fight and do away with this troublemaker.'

'Simple and direct but one problem,' said the Mother Goddess, 'you don't know who the enemy is. Focus on assisting the Atlanteans as they need it.'

'The Moirai told us not to interfere,' Apollo said, arms crossed against his chest.

'My dear boy, you already did,' she said. 'You will refrain from meddling and allow the events to unfold. Helping is another matter; provide aid as required.' The Mother Goddess stepped closer to him and added in a soft voice, 'She will come to you. Let her complete this journey for she must learn her limitations. Nonetheless, if you in any way harm Evandros I will cast you beyond the realm of Tartaros for eternity.'

Apollo swallowed and gave a curt nod. The Mother Goddess, satisfied, turned and walked back to the centre of the room. She shimmered, and white light encased her form.

'I'll be watching.' Then she was gone.

Zeus lowered himself onto his throne, his mind racing, replaying what Mother said. Did he read the signs wrong? He thought he covered everything and all possible outcomes. What did he miss? His plan was sound with a high probability of a successful result. He made allowances for fatalities, for in times of war there is always death. There was something he did not account for but what was it?

'What have we done?' Demeter said as she hugged herself.

'I will kill the Moirai,' said Ares in a clipped tone, hand clasped tight on the hilt of his sword.

'That will not solve the problem,' Hestia said, face white and taut.

'There will be no killing,' Zeus said in a quiet but firm tone. He stood. 'We cannot change what is done. Let the events unfold as they must.'

CHAPTER THIRTY

When he first started working on Gelon's ship Evan watched for hours, awed by how much traffic came and went from the harbour. He did not expect it to be so busy and wondered what other surprises to expect. Reading and learning of the past did not prepare him for these experiences. Most merchant ships docked in port had colourful masts, and symbols or crests denoting their origins or ownership. Many were laden with cargo, bringing goods to sell much as their employer had, and others came to buy. The warehouses were stacked with merchandise ready for export across the Mediterranean.

During one of their breaks between shifting urns, Evan and Phameas approached captains and asked whether they took passengers. Evan spoke to four captains without success. He was walking back to Gelon's ship when Phameas hurried towards him, a big grin plastered on his face.

'I think I found our captain,' he said with breathless excitement. 'His name is Banipal and he sounded interested in making extra money.'

'Let's go and chat with him.' Evan followed Phameas. They passed the warehouses and headed towards the entrance of the port and the berth of a black hulled ship.

'Hallo, Captain Banipal!' Phameas called out.

A tall slender man conversing with another on deck ceased talking and turned. He wore a tunic in various shades of red and a conical hat. His angular face was hidden beneath his beard, fashioned in four rows of tight curls.

'This is the friend I mentioned to you,' said Phameas, pulling Evan alongside. 'Permission to come aboard, Captain?'

The captain's black eyes studied Evan, his face unfathomable. Evan resisted the urge to squirm under the other man's scrutiny and after a long period, the captain nodded. He resumed speaking to his companion while they boarded the ship. As the two approached, the man who spoke with the captain moved on. He gawped at Evan as he passed by.

'Captain, this is Evandros. I told him you may take passengers,' said Phameas.

'I've taken paying travellers in the past,' the captain said with a nod.

'What has Phameas told you?' Evan said.

'You require transport to Egypt and need to stop at Kyrene to pick up companions.' Banipal turned to Phameas, who nodded. 'Is that right?'

'Yes,' said Evan. 'How much for seven passengers?'

'Two shekels per day a person.'

'How long will the journey take?' Evan's brow furrowed.

'If the gods are with us and the winds are fair, three to four days.'

Evan did a quick calculation and estimated it would cost around fifty-six shekels if it took four days. There wouldn't be much change left for food and board or much else.

'When do you plan to leave?' Evan said.

'It will depend on how quickly I sell the merchandise. Come back in two days. I will know by then.'

Evan thanked the captain, the two disembarked and headed back to Gelon's ship.

'I don't think we've earned enough money for the fare,' he said.

'I still have a little money from the wages the captain paid me,' said Phameas.

'You better hang on to that, we may need it later on,' said Evan.

'We could offer to be rowers,' Phameas said, 'in exchange for a reduction in the fare.'

'There's no harm in asking. We need a backup plan just in case the captain doesn't agree.'

***

Two days later, Evan and Phameas took a short break from moving pithois and went to see Captain Banipal. When they reached his ship, the captain was standing on the pier speaking with an officious looking man. His arms were crossed and a deep scowl marred his face.

'This does not look good,' Evan said.

The official then scribbled something on his wax tablet, nodded at the captain and moved onto the next vessel.

'We can come back later if this isn't a good time, Captain,' Evan said.

The expression on Banipal's face didn't lessen as he turned his angry gaze on Evan. 'The Harbour Master likes to flaunt his power and assert his authority at any given time. At present, he is collecting port taxes and explained the government has added a new tax. Now we must pay a tariff on the goods sold. How is a man to earn a living if the government keeps inventing new ways to collect money? It will not surprise me if one day they find a way to make us pay for breathing air. They will drive honest and good merchants away with this extra financial burden. Now, I don't intend to give the authorities any more of my hard earned money. I plan to set sail in four days.'

'So soon.' Evan pursed his lips.

Banipal shrugged. 'You asked for passage.'

'It's just we need to inform our employer we are leaving,' Evan said. 'He offered us work when we needed it and deserves notification of our departure. Besides, we want to make you an offer.'

The captain narrowed his eyes and clasped his hands behind his back. His hard gaze did not leave Evan's face. 'What is this proposition?'

'We don't have enough money to pay you the entire fare. We are short by ten shekels. Phameas and I are rowers and in exchange for the difference owed, we extend our services while on board.'

Banipal's unsmiling face made Phameas fidget so much so it began to rub off on Evan. He wanted to tie Phameas up to make him stop.

'I accept your offer,' Banipal said at length and pointed at Evan. 'For being upfront and honourable. We'll be shipping out early morning, so make sure you are here otherwise I leave without you.'

'Thank you, Captain. We'll be here.' As the two turned to leave, Evan added in a low voice. 'We'd better tell Gelon today we are going.'

Their employer wasn't too pleased when told of their departure and offered to increase their wages if they stayed.

'Gelon, you have been good to us and if the circumstances were different we'd be happy to remain in your employment for a while longer. However, Zeus made it clear I need to rescue fellow travellers...'

'Almighty Zeus spoke to you?' the merchant said, recoiling.

Evan suppressed the urge to roll his eyes. 'Yes, he told me they were in trouble and to liberate them.' He hadn't wanted to mention Zeus or the mission but knew it would influence Gelon.

'You must be someone he considers important,' Gelon said in awe. 'I do not dare stand in the way of Zeus' messenger, so you must do as he commands. Before you leave, let me offer you a small bonus and please tell Zeus I am a faithful follower.'

CHAPTER THIRTY-ONE

A day out from Carthage, Banipal sent for Evan. He was piloting the
ship, using the two steering oars Evan now realised was a common
apparatus during this time.

'Captain, you asked for me?'

'Who are these people we are stopping to collect in Kyrene?'

Evan grimaced. It was a question he'd hoped to avoid. He didn't
know them and any answer he gave would sound false. He scratched
the back of his head and decided to tell Banipal what Zeus showed
him.

'We were on a ship when a gigantic octopus split it in two. Everyone on board was killed except for a few of us.'

'How did you become separated?' Banipal stared at Evan, his eyes
unblinking and unyielding as black tourmaline.

'That, I don't recall. The crew on Phameas' ship found me unconscious; there was no one else.'

'Tell me then, how is it you know where they are?'

Oh, oh! Evan's mind froze. How did he answer this one? He
chewed the inner part of his cheek. What the heck, he'd just give the
same spiel he gave Gelon.

198

'Zeus told me where to find them.'

Banipal frowned. 'Who is Zeus?'

Evan resisted the urge to groan. 'He is a Hellenic God, much like your Baal.'

'A god spoke to you?' the captain said, raising a single eyebrow.

'I realise it sounds absurd given that you don't know me but those who do will tell you I am sincere. I'm not one given to fanciful explanations. In fact, I pride myself on being truthful and reliable, a reputation which has made my business a success.'

Banipal's silence spoke volumes.

'I'd have thought as a sailor you'd honour the gods.'

'I offer libations and sacrifice to Yamm for safe passage on the sea each time we depart and arrive at a port,' Banipal said. 'Though I have not had a god speak to me. That I must concede is a different matter.'

'You're lucky,' Evan said, lip curling. 'It's not that wonderful. Believe me when I say you're not missing anything worthwhile.'

'I still find it difficult to reconcile,' the captain said with a shake of his head.

'That is understandable. Up until a few months ago, I thought the same thing, and now my life is turned upside-down. I can't wait for this nightmare to be over.'

**

Evan stared across the turquoise sea and in spite of its beauty he yearned to be home. He shut his eyes and breathed in the sea air hoping it would cleanse the helplessness that threatened to overwhelm him. He now understood what a fish must experience when taken from its home.

'Master Evandros! Something is happening,' said Dexion, shaking him. Evan blinked and realised he had fallen asleep. It took a few minutes to clear his head.

'What's going on?' he said.

The crew was hurrying back and forth, and a few hoisted the sail as the smaller men climbed the mast to adjust the ropes. Others rushed to the oars while half were arming themselves with weapons. Evan stood and reached out to grab the arm of a sailor.

'What is it? Are we hit?'

'Pirates!' the sailor shouted and yanked his arm free. He pointed to a ship to the lee side sailing towards them at top speed.

'Pirates...' Evan's skin chilled and his stomach fluttered. 'Where is Phameas?'

'He's rowing. You must arm yourself!' Dexion took his hand and pulled him below deck to where he stored his bag and weapons. 'Quick! There is no time to waste!'

'I have no idea how to use these!' he said, voice rising in a panic.

'Slip your arm through the straps at the back of the shield. Use it to protect yourself and swing the sword!' Dexion said with grim determination. He pulled out a dagger from the folds of his tunic.

They were thrown to the floor, and the dagger clattered across the wooden planks. Evan's head slammed against the deck. The sound of wood splintering and cracking reverberated. There were shouts and the clashing of swords rang loud. Evan scrambled to his feet and swayed. He clutched his head. It took a few seconds before the wave of dizziness passed. He slid the shield onto his arm and picked up the sword. He shook his head, not able to see what help he could offer.

'Are you all right Dexion?' He looked at the boy. Dexion clutched the dagger, his knuckles white, and nodded. 'Stay close.' He had no clue why he said that. He'd be lucky even to scratch someone let alone to come out alive.

Evan poked his head out of the manhole, and his eyes widened. Banipal brandished a wicked looking curved sword, shouted orders and then ran the weapon through a pirate. The captain planted a foot on the dead man, pulled out his sword and moved on to fight another. Grappling hooks held the two ships together. The pirates clambered on board and attacked fallen crew-members not recovered from the impact.

Evan's mouth went dry, heart beating as fast as a rabbit's, and his body trembled. He had never been squeamish or shied away from threatening situations but this was a different matter. As he watched, it was obvious the pirates had the upper hand. The tactic of ramming the ship had the intended effect as Banipal's crew struggled against the marauders. A hand grabbed his leg and squeezed. Evan jumped and slipped. Blood thumped in his ears and he found it difficult to breathe. He thought his heart would stop.

'You must go and help!' Dexion said.

'But...'

'People are dying!'

He shook his head. 'I can't do this!'

'You can and will,' said Dexion. 'It's your destiny to be a great warrior.'

'This is ridiculous! I have never held a sword let alone fought with one!' Evan said.

'No matter how much you protest, this is your reality! Right here and now! Stop being stubborn and get out there!'

Evan's chest heaved. He gritted his teeth and pointed the sword at Dexion. 'This conversation is not over by any means.' He looked up. The sound of swords clanging and screams of wounded men pierced his ears. He took in a deep breath and burst through the manhole, coming face to face with a brigand. The look of surprise on his face would be laughable if Evan was in a humorous mood. His eyes bulged, and he clutched his throat. The tip of a dagger protruded, and blood spouted from the pirate's neck like a fountain. He fell flat on his face with a thud. Evan stared at Dexion. He did not see when or how the boy slipped behind the pirate and killed him. Dexion moved quickly, recovered his dagger, gave Evan one last look and hid behind a stack of wooden crates.

'What the hell am I doing in this godforsaken place?' he said, shouting up at the sky.

'Master Evandros!'

He turned in time to see a pirate running at him. More out of instinct than experience, Evan thrust the shield out in front of his body. The sword hit the shield with a loud thump. Evan's arm reverberated, his fingers tingled from the blow. His attacker drew his weapon across to strike again. Evan thrust his shield to the other side, deflecting the blade. Quick as a snake, the pirate struck again.

His arm burned and numbed in the same instance. Warm blood ran and dripped from his elbow onto the deck. The cut, not deep, sliced his bicep.

Blood roared in his ears, and the hair-raising shouts faded. Evan clenched his hand on the sword's hilt and swung. The pirate parried and slashed. Evan used the shield to force him backwards then swung his sword. Bit by bit, he edged his opponent back until they could move no more. The pirate was pinned against the starboard side of the ship. Evan slammed the shield into the man's body, knocked him on the head with the hilt of his sword and pushed him overboard.

He pivoted to find another pirate swinging a sword at him. The weapon bounced off the shield and ricocheted, the blade biting into the man's face. He had no time to take in what happened, finding himself defending a blow from a new attacker. They exchanged a series of strikes, sparks flying. The pirate's sword broke. He stared at Evan, and then his face went slack. Evan pulled his sword out from his stomach and the raider crumbled to the floor.

From the corner of his eye, he saw another hurtle towards him, sword held out like a spear. Evan bent at the last second. He straightened as the pirate ran into him and thrust the man into the air. He fell onto his back with a thump. Evan, his hand clutched around the hilt, drew the sword up and plunged the blade into his chest. Blood spurted from the wound and sprayed Evan.

The deck was slippery with blood. Dead marauders outnumbered the sailors. The pirate captain yelled to retreat. Confusion followed as they tried to fight their way back to their ship. The rope of the grappling hooks was severed, and the pirates pulled away. Banipal's crew killed those stranded.

Standing from one end of the ship to the other, the crew thrust their bloody swords towards the sky and shouted triumphantly. Banipal, blood spattered over his face and clothing, grinned, the expression fearsome.

CHAPTER THIRTY-TWO

In the wake of the skirmish, the injured men had their wounds stitched and bound. Those who died were wrapped in linen and cast into the sea after an offering to Mot, God of Death and Melqart, King of the Underworld. The decks were scrubbed and washed and order restored.

Evan did his best to remove evidence of blood from his clothes and body but the smell of iron and excrement he could not erase from his memory. He'd never killed anyone before or even seen someone die. The look on their faces at the realisation of their demise was one he did not expect. He did not belong here. The knowledge he had from this time was from books he read and studied. The theoretical and educated findings of how people lived and behaved was a stark contrast to what he faced. He had to find a way home. The question was how? He looked for Dexion and found him throwing a bucket of sea water across the deck. The boy straightened, turned and gazed back, his honey-brown eyes appearing to understand what he wanted. If one person had an idea how he could return, it was the young oracle.

The captain ordered the sails hoisted and rowers to cease, and the moderate winds helped the ship cruise. Evan and Phameas headed for the prow, sat and waited for the other oarsmen to finish taking their share of the water.

'What can you tell me about Kyrene?' Evan said drawing up his knee and resting his arm atop.

'It is one of the few cities colonised by Greek peoples who came from one of the small islands around two hundred years ago. The name of the harbour, Apollonia, honours one of their gods,' Phameas said.

Evan's eyes lit up. 'I read this in a book. The people were from Thira. Terrible droughts affected the island and they petitioned the Delphic Oracle. She instructed them to settle in a place far from their home, and gave them directions where to go.'

'You seem to know quite a bit,' Phameas said, tilting his head.

'Most of the information comes from books I've read. It's not the same as going to a place and experiencing it yourself. While you were with your captain, did you stop at Kyrene?'

Phameas nodded. 'Once, that was enough.'

'Why's that?'

'Kyrene is not the most pleasant place to visit,' Phameas said, frowning. 'The king is very greedy and has the penchant to kill people without cause.'

'And you're telling me this now!' Evan said. 'Why didn't you mention this earlier?'

'What difference would it make if I did or didn't, we were going anyway.' Phameas shrugged.

'Haven't you heard of the expression "to be forewarned is to be forearmed"?' Evan ran a hand through his hair. 'It is better to be aware of what we are getting ourselves into! If the king is as you say, there could be trouble. Cripes.'

'I'm sorry, Evandros, I didn't think it mattered,' said Phameas, lowering his head. 'I thought it was more important to rescue your sister and companions.'

Evan rubbed his brow and bit his lip. He put a hand on his friend's shoulder. 'I'm sorry Phameas, I didn't mean to be so harsh. You are right. But if in future you have knowledge of a place or someone, please don't keep it to yourself. Doesn't matter if you think it trivial, tell me regardless. Agreed?'

Evan put out his hand. Phameas looked at him and his extended hand. He gave a small smile and a nod.

'Agreed.' He put out a hand near Evan's.

Evan grabbed his hand and shook it.

'Good.'

They sat in silence and stared across the deck. A majority of the men vacated the water urn, with a few lingering and chatting near-by.

'Let's go get a drink,' Evan said, getting to his feet.

The rest of the voyage was uneventful. Within days the captain guided the ship into a channel which narrowed and opened into a large natural harbour. Banipal steered towards an empty berth and a few men threw anchors over to slow the ship's progress. The hull bumped against the pier and when the ship settled three men jumped onto the jetty. Thick rope was thrown to them and the sail-ors made quick work of securing the ship.

Banipal gathered his crew, and gave instructions before granting them a few days' leave. After the battle with the pirates the men were more than eager to spend time enjoying a well-earned break. He then turned to his passengers.

'I suggest you head into the city at daybreak,' he said. 'It will take you one to two hours to walk there. Odds are you might not get an audience with the king. I find people are much more agreeable in the morning; by the afternoon their temperament can be fractious.' He gave a nod, moved to disembark but stopped and looked back at them. 'The king is reputed to be unstable and a number of political factions are fighting with each other. The people are suspicious of strangers so it will be in your best interest to remain alert.'

CHAPTER THIRTY-THREE

The trio heeded the captain's advice and departed the next day as the sun began its ascent. They followed the main road south west out of the port town and travelled towards the foothills, the site of the city of Kyrene. The road between the two settlements was wide and paved. Under the soles of his sandals, smooth rounded cobblestones pressed underfoot and shifted over a slight dip where the stones laid next to each other. He marvelled at how uniform it looked. As far as he could see, there was not a stone out of place. He, as did most scholars, considered the Romans as masters at road making but they hadn't conquered this region yet.

'Is the city still run by the Greek settlers?' said Evan.

'For now it is, though the Persians controlled the city for a short while. The inhabitants rebelled and later the Egyptians tried to rule them. It has a long history of conflict and as the captain mentioned, the citizens are unhappy,' Phameas said.

Evan had learnt while studying Ancient History that Kyrene was one of three Greek settlements in the region. It happened not long after the original migrants from Thira had settled and their leader

Battos died. The king's three sons argued as to who succeeded their father.

They had been walking for an hour and stopped to have a drink of water. Their destination lay just ahead, the city built on the crest of two hills, protected by a wall. A large temple sat on the akropolis and if memory served him, it was dedicated to Zeus.

'If only the people saw you for what you really are,' Evan said, muttering to himself and shaking his head. Overhead the sky greyed, and the clouds gathered.

Phameas and Dexion glanced up, startled by the sudden change.

'Oh dear, one of the gods is pretending to flex their muscles,' Evan said, words dripping with sarcasm. A white flash of light streaked across the leaden sky, followed by a thunderous crack. The ground shook.

Phameas' eyes grew wide and he began murmuring words of prayer to Baal-El. Dexion's face paled. He turned to Evan, his eyes filled with concern.

'We should get moving before it starts to...' Evan paused as the first drops of rain fell. 'Never mind.' He started walking again, and the rainfall increased. 'Good to see you have a sense of humour,' he said, shielding his eyes as he looked up at the sky.

When they reached the outskirts of the city, the downpour lessened but they were soaked. Their clothes stuck to their bodies like a second skin. Evan now understood why dogs shook their bodies from head to tail after such a deluge. He considered taking his khiton off and wringing it out. He scouted ahead and slowed his pace until he stopped. Evan clapped a hand to his forehead, gaping at the entrance. It was colossal; bigger than the triumphal arches the Romans had left. It had eight columns, four at the front and four to the rear, which supported a stone roof. Phameas and Dexion walked through the gateway and glanced back when he hadn't moved.

'Master Evandros, are you all right?' Dexion said, taking a few steps towards him.

'What? Oh, yes. I'm fine,' he said, feasting on the structure and drinking in the details. 'I didn't expect the entry to be so impressive.' He reached out and touched the nearest column. The fluted pillars were smooth under his fingertips. Each drum fitted with such precision there wasn't the slightest gap between them. 'Remarkable.'

He craned his head back and gazed up at the roof, taken by the sheer size of the blocks and craftsmanship used to build it. He walked a few paces backwards, calculating how the engineers worked it out. Every section of the gateway was symmetrical and proportionate in design.

'Evandros, we should keep moving.' Phameas' deep rasping voice startled him.

'Oh... sorry, yes we should.'

He crossed over to where Phameas and Dexion waited and stopped mid-way. Evan cringed. Marble statues with solemn expressions, painted in bright primary colours, adorned each side of the road.

No wonder they're not happy, he thought, I wouldn't be either, painted in garish shades!

Along the main road, the statues gave way to small shrines. A group of citizens placed offerings at the foot of a stela. They stared at the trio as they walked past, their eyes cold and hostile. Much further along, simple houses lined the way; square shaped and flat roofed with a central door that opened onto the street. The road veered to the right, and they came to a crossroad. People bustled to and fro, intent on their business, the drone of their voices filtering into the air. To their left loomed the akropolis, big and silent. The temple, the biggest building on site, was a symbol of the people's devotion to the patron god.

'Now to find the palace,' Phameas said.

'One way to find out is to ask,' Evan said. He saw a person passing close by, dressed in a lime coloured full-length khiton and a wide-brimmed headpiece. Evan walked across and reached out with a hand. 'Excuse me, could you tell me where I may find the palace?'

'You are standing in my way.' The man sniffed in disdain. He then looked up, and his eyes widened. He took a step back and hastened away, running and stumbling at the same time.

'Was it something I said?' He looked at his friends.

Phameas shrugged and shook his head. Dexion gazed after the man, somewhat bemused. He approached another person and got the same response, except the man almost tripped on his clothes trying to get away.

'You try, Phameas,' Evan said, throwing his arms up in the air.

The sailor took the lead and walked up to two men. He spoke and pointed back to Evan and Dexion. The men turned, saw Evan, shook their heads and sped away. Phameas returned, perplexed.

'What is wrong with these people?' said Evan flinging an arm behind at the retreating residents. 'Come on, looks as if we have to find it on our own.'

They continued along the road and proceeded to the busy part of the city. People turned and pointed, whispering to each other as they passed. The citizens gave them a wide berth, clearing the road ahead the further they progressed.

'This is ridiculous!'

'It's you they're running from. You are scaring them,' Phameas said, tapping his fingers against his lips.

'Me? Why on earth are they frightened of me? I'm easy going and pleasant!'

'No idea,' the sailor said, 'but each person we've spoken to took one look at you and fled. Now everyone on the street is leaving.'

'That is ludicrous. How can I be a threat?'

'Perhaps it's more than just you,' Dexion said in a quiet voice.

'What do you mean?' Evan said.

'Let me go and find out where the palace is and learn what else is going on,' he said. 'Adults tend to ignore children and talk more.' He pointed. 'Wait for me in the shade of the theatre. I'll be back soon.'

He scampered away before Evan could stop him. The boy was soon swallowed by the crowd that converged in the large square at the end of the street. Evan and Phameas walked over to the theatre and sat on the ground. The shade shielded them from the sun and the strange behaviour of the citizens.

'Do you have any ideas as to why they're acting oddly?' Evan said to Phameas.

'No,' Phameas said, shaking his head. 'Dexion will return soon and tell us.'

Evan leaned his head back against the stone façade and gazed up at the blue sky, marred by a few pristine white fluffy clouds. It was a stark contrast to their trek to the city; as if a tap was turned on then off. Did Zeus make it happen, or was it pure chance? He opted for the latter. He rubbed his face with his hands, all of sudden feeling tired. Evan scrunched his nose and made a mental note to shave when the chance arose. He didn't like to leave facial hair to grow too long. Phameas elbowed him, disrupting his musings.

'Dexion is returning.'

'What is it?' he asked the boy. The expression on his face made his stomach flutter.

'There's an execution at sundown of the three men captured by the king's soldiers and the female held as a concubine,' he said.

'And?'

'They described men and a woman who match your appearance: tall, powerful with ice blue eyes. That's why the people ran away from you. They didn't expect another of the foreigners' kind to arrive here.'

'Is it possible the king knows of your presence?' said Phameas his face grim.

'This changes things,' said Evan. 'If the king is unstable as you and Banipal state, odds are he won't be keen on negotiations. Not if he intends to execute these individuals.' He paused. 'Did you learn where the palace is?'

Dexion pointed towards the akropolis. 'It's at the foot of the hill, opposite the agora.'

'What do you plan to do?' Phameas asked.

'Ask the king to release them.'

'And if he doesn't?'

Evan hesitated. What would he do? He didn't know these people, yet Zeus demanded he rescue them. He told him they were important for the recovery of sacred relics and to prevent the rise of a new religion. Was that even possible? It had happened. Can't change history. Or can you? Besides, he did not appreciate innocent people killed for no reason and a woman enslaved for the pleasure of the king. He glanced over at Phameas and Dexion who still waited for an answer.

'We improvise,' he said.

CHAPTER THIRTY-FOUR

Evan, flanked by Phameas and Dexion, left the shady recesses of the theatre and made his way up the road towards the agora. The busy street cleared on seeing them charge forward, the people flooding to the sides. In their wake, the crowd followed, though no one dared to approach.

They crossed the agora and proceeded towards the palace. Evan took a quick mental note of the number of guards and where they stood. Before they reached the foot of the stairs he said, 'You don't need to come with me...'

Phameas shook his head. 'I'm coming.'

'Me too.'

'There's no need for you to get involved here.'

'But we are, since the day we met!' Phameas said, eyes flashing.

Evan gave them a fleeting look. They'd be at the steps soon. 'Right then, keep alert.'

A few of the guards marched towards them, hands on the hilts of their swords.

'He looks just like those others!' Evan heard one say.

They scaled the steps and stopped when face to face with the armoured troop.

'I want an audience with your king,' he said.

'The king isn't receiving any petitioners this morning.'

'Then you can give him a message.' Evan waited and stared at the grizzled warrior standing before him. The man, though much shorter, was stout and strong, and his eyes buried beneath bushy eyebrows were keen and calculating.

'What is it?' the guard said in a terse tone.

'Is the king a devoted follower of Divine Zeus?'

The guard narrowed his eyes at Evan. 'We all are.'

'I am here as an emissary of Divine Zeus. Tell your king if he doesn't release those he holds captive, my people, the King of the Gods will show his displeasure.'

The guard's lip curled. 'What has addled your brain? Been in the sun too long?'

Evan leaned towards him. 'If you do not give the king my message, then you will suffer the consequences.' He lowered his voice. 'I will eviscerate you here and now.' The man flinched as he felt the point of the dagger Evan held against his ribcage.

'My men will kill you the instant I fall.'

Evan smiled. 'That is possible but not expected, for I believe you value your life over theirs.' He prodded the knife deeper into his side. The guard sucked in a breath. 'I am a reasonable and level headed man but recent events have made me short-tempered. In fact, I am furious and there is no knowing what I may do. Now, I will ask you one more time. *Please* give the message to the king.' He moved back, sheathed the dagger beneath his tunic and eyed the guard.

'I don't have time for niceties. I suggest you move with haste.'

The man scowled at him, hand tightening on the hilt of his sword.

'Now is not the moment to be a hero,' Evan said in a soft voice, eyes glinting.

The other drew himself up, spun on his heel, barked out orders to his men and strode away with quick steps. The remaining sentries closed in to form a line facing Evan and his friends. Phameas, with an eye on the armed men, sidled up next to Evan.

'What did you say to him?' he said, unable to keep the surprise from his voice.

'If you use a particular tone when speaking, what you say has more meaning. Something I learned from watching Robert DeNiro.'

'Ah... Who?' said Phameas.

'The king will grant us entry,' Evan said.

He clasped his hands behind his back and stared at the guards. He stood, not moving or blinking an eyelid. Dexion soon grew tired and sat on the step. Phameas, bored with waiting, turned around to look over the agora and various buildings. The guard standing in the centre clenched his jaw, and his eyes scanned right then left. Those next to him twitched, mouths drawn into a thin line. As each man grew restless, Evan remained still and watching. A voice cut through the edgy atmosphere, and the men, quick to reassert themselves, stepped aside.

'The king will see you.'

Evan gave the returning guard a nod. Dexion scrambled upright and hurried to his side, and the three followed the sentry into the palace. Large, ornate wooden doors opened as they neared.

'I hope you know what you are doing,' Phameas said in a whisper.

They were led into the throne room where the king's royal guard lined the way. Evan counted them as they walked towards the king seated on the throne. The king sat on an oversized throne, his toes just touching the floor. He reminded Evan of pictures of Henry the Eighth, overweight with a puffy, red face. His face glistened with perspiration, making the veins on his nose stand out. A man destined for a heart attack, thought Evan. His mousy brown hair was thinning, which he tried to hide by combing his hair forward.

His small brown eyes flitted from Evan to his warriors. On his left sat the High Priestess, whom Evan recognised from his dream and Zeus' visions. Although her face remained neutral, her eyes gazed at him with uncertainty. On the king's right stood the tallest man Evan had seen so far, though not as tall as him. He was barrel-chested and wore a olive coloured loin-cloth.

'Thank you for granting us your time,' Evan said with a slight bow of the head.

'My man Chiron convinced me I didn't have a choice.'

'There is always a choice, but it depends on what outcome you prefer,' said Evan.

'Why are you here?'

'I believe you know the answer sire; the question you should be asking, is, are you ready to release them?'

The king burst out laughing.

'Why in the gods would I do that?' the king said, face filled with mirth.

'As I told your man Chiron, Divine Zeus has sent me here to retrieve my companions and if you do not free them, you will pay the price.'

The king laughed again. 'You are very funny. I should hold you to be my court jester. Or shall I mete out a fitting punishment, as your fellow companions soon learned. They had to be subdued. The big one, Homer I believe his name is, became troublesome. Belos here had to take steps to bring order.' The king snapped his fingers.

From a doorway to the left of the throne, two soldiers struggled to carry the dead weight of the one called Homer. His head hung low and his feet dragged along the floor. His head lolled back. Evan drew in a sharp breath. His eyes were swollen shut, his nose broken, mouth split in two places and black and blue bruises covered his face. His throat was red and engorged. Evan wondered how he still breathed. Behind them, two more soldiers brought out another man whom he recognised as Hektor, his ankles and wrists shackled. His face lit up when he saw Evan. Shuffling in his wake came the third Atlantean called Leander, also chained and flanked by soldiers.

'Evandros!'

One of the soldiers punched Leander in the face. Both he and Hektor were covered with the remains of dried blood. Their bodies bore the weight of bruises which turned the colour of their skin into a mottled blue and yellow.

'Release them to me,' Evan said between clenched teeth.

The king smirked, and sat back his hand stroking the arm of the High Priestess. She wrinkled her nose but did not pull her arm away. 'You are as stubborn and stupid as your companions.' With a wave of a hand, he added, 'Can't you see you're outnumbered?'

'Do you think I'd come unarmed and without the support of Zeus?' Evan tilted his head. 'You have underestimated me.' He then glanced over at the High Priestess and closed his eyes. 'Now is a good time to intervene, Mr Pantokratora,' he said under his breath.

The air grew still and quiet. The hem of his khiton stirred as if a cat brushed against his leg. His skin tingled and the hairs on his arm stood on end. The sound of everyone breathing, the tempo of their heartbeat, and the whisper of insects moving amplified. Then he heard a familiar voice. He opened his eyes.

'You have wronged the gods by seizing our children.'

The king's face blanched. 'Al... Al... Almighty Zeus...'

'My son and his companions will leave now.'

'Son...?' The king's face went slack.

'As punishment for your iniquity you will sacrifice a bull every day at my altar. In addition, you will offer a token of worth from your immense treasury on the winter and summer solstice till your death. If you fail to follow my decree, your life will be forfeited.' Zeus turned to Evan and glowered. 'We will speak of this later.' Then he vanished.

'Who was...?' Phameas gaped at Evan. 'You are a god!'

'I am as human as you are,' Evan said, shaking his head.

'Divine Zeus is your father,' said Dexion in surprise. 'Now it's beginning to make sense.'

'I am glad it does but this is not the place to discuss my parentage. We need to leave. Phameas, go help with Homer.'

Phameas nodded and half walked, half ran over to the three battered men. Evan stomped over to the High Priestess and held out his hand. 'Time to go.'

She gazed up at him, her eyes searching his.

'There's a physician called Ariston who's been treating Homer. We need the herbs he's been using.'

'That quack! I will kill him!' the king exploded. Evan looked at him, he cringed and tried to withdraw as far as possible.

'Did this man touch you?' Evan asked, his cold hard gaze fixed on the king.

'No Evandros, he did not.'

Evan continued to stare. The king's breathing was quick and shallow. He began to tremble, his jowls quivering.

'Master Evandros, Phameas and the others are by the door.'

He straightened but did not take his eyes off the cowering king. 'We are leaving. If your soldiers follow, their deaths will be on your head.'

He took the High Priestess by the elbow, wheeled around and strode towards the entrance where Phameas and Hektor stood, holding an unconscious Homer. Dexion and Leander waited alongside them, faces bleak as they stared at the guards.

CHAPTER THIRTY-FIVE

'Where do we find this physician?' Evan asked when they emerged from the throne room and head for the stairs.

'He said he lived a good way from the royal palace but I'm not sure where exactly,' Leander offered. They were staring at him. Evan shifted from one foot to the other and avoided making eye contact. He turned his attention to Homer. Phameas' face was going red.

'Here, let me help.' He took hold of Homer's arm, lifted it away from Phameas' shoulder and placed it over his. 'We can't carry Homer all the way to the port. We need a horse and cart. Dexion—' the boy trotted over, '—the people responded to you. Find out where the physician lives and see if you can persuade someone to lend us transport.'

He nodded and sped away, ran down the stairs and across to the agora.

'There's a ship waiting for us and the captain is expecting us by the end of the day.'

Evan, not knowing what else to say, focussed on tracking Dexion as he threaded his way from stall to stall. 'Oh... this is Phameas, a good friend of mine and the boy is Dexion.'

The High Priestess studied him as if she knew something was not right. He couldn't agree more with her. Then a thought struck him.

'Didn't you have weapons?'

'The king's guards took them,' said Hektor.

'We need to get them,' said Evan. 'Wait here and I'll talk to the king.'

'I'll come with you,' Leander said.

'Let's lay Homer on the ground. If Dexion is successful, he'll return with the location of the doctor and transport.' He and Hektor lowered Homer onto the terraced flagstones. 'Shouldn't be too long, otherwise call in the cavalry if we're not out in fifteen minutes,' he joked.

'What?' Hektor said, head pitching back.

'It's a figure of speech. Sorry, it was lame,' he said with a sheepish shrug.

'Lame? What is lame? Have you hurt yourself?' Hektor said, puzzled.

'Never mind,' Evan said. 'Best we see the king before he changes his mind.'

The guards hadn't returned to their posts. He and Leander strode across the portico, passed through the still open doors and re-entered the throne room. The king was engaged in an excitable and animated conversation with his advisors. He gesticulated and his angry voice rose, punctuating each word with venom.

'I'm not interested in excuses! I want that man dead! I want them all dead!'

'Looks like we may be too late,' Leander said.

'Would you be referring to me?'

Evan's voice cut through the atmosphere like the crack of a whip. The king rose out of his seat as if to run away, his complexion paled and eyes grew to the size of golf balls. The men closest to him shrank back and tried to fade into the rear wall. Leander glowered at the retinue of advancing guards who halted mid-step.

'I am a tolerant man but I do detest people who go back on their word. It is the most despicable and offensive conduct by any person. Shall I call on Divine Zeus once again? I'm sure he'd want to know your new plans.' The tension in the room escalated; one could taste the hysteria in the air. Evan took a step. The king scampered behind the chair. He peered from behind and cowered as Evan moved closer. 'No? Let me get to business then. You have taken possessions from my companions that do not belong to you. I want them back and your best cart and horse.' The king cringed as Evan came to stand next to the throne. 'And I want them now. Have your men bring them to the entrance. We—' he sat on the throne. Leander took his cue from Evan and sat next to him. '—will wait here.' As an afterthought, he turned to the trembling king. 'And we need supplies: food, water and blankets.' He settled back into the throne. 'I suggest you instruct your soldiers to get moving.'

***

When Evan and Leander re-joined the others, Dexion had returned and two horses and carts waited at the base of the steps. Next to one stood the king's guards, one holding the reins and the other by the cart. Phameas beamed at Evan and Hektor gave him a grim smile of acknowledgement.

'Time to leave,' he said. He handed the axe to Leander and with Hektor, they carried Homer down the steps and loaded him into the back of the royal cart. 'High Priestess, you ride in the other cart.'

'I will travel with Homer,' she said.

'All right.' He helped her onto the wagon. She moved to the end and with care lifted Homer's head. She then sat with his head on her lap.

Evan turned to Dexion. 'Did you find out where the physician lives?'

The boy nodded. 'He lives on a street called Valley Road. We follow this and turn left where two streets meet. His house is closest to the Temple of Apollo.'

'Well done Dexion and nice work on getting the horse and cart.' He looked over at Hektor and Leander. 'Why don't you ride in the cart?'

'I can walk,' Hektor said, straightening, clenching his jaw.

'I don't doubt it,' Evan said. 'We'll take turns. You take the first half of the journey, and then walk the second leg.'

'Come on, Hektor,' said Leander, putting a hand on his shoulder. 'That is a reasonable proposal; besides Evandros is concerned for our wellbeing.'

'All right,' said Hektor with reluctance. 'But I will ride in the wagon for just the first stage of the journey,' he added, shaking his finger at Evan.

'Of course. Now to the doctor's place, get what we need and leave for the port,' said Evan. 'Phameas, you take the reins and lead that horse and I'll take this one. Come on Dexion, you can ride on the horse.' Evan lifted the boy onto the horse's back. He held out his hand for reins. The guard gave him the straps and stepped aside.

The physician's home was the only one within the vicinity of the temple. As they pulled up outside, the High Priestess proposed she should confer with the doctor.

'It's better if I speak with the physician alone,' she said. 'He and I discussed how best to treat Homer and he trusts me.'

'Not sure that's wise.' Evan frowned.

'He is a healer. I will be safe,' she said.

'Regardless, you're not going alone. Phameas and Dexion will go with you,' he said.

'But...'

'Either it's them or me.'

'It is unnecessary.'

'Humour me,' he said, his gaze hardening.

Her brow creased and eyes narrowed. Then with dignity and poise, she lifted Homer's head and extricated herself from the cart. Phameas gave Evan a searching look.

'Got your dagger?' he mouthed to the sailor. His friend frowned and nodded. 'Be prepared,' he added. Phameas and Dexion trailed behind the High Priestess. She glanced back at Evan, the expression on her face unreadable, and then turned to knock on the door. A slave opened the door, stared at the trio and listened as the High Priestess explained her visit. He stood aside and granted them entrance. Before the slave closed the door, he spotted Evan, Leander and Hektor. His eyes widened and he slammed the door shut.

'What a strange reaction,' Evan said.

'It's been this way ever since we arrived,' Leander said. 'Not sure why they behave in that manner.'

'They have never seen the likes of us before,' said Hektor with a derisive snort.

'I am sure it's not that,' Evan said.

'What of your experiences then? What happened to you after the ship sank?' Hektor asked, tone curt.

'We searched the wreck but couldn't find you. We thought you died along with the crew until the High Priestess said you were alive. Divine Zeus visited and told her you were coming,' Leander said in a calm tone.

'I have no memory of the voyage or of the accident,' he said. Which he didn't, for how could he remember something that didn't happen? 'I awoke on a ship Phameas worked on. We sailed to a place called Rusaddir where we met Dexion then onto Hippo Regius and arrived at Carthage. Zeus visited me while on the ship and told me where you were held captive. And here we are.' He threw out his arms and let them drop. 'That's all there is to tell.'

'We're fortunate you came when you did,' said Leander with a grateful smile.

'Thank the Mother Goddess,' Hektor added in a mutter.

'With regards to finding the relics, one may be in Thebes, Egypt,' Evan said.

'How did you learn of the actual location?'

Evan spun around. He didn't hear the High Priestess walk up behind him. Phameas lagged behind, carrying a large black bag made from canvas and Dexion carried a similar but smaller one.

'At the library in Carthage,' he said. 'The source mentioned the Temple of Amun-Re in Thebes where a golden serpent may be found.'

'Did something else happen while you were there?' she said, as her gaze bored into his.

'No.'

The High Priestess studied him, her gaze searching as he stood there with a deadpan expression.

'Did you get the necessary medication?' he said, breaking the long silence.

She nodded. 'The physician was generous in giving what we need to help Homer.'

'Right. Good. Best we move on or the captain may think we decided to stay.'

When the High Priestess turned and walked to the cart where Homer lay, Phameas beckoned Evan with quick, sharp flick of his head. He went over to check the horse's harness.

'What is it?' he asked in a low voice.

'She's not what she appears. She made Dexion and me wait in the courtyard while she met with the physician. When they both returned, the look on the man's face was one of fear. He was more than eager to give what she wanted.'

Evan patted the horse and nodded. 'Everything good here.' He handed the reins to Phameas.

CHAPTER THIRTY-SIX

The journey back to Apollonia was quicker and before long they arrived back at the harbour. Banipal supervised the supplies loaded on board as they approached the ship. He turned around hearing the repetitive clap of hooves on the cobblestones. Evan lifted a hand of acknowledgment then became perplexed on seeing the captain scowl. He glanced at Phameas who shrugged. They came to a stop, and the two approached him.

'Is there something wrong?' said Evan.

'You did not mention two of the passengers were a woman and a dead man!' Banipal pointed. They watched Leander help the High Priestess dismount from the cart.

'The man is unconscious and not dead,' Evan said. 'What is the problem with a woman being on board?'

'Women bring bad luck.'

Evan looked to Phameas who nodded. 'Would it help to know she is a High Priestess?' He then added as an afterthought, 'Oh and she is my sister.'

'You should have told me!' Banipal's anger waned a little.

'I didn't think it was an issue. My apologies, Captain.'

'If anything happens to my ship and crew while she's on board, I will curse you, your friends and family for eternity.'

'Would you consider extra payment for this oversight?' Evan offered.

'Ten shekels,' was the captain's prompt reply.

Evan grimaced and nodded.

***

After a day at sea, Banipal navigated the ship towards the mouth of a river. Along the water's edge, the land was rich and verdant, teeming with birdlife, both big and small. He steered towards the embankment and ordered the anchors thrown over. The vessel slowed and came to stop when the prow hit the ridge.

'Why aren't you sailing into the tributary?' Hektor asked.

'The river is shallow in parts and my ship won't be able to pass. The Egyptians use barges and smaller boats to sail on the Nile,' Banipal said in a flat tone. 'These waters can be treacherous. It would be wise to either steer clear or travel on a vessel.'

'You're going to leave us here?' Evan asked, dumbfounded. 'How do you expect us to travel with an unconscious man?'

'There are many settlements along the waterway. The closest town is Khito. It's a few hours' walk. There you should find transport,' the captain said. 'Make sure you don't wander too close to the water's edge or one of the river's beasts will eat you.'

'Are you serious? We paid you good money.' Evan glowered at the captain.

'You wanted to come to Egypt; well here we are.' Banipal spread his arms. 'Now disembark from my ship. I'd like to sail back to sea.'

'You are not an honourable man,' said Evan, clenching his hands.

'Come Evandros, the captain has fulfilled the agreement. It is time for us to depart,' the High Priestess said, coming to stand next to him.

'If our paths ever cross again, you will regret this day ever happened,' Evan said in a tight tone.

Banipal didn't waste any time in leaving once they were on shore. Planks were hoisted and long poles thrust over the side to push the ship from the escarpment.

'I'd have loved to punch him in the face,' Evan said as he and the others watched them sail away.

Hektor agreed. 'Yes, he deserved nothing less.'

'The gods will punish him,' said the High Priestess turning away.

Evan snorted. 'If only that was true.'

'What beasts was he talking about?' Leander asked as he bent to help Hektor carry Homer.

'Crocodiles and hippopotami,' Evan answered.

'What do they look like?'

Evan thought he was jesting but from the expression on the other man's face and that of Hektor and the High Priestess, they didn't know.

'The Nile crocodile, the largest reptile in this region, can grow up to six metres in length. It captures a prey in its jaws and drags it back into the water. Then it spins, crushing the body and buries the carcass in the riverbed to eat later when it has decomposed.'

They all stared at him.

'And the other animal, the hippopotami?' Hektor said.

'Big mammals and known as the river horse but doesn't look like one. They spend most of the time in the water and are territorial.

They eat plant life but there have been incidents where they've knocked boats over.'

'How is it you know this information?' Leander said. 'As Master of the Water, I have never heard of such animals or behaviour.'

Great. Thanks Zeus for putting me in this awkward position.

Evan's mind whirled with possible explanations but none sounded plausible or convincing.

'Evandros has access to sacred ancient writings as Master Scholar. Perhaps he read the information in the text on these water creatures,' the High Priestess said.

Evan nodded, relieved and grateful for the High Priestess' interjection. 'Yes an obscure manuscript on Egyptian wildlife.' Eager to deflect further questions he added, 'We can't travel with Homer while he's in this condition. Phameas, Dexion and I will go to Khito and find transport. While we are away, I advise you to rest in the shade of the trees.' He lifted the bag off his shoulder and pulled out rations he'd managed to scrounge from Banipal's stores. He handed them to the High Priestess. 'We'll bring back more food.'

From the scowl on Hektor's face, he did not appear to be happy about the arrangement. Leander tapped him on the shoulder and pointed to a cluster of trees a few metres away.

'We'll follow the river,' Evan said to Phameas and Dexion.

'What of those beasts?' Phameas said, alarmed.

Evan shrugged. 'Watch where you walk.'

Phameas muttered and shook his head. They set off southwards, keeping to lush verdant growth fed by the Nile. West of the river just beyond the fertile land rose the desert. Yellow and red hues marked the terrain in a permanent sunset. Never had Evan seen such contrast in landscape. This was not what he had in mind as his first trip to Egypt.

After an hour of walking, Evan came to a stop.

'Anyone want a drink?' He held the water skin out to Dexion.

'You don't appear to be too comfortable in the company of your companions,' Phameas said. Evan glanced away, not wanting to meet his curious expression.

'I am not the same man who left with them. They are strangers to me.'

'Even the High Priestess? Your sister?'

He watched as a pied kingfisher dived into the river and in a short time emerged with a fish. It flapped, powerless in the bird's powerful beak. The bird took flight and landed on the limb of a tree.

'I don't remember anything or anyone prior to your captain hauling me out of the sea.' He turned to Phameas. 'I can't remember something that didn't happen.'

Phameas frowned. 'What do you mean?'

'Forget it,' Evan said taking the water skin from him. 'Let's keep moving.' He thrust the water container into the bag and marched off. Phameas stared after him, bemused.

'Do you know what he meant?' he heard Phameas ask Dexion. 'Well?'

'It's not my place to say,' Dexion said. 'Only that he's not the man they believe him to be.'

CHAPTER THIRTY-SEVEN

They returned hours later, Evan leading a donkey pulling a make-shift rickety cart. Phameas walked on the other side of the pack animal, while Dexion rode in the wagon, sitting amidst a generous supply of food. Leander stood first, followed by the High Priestess then Hektor.

'You have done well!' Leander said, walking over and looking into the cart.

'How did you procure all this?' Hektor asked as he picked up a loaf of bread.

'Dexion has a unique ability to convince people to give. Besides we had very little money left over which went to pay for our new transport.' Evan picked up a jar. 'In this is beer. We also have dried figs, pickled vegetables and loaves of bread. No meat but we can catch fish from the river.' He pulled out a roll of twine. 'Speaking of which, I'll see if I can get some for dinner.'

'Have you taken leave of your senses?' Hektor said, astounded. 'One of those beasts may attack you!'

'I'll bring my sword with me.' Evan smiled. With twine and a basket in hand, he headed for the river.

'I didn't believe you when Divine Zeus told you he's different but after what I have seen and heard, I do now,' Hektor commented to the High Priestess and Leander, his attention on Evan strolling away. They didn't see the look exchanged between Phameas and Dexion. 'Is he going be able to fulfil his part in the quest?'

The High Priestess gazed at the retreating back of Evan. 'Divine Zeus said he can, that's all we need to accept as true.'

***

At the break of dawn and after a quick meal of bread and olives, they set off southwards. Before long the heat of the sun was in full force so even the shade from the trees offered little respite. They bypassed the settlement of Khito and journeyed to the next town to make their stop. Evan handed the reins to Phameas and dropped back to the cart where the High Priestess nursed Homer.

'How is he going?' he asked her.

She was wiping Homer's face with a damp cloth. 'He still breathes, which is a good sign.'

'How did it happen?'

'The king laughed when we told him where we came from. He'd have Belos and his guards beat Homer, Hektor and Leander each time they spoke the truth. After many encounters and realising the thrashings had no effect, the king ordered Belos to strike at their heads.' She turned to Hektor and Leander who kept pace alongside. 'You can still see the effects of the harsh treatment on their faces.' She glanced down at Homer, tears welling in her eyes. 'Homer suffered the most. Belos crushed his windpipe, but dear brave Homer fought back and threw him across the room. The guards rushed at Homer with swords, and his body bears the wounds inflicted. The king later chained Homer to a post and had him clubbed until he passed out.'

'He punished you for speaking the truth?' Evan said, incredulous. 'We were told the king was despotic, but this was extreme. It doesn't make any sense.'

'It would appear the fate of our people and destruction is folklore, a story.'

Evan wanted to say more but if he did it would reveal the depth of his knowledge. He saw how they reacted when he explained about the animals and decided to keep silent. All of a sudden, the cart lurched. The donkey reared and brayed, eyes wide. Phameas tried to shorten the lead, but the donkey bucked. It turned and tried to run. Evan leapt and wrapped his arms about its neck, feet skidding in the dirt to slow it down. Phameas pulled hard on the reins. The donkey whipped its head from side to side, knocking Evan off his feet. Leander rushed to the other side and placed a hand on its forehead. He spoke in its ear in a soothing tone. After a while the pack animal calmed.

'What in the name of Zeus is the matter with it?' Hektor said, brushing the dirt off his khiton. He got knocked over as he tried to steady the cart.

'Nice work,' Evan said looking over the donkey's head to Leander.

'Master Evandros.' Dexion tugged at his tunic.

Evan turned. He looked to the sky where he pointed. He shielded his eyes. 'What is that?'

The donkey trembled. Leander stroked its back and put an arm about it.

'Can you hear that?' Leander asked in a low voice.

Evan nodded. A chill slithered up his spine at the sound of keening. The ear-splitting squawk was not familiar. Not knowing why, he pulled the sword from its scabbard.

'Arm yourselves.'

Three dark bodies flew towards them, their screeches piercing as they neared. The donkey stamped its hooves. Leander clasped its head in his hands, gaze focussed on the animal's and then its head drooped. As the three flying creatures drew nearer, Evan stared and rubbed his eyes. He blinked.

'No way! They can't be real!' he said, his heart thudding as fast as a stallion racing up a hill. His blood went cold as one broke formation.

'Gods! Soul-eaters!' Phameas said with a shrill voice.

'Harpies!' the High Priestess screamed.

A harpy swooped down, its mouth open wide, razor-sharp teeth gleaming. Hektor swung his axe at it. The winged monster swept by and banked right, then came back. It reached out with its talons. Evan ducked low. Hektor swung again. The harpy shrieked. A claw fell a few feet from him. As it soared, hot blood splattered over them.

Another attacked. Leander showered it with arrows. One pierced a wing. The harpy wobbled. It swayed from side to side for some distance before the beast regained control. The third one came at them with an ear-splitting squeal. Phameas and Evan thrust their swords but missed. The predator wheeled around flying low. Hektor threw the axe. It swerved and charged. The harpy extended its talons and grabbed Evan. Its claws bit into his skin as they squeezed his shoulders. The soul-eater began to ascend at a high speed.

'Evandros!'

He twisted and turned, trying to get free but the sharp talons cut into his flesh. Arrows zipped past. Each one found its mark. The harpy's torso was soon riddled with the projectiles. Its claws cut deeper into his skin. Evan swung his sword. The winged creature squealed. It took him a few seconds to realise he was falling, and fast.

'Sweet mother of God!' He propelled his arms and legs as if to stop the inevitable from happening. His heart swelled as if it would burst from his chest.

'Brave Evandros, do not worry,' said a voice. Warm arms embraced him. The sweet scent of ambrosia and honey filled his nose. The rapid descent stopped and he realised he no longer plummeted to his death.

'Who are you?'

'Hush.'

Before long, his feet touched the firm ground. Soft lips touched his and then they were gone.

'Evandros!'

He turned, a little dazed, his heart still racing. The High Priestess, Dexion and Phameas ran towards him. Leander and Hektor stayed by the wagon, their faces tilted upwards, scanning the sky. Dexion flung his arms about Evan's waist and the High Priestess threw her arms around his neck.

'For a while there, I assumed we'd never see you again,' Phameas said, face pale. 'Soul-eaters are treacherous creatures and no one ever survives when they capture their prey.'

'Mother Goddess! And when we saw you fall, I thought you were lost to us,' the High Priestess said, her voice wavering.

'I must admit, it crossed my mind that it was the end for me,' he said with a nervous laugh, 'but someone caught me and well, here I stand.'

'Who?' Phameas asked.

'I don't know.' Evan shook his head. 'It was a woman.' He then described her scent but omitted to say anything about the kiss. The lingering softness of her lips stayed with him.

'She is a goddess,' the High Priestess said, letting her arms drop. She stared at him. 'I wonder which one?'

Evan raised his brows and shrugged. 'If it was a goddess who saved me, I am grateful she did.'

'A goddess?' Phameas beamed and slapped him on the shoulder. 'Didn't I say from the first time we met the gods favour you?'

'Somehow I don't expect that's the case,' Evan said. He glanced down at Dexion who clung to him. 'It's okay Dexion, I'm fine.' Evan gave the boy a reassuring smile.

Dexion nodded and let go. 'The one who saved you is a goddess,' he said looking at Evan, 'but she remains apart from the other immortals.'

'Are you able to see why she did it?' Evan was curious as to who his mysterious saviour is and why she rescued him and not Zeus who claimed to be his father.

'No,' Dexion said. 'I do get a sense she is interested in you.'

'Well, not sure how to respond to that bit of news.'

'How do you know this?' the High Priestess asked Dexion.

'I am aware of her presence. She's been with us for a while but until now kept her distance, observing.'

The High Priestess regarded Dexion in silence and then she smiled. For the first time since her liberation from the clutches of the tyrant king, the High Priestess looked hopeful and optimistic. 'You have travelled quite a distance to be here.'

'It is where I must be.'

Evan scratched his stubbled jaw. 'What are the two of you discussing?'

'Your young friend's gift is fortuitous.'

Evan looked at Phameas whose puzzled expression mirrored his own.

'Come along,' she said, taking Dexion's hand. 'We want to reach the next town before nightfall.'

'What was that about?' Phameas asked Evan as they watched the two walk back to where the others waited.

'No idea but there's more to Dexion than we expected.' He searched the ground.

'What are you doing?'

'I dropped my sword after the harpy let me go.' Evan circled one way then the other. 'Ah... there it is.' The sword lay hidden in the green foliage but the glint of the blade reflected the sun's light. He strode over and picked it up. 'How odd.'

'What is it?' Phameas asked.

'There's no blood on it and am certain I wounded the harpy.'

His friend stared at the blade, looked at Evan and then back to the weapon.

'This, my friend, I suspect is the beginning of strange occurrences,' he said.

Evan slid the sword into the scabbard. 'Welcome to my world.'

'Any ideas on who sent those harpies and why?' Evan could not shake the feeling the attack wasn't a coincidence. Would they have acted of their own accord? Did they know how and where to find them?

'I remember my father telling me stories when I was a boy of the many magical creatures that roamed the earth during the time of the gods. He told me the harpies were Divine Zeus' hounds, they do his bidding and take things, even humans,' Leander said.

'I find it difficult to even consider Divine Zeus instigated their attack,' said Hektor. 'Why endanger us? It negates the purpose of our being here.'

'I agree with Hektor that Divine Zeus and the other immortals had nothing to do with the harpies,' said the High Priestess. 'Even so, it would be unwise to ignore the possibility there may be others who want to stop us. We cannot afford to become complacent.'

'The question is who'd benefit from stopping us finding the sacred relics?' Hektor said.

'For one the Christians,' said Evan.

'Who?' Leander said.

'A religious group who have faith in and worship one god.'

'Why would they do that?'

'It is their belief, the one they call the Messiah, is a son of God and sent to earth to save humanity from all manner of sins.'

'The gods do that now,' Hektor said with a sniff.

'The Christians are of the opinion he forgives people for their transgressions and saves them from damnation.'

'If a person does something wrong they should be punished,' said Hektor.

'It enables people to draw strength from this man who, through his actions, shows devotion and compassion to the human race.'

'Are they a strong force?' the High Priestess asked.

Evan said, 'You could say they are.'

'So we must find the relics,' said Leander.

'And soon given what Evandros is saying,' Hektor added with a dark scowl. 'I, for one, do not want our gods replaced.'

'Nor do I,' Leander said with a firm nod. 'With the gods gone, our people cease to exist.' He turned to the High Priestess. 'What is Mother Goddess' view on this?'

'She supports the gods in their claim and the need to find the relics.'

'Then we do everything in our power to stop the fall of our lineage,' said a grim Hektor.

The donkey refused to move. Both Evan and Phameas pulled and pushed the pack animal but it did not budge.

'Here, allow me,' said Leander walking over.

'I hope you have better luck than us,' Evan said handing him the reins. Both he and Phameas stepped back. Evan watched Leander speak into the animal's ear. He stroked the ears and neck as he spoke in a soothing tone. Then the donkey shook its head. Leander smiled and looked up at Evan.

'He's ready to go now.'

Leander held the reins loose in his hand and began to walk, and the donkey trotted alongside. Evan and Phameas stared, mouths gaping. Dexion stifled a laugh; the High Priestess had a small smile on her face and Hektor's mouth twitched.

'I wonder if he can charm a snake,' Evan said as they fell in step behind the cart.

The further south they travelled, the more the desert encroached and the fertile land narrowed. Plant life throve along the river and in the water; tall, slender stems topped with a thick cluster of thin green spindle fronds. Pink and white lotus floated on the water and a variety of grasses, shrubs and trees broke the austere landscape.

They happened across an oasis, where lofty date palms with umbrella shaped fronds created a cool haven. A pool of fresh water sat amidst the trees. Here they replenished their water containers and refreshed before continuing their journey.

Farm lots began to appear on the fringes of the river where workers were busy harvesting crops. Wheat, barley, flax, beans, lettuce, peas and radishes grew in abundance in the rich black earth. Small dams were dug from the earth and fed from the Nile, with handmade wooden sluices irrigating the land. Here they stopped and enquired after a boat and offered in exchange the donkey and cart. The farmer was at first not keen on the trade as he owned an ox, but Evan explained the benefits of the pack animal and convinced him otherwise.

The boat, more resembling a barge, had a crude hut-shaped shelter in the centre and two long poles. Once everyone was on board, Evan and Phameas used the poles to push away from the levee.

'We can use the current of the river,' Phameas said as he steered the boat to the port side. 'Plus it will give us a break from rowing.'

'A good idea,' Evan agreed.

'Do you know where Thebes is located?' the High Priestess asked.

'It is long way south of here,' Evan said.

'How long will it take?'

'At current speed, it may take ten to sixteen days. We won't be able to sail at night. We don't want to disturb the hippopotami or we'll end up in the water.'

As they coasted downstream, the landscape changed from farmland to towns. Simple, sturdy mud-brick homes with pens that housed cattle, sheep and goats dotted the way.

'Dexion?' Evan beckoned. The boy turned with a questioning look. 'See if you can catch fish for us to eat.' He handed Dexion a roll of twine.

They continued along the river over the next few days, a routine marked by the sun's rise and descent. Evan took notes and drew what he saw when not steering or rowing the barge, marvelling at the sophistication of Egyptian ingenuity.

'Ah... Evandros, we have a problem,' said Leander. Evan looked up from his drawing. 'We're taking on water.'

Evan put the tome aside and joined Leander. 'Great, just what we need. Head for the shore.' Phameas moved to his side. Evan glanced at him. 'What do you think? Can the gap be sealed?'

'All we can do is tighten the existing seams,' he said, 'and ask the gods to get us to the next town where we can get supplies to fix it.'

On reaching the shore, everyone disembarked and the four men hauled the waterlogged vessel onto the land. Under Phameas' instruction, Hektor and Leander squeezed the planks together while Evan pulled the swollen rope tighter. He handed the extra length to Phameas who with deft fingers knotted the cord. They repeated the task for each plank and had almost finished when there was a resounding crack.

'Oh... that is not good,' Evan said.

He and the other three stared at the broken board.

'I am surprised this didn't happen earlier. This particular wood is brittle and doesn't last long,' Phameas said.

'Can it be mended?' Leander asked.

Phameas shook his head. 'We don't have tar to patch the break.'

'Will it still float?' asked Hektor.

'For a small stretch, but it will take on water and we may not be able to reach land faster than it sinks.'

'What if we collect resin from the trees?' said Evan. 'Will that give us enough to seal the break and time to reach the next town?'

Phameas frowned. 'Not sure. It may work but it needs to harden on both sides.'

'The sap from a pine tree is the best but we'll take what's available. We collect as much as possible and heat it over a low flame,' said Evan. He grabbed a couple of bowls, handed one to Leander and the other to Phameas. 'Let's get to it.'

Splitting into two groups they moved from tree to tree extracting resin. Evan combined the amber liquid into one bowl and heated it over a small fire Dexion prepared. He stirred the extract with a stick until it thickened.

'We need to move quickly,' he said looking up at the others. 'Once this starts cooling it sets and is hard to spread. Phameas, apply it to the top first then we will turn the boat on its side so you can smear the rest on the bottom.'

Phameas nodded and held his hand out for the bowl. He set off at a quick trot, the others on his heels. It didn't take him long to apply a liberal quantity of the resin into the break. He stood back as the three big men lifted the boat. Phameas sneaked beneath their arms, scanned for the damaged board and smeared the rest into the crack and along the length. He ducked back out, and they eased the boat onto the ground.

'Will it work?' asked the High Priestess. She had followed them and watched as they mended the boat.

'It is a temporary fix,' Evan said. 'Just to be safe, we should stay here the night to allow the mixture to harden.'

The following morning they got up as the sun peeped over the horizon. Phameas checked the gaps between the boards and the break. He pressed his hand down on it and grunted with satisfaction when it didn't give way. He nodded to the others. They loaded Homer onto the boat. The High Priestess was next to board and then Dexion. The men pushed the barge back onto the water's edge, scrambled aboard and before long were drifting on the river.

During the voyage Evan and Phameas made regular checks on the mended plank and each time came away satisfied. Leander and Hektor relieved them from steering the barge and Evan took the opportunity to sit back and take a nap. Since his nocturnal exploits and displacement, he hadn't the time to digest what had happened. Even as he closed his eyes, Evan still found his predicament difficult to accept. He was living and breathing in a different time and interacting with people who belonged in the texts of ancient history. Would he ever return home?

He fell into a deep sleep, lulled by the gentle lapping of water against the hull of the boat and the quiet chatter of his companions. A face appeared in his dream, the most stunning woman with long, wavy auburn hair and light grey eyes. Then he was standing at his desk, flicking through designs of his latest project. The sound of fingers pounding on keyboards and phones ringing made him turn.

'Hey boss, do you have the latest calculations for the dimensions of the library?'

'Huh?' He blinked.

Jerry snapped his fingers in front of his face. 'Are you okay? Did the doctor find out what's causing your blackouts?'

Evan gaped at him, his mind unable to comprehend what happened. 'What? Where am I?'

Jerry frowned. 'You're at the office. Don't you remember getting a lift in with Alex?'

Evan's heart pounded. He whipped his head from one side to the other. He was back in his company office that overlooked the Swan River, surrounded by desks, computers and his staff. The familiar cushioning of his chair rocked under his weight as he sat. He glanced at the papers he clutched in his hands. Not the black tome but building specs and drawings of his latest project.

'Am I really here?' He lowered his gaze and saw he was wearing tailored pants and a blue cotton shirt. He touched the clothes, the fabric smooth under his fingertips and quality very different to the heavy linen of the khiton.

'Are you sure you should be here?' Jerry said, forehead wrinkling.

'I...'

Someone was shaking his shoulder. Evan's eyelids fluttered.

CHAPTER THIRTY-NINE

'Evandros!'

When he opened his eyes, he half expected to see Jerry standing before him but he saw Phameas' animated face.

'How can this be?' He sat up. The hardness of the wood pressed beneath his backside and the hot sun bore down on his head. Mere moments ago he was back in his own time and place of work. Did he make it happen? And if he did, how? He had returned home, even if for a moment. He must work out how it happened in order to try again. Preoccupied, he didn't notice what grabbed everyone's attention until he heard the excitement in Dexion's voice.

'Look!' Dexion pointed.

He turned absent-mindedly, blinked and stared.

'It can't be...' he started to say, his eyes growing wider the closer they sailed.

Ahead, on the eastern embankment, was a large city complex. Massive walls surrounded the buildings, and held the extensive desert at bay. A canal fed from the Nile led to the metropolis. Phameas took control of one of the poles and guided the barge towards the waterway.

'Gods! It must have taken generations to build,' said Hektor.

Outside the walls was a series of smaller buildings, two storeys and a large number of single storeys. A range of trees including palm trees had been planted in and around the dwellings. They reached a large port, with a smattering of big and small boats tethered to the dock. Evan caught a glimpse of two colossal statues and two enormous pillars positioned on either side of an entrance to an enclosed precinct.

'The city of Memphis, home of Khufu. Oh my God!' he said in awe. 'This is the location of the pyramid of Giza and the Great Sphinx!' he added in an excited voice.

'Pyramid? Sphinx?' Leander said.

Evan nodded, eyes sparkling. 'The pharaohs built pyramids for their tombs as a means of connection with the gods. There are hundreds if not thousands of pyramids throughout the land of Egypt. And the Sphinx is a large statue with the head of a man and the body of a lion, sculpted from stone. Incredible works of engineering.'

'How is it you know this?' Hektor asked.

'I read it,' Evan said his eyes devouring and drinking in the vista. 'Come on, let's go take a look.'

'We need to find accommodation, a place for Homer to rest in comfort and a doctor to check on him,' the High Priestess said.

'Oh... of course,' said Evan, shoulders drooping.

'We can't carry Homer while we search for a hostel,' Leander pointed out. 'The sensible thing to do is a few of us go.'

The High Priestess concurred. 'That is a good idea. I'll stay here with Homer.'

'I'll stay as well,' Leander said, glancing over at the High Priestess.

'I must check the state of the repairs and chat to the Harbour Master about where to get tar to seal the damaged plank,' said Phameas.

'Then it's up to us to find lodging and a doctor,' Hektor said, looking at Evan and Dexion. 'Come along.'

Hektor stepped off the barge. Evan's jaw tightened but he did not utter a word. He waited until Dexion had alighted and then followed. A well-trodden dirt road, one side lined with palm trees four rows deep, led from the port to the lower part of the city.

'This must be the workers' quarters,' he said casting an expert gaze at the simple dwellings.

Evan observed the state of ruin and disrepair of the homes, only a few of which were inhabited. It must have been once a wonderful, thriving and vibrant city. Now the skeletal ruins of buildings inhabited the land.

What struck him was the haphazard alignment of the streets. Some ran in angles and others in a grid-like formation. All were narrow, just wide enough for two people to walk alongside. It gave Evan the impression there was no planning involved, and the buildings erected ad hoc.

'Doesn't appear many people live here anymore,' said Hektor as they passed a house with a part of a wall missing.

'Perhaps there wasn't enough work, and they moved on,' Evan said.

'It must have been once a grand city by the number of houses,' Hektor added. He pointed. 'What would be behind that wall?'

'The pharaoh's palace and the temples. The fortifications protected royalty, priests and priestesses, the wealthy and those fortunate enough to live inside the compound.'

'What of the citizens outside the walls? Wasn't the pharaoh concerned for the welfare of these people?'

'Of course, their adulation was very important to the pharaoh,'
Evan said. 'In spite of this, the security of the palace and temples
were the primary importance. They were the figureheads for Egyptian rule. Without them, their power diminishes, which suggests
that's what occurred here.'

They approached the enclosed complex, from which loud hum-
ming pulsated. The monumental gateway had painted reliefs depict-
ing scenes of a pharaoh engaged in various ritualistic activities. Evan
recognised the image of a hippopotamus though he could not work
out what the tableau represented. Remnants of yellow, blue, green
and red were still embedded in the artwork. Evan reached out and
touched the decorated block.

'It must have been magnificent when completed,' he said, closing
his eyes and taking a moment to visualise how it may have looked.

'From the noise inside, this must be where the people are,' said
Hektor. 'We may find a place to stay the night.'

Inside the precinct were lush gardens and trees and pools of water. There was a large, elaborate building surrounded by walls and a
series of smaller walled off areas. Inside each were mastaba constructions.

'This is the royal quarters,' Evan said.

'Why is that?' Hektor asked.

'Can you see those massive statues and plinths on that wall?'
Evan pointed. Hektor nodded while Dexion tiptoed to see. 'Ramesses
II commissioned those in his likeness.'

'Why did they build such colossal figures?' said Dexion.

'It showed their power and kinship to the gods.'

'They likened themselves to the divine?' Hektor said, gaping.

'The pharaohs were considered their offspring, hence they were both gods and kings of Egypt, supreme rulers.'

'Did they worship many gods?' Hektor asked, staring at the statue.

'A great many,' Evan said. 'They were both human and animal, sometimes sharing the one body. Amun-Re was their sovereign god and worshipped by everyone. Each divinity had a particular function in the lives of the Egyptians and the more important ones had temples.'

'Much like Zeus and the Olympian gods,' Hektor mused.

'There are a few people over by that low building.' Dexion observed.

'Let's go talk to them,' said Hektor, striding ahead.

Evan clenched his jaw and took a deep calming breath. He disliked the way Hektor presumed to take charge and expected everyone to obey his directives. Evan believed people earned respect first by showing consideration and paying attention to others. From their behaviour and what they had said, these companions had done little to inspire his confidence. If every Atlantean acted this way, no wonder their world had been destroyed.

'Master Evandros, are you coming?' said Dexion.

'Do I have a choice?' he said under his breath. He trailed behind Hektor. Dexion walked alongside and kept looking up at him, as if he sensed Evan's displeasure.

Hektor stood with a group of men, head and shoulders taller than them, talking and gesticulating in the direction of the port. The Egyptians stared, perplexed, and shrugged. They turned to each other nonplussed.

'What is the trouble?' Evan asked.

'They don't understand what I am saying,' Hektor said, flinging a hand out at the men in frustration.

'Not surprising, they speak a different language,' Evan said in a mild tone. 'Let me try.' He bowed towards the men and when he straightened smiled at them. 'Greetings honoured men; we are strangers to your glorious city and have travelled far. We seek a place to sleep and a doctor for our companion who is unwell. Can you help us?'

'You speak in a strange dialect,' one remarked.

'My apologies, I did not mean to offend.'

'You haven't but your friend was rude,' said another with a sharp tilt of his head at Hektor.

Evan suppressed a grin. 'He's not my friend, just a travelling companion. I am sure he meant no disrespect. He's neither familiar with your customs nor versed in your vernacular.'

'Then he is fortunate you are with him!' said the first man.

Evan bowed. 'Thank you.'

'How sick is your companion?' the Egyptian asked.

'He is unconscious.'

The man clasped his chin, tapping a finger over his mouth. He then dropped his hand, looked at his friends and said one word. Their faces brightened and nodded. He turned back to Evan. 'There is one who can help, a physician called Neshi. He lives over by the white walls.' The man pointed behind the complex. 'As for accommodation I have a friend who owns a hostel; his name is Ani. His place is just behind the merchants' quarters. Tell him Ishpi sent you.'

'Thank you Ishpi, may your gods honour you and your family in the afterlife.'

Ishpi beamed and bowed. He then proceeded to give detailed directions to the physician's home and to his friend's hostel. Evan acknowledged each man with a nod and said farewell. He headed for the gateway, and Dexion and Hektor walked beside him.

'How is it you could converse with them?' Hektor said, casting him a bitter look.

'My experience with Phameas and Dexion and exposure to various places we've visited provided opportunities to learn. Egyptian is not straight forward; it is a mix of Semitic and Hamitic words.' Evan did not want to reveal how easy it was for him to speak different languages. For one, he didn't want to reveal where he learnt them, and two, he really enjoyed irritating Hektor.

CHAPTER FORTY

They followed Ishpi's directions and came to a standstill.

'Well, this is a dilemma,' Evan said.

Everywhere they looked were white-walled streets.

'Time to knock on doors and ask,' he said. He walked up to the first house and rapped on the wooden door. No one was home. They moved on to the next house and received the same response. Dexion grabbed the corner of Evan's khiton and tugged.

'What is it?' he said.

'What about him?' Dexion indicated across the street.

A man, in his twilight years, sat cross-legged against a wall and looked to be sleeping. He was bald with chocolate coloured wrinkled skin.

They walked over and stopped a few paces from where the man sat.

'Good sir, could you direct us to the physician Neshi?' Evan said.

He glanced up, blinked and his eyes grew wider. The white of his eyes glowed like headlights. 'Go to the end of this street and turn right. The physician lives in the third house but you won't find him there. He will be at the House of Sekhmet tending to the sick.'

'Where is this house?'

'By the Temple of Great Ptah.'

The old man then gave them directions to the compound. Evan thanked him and left the man to resume his daily slumber. They followed the length of the walls that enclosed the royal buildings.

'Who is Ptah?' said Dexion.

'He was the first god of the Egyptians, the creator of the other gods and every living thing,' Evan said.

West of the city lay lush and thriving farm lands, irrigated by an intricate formation of channels fed from the Nile. They reached the end of the royal complex, rich with a garden replete with palms, acacia, tamarisk and fruit trees amongst which flowers grew. Beyond were the temple grounds and according to the instructions given, a gate faced the Nile River.

The walls had lost their grandeur and lustre over the thousands of years, yet their magnificence was still visible. Just as the old man told them, at the northern gate, were two huge perfect sculpted like-nesses of Ramesses the Second and a sculpture of Ptah. Evan saw how time, weather and human interference had taken a toll on the large stone statues. The hieroglyphs had lost their pristine definition yet even now the colour was evident. Cracks in the red granite of the statues threatened to dismember the figures at the waist. Even the walls had not escaped pillage and erosion.

'A masterful construction,' Hektor said gazing at the huge en-trance. After a few moments he headed for the gate.

'Wait!' Evan grabbed his arm.

Hektor's jaw tightened.

'Look at that lintel,' Evan pointed. 'It is split and judging from the position it is not in alignment and could fall. The lip of the beam is sitting on the edge of the supporting wall. This is the reason the old man told us to enter via the main gate facing the river.'

Hektor yanked his arm from Evan's clasp and stomped away.

'I preferred it when it was just the three of us,' he said to Dexion in a murmur. 'Much easier and less tense.'

'They need you and you need them.'

'Be better if I wasn't here at all.'

'This is where you are meant to be.'

'You and Zeus may believe so but I don't.'

Evan and Dexion trailed after Hektor, allowing the distance between them to grow. A whitewashed rundown paved road ran parallel to the defensive wall, wide enough for chariots and royal processions. The fascia of the compound was further reinforced by turreted pillars two metres apart. The western gate nestled in the middle, a monumental façade that towered over the walls. In the centre was the main entrance, adjoined by two smaller entries. Two huge statues were erected in front of the main opening, each flanked by three somewhat smaller figures. Sphinxes lined the path into the sacred precinct. To the left on the main wall was an image of a pharaoh on his chariot leading his army into war. On the right, the same pharaoh posed, smiting his enemy.

Evan reached out and touched the paw of a sphinx, the stone warm from the heat of the sun. If anything good had come out of this crazy situation, he thought, it was seeing the magnificence of Egyptian engineering and statues. They continued along the avenue of the sphinxes and came to the forecourt of the temple grounds. Evan gazed up at the silent stone sentries.

'What I'd give to take a photo!' he said. 'I knew these were huge but did not expect them to be monolithic!' He was not a short man but felt dwarfed standing by the plinth and statue, his head level with the knees.

'What's a photo?' Dexion said.

'Oh... ah... I meant drawing,' he said, moving on. He chided himself. He needed to be more careful when he spoke.

They entered the darkened gateway. The temperature dropped and cooled his skin, the depth and width of the pylon a temporary refuge from the sun. Evan shielded his eyes as they moved from the dimness back into the bright daylight and spots impeded his vision for a few seconds.

'This is extraordinary!' he said when his eyes readjusted to the sunlight.

Though neglected, the Temple of Ptah exuded splendour. Further along were more temples and buildings, their condition much worse. In spite of the derelict condition, it had an air of reverence. People gathered outside various temples. A few held baskets of food and others, trinkets.

'Did the old man give the location of the temple of Sekhmet?' Hektor asked, turning to Evan.

'No, though she's associated with the god Ptah. Odds are her temple may be built next to it or inside,' he said.

'Which one is this god's temple?'

'It is over there.' Evan indicated.

Hektor turned away and walked towards the temple. Evan screwed up his face and followed with heavy steps. The gateway to the sanctuary was built in the same manner as the western entrance, a little shorter yet impressive. The fascia was carved with four vertical stripes on each side. Three quarters of the way up the wall broken wooden apertures jutted; once affixed with masts and flags. The parapets were constructed from blocks of stone and engraved with images of the god and reigning pharaoh.

They passed through the entry and came to a pillared hall. Large columns four across and four deep were surrounded by thirty-four smaller ones on three sides. Another opening lay straight ahead. The sound of muted voices drifted towards them the nearer they got to the doorway. A group of people sat cross-legged on the floor by a smaller building. A statue stood adjacent and bore the head of a lioness and the body of a woman.

'That is where we will find Neshi,' said Evan.

Once again, Hektor took the lead. He picked his way through the sitting people, ignoring their looks of outrage and rumblings of discontent. Evan bowed and offered apologies as he and Dexion followed Hektor's trail of disregard. He entered the small building, and they hurried in after him.

Evan's eyes adjusted to the murkiness of the interior. He shivered, surprised how much cooler it was indoors. He scanned the room, and took note of the worn sparse furniture. The stone floor was scuffed and uneven in places, ground down by the traffic of feet. The walls were plastered and decorated with pictograms and hieroglyphs which depicted images of the goddess Sekhmet receiving petitioners. A golden statuette sat on the altar surrounded by gifts from supplicants. At the base of the altar, a short, bald man sat on a mat, his skin the colour of chestnut. His features were pointed, like those of a rat, and dark intelligent eyes locked onto the interlopers.

'Who are you and why have you disturbed the House of Sekhmet?' he demanded.

Evan bowed. 'Our apologies, we mean no disrespect to your goddess. My companion is not aware of your customs. He is concerned for a man in our group who's been unconscious for many days. We come seeking the physician Neshi with the hope he can help.'

'How long has he been this way?'

'At least ten days.'

The Egyptian's brows puckered. 'What happened to him?'

'He was hit on the head.'

'What is he saying?' asked Hektor, tone curt.

'He wants details on what happened to Homer.'

'Is he always like that?' the Egyptian asked, nodding at Hektor.

'Since I've known him,' Evan concurred.

'Maybe he should have been the one knocked out.'

Evan suppressed the urge to grin and said instead, 'I see the physician is busy but when finished here, is he able to take a look at our companion?'

'It will be a number of hours. Where are you staying?'

'We're looking for a place to stay but our fellow traveller is at the port with the rest of our group.'

'Right, now move on,' he said, waving them away.

'Our deepest thanks... physician,' said Evan and backed out, indicating to the others to follow.

The Egyptian appraised Evan with renewed interested, and as he turned to his next patient, the corners of his mouth curved.

'What did he say and is the physician coming?' Hektor said when they emerged from the shrine.

'As soon as he has finished here.'

'That's not acceptable! Homer needs help now.' Hektor spun on his heel. Evan, quick as a snake, grabbed his wrist. Hektor turned, eyes blazing and wrenched back his arm. Evan tightened his grip.

'You have offended the customs of the people with your arrogance. We are guests in this country and you will honour their ways, just as you expect them to respect yours,' Evan said through clenched teeth. 'We are leaving.'

The two stared at each other. The air crackled with tension. People backed away, clearing a space between them and the tall men. The physician stood in the shadows of the doorway and watched. Evan squeezed Hektor's wrist, fingers biting into his flesh and then let go. Hektor's chest heaved, and his upper lip curled, as he bared his teeth. Evan waited, fists at the ready. Hektor then stormed past, bumping him hard against his shoulder, and left the precinct.

Evan relaxed his hands and caught sight of the physician standing by the door. The Egyptian gave a nod and disappeared into the gloomy confines of the shrine.

'Come on Dexion, time to leave these good folk in peace.'

CHAPTER FORTY-ONE

Phameas had a wild look on his face and was relieved to see Evan and Dexion return. He hurried to meet them. They huddled together metres away from the barge. Evan glanced over his shoulder. Hektor turned his back. Leander's contemplation of him lingered and he dropped his head when elbowed by Hektor. The expression on the High Priestess' face was unreadable. She then returned her attention to Homer.

'I gather Hektor's version of events was unfavourable.'

'He doesn't want you here. He says your behaviour is an affront to the gods.'

Evan shrugged. 'Fine by me. Let's get out of here.'

'Now?' Phameas said, surprised.

'Now. Go get your things. We'll stay here the night and decide what to do next.'

'What about finding those sacred objects?'

'They can find them.'

'Are you sure?'

The muscles on Evan's face tightened. 'I am not going to stick around with a group of ungrateful people.'

'Right... well then, let's go and get our gear from the barge.' Phameas took a few steps and then looked back at Evan. 'Are you coming? You know I can't lift that shield and sword of yours.'

Evan scrunched up his nose. 'Damn it.' With quick long strides, he headed for the barge. Phameas and Dexion half ran and half walked to keep up. He strode past the others without looking or saying a word to them and stepped onto the boat. He did not waste any time in collecting his belongings and within minutes was back on the pier.

'Where are you going, Evandros?' The High Priestess blocked his path.

'The physician will be here to check on Homer soon. Follow this river downstream and in seven to ten days you should reach Thebes,' he said, staring over her shoulder.

'Aren't you coming with us?' she asked.

'Keep the food and use the line to catch fish.' He stepped around her.

'We need you. Without your expertise we cannot complete the quest of the gods,' she said.

He stopped and looked back at her. 'You don't need me. Good luck.' He marched on.

'You are one of us. You are my brother.'

He hesitated, lowered his head for a moment then continued walking, Phameas and Dexion jogged to catch up.

'Evandros!'

The three kept going. Evan maintained a steady pace, his attention focussed on the street ahead. The path veered right, away from the port and the Atlanteans. Within minutes they reached the outskirts of the workers' village, a collection of single storey homes.

'Where are we going?' asked Dexion puffing as he trotted along-side Evan.

Evan glanced at him and noted his red face. He slowed down.

'Sorry.'

Phameas' face had a sheen of perspiration and he was breathing fast.

'No idea,' he admitted with a cough and averted his eyes. 'We'll go to the market and get food.'

'Good, but we get to set how fast we walk!' Phameas said.

Evan grinned. 'Fair enough.'

Later that night, in a small room of a hostel, the three were asleep when a blue light hovered over Evan's face. It cast an ethereal glow over him and the wall behind Evan. He murmured in his sleep and frowned, swatted at the light and turned onto his side. The light grew brighter and drew closer. Evan's eyelids fluttered.

'EVANDROS!'

He bolted upright, eyes wide, heart beating so hard he thought it would burst from his chest. Dazed, he shook his head and wondered what he was dreaming to jolt him awake. His eyes adjusted to the gloom and saw a figure standing at the foot of his bed. He crossed his arms.

'What an unexpected surprise,' he said.

'You will re-join the other Atlanteans and lead them to Thebes,' Zeus said.

'No, I will not,' Evan said shaking his head.

'You do not have a choice in this matter,' said Zeus and his eyes glinted.

'That's where you are wrong, I do have a choice and I choose not to return.'

'You will do as I say.'

Evan flung the coarse woollen blanket off, swung his legs over the side of the bed and stood toe to toe with Zeus.

'They do not need me and nor do they want me,' he said. 'They are more than capable of finding whatever you require. Besides I don't have time to babysit a group of ungracious and conceited individuals. Just put me back in my own time, please!'

Zeus' face softened. 'You alone are the one who can find the sacred relics. Your knowledge and intellect is needed. Your fellow Atlanteans will learn to accept the person you are now.'

'Oh yeah, Hektor is a real charmer.'

Zeus chuckled. 'He has his father's disposition, quick to temper and to fight. I am surprised he did not lash out and hit you.'

'You know about that?'

'Of course.'

'So why didn't he?' Evan said.

'You are my son.'

'Herakles was your son, and that didn't stop powerful people from attacking and wanting him dead.'

'It was his destiny to face those trials,' he said in a grave tone.

'Being your "son",' Evan emphasised with his fingers, 'doesn't inspire a lot of confidence. Not that there is any evidence to suggest I am.'

'The sword and shield are made for you and no other can wield either; not even your fellow Atlanteans. The Phoenician cannot hold them.'

'That doesn't mean no one can,' Evan said.

'You will soon realise what I am telling you is the truth,' Zeus said. 'The High Priestess will arrive in the morning.'

'What? Why did you tell her where we are?' Evan crossed his arms.

'Without you the relics cannot be found, and she knows this. Hektor's been dealt with and is no longer a problem.'

'I could handle him.'

'Nevertheless, he understands what is expected of him. You will lead the others and complete the quest.'

'If I do this, I want something in return,' Evan said.

Zeus clasped his hands behind his back. 'What would that be?'

'Once these items are found and returned to you, I want to go back to the twenty-first century.'

Zeus studied his son for a long while and then inclined his head. 'If that is what you want.'

'It is,' Evan affirmed with an emphatic nod.

Evan blinked. Zeus had left. He sat on the edge of the small bed, replayed their conversation and a smile spread across his face. All he had to do was find the relics, and he got to go home. How hard could that be? He looked over at the slumbering forms of Phameas and Dexion. They would join him, even if they didn't understand why he changed his mind. Morning was still hours away. He lay back on the bed. He'd tell them then.

Evan tossed and turned, excited by the prospect of returning home. He gave up on sleeping, too wound up, his mind on what he would do when back home. First, he would write his experiences and pass it off as fiction. No one would believe it was true.

The rosy hue of the morning sun cast its rays through the window and warmed Evan's cheek. He had spent the rest of the night seated on the bed, legs crossed, leaning against the wall with his eyes closed, thinking. He heard the others stir and opened his eyes. Dexion was the first to waken. He stared at a relaxed and serene Evan.

'What's happened?' he asked, sitting upright.

'We're going to re-join the others.'

'Huh?' said a groggy Phameas. He sat up and gazed at Evan with bleary eyes. 'What was that?'

'He said we're going back,' Dexion said.

Phameas scratched under the pit of his arm. 'I guess you must have a good reason.'

'To return home, I need to locate the relics.'

'How did you figure that would work?' said Phameas with a yawn.

'Something a person told me which I had overlooked,' Evan said.

'Right, we should head back so I can repair the barge, otherwise we won't make it to Thebes.' Phameas yawned again and shook his head. As they packed their blankets, there was a knock at the door. Phameas went over and opened it. He gazed at the newcomer, and without saying a word stood back to allow her to enter. The High Priestess crossed the threshold, her eyes meeting those of Evan.

'Divine Zeus said this is where I may find you,' she said.

Evan did not comment and ignored the questioning glances from his friends.

'Hektor is finding it difficult to come to terms with how different you are. We all are.' She paused. Evan remained silent. 'Please give us time to become reacquainted and to adjust to being together once again. We cannot succeed without you. Will you come back and help us find the relics of the Mother Goddess?'

'I will help recover the objects and afterwards, we part ways.'

'If that is what you wish,' said the High Priestess, taken aback.

CHAPTER FORTY-TWO

No one spoke on the walk back to the port and the silence grew more uncomfortable with each step. The High Priestess' face brightened as soon as the barge came into sight and she quickened her pace. Leander emerged from beneath the canopy, the first to see them. His relief was apparent and he disembarked from the boat. His attention centred on the High Priestess' every move.

He nodded at Phameas and Dexion. 'Welcome back,' he said to Evan when they came within earshot.

'Are you sure?' Evan shot back.

'Evandros.' The High Priestess' brow drew into an angry line. She grabbed his hand and pulled him a few feet away and out of earshot of the others. 'You may not be happy to be here but you agreed to return and help. For the sake of this errand, put aside your resentment and understand this dilemma is not of our doing. We may have to face many challenges during our expedition and fighting amongst ourselves will not make it any easier.'

Evan worked his jaw back and forth, teeth gnashing. 'Fine,' he said after a long few moments. 'We'll work together but if Hektor ever so much as says something contrary, I will punch him.'

'He is aware,' she said.

'Did the doctor come to see Homer?' he said, changing subjects.

She nodded. 'He did. The physician gave me powder to mix with water and showed how to administer the liquid. He indicated it may take a few days for the medication to work.'

'Phameas needs to strengthen the repairs we made to the barge otherwise it will not make it to Thebes and back,' he said. 'It needs to be emptied so we can pull it onto the ground to dry out.'

'Then that's what we'll do,' she agreed. 'I will tell Leander and Hektor to transfer Homer.'

'I will go and speak to the Harbour Master and ask for help to move the barge,' he said.

Evan, Phameas and Dexion set off towards a large rectangular building. Twenty minutes later, they returned with the Harbour Master and a small contingent of men who carried thick rope, logs and planks. The High Priestess sat with Homer under a tent erected by Leander and Hektor, surrounded by their belongings.

The Egyptians set to work securing the boat with the rope, and then laid the planks on top of the logs. They spread themselves on each side with the rope in hand. Evan and Phameas joined the queue. Moments later, Leander and Hektor came and stood behind the workers. Evan glanced over his shoulder and acknowledged them.

The Harbour Master bellowed a command, and the Egyptians pulled the rope taut, planted their feet apart and hunched over ready to pull. With another shout from the Harbour Master they heaved. After many grunts, puffs and much sweat, the barge was hauled from the canal. Water pooled beneath and cooled the ground, fine mists of steam rising into the air.

Evan, hair damp and tendrils of perspiration trickling down the side of his face, beamed. He walked over to the Harbour Master, clasped his hand and shook it. The Egyptian was at first unsure and then grinned. Evan then shook each man's hand and thanked them for their help. The Harbour Master, taken by Evan's gesture, offered a few of the men to remain behind to help repair the barge.

'What was it that you did with those men?' Leander asked when the Egyptians left.

Evan didn't understand to what he referred until the Atlantean moved his hand up and down. 'Oh, you mean the handshake?' Leander nodded. 'I wanted to thank them for their help.'

'I've never seen anyone do that,' he said.

Great, how to explain this one? 'Oh, it's not common but a few people use it to show gratitude,' Evan said with a careless shrug.

'How is it you know of it?'

'I must have seen someone do it.' He moved towards the barge in the hope Leander wouldn't follow and ask more difficult questions. He crouched beside Phameas to take a look at the damaged section. 'Does it need much work?'

Phameas lay on his back and shuffled beneath the elevated vessel. He knocked at the hull and the two pieces came away, falling near his face. He turned to Evan. 'We're going to be here at least a few days.'

'Tell me what you need and I will ask the men the Harbour Master was kind enough to leave with us.'

Phameas shimmied out from under the boat, stood and brushed off the dirt from his backside. He explained what he needed and Evan relayed the details to the Egyptians. They nodded, gestured and spoke with enthusiasm and before Evan said anything else, they trotted away.

'Where are they going?'

'Off to get supplies. I'd better inform the High Priestess.' He sauntered across to where the High Priestess, Leander and Hektor sat with Homer. 'We may be here longer than expected. The men have gone to collect items to fix the boat but we can't start the repairs until the wood has dried. We should find accommodation so you don't spend another night out here.'

'What about where you stayed?' the High Priestess suggested.

'I'll go and ask the innkeeper and find out how many rooms he has available.'

'May I come with you?' Leander asked, getting to his feet.

Evan hesitated, and glanced over at the High Priestess who gave an imperceptible nod. 'Sure.' He ducked out from under the makeshift tent. 'Dexion! Want to come along for a walk?'

Dexion scampered over. 'Where are we going, Master Evandros?'

'Back to the inn to check whether there's enough room for everyone.'

'We're going to need more money,' he cautioned.

'I know,' Evan agreed. 'What if we take a detour to the merchants' quarters?'

Dexion's eyes sparkled. 'Are you sure?'

'This time I will make an exception.'

Dexion rubbed his hands together and grinned.

Evan and Dexion exchanged banter during the walk and at times spoke in the boy's native language. Yet, Leander's presence reminded

Evan of the uneasy alliance with the Atlanteans and they were mindful to include him in their discussion.

'What if we got horses?' Dexion was saying. 'They make travelling easier and quicker.'

Evan agreed. 'Quite, though expensive to buy, feed and look after. We don't have the money and besides, water and food comes first.' He turned to Leander. 'What do you think, Leander?'

'Wonderful animals and useful,' he said. 'The question remains as to where can we buy them? I haven't seen many horses since arriving in Aegyptos. And if currency is an issue, why don't we ask the gods? After all, we are their children.'

'An interesting idea but I don't think that is an option,' said Evan.

'Why not?'

'I'd expect they want us to work it out for ourselves otherwise why haven't they offered to help?'

'A fair point,' Leander acknowledged, 'but have you tried asking the gods?'

'No.'

'If you don't mind, I'll confer with the gods.'

'Sure, go for it,' Evan said with a wry smile and shook his head. A few paces along he realised Leander had stopped. He turned and looked at him astonished. 'Are you going to ask right now? Here?'

'We need money, don't we?' He said looking from Evan to Dexion.

'Yes, but...'

'I will ask.' Leander closed his eyes, tilted his head skywards, hands at his sides, palms facing outwards. He stood still and silent. Minutes passed and Evan began to fidget.

'How much longer is this going to take?' he grumbled.

'Master Evandros...' Dexion began to say.

'What on earth?'

Leander was shrouded in a white glow. They watched, stunned, as the veil of light shimmered and pulsed. It then faded and Leander opened his eyes.

'What is the matter? Did something happen?' he asked, concerned by their expressions.

'You,' Evan said waving a hand at Leander, 'were cloaked in a white light. Didn't you feel it?'

'Is that all?' he said, the corners of mouth curving into a crooked smile. 'The light protects us from being harmed by malignant beings and paves the way to communicate with the gods. We carry the white light within us; haven't you felt or used yours?'

'Can't say I have,' Evan said. 'My experiences aren't as collaborative.'

Leander gave him a puzzled look.

'What response did they give you?' he said, arms crossed.

'I reached out to my forefather.'

'And who would that be?'

'Divine Apollo.'

'Did he give you an answer?' said Evan with heavy scepticism.

Leander didn't react to the scorn in Evan's tone. 'Not in so many words. He did show me where the money is stored. Are there temples nearby?'

'Yes, but that is considered stealing.'

'This temple hasn't been used in over a hundred years, and the money is hidden and forgotten.'

'It's not right to take what isn't ours.'

'If no one knows about it, how can it be theft?'

'It belongs to the people of Memphis,' Evan said.

'How is it different from having Dexion rob honest and hard-working people?' Leander pointed out.

'You understood what we were saying?' Evan asked, taken aback.

'I may not be as experienced as Dexion, Phameas or you but I grasped the inference. We need money and at least this way, innocent people aren't taken advantage of.'

Evan clasped the back of his neck and gave it a squeeze. His dropped his hand and nodded. 'Which temple is it?'

'I'll recognise it when I see it,' Leander said.

'We'd better get to it, as we still need to see the innkeeper about boarding.'

CHAPTER FORTY-THREE

It didn't take long to reach the temple compound. Evan led Dexion and Leander through the western gate which was more elaborate than the eastern gate. Not wasting any time to stop and admire the impressive entrance, they passed through the gateway and came to a halt.

'Which one is it?' Evan said to Leander.

Leander scanned the vast grounds, skimming past the massive statues and plinths. He pointed. 'It's that building over there, next to that statue.'

An elephantine sculpture of a pharaoh stood crosswise from their position. Evan identified it as Ramesses. The statue was famous in his timeline and to view it in its magnificence was awe inspiring. As much as he wanted to stop and study it, Evan pushed the thought aside and focussed on retrieving the money before being apprehended by the authorities.

They approached a covered colonnade. The entrance had a different orientation to the temple opposite and faced west. They left behind footprints on the paved walkway, where dirt and sand had accumulated over the years of disuse. The path led to a chamber where a large rectangular stone table sat at its centre. On either side a step jutted out. At one end was a stone circular tub with a spout above and beneath a hole drilled through the marble.

'Wonder for what purpose they used the table?' said Leander, and his voice reverberated in the room.

Evan ran a hand over the smooth stone and examined the tub and spout. Constant use had discoloured the interior of the container and outlet.

'This was where the Egyptians sacrificed the Apis bull,' he said. 'They believed the bull acted as an agent between the people and the supreme god and connected to the pharaoh. It symbolised the king's power, courage and virility.'

'Similar to how we revere the bull by leaping over it though the animal isn't always sacrificed to Divine Poseidon,' Leander said.

'You leap over a bull?' Dexion asked, eyes bulging.

'Every Atlantean learns to jump over a bull.'

'Why?'

'It unifies us with our god Poseidon.'

'How do you...' Dexion demonstrated with his hand leaping over an imaginary bull, 'you know, jump over a bull? Is it standing still or charging?'

'You run towards the bull as it charges, grab the horns and somersault over its back,' Leander said.

'I'd love to see that!' Dexion said in an eager voice. He turned to Evan, his enthusiasm brimming. 'Have you leapt over a bull?'

'I...'

'As I said, *all* Atlanteans perform the leap,' Leander said.

'Would I be able to learn how?' said Dexion.

'When we get back to Atlantis, I will show you,' Leander said with a warm smile.

'I can't wait!' Dexion turned to Evan. 'Did you hear that Master Evandros, Leander is going to show me how to leap over a bull.'

'I did.' Evan ruffled his hair. 'But before you learn a new skill, let's test the one you excel at,' he added with a wink.

Dexion was bouncing with excitement as they walked away from the altar of Apis.

'Now where to next?'

'Just before a hall with pillars is a small building with a tall obelisk in front of it. Inside is where we will find the money,' Leander said.

'Lead the way.' Evan indicated, with his palm facing upwards.

Leander continued along the passageway and turned right. The deeper they went, the dimmer it became. After a few more twists and turns they were cloaked in darkness.

'A torch would come in handy right now,' Evan said in a dry tone.

'I may have something that will provide light,' said Leander.

Evan heard him rummaging, the noise loud in the preternatural silence.

'Sorry, I must have left the fire stones with the others.'

'Fire stones?'

'Yes.' Evan could picture Leander nodding his head. 'When you rub the stones together they emit a light.'

'We'll have to continue without light, but our eyes should adjust,' Evan said.

'We should hold hands so we don't get separated or lost,' suggested Leander.

'Right.'

'Is something the matter?' Leander asked.

'No, no. I'm good,' Evan said, glad for the obscurity. 'Where are you Dexion?'

'Here.'

Evan reached out to his left. 'Take my hand and you hold onto Leander's.'

They forged ahead taking small steps, linked together. No one spoke, not wanting to break the spell of unity or the concentration needed to keep moving without falling or running into a wall. To Evan the gloomy atmosphere was oppressive and felt as if they were going deeper into an abyss, where nothing lived or breathed.

'There's light ahead,' Leander said, breaking the funereal peace. His pace quickened. A shaft of sunlight streamed through a hole in the roof and flooded the corridor. Evan's eyes contracted, and black spots filled his vision, blinded by the shock of the bright light. He blinked and bit by bit as his sight adjusted, objects and images painted on the walls and columns became clearer.

He did a quick scan and something caught his attention. He let go of Dexion's hand, stepped over to a column, bent and peered behind it.

'Aha!' Evan grabbed a wooden rod wound with cloth, stood and swung around. 'We need something to light it.' Around them was rubble, debris from the broken roof. He slapped himself on the forehead. 'Idiot.' He picked up two good sized stones and placed the torch on the ground. He knelt and struck the rocks together, one sliding against the other. He was not sure how long he kept striking the two stones and grimaced as the small pebbles pressed deeper into his knees and shins. He gritted his teeth, pulling his face into a grimace.

'Come on!' He was ready to give up when a small spark flickered. It hit the dry material of the torch. Nothing happened. He sat back on his haunches. 'What I'd give for a box of matches.'

'Look!' Dexion said, excited.

A wisp of smoke escaped from the fabric.

'Excellent!'

Evan leaned forward, pursed his lips and blew a gentle breeze that caressed the skin. A faint yellow glow formed. He did it again. The flicker of light grew and began to spread. Evan picked up the torch and within seconds the entire head glowed in an orange flame. He grinned, pleased with himself.

'Keep on the lookout for another torch,' he said and then held it out to Leander. 'I hope this pillared hallway isn't too much farther away.'

Leander, with torch in hand, led them away from the sunlight and further into the temple. The flickering light of the torch illuminated their path and cast their elongated forms on the walls. They turned another corner and Evan spotted a torch sitting in an alcove on the wall. He swept past Leander and plucked it from the niche. Leander thrust his torch towards the one Evan held. The dry tinder smouldered and soon caught fire. The extra torch bathed them in warm light and increased the circumference of illumination.

'Let's get on with this,' Evan said. 'You notice anything familiar?'

'No,' Leander said, mouth down-turned.

Evan drew in a deep breath. 'It would have been easier and quicker to go with our original plan than trekking through this old temple with no idea where we are going.'

'I am sure we're heading in the right direction. Divine Apollo would not give false information,' Leander said with confidence.

'We need to find the money first,' Evan said. 'And I hope you remember how many left and right turns we've made. I don't want to get lost in here.'

'Don't you have the ability to recall everything you see and read?' Leander said, brow arched.

'Yes, well...' He gestured with his chin. 'Lead on.'

How much time passed, Evan could not say but then he detected a glimmer of light. The closer they got the brighter it became so much so the torches weren't needed. Evan placed his torch in an empty slot in the wall and Leander did the same. They approached the doorway and crossed the threshold.

'Mother Goddess!' Leander said, mouth falling open.

Before them stood the pillared hallway, four columns deep and eight across. The breadth of the bottom drum was such it needed at least three people holding hands to encircle the base. Scenes of the pharaoh and the Apis bull were etched into each and painted in vibrant colours of cerulean blue, ruby red, sunflower yellow, and forest green. Evan had read how historians, archaeologists and engineers speculated about the various ways the Egyptians constructed their pyramids, temples and palaces. He had his own theories as well but standing here and seeing it, he questioned even those. The word "ingenuity" came to mind.

'That's the building!' Leander pointed and hurried to a small, nondescript structure tucked in a corner, dwarfed by the hypostyle façade.

In comparison to other elaborate creations, it was plain. No pictorial features adorned the walls or the doorway. There was no indication who built it or which god it served. That struck Evan as odd. Why did the Egyptians construct such an ordinary and simple building? He wandered around it.

'This is very old,' he said. 'The stone is more eroded than the other structures and the technique is different.'

'How old?' Leander asked.

'Hard to say, maybe two thousand to four thousand years old,' Evan said.

Dexion gave a low whistle.

'The rest of the complex was built around this. It must be very sacred if it still remains,' Leander said.

'But why did the people desert the temple if it's so sacred?' asked Dexion.

'Egypt was unable to retain the authority it had and weakened, and neighbouring empires invaded. Memphis was once a very powerful city and though we can admire the splendour left behind, the Egyptians are no longer in control.'

'How can you know this?' Leander asked, words laced with incredulity.

'You may not have noticed but there was graffiti on the walls outside the western gate that was not Egyptian. It's Persian.' He squinted. 'We're going to need the torches.'

'I'll get them.' Dexion trotted back.

'How do you know so much when we've had no interaction with these lands for thousands of years?' Leander asked, mystified.

'Captain Sostrate and his predecessors brought back information from their journeys, detailed information on the developments of the lands,' Evan said turning to watch Dexion, wishing he'd return soon. *Thanks Zeus, I appreciate the tight spot in which you've placed me.*

'Yes but...'

'Great, here comes Dexion. Now we can search for the money your divine predecessor said was here.' Evan left Leander standing by the doorway and met Dexion part of the way. 'Don't ever leave me alone with these people again!' he said softly, grabbing one of the torches.

'Master Evandros?'

'Let's get this over with.'

Before they entered, Evan turned to Leander. 'Any ideas where to begin once we're inside?'

'Divine Apollo showed me the location of the building, not the interior,' he said. 'It's not very big, so finding the money shouldn't be hard.'

'If that were the case, someone would have found it a long time ago,' Evan said. He gazed into the murky interior. 'Odds are it is well hidden. Search every corner, every nook, the walls and floor.' He strode through the doorway, Dexion right behind him. Leander followed, torch held aloft.

The room was sparse except for a granite statue at the far end, the same height as Dexion. Evan and Dexion examined the left side of the room and Leander the right.

Evan ran a hand over the wall, with slow strokes, shuffling along centimetre by centimetre. The wall was smooth under his fingertips and where the blocks met there was a slight indentation. He came across an alcove, empty except for the accumulation of dirt and dust. From the depth and length of the nook, it may have been used to store urns or to house oil lamps. The purpose of the room was not clear but Evan surmised people once worshipped a very old deity. He inspected the interior and rapped his knuckles against the sides and backing.

'Why are you doing that?' Dexion asked.

'To check for a false partition. There might be something hidden in the walls,' he said. 'If you were to hide valuable items where would you put them?'

Dexion glanced around, and then pointed.

'In the statue.'

'Too obvious; that's the first place treasure hunters consider. If you wanted to make sure no one found the valuables, where else would be a good place to conceal it?'

The boy had another look and Leander, who overheard their discussion, sidled up next to them.

'Perhaps that's the point. If everyone thought that, then the statue is the perfect location to hide the treasure,' Leander said.

'It's possible,' Evan agreed with a nod, 'and we should take a look.'

While Leander examined the statue, Evan walked to the rear of the plinth. He tried to push it, and then stood back studying both objects. Leander had less success with the statue.

'I guess you were right,' he said drawing his lips into a thin line. 'The money's not here.'

Evan took a step back, his attention fixated behind the statue. He moved a few paces forward, stopped in front of the wall and tilted his head from one side to the other.

'Hmm... interesting,' he said with a murmur. Not saying a word to the others, with a hand outstretched, he closed his eyes and marched towards the stone wall.

'Master Evandros, if the statue isn't the location, then where do...' Dexion's voice trailed off as he gazed at the empty space where Evan had stood. 'Master Evandros?'

Leander poked his head around the statue. 'Evandros?' He walked to the rear of the statue turning his head one way then the other way. 'Evandros!' He did a complete circuit, and then came to a stop next to Dexion. 'He was right here!'

'Dexion! Leander!' They spun at the sound of his voice. Evan materialised out of nowhere behind them. His eyes were sparkling, face lit up. 'You've got to come with me!' He beckoned and then disappeared again. Dexion and Leander stood dumbfounded. Evan reappeared, the lower half of his body concealed by the wall.

'What are you waiting for? Come on!'

Dexion took a hesitant step. Evan grabbed his arm and pulled the boy behind the wall. Leander gaped.

'Are you coming? Believe me, you don't want to miss this,' Evan said beaming.

Leander did not move.

'Oh, for goodness sake.' Evan emerged from the interior of the wall, took a stupefied Leander by the wrist and led him into the wall. Leander stumbled after him. Evan followed the narrow passage for a few metres then began to descend a series of steps. Dexion scampered after him as a bedazzled Leander staggered after them.

When he caught up, both Evan and Dexion had their backs to him. A golden glow greeted him as he drew up alongside them.

'Mother Goddess!'

Strewn on the floor lay gilded wooden statues of various gods and goddesses, golden goblets, an ivory headrest, a golden head of

Horus, jewellery, incense burners, golden tripods and urns filled with coins.

'Hard to believe this is just lying here,' Evan said in a hushed tone.

'A tragedy must have befallen the priests for these offerings to be forgotten,' Leander said.

Dexion, drawn to the pile, stepped towards the treasure, kneeled and grabbed a small golden rectangular box. He turned it in his hands. The sides were inscribed with Egyptian hieroglyphs as was the lid that had a scarab beetle on top. He looked over as Evan squatted next to him.

'We take nothing except an urn with coins,' he said. 'The people offered these objects to the gods so their petitions were listened to and here they will stay.'

'But those people are dead,' Dexion said, staring at the precious hoard. 'What good is this treasure to them now?'

'A fair point but we must respect their wishes. The Egyptians believed in the afterlife and this was their way of securing passage for a new beginning.' Evan placed a hand on his shoulder. 'It is tempting to take what is here but we can't. Besides, Leander was shown only the coins and nothing else. Don't you think if Apollo wanted to reveal the rest of the valuables, he would have?'

Dexion screwed up his face and then sighed. 'I guess.' He placed the box back on the pile.

Evan smiled and patted his shoulder. 'Good lad. Now why don't we take what we came for and return to the docks.'

CHAPTER FORTY-FOUR

Phameas was the first to catch sight of Evan, Dexion and Leander. He placed the tar and tools on the ground and went to greet them.

'I was beginning to worry something had happened to you,' he said, his eyes flicking from Evan and Dexion to Leander.

'Everything is fine. As a matter of fact it's outstanding.' Evan lifted the bag from his shoulder. It clinked as he set it on the ground. 'Take a look.'

Phameas bent and flipped the flap open. He whistled, and looked up at Evan, eyes wide. 'Where did you get the money?'

'We were guided to the location,' Evan said.

'You should have seen the treasure Phameas!' Dexion blurted. 'Piles and piles of gold!'

'What is this about treasure?'

They turned at the High Priestess' voice.

'Evandros expressed concern with our lack of currency and I communed with Divine Apollo. He showed me where the money lay hidden and as Dexion says, there were more riches,' Leander answered.

'We didn't take the treasure,' Dexion was quick to say. 'Master Evandros didn't let us. He said they were sacred offerings from the people to the gods.'

The High Priestess appraised Evan. He didn't say a word. 'We do not want to offend the Aegyptians or their gods by taking what is theirs.' She directed her next question to Evan. 'Were you able to secure rooms for us?'

'I have and told the innkeeper we may need to stay a few nights.'

'Evandros managed to hire a donkey and cart from a merchant to carry Homer. He'll be here soon,' Leander said.

'Best get your gear together,' Evan said. 'Phameas, how are the repairs?'

'Those Egyptians are good workers. We managed to plug the holes and affix a new plank. Tomorrow, we'll test whether the barge floats and if there's leakage from the mended sections. It will take a few hours to determine whether the repairs worked and if it does we can set sail,' Phameas said.

'Nice work, Phameas.' Evan smiled at him.

Phameas drew himself taller and beamed.

***

The following morning Evan, Phameas and Dexion left the hostel early for the docks. The Egyptians who'd assisted Phameas the previous day were waiting by the boat. Evan greeted them and set to work to prepare the barge for launch. The slipway was checked and swept.

'Time to test if the new planks and patching works,' Evan said.

Evan stood at the rear, Phameas and the Egyptians gripped the sides. Hektor and Leander arrived just as they began to push the barge. They hurried over and took positions by the Egyptians on the slipway. The wooden frame creaked under the force but the only movement was their feet giving way on the stone pavement. The flat hull resisted. The air filled with heavy breathing and grunting as they renewed their efforts. There was a slight shift. Evan, head lowered between his shoulders, gritted his teeth and pushed harder. After a few steps the barge began to move more easily, and the prow hit the water with a resounding splash.

The Egyptians whooped and jumped, their faces shining. Evan thanked each man with a handshake and gave them a silver coin apiece. They bowed over and over, giving thanks. One grabbed Evan's hand and uttered a few words. Evan held the man's hand in both of his and bowed. The Egyptian smiled and left, trailing behind his fellow workmen.

'What did he say?' Phameas said.

'He asked the goddess Hathor to protect us while on our journey,' he said, tone reflective. 'In any case,' he added, turning to Phameas, 'now it's a waiting game.'

'What's a waiting game?' Leander asked. 'How do you play it?'

'It's an expression used when you have to wait for something to happen,' Evan said.

'I understand, we're waiting to ensure the repairs on the boat are successful,' he said. 'An unusual turn of phrase but an apt description.'

'There's not much to do except sit and wait,' said Evan. 'There's no need for all of us to stay here.'

'We should return to the hostel,' Leander said to Hektor. 'The High Priestess has been on her own for a while and she may need our help.'

Hektor stiffened. Leander's brows arched ever so slightly. Evan took note of the exchange. Hektor then nodded.

'Will you send a message to us if the news is good?' Leander asked Evan.

'Of course, I'll have Dexion keep you informed.'

Once the two Atlanteans were out of earshot, Evan turned to Dexion.

'I want you to follow them back to the hostel and listen to what they say. I don't need to tell you to be discreet, but keep out of sight.'

Dexion dashed away and melted into the shadow of the maritime buildings.

'Are you expecting trouble?' Phameas asked.

'Not really.'

'Then why have Dexion spy on them?'

'A precaution. People tend to express their true natures and opinions when alone. During these situations information is revealed, and I'd prefer to be aware of what is going on than being surprised.'

'They're your people, so why don't you trust them?' Phameas said, perplexed by Evan's actions and taciturn attitude towards the other Atlanteans.

'How can you trust someone when you aren't familiar with them?'

'You still have no memory of your past? I thought being reunited with your countrymen may trigger familiarity or at least a sense of recognition.'

'The past I remember has no direct connection with them,' Evan said.

'I don't understand.'

'Yes, well neither do I. What I can tell you is these people are strangers to me.'

'They know you,' Phameas pointed out. 'They recognised you straight away when we walked into the palace at Kyrene.'

'The person they were acquainted with doesn't exist.'

Phameas recoiled. 'But...'

'Look, can we not discuss this any more?' said Evan his face set like a marble statue. He turned on his heel, walked to the boat and checked for leaks.

Phameas put a hand on his hip as he gazed at his friend. He stood there for a while before letting his hand fall to his side and joining Evan.

***

Dexion returned a while later and sat next to Evan. He took the proffered water container and had a drink.

'What did you hear?' Evan asked as Dexion returned the container.

'Hektor is not happy you are in charge.'

'That's not surprising.'

'Leander was at first concerned, but after spending time in the Apis temple with us looking for the money, he believes you are the right person to lead.'

'Huh, that's surprising,' Evan said. He drummed his fingers on a knee. 'Did the High Priestess speak?'

Dexion hesitated.

'What is it?'

'I heard her say you are not the man who left Atlantis with them. She believes her real brother is dead and you are a pretender placed here by Divine Zeus. She plans on seeking counsel from the Mother Goddess.'

Evan sat back and mused over this latest revelation. He smirked and shook his head.

'Why are you smiling? The High Priestess thinks you are an imposter,' Phameas said, bothered by Dexion's report.

'The High Priestess is very astute and her brother isn't dead, he's been replaced.' Evan looked at Dexion. 'Have you had any further premonitions?'

'Not ones that make sense. I've been receiving strange visions, glimpses in fact. I don't understand what they mean.'

'Such as?'

'There were images of you wearing strange clothes. In another you were sitting in a...' he frowned. 'I'm not sure how to explain it but it had wheels and moved.' Evan smiled. 'I saw Phameas and me with you in a place where there were roads, black tongues crisscrossing the land. Lots of unusual houses and tall buildings that had walls like mirrors, those same moving objects and our clothes different.'

'What in the name of Baal is that supposed to mean?' Phameas said looking from Dexion to Evan.

'No idea,' Evan said, 'but I am familiar with the places and descriptions you've mentioned. You remember I told you I was not from this place and time?' Dexion nodded. 'It is true, this is not my reality.'

'Yes, but the prophecy showed you did once come from here,' Dexion said. 'The man I envisioned and you are the same person and yet not. I don't know how that happened, I have not been shown.'

'How can you tell this other guy and I are one person?' Evan frowned.

Dexion waved his hand in a circle in front of Evan. 'You have the same aura.'

'Aura?' Phameas said.

'Everyone has an aura, an energy that covers your body. I see the colour of your aura.' He nodded at Evan. 'Most of the time yours is gold.'

'What's mine?' asked Phameas.

Dexion leaned back and studied him for a few minutes. 'Green.'

'What do these colours mean?' Evan said, turning up his nose at the idea.

'It doesn't work that way, the colours give me a sense of a person.'

'What does that mean?'

'Your aura has a strong connection with the need to protect people and possesses divine guidance while Phameas' aura is in harmony with nature, a warm and social person.'

Phameas sat back pleased and crossed his arms. 'By Baal, I don't understand how this sight of yours functions, but it's uncanny how right you are.'

Evan glowered. He did not agree with Dexion's perceived summation. To do so meant accepting what had taken place.

'Master Evandros, I realise you find this difficult and as much as you don't want to be here, it's where you belong.'

'I don't accept that,' he said, thrusting his chin upwards. 'One way or another, I will return home.'

'What happens to us when you do?' Phameas asked. 'I left everything to come with you and what of Dexion?'

'I didn't ask you to join me,' Evan said, scowling.

'No you didn't. I wanted to because I thought our friendship meant something but it appears I am wrong.' Phameas stood and glared at Evan. 'Friends don't abandon one another.' He stalked off, arms swinging with each stride.

'You've got something to add?' Evan said in a clipped tone.

'You don't have many friends here, so perhaps it's not a good idea to lose the ones you do have,' Dexion said. 'Phameas left everyone and all he knows to be here with you. How many people have you met who would do that? You should apologise and tell him how you value his friendship.'

'What of you? Do you want an apology?'

Dexion shook his head. 'I am here because I must, Phameas is here out of choice.'

'Are you sure you're only eleven years old?'

'Here and now I am,' he said.

Evan appraised him for a few minutes. 'So are you a manifestation of a god?'

Dexion smiled. 'No. I have the ability to foresee events but that's all. I don't always understand the messages such as the one I explained earlier and I am never wrong.'

'Huh… do you enjoy having these visions?' Evan said. 'Doesn't it get tiresome? Don't you want a normal life?'

The boy shrugged. 'This is who I am and know no other way to live. It's a part of my life and a gift from the gods.'

'Did your mother or father have this ability?'

'Not that I am aware of,' Dexion said, 'but they died before I had my first vision.'

'Interesting.' Evan studied Dexion. 'Can you remember when it happened?'

'I do,' he said with a pained expression, 'it was two days after my parents were killed.'

'What did you envisage?'

'The master's death, and five days later I slit his throat.'

Evan put an arm around the boy's shoulders and they sat in silence and stared at the mirrored surface of the Nile River.

CHAPTER FORTY-FIVE

'I'm pleased to say the repairs to the barge are holding,' said Evan after examining the barge. 'Go tell the others we're ready to leave.'

Dexion nodded, spun on his heel and sprinted along the length of the stone jetty, weaving and dodging the harbour workers. Evan spotted Phameas loitering outside the Harbour Master's building. He chastised himself for upsetting his friend and strolled over. Phameas saw him approach, and his face hardened.

Evan stopped, cleared his throat and shuffled.

'Phameas, I am sorry for what I said earlier. I am grateful you are here and should have said as much. We are a team, the three of us, and wherever this journey takes us, we're in it together,' he said. 'I will tell you the full story when I have worked out what is going on.' Evan put his hand out. 'Friends again?'

Phameas' arms dropped to his sides. 'You ought to work out who is a friend and who isn't.'

'I do know who my friends are, Phameas. This predicament I am in is complicated but I promise to explain it to you.'

Evan kept his hand out. Phameas' shoulders relaxed, he grinned and shook his hand.

'Now, the boat is floating, yes?' Phameas said.

'You did a brilliant job fixing it,' said Evan beaming. 'I've sent Dexion to get the others.'

'The Harbour Master gave me a few tips for sailing,' Phameas said and recounted the conversation as they walked back to the vessel.

They were loading and preparing the boat for the voyage when Dexion returned with the Atlanteans. Leander led the donkey and wagon with Homer and the High Priestess while Hektor walked alongside.

'You did a masterful job with the boat,' said Leander smiling.

'Credit goes to Phameas,' Evan said. 'He's the one with the experience and skills.'

'How long will it take to sail to Thebes?' the High Priestess asked.

'The Harbour Master told Phameas it could take fourteen days.'

'Why so long?' Hektor said.

'It is safer to sail by day. We are lucky as this is the period of the inundation. If it was during the dry season the crossing would take two months.'

'Doesn't the river stay the same throughout the year?' Leander said.

'No, the water recedes during the drier months and the currents run slower.'

'Extraordinary, we don't have a river that floods on an annual basis on our island,' Leander said, facing the canal. 'I'll have enough time to learn more about it.' He turned to Evan. 'What else do you know on the life of the river?'

Evan hesitated. He wasn't sure whether Leander's interest was genuine or a way to expose him. The earnest expression on Leander's face gave him the answer.

'A bit of general information.'

'Anything to help me understand the river's nature,' said Leander, eyes shining. 'Now what can we do to assist?'

'The supplies of food and urns of water need to be stored on the boat. First, we should get Homer aboard and out of the sun.'

Before long they coasted down to the mouth of the canal that connected to the river. Evan and Phameas worked hard to turn the boat upstream, their faces and arms glistened with perspiration.

'Sail up!' Phameas called out.

Dexion and Leander removed the rope and Hektor hoisted the mast. The breeze was slight but enough wind caught the square sail, making the job of poling the boat easier. Dexion sat at the prow, leaned over with an instrument and tapping it at various intervals. The sound it made was wide-ranging.

'What is Dexion doing?' Hektor asked.

'He is making sure the water is deep enough for the boat to pass. With the shifting sand deposits we could get stranded on a sandbank,' Evan said. 'The sound indicates whether it's shallow or not.'

'And if we do hit a sandbank?' asked the High Priestess.

'The river beasts will have a feast,' Phameas said.

Hektor shuddered. 'When this quest is over, I will never step foot on another sailing vessel. The waters are too treacherous!'

Evan gazed at the extremes of the land. The terrain was green and fertile on either side of the river, and beyond was the ever threatening perpetual and expanding desert. The multitude of farming lots made a striking contrast to the monuments of sand. In the fields he saw people sowing seed and others harvesting barley and wheat crops. He thought back to his own time and of the turmoil that consumed the country.

'Is something the matter? You look sad,' Phameas said.

'I am reminded of how fragile this land is in the beauty of the surroundings and the magnificent buildings. I wish there was a way to protect it from human nature.'

'It is the character of people to do terrible things and no matter how one tries to reason with them, they cannot be stopped,' Phameas said.

'You are right,' agreed Evan. 'There is an innate need to dominate and conquer and the threat of being controlled by others forces retaliation. Then comes the devastation of lives, incredible buildings and innovation lost forever.'

'Is that what you predict? The end of what has been created here and now?' asked the High Priestess.

Evan hadn't realised she had moved closer to where he and Phameas were standing with the poles, guiding the boat. His attention was on the scenery and the remarkable pyramids that dotted the landscape.

'It's more of a fact,' he said.

'How can you make such a statement?' she said.

'There is a saying "nothing lasts forever" and even buildings, big and enormous as we've seen do not last. Time does that,' he said choosing his words with care. He did not intend to give her any more clues as to his true self.

'Time is the enemy of all,' she said with a nod and turned to face the passing vista.

'How is Homer?'

'He continues to sleep,' she said, her head bent. 'It is difficult to know whether he is aware of us. He does not respond when I speak to him.'

'With the beatings he suffered, perhaps his mind is protecting him while his body is trying to heal,' said Evan.

The High Priestess turned her head. 'The mind healing the body, yes it is possible that is what is happening. You know this from your readings?'

'No, Zeus told me,' he lied.

'Oh... then that is good news,' she said, her sharp gaze boring into his. 'This means Homer will waken.'

'When he has healed from within,' he said in a light tone.

She held his attention for a while longer, her eyes searching his, and moved away when she didn't get a reaction. Evan clutched the pole so the skin on his fingers stretched tight but kept looking straight ahead. There was no way he was going to give her or the others any more clues if he can help it. He sensed Phameas glance at him but was grateful his friend remained silent and did not ask questions.

Sometime later Phameas pointed to the orange reddish hue on the horizon.

'We should steer for the bank.'

'Good idea.'

'Drop the sail!' Phameas ordered.

Evan plunged his pole into the water and lodged it into the silt of the riverbed. Phameas laboured to turn the barge towards the embankment. Together they manoeuvred the vessel towards land.

'Leander and Hektor, grab those ropes on either side and jump in the water to pull the boat in,' said Evan.

After securing the boat, they moved Homer off and away from the river side. They set up camp and began roasting the fish Dexion caught while they sailed.

'Now tell me about this river,' said Leander popping a piece of succulent white flesh of the fish into his mouth. 'From what I can tell it flows south to north. Most unusual.'

'The river is fed from mountains south of here, around six and a half thousand kilometres away. Every year the Nile swells from the south and floods the northern lands.'

'What happens when the water decreases?'

'Rich fertile soil remains and the farmers sow their crops, a busy time for the Egyptians.'

'How long does the flood last?' the High Priestess asked.

'It depends on the overflow. If the river rises too high it can destroy villages, not enough water, then drought and famine. Many cities like Memphis are built on high ground so when it floods, the people and buildings are safe.'

'It is a very long river,' said Leander in awe.

'Indeed.'

***

The morning sun cast myriad shades of peach and gold, a glorious reflection against the sprawling arid plains. Careful not to wake the others, Evan trod lightly and wandered a short distance from the campsite to watch the birth of a new day. Being here and having these experiences had given him a new appreciation of the ancient world. Their relationship and respect for the environment could teach future generations how not to abuse the fragility of nature. He took in a deep breath and lifted his face to the sky. The pristine air and the cloud-free blue sky were as tangible as the swollen river and the contrasting surroundings. It was as if the land had two hearts, the fertile Nile which gave life and the desert that condemned it.

CHAPTER FORTY-SIX

'Do you think we'll find the golden serpent in Thebes?' Leander said. He stood with Phameas and Evan at the stern of the boat. Trickles of sweat ran down their faces as they hoisted and plunged the poles into the river.

'We know what we're looking for which makes the search straightforward,' said Evan.

'How can you be sure?'

'The librarian at Carthage was confident with his interpretation of the text and the location of the golden serpent. The Temple of Amun-Re in Thebes was the last known location of the object. He said it was a great city, the political and religious centre of Upper and Lower Egypt. It now functions as a place for the Egyptians to venerate the gods.'

'He remarked it once held great many riches such as gold, emeralds and precious stones,' said Phameas.

'Once? What does that mean?'

'The tombs of the pharaohs and temples were looted by conquerors and thieves,' Evan said, shrugging.

'That's it then,' Hektor said from beneath the canopy. 'We're not going to find the golden serpent, it is long gone.'

'It is there,' said the High Priestess. Her conviction was so adamant no one dared to challenge her.

The days on the river seemed never-ending, one merging with the next. Dexion was charged with fishing, the High Priestess tended to Homer while Hektor and Leander exchanged places with Evan and Phameas to pilot the barge. Evan was dozing when his slumber was disturbed.

'By Zeus!' Hektor said.

Evan jolted upright, took one look at Hektor and Leander's astonished expression and turned to see what captured their attention. He sprang to his feet.

'Moloch!' said Phameas standing next to Evan.

'Is that Thebes?' Leander said in a hushed tone.

Evan nodded. 'The City of Amun-Re.'

Even from a distance its magnificence was spellbinding. They watched in silent reverence as the city grew before their eyes.

'We need to prepare for docking,' said Phameas and moved to reclaim one of the poles. Evan stood for a few more minutes gazing at the sight and then took over from Leander.

The main sail was lowered and furled. Dexion had rope in hand ready to jump onto the pier and secure the barge. Phameas' years of experience at sailing came to the fore as he guided the riverboat into an empty dock and hit the side with a gentle bump. Evan threw a second rope to Dexion who had leapt as soon as they were within reach. The boat fastened to the jetty, and they were able to disembark.

'How will we identify the Temple of Amun-Re?' said Hektor.

'I think we'd spot it straightaway,' Evan said. 'It's the most important building and the biggest.'

'Someone will need to remain here with Homer,' the High Priestess said.

'We'll stay here and the three of you go,' suggested Evan.

'No,' she said. 'You can speak Aegyptian so you must come.' She turned to Hektor. 'I'd like you to wait here with Homer. We'll return when we can.'

Hektor's eyes flashed for a second but he did not comment. Instead, he gave a curt nod.

'Dexion and I will go to the market. We need to replenish our food stocks plus it will be good to have fresh fruit and vegetables for a change,' Phameas said.

'Looks as if it's just the three of us,' said Leander in a light-hearted tone. He pointed to a wide path. 'I presume that will lead us somewhere?'

'We shall find out soon enough,' said Evan with a resigned sigh.

They walked up the white limestone avenue that intersected a paved walkway and ran parallel with the river.

'Goodness! What are those statues? They go on forever!' Leander said, coming to a stop.

'They're sphinxes,' said Evan.

'They don't resemble the ones we are familiar with,' said the High Priestess.

Over one hundred sphinxes lined each side, a multitude of obedient watchdogs. Identical features gazed out from a human head set on a lion's body. They continued along under the perpetual and serene gaze of the sphinxes. They came to an entrance at the end of the laneway where two gigantic statues, flanked by four smaller ones, two on either side. A pair of huge obelisks augmented the entry and juxtaposed the seated statues, and the spires pierced the sky. Hieroglyphs inscribed on the obelisks and the long defensive walls presented a tableau of a pharaoh's achievements.

Evan stopped for a moment, taken by the grandeur and detailed workmanship. The colours may have faded, but it was easy to imagine how vibrant they must have been.

They crossed the forecourt. To their left was a shrine and along the walls were massive columns. The sanctuary, divided into three smaller memorials, had large statues standing to attention and as observant as watchmen. On the right was a temple, which merged seamlessly with the complex. The quantity and quality of the monolithic monuments, both pillars and figurines, was overwhelming. Their stature shouted a god-likeliness and omnipotence. Evan touched the foot of the nearest one. The stone was cool and smooth. He closed his eyes and drank in the heady feeling of euphoria.

'Hektor would be impressed by the workmanship and engineering of what is here,' Leander said in a low voice and ran a hand over the base of a column.

In the centre of the enclosure was a colonnade that led into another building. Evan kept going, walking through the portico, and came to an abrupt stop, puffs of dust swirling at his feet.

'What's wrong?' Leander said as he came up behind him. He drew a sudden breath.

'Great Mother!' said the High Priestess.

A forest of columns, carved and placed with such precision filled the room. Every which way Evan turned, vivid images leapt out from every pillar and from the walls. Sunlight streamed in from the windows illuminating the room.

'How in the name of the gods can anyone describe this place?' said Leander, gripped by the scenery.

Evan shook his head, unable to speak. He had never seen anything like it, except for pictures in books and on the internet. It took his breath away. He wanted to know how the Egyptians constructed the buildings and how long it took. The historians and archaeologists made educated guesses based on what they found. But standing in the midst, Evan believed the secrets of construction were more elusive than ever.

The hair on Evan's nape prickled. He took a small step to the side and with a slow turn of his head, from left to right, scanned the columned hall. From the corner of his eye he saw a dark shadow. He turned and saw nothing. He drew his sword, the sound of ringing breaking the reverential tranquillity. Leander moved closer to the High Priestess and held out a small dagger.

'One may not bear arms within the great Temple of Amun-Re.' A bald Egyptian appeared out of nowhere and stood between two pillars. He wore a white linen kilt with a white sash over his chest. A large hooked nose dominated his otherwise small facial features. 'What brings you to the Temple of Amun-Re?'

The High Priestess placed a hand on Evan's forearm. 'Tell him we seek an audience with the High Priest of Amun-Re.'

Evan nodded and relayed the message.

'And why do you come?'

'We seek a sacred relic.'

The priest appraised the High Priestess, his face giving nothing away. 'To which god does this object belong?'

'The Mother Goddess, patroness of our home.'

'And what are you to this goddess?'

'I am High Priestess.'

He bowed before her. 'Please wait and I will commune with the High Priest.'

The priest withdrew amongst the columns as silently as he had appeared. Evan craned his neck and tried to keep an eye on him but the forest of pillars concealed his movements. He gave up and while they waited he studied the hieroglyphs, moving from one huge stone column to the next.

'The writings depict the pharaohs being purified by the gods. It shows their coronation and presentation of the sceptre as they become king and god of the land. The images on the walls show the victorious battles led by the pharaoh of the time,' said a deep voice. They spun around. A tall, muscular Egyptian stood a short distance from them. He too wore a white linen kilt but over his shoulder he had a leopard fur sash. 'Please put away your weapons. You won't need them here. You're in no danger here in the house of Amun-Re.' He gave them a reassuring smile. Evan gave a slight nod and slid the sword back into the scabbard. Leander sheathed his dagger. The Egyptian stepped forward. 'I am Sethe, High Priest of Amun-Re.'

The High Priestess acknowledged him with a quick bow of her head. 'I am Alexina, High Priestess to the Mother Goddess. These are Evandros and Leander, my companions.'

'My priest tells me you are seeking a relic belonging to your goddess.'

She nodded. 'We were informed the sacred object is here.'

'What is the object?'

'A golden serpent.'

The High Priest smiled and shrugged in apology. 'I'm afraid there's no such relic here. I've been high priest at the temple for the last ten annuals and haven't seen a golden serpent. The treasures that once were here are long stolen. Nuwe has returned to the rule of the pharaoh but the temple was pillaged and plundered for the last seven hundred years.'

'May we search the premises, with your permission of course?' she said.

'That's not possible,' he said and shook his head. 'Only priests and kings have the right to enter the sacred grounds of Amun-Re.'

'We have travelled far honourable High Priest, and we cannot leave without the relic. Our people and home will be destroyed if we fail,' she said.

He shrugged. 'The plight of your people is unfortunate but our laws are sacrosanct. If I allow you to enter, it is I who is then punished.'

'You must understand, our gods commanded us to find the golden serpent. If we disobey, we will suffer great consequences. We don't mean any disrespect to your god, but may we make an offertory which will appease Amun-Re?'

'What are you willing to present?' He glanced down at his hands and then looked back at the High Priestess as if bored.

'We have old and precious documents that may interest you.'

'My people have the oldest parchments in the world,' he said with a smirk. 'What possible worth would yours have to us?'

The High Priestess gave him a benign smile. 'Our ancestors charted the world and great oceans and listed locations of prized metals and untold wealth.'

The High Priest's eyes sparked and then just as quickly, he resumed his serene poise.

'Evandros, give the High Priest the map.'

He grimaced. She turned to him and arched a brow.

'What if we gave him money instead,' he said, pleading.

Her face hardened. 'This is far more important. Hand him the map.'

With great reluctance, Evan lifted the bag from his shoulder, opened it and grabbed the largest of the scrolls. A sense of devastating loss came over him as he held out the document. The face on the High Priest was impassive but his eyes gleamed as he took the proffered chart.

'I'll take you to the holy centre of the Temple of Amun-Re.'

Evan straggled behind. The High Priest led them through one remarkable building after another, until they arrived at a small grey one. Two obelisks stood before the doorway.

'Thutmosis the First erected these and dedicated them to Amun-Re. Each pharaoh has since added dedicational buildings or a monument as a tribute to our mighty god.'

'May we enter?' the High Priestess asked.

He stood aside to let them pass. Evan pushed open the wooden doors, stepped across the doorsill and descended the few stairs. A fresh, fruity, pine-lemon bouquet with woody undertones of incense lingered in the air. They moved into the semi-dark shrine, torches ensconced along the walls providing scant light and casting long shadows. The small room was rectangular in shape and an altar faced the doorway. On it was a wooden statue of the god sheathed in gold, and a platter of fruit.

They explored the temple in silence. Evan headed for the altar, peered beneath, and ran a hand under the tabletop. The marble was cold and smooth. He stretched his arm further and recoiled at the touch of cobwebs. He wiped his hand on his tunic and turned to the statue, checked behind it and around the plinth. Nothing. He scanned the ceiling, searching for crevices, but did not see any. He checked the nearest wall and placed his hands against it. Under his palms he felt the raised textured surface and the joins in the stone. He progressed along the length of the wall, hands exploring every section.

'It's not here,' he said in a flat tone, his voice echoing in the small room.

'Where do we look now?' said Leander, turning to Evan.

'With the High Priest's consent, we examine every room.' The High Priestess was by the door, her attention fixed on the Egyptian. He gave a short nod. 'We'll split up, that way we can cover more ground and quicker. When you are done, we'll meet back at the forest of columns. If you find the sacred relic, remember not to touch it. Leander, you search the entrance, Evandros the rear, and I will return to the main hall.'

She turned and exited the temple, the High Priest walking alongside. Leander hastened after them, and Evan went in the opposite direction towards another massive doorway.

'The Egyptians really had a thing for pillars,' he muttered as he entered the next building. 'And big!' Evan looked up at the cedar ceiling, the wood faded over the centuries but still in good condition. He pulled out the tablet and with quick strokes sketched what he saw.

Evan inspected every passageway he stumbled across, climbed stairs and squeezed into narrow openings. A few passages, where the roof had collapsed, were impassable. He returned to where he started and shook himself like a dog. Dust and dirt spread around him in a cloud. He brushed the cobwebs from his hair and jumped up and down to shake out any insects. He did not want uninvited guests to use his body as a new place of residence.

'This is a complete waste of time!' he said, banging his hand against the wall. He poked his head into a small room. 'This is a joke!'

He mumbled away, harsh words and expletives rolling off his tongue. The continued lack of success made his blood simmer.

'Enough of this nonsense!'

Evan hit his head on a low doorframe. He winced and swore, clutching his head. He backed out and turned. Evan recoiled and missed hitting his head again. A blue nimbus shrouded a large form. He rolled his eyes as the circle of light dimmed.

'Oh wonderful! Now you show yourself. Thanks for helping out when the monsters attacked us. You have impeccable timing.' Evan strode away and peeked into the next doorway.

'Stop being impertinent! You were never in any danger. I had every confidence you'd free yourself.'

'And save myself from plummeting to my death?' Evan said with a harsh bark of laughter. 'Thanks *Dad.*' The sarcasm dripped like venom. 'In any case, it doesn't matter, someone saved me.'

'What? Who?' Zeus clenched his jaw.

Evan shrugged. 'Whoever it was is someone with your capabilities. They smelt nice.' He crossed his arms and stared at Zeus. 'Why are you here?'

Zeus frowned and his lips pressed together. He glanced at his son. 'The object you are seeking is here. Go back to the hypostyle hall, there you will find the golden serpent of the Mother Goddess.'

'If you knew it was here all along, why didn't you tell me? Could have saved us a lot of time.'

'We aren't sure where the object is,' Zeus said. 'We can offer assistance and nothing more. I could only help now as you discovered the location.'

'This is ridiculous! Why don't you find these objects, sort it out yourselves and be done with it?'

Zeus sighed. 'As I showed you, we cannot retrieve the sacred items. To do so would confirm the consequence we are trying to prevent. We don't want to disclose the whereabouts of the relics to another seeker who wants to block our efforts.'

'Have you discovered who this individual is? Are they like you?'

'Not as yet,' Zeus said, face closing over. 'Be wary of anyone who offers gifts my son and always keep your weapons with you.' Then he departed.

'You can't just leave with that!' Evan shouted. 'Come back and tell me what the hell is going on!' He punched the nearest wall. 'God damn it!' Jaw clenched, he set off for the hypostyle hall. By the time he reached the multi column building, his anger ebbed. He stared at the thick cluster.

'This is just brilliant,' he said shaking his head. 'How do you find one needle in a bunch of haystacks?'

'Evandros? What are you doing here?' Evan spun around at Leander's voice. He tilted his head. 'What is wrong?'

'The golden serpent is in this room,' he said.

'What makes you think the relic is here?'

'I had a visit from dear ole dad and he told me.' Evan shook his head as he did a slow turn. 'This is not going to be fun.'

'Divine Zeus came and told you?' Leander said.

'He did, although he didn't give me any hint as to where the relic is in this room.'

'I have searched rooms hidden within walls and outside the walls finding nothing,' he said.

'Even the columns?'

Leander nodded. 'As far as I could check. The uppermost parts are beyond my reach. We need scaffolding to reach the top.'

'Scaffolding... no doubt that's what they used during the construction of this hall and the other buildings.' Evan had an arm crossed against his chest, the other raised with a hand at the corner of his mouth.

'Hektor is an engineer; he'll figure out what needs to be done,' Leander said. 'What if I return to the boat and get him?'

'Sure, why not.' Evan had an idea but opted to go with Leander's plan to try to get along with Hektor.

CHAPTER FORTY-SEVEN

Evan weaved in and out of the columns, touching them as he mean-
dered past. The colourful hieroglyphs were still as dynamic as the
day they were painted as was the entire room. He strolled back to the
front of the hall, sat on the stone floor and began to draw. His mind
went through a number of scenarios on the construction process.
The drums on each were massive and must have weighed tons. He
closed his eyes and tried to visualise the various techniques the
Egyptians may have used to build the enormous buildings. A
memory tugged at the deep recesses of his brain, something he read
in a book or was it a magazine?

'What are you doing?' a voice said.

Evan's heart started racing. He turned to see the High Priestess
and the Egyptian High Priest standing behind him.

'I was contemplating how the buildings, pillars and statues were
placed into position,' he said, getting to his feet.

She looked past him, turning her head from one side then to the
other. 'Where's Leander?'

'He's gone to get Hektor.'

'Why?'

'Zeus paid a visit and confirmed the relic is here and in this room. Leander thought Hektor may come up with an idea on how to reach the top of the pillars and ceiling to search them.'

'Divine Zeus was here?' she said taking a step back.

'Uh huh.' He glanced over at the dense cluster. 'It's going to take a while to check each one. There must be over a hundred columns.' He looked over his shoulder to the Egyptian and asked if he knew how many there were. Evan gave a low whistle and turned back to admire the room.

'What did he say?'

'There are one hundred and thirty-four pillars. The building was commissioned by Sety the First and added to by his son Ramesses the Second.' He gazed at the room. 'The search could take weeks so we'll need somewhere to stay.'

'Not far from the port is a hostel,' the Egyptian said when Evan asked.

Evan nodded his thanks. 'Now to wait for Leander and Hektor.'

'We're here!' said Leander with a wave.

'Great Mother Goddess!' said Hektor, jaw falling open.

'I did try to explain the room to Hektor but my description wasn't very good,' Leander said with an apologetic smile.

'What is the purpose of the room?' Hektor said, stepping forward.

'This is the home of our god and creator of the universe,' said the High Priest. 'The sanctuary is the embodiment of Atum's awakening and the bringing to life his children who rule over our world. This multi-pillared hall represents a papyrus field, the edge from which the greatest of gods built his home. The furthest of sacred chambers is where He roused from his slumber.'

The chamber took on a new meaning for Evan standing amidst the richness of the temple. Each building told a story: the journey of the gods, the pharaohs' accomplishments and the life of their worshippers.

'May I look around?' Hektor said.

'Of course.' The High Priest extended a hand.

While Hektor moved around the room, the others waited and watched. Fifteen minutes passed before he re-joined them.

'We're going to need a ladder, it's the only way to reach the top,' he said. 'We could use rope and lever someone from the ceiling but that won't be practical.'

'Where in the name of Zeus are you going to get a ladder that reaches that high?' said Leander.

'I will make one,' Hektor said without blinking an eye.

It took two days to make the ladder. Everyone helped to chop down palm trees, cutting the wood into lengths and dividing it into smaller parts. By mid-afternoon on the third day the ladder was ready. Due to the weight and length of the ladder, the four men needed to carry it. Dexion remained with Homer at the hostel while the others returned to the Amun-Re's Temple and the hypostyle hall. Space was tight with very little room to move a long object. It took several attempts to shift the ladder upright, as the top half kept swinging away. Heavy breathing and grunting filled the room. Sweat trickled down Evan's face as he and the others tried to lever it into position. Phameas' cheeks puffed out as he strained to hold his end; the muscles in Leander's neck stuck out like thick cords as he struggled to control the swaying; Hektor gritted his teeth and puffed and snorted like a bull pawing the ground. Then the ladder fell against a column. They heaved a collective sigh of relief.

Leander shook his arms. 'How many times do we need to shift this thing?'

Hektor gave him a dark look.

'Just asking. Took a lot of effort to set it up,' Leander said. 'Who's going up?' he added, glancing away.

'Evandros, you scale the ladder,' Hektor said, eyes averted and fixed on the furthest point of his contraption.

'Me? It's your creation, Hektor. You should climb it.'

He shook his head. 'You're lighter than me.'

'Oh Mother Goddess! I will go up!' said the High Priestess, exasperated.

'No need, High Priestess,' Hektor said, cheeks flushed.

'All right, I'll go,' Evan said. 'Been on taller buildings than this anyway,' he said under his breath as he clambered up the ladder.

'What was that?' Leander called up at him.

'Nothing!'

When he reached the top, his head brushed the ceiling, and Evan took a moment to admire the artwork. From the ground they were beautiful but up close the images were astounding.

'Are you all right, Evandros?' Phameas said.

'I'm fine,' he said looking down. 'Cripes, that is a long way to the ground.' He closed his eyes.

'Evandros, you can't see anything if your eyes are shut,' said Leander, the mirth in his voice unmistakable.

'I'm aware of that, Leander!' he said, biting back. Evan's head stopped swimming. He took a deep breath and opened his eyes. He concentrated on the image in front of him, inspected the others and moved down a step. Rung by rung, he descended the ladder hoping one might represent the golden serpent.

'There is a major flaw in this method,' he said dismounting. 'There are masses of snakes on the columns.'

'The image will be different to the others,' the High Priestess said with conviction.

'How can you be sure?' Evan asked her.

'You will recognise it.'

He grabbed hold of the wooden frame. 'Fine. Let's move the ladder.'

They got more adept and quicker at relocating the ladder from one column to the next. The process of scrutinising each image was painstaking and slow. How many hours had passed, Evan wasn't sure. The pictograms blurred, and he struggled to refocus. He stole a look out the window and noticed the shadows lengthening.

'This is the last one for the day,' he said, calling down at them. 'The sun is setting and soon it will be hard to see the drawings. We'll have to come back tomorrow.'

'What if we get you a torch? Will that help?' said the High Priestess.

'With or without a torch it won't make much difference. I am too tired to keep going,' he said.

'I will take over,' Leander said.

'All right.'

Evan had stepped down a few rungs when a strange icon caught his attention. The image was faint, the paint washed out. He leaned closer. It was an outline of a woman holding an object in each hand. The profile and artwork did not match the Egyptian hieroglyphs. It appeared to be added later, set into the column and then painted. He traced it with a finger. The figurine was embedded into the stonework. He prodded it but it did not budge. He recognised the picture straightaway.

'What have you found?' the High Priestess said.

He glanced at the expectant faces below and grinned. 'You were right, she was easy to spot.'

Leander and Phameas laughed with delight. Hektor gave a nod of acknowledgement and the High Priestess had a small smile on her face. Evan pulled out his dagger and with the tip removed the sand lodged around the image. He worked at it until he could slip part of the blade under the base. It moved a little. Encouraged, he slid the blade back and forth, fine granules of sand wafting into the air. With the tip of the knife he tried to edge the statuette out from its niche. He felt it budge. He kept at it until the figurine began to protrude from the column. With clawed fingers Evan gripped it and pulled, but it refused to shift. He tightened his grip, gritted his teeth and yanked it out.

'Whoa!' Evan's arm flung backwards, object in hand. The ladder lurched away from the column.

'Evandros!'

With his heart in his throat and galloping like a furious horse, he tilted forward. The ladder fell back against the sturdy pillar.

'Bloody hell.' He leaned his head against the cold stone, his heart still racing.

'Evandros, are you all right?' called up Phameas.

He nodded. 'Yes, I'm fine.' He drew in a shaky breath, lifted his head and peered into the dark vacant cavity. A mound of sand filled the rear of the nook. He cleared it away until he saw something glitter. Mindful not to touch it, he grabbed the pouch made from rabbit skin tied to his belt. He reached in. His knuckles scraped against the narrow enclosure, clutched the item and extracted it with care. He pulled the sides together and drew the string. His legs still wobbled as he descended with slow and steady steps.

When his foot touched the ground he wanted to kiss it but instead handed the bag to the High Priestess. She opened it and Leander, Hektor and Phameas stepped closer. She withdrew the serpent and held it out for them to see. It was exquisite, the details lifelike and it appeared as if it would curl around her arm. The High Priestess looked up at them, her eyes bright and shining.

'The sacred serpent of the Mother Goddess has at long last returned,' she said in a reverential whisper. She turned the relic in her hands with tenderness and adoration, stroking the golden head.

'Glad that's over,' said Evan. 'Time to leave and work out where to go next.'

'Yes, we must discuss our next destination,' the High Priestess agreed, and opened her bag to slip the relic inside.

'No! You will not take the treasure! It belongs to us!' the High Priest said, screaming. He snatched the object from the High Priestess and turned to run.

The golden serpent stirred. Startled, the Egyptian froze. The serpent hissed and grew bigger. It coiled and tightened its body along the length of his arm and raised its head. A golden tongue flickered from its mouth. Its eyes gleamed. The Egyptian recoiled and tried to fling the snake off his arm. The serpent grew larger. It struck, and sank its fangs into his neck. The High Priest gave a short shriek and collapsed.

Dead.

His body withered and blackened, then crumbled into dust. The golden serpent lay inert on the floor where it had fallen. The Egyptian priests, who accompanied the High Priest to oversee the search, fled, wailing and screeching.

'So... that's what happens,' Hektor said.

They stared at the blackened outline of the High Priest, the only evidence he ever existed.

CHAPTER FORTY-EIGHT

The return to Memphis was quicker than the journey to Thebes. The currents of the river ran southwards and hastened their trip. On arrival, the Harbour Master came out to greet them and chatted away with them as if they were old friends. He had one of his workers retrieve a donkey and cart for Homer and the High Priestess.

'What did you think of our holy city?' he said to Evan.

'It is magnificent.'

The Harbour Master beamed. 'When Memphis was the centre of Egypt it rivalled all other cities.'

'It still does,' Evan said. 'Tell me honoured sir, where can we go to enquire as to the past?'

'The priests are the keepers of lore. Go to the Temple of Ptah, and a priest may be able to answer your questions.'

With Homer loaded on the cart and the High Priestess sitting with him, the group set out for the same hostel.

'What do you hope to learn from the priests?' Leander said as he walked alongside Evan.

'If they have any knowledge of Atlantis and whether there was any interaction between the two peoples. The Egyptians are very good at keeping records and there's a chance to learn where the next object is located.'

'And what if they don't have the information, what do we do next?'

Evan stared ahead and sensed the others were listening and anticipating his response. 'Let's wait until we visit the priest.'

The innkeeper appeared pleased to see them again and did not hesitate in allotting rooms. While the others settled in, Evan set off for the temple with Phameas and Dexion in tow. On arrival, they had to wait until the priests were available to hear their petition. They sat in the shade of the building out of the sweltering heat and humidity. Half a day passed before someone came out to summon them.

'That was disappointing but I guess we have our next destination,' said Evan as they left the compound.

'When do you want to leave?' Phameas asked.

'There's nothing to keep us here, but we'll stay a day or two to stock up on food and water.'

They chatted as they walked back to the hostel. Leander spotted them and went to greet them.

'What is wrong? Has something happened?' Evan said.

'In a way. Homer has woken,' he said.

'That's great news!' Evan frowned as Leander hesitated. 'How is he?'

'Homer has lost the ability to speak,' said the High Priestess, stepping out from behind Leander. Her face was drawn and saddened. 'The damage to his throat is much more serious than first expected. Other than weakened by lack of food and the length of time being asleep, he is fine.'

'How will he communicate?' said Dexion.

'He'll need a stylus and wax tablet,' she said.

'I am glad he has wakened,' said Evan. 'He'll be only able to eat soft foods?' The High Priestess nodded. 'Can he travel?'

'Yes, but not on foot.'

'That's understandable. We'll be sailing on the river for a while yet so he'll have time to recover. As to his dietary needs, we'll head for the marketplace and check what is suitable.'

'What did you learn from the priests?' she said.

'They didn't know much except there was a civilisation and land destroyed by the gods' millennia ago. They suggested going to Sais. The priests there interacted with the survivors.'

'How far is this place?'

'Four to five days sailing.'

'Before you leave for the market, would you like to visit with Homer?' the High Priestess said, her forehead creasing.

'There's plenty of time to catch up, and the market won't be open for much longer.'

'Just a few minutes,' she said her eyes glinted. 'He said during our captivity you'd come and rescue us.'

'He did?'

'He was convinced you'd find us,' Leander said.

Evan pressed his lips together and then sighed. 'Lead the way.'

He followed the High Priestess into the small room where Hektor sat with Homer. He was sitting on the bed, leaning against the wall. As soon as Homer saw Evan, his face lit up.

'Homer, it's good to see you awake.' He was rewarded with a warm but tired smile.

Homer beckoned him. Evan stepped closer to the bed. Homer gestured a second time. Evan leaned forward. Homer put his hands on either side of Evan's face and peered into his eyes. Minutes passed, and then Homer nodded and smiled. He closed his eyes and his hands flopped onto his lap. He propped his head against the wall, as if the weight was too much to bear. Evan straightened and stared at his peaceful face.

'I will return in an hour,' he said in a soft voice and left the room.

***

Evan and Phameas loaded the cart with goods Dexion, Leander and Hektor handed them. Homer emerged from the room using the wall as support. Leander hurried to help, but he waved him away. The High Priestess walked with him. Homer shuffled his way to the cart and clutched the sides. His face was pale and had a light un-healthy sheen.

'Come and sit,' said Evan, patting the corner of the crude wagon.

Homer shook his head. He pulled out the wax tablet, wrote a few words and held it out for Evan to read.

'You won't be in the way,' Evan said, shaking his head. 'Now sit before you fall down.' He took Homer by the elbow and sat him down on the end of the cart. Homer gave him a grateful smile. 'We won't be much longer.'

The last of the stock was packed onto the wagon, and they were ready to leave. Evan turned to the High Priestess.

'We left you a space to sit next to Homer.'

'I will walk,' she said.

'If you wish.' Evan looked at Homer. 'More room for you. You can sit across the length of the back.'

Homer grinned, lifted his legs and rested an arm on the frame of the cart. The High Priestess watched the exchange between the two.

'Hang on,' Evan said, warning Homer. He took hold of the reins and with a gentle slap on the donkey's rump, prodded the animal into moving. Dexion sat on the animal's back, Phameas walked next to Evan and Leander on the other side. Hektor and the High Priestess followed the cart.

By mid-morning they left the megalithic structures of Memphis and sailed northwards for the city of Sais. The land changed from vast sandy outcrops to verdant terrain and extensive farmland.

'Did the priest give you any pertinent details on Sais?' the High Priestess said as they entered their third day of sailing.

'The city is very old, more so than Memphis and considered the main capital of Egypt in this region. It lost prominence for a few centuries until King Tefnakhte re-established its position. Today it is one of the royal sites of the ruler Ahmose the Second.'

'And of the information we seek?' she said.

'I was just getting to that,' said Evan. 'He suggested we visit the Temple of the Goddess Neith and speak to one of the priests there.'

'Why this particular city?' said Hektor.

'On a visit to Sais, he was told a story about a group of people from the sea who sought help. They arrived not long after the world descended into night-time during the day,' Evan said.

'How is that possible? Darkness during the day,' said Phameas, tilting his head to the side and tugging his ear.

'When the gods destroyed our home, day became night. The world was without light for many days,' said the High Priestess.

Phameas whistled. 'What did your ancestors do to anger the gods?'

'Hubris,' Leander said in a flat tone, the usual twinkle in his eyes absent.

'We are no longer driven by self-importance or insolence. We live according to the doctrine of the gods,' said Hektor, tone clipped and face stiff as a plank of wood.

The High Priestess patted him on the hand. 'Phameas was not making a judgement by his question and has the right to ask why.' She turned to the Phoenician. 'Our predecessors revered the gods and lived in harmony for many thousands of years, and then they became greedy. They were a powerful nation and did not hesitate to conquer others to obtain land and wealth. Hostility replaced peace, and they neglected to pay tribute to the gods. To punish them for their acts of betrayal and to restore the good of the world, the gods caused the earth to rebel and engulf their home.'

'Moloch! Your gods are unforgiving,' said Phameas swallowing hard.

'As Hektor pointed out, our people are no longer driven by insolence or self-importance,' she said.

Phameas lifted a single eyebrow. 'How is it you are here if the gods devastated your home and killed every person?'

'Our forebears,' she waved a hand at her fellow Atlanteans and Evan, 'managed to escape on ships and were fortunate not to be destroyed by Poseidon's waves. Not every ship managed to avoid his wrath. Many of our ancestors got lost and were never seen again.'

'I, for one, am grateful you have changed. Having said that, if you behave in a contrary manner, I'm leaving and I'll be taking Dexion with me,' said Phameas in mock horror.

Evan grinned and thought if he could, he'd go now.

By day five, they came to a tributary. One branch went west and the other straight ahead. Evan and Phameas steered the barge into the latter branch as instructed by the priest in Memphis. A few hours later, the outskirts of the workers' village came into sight. Just metres along, they sighted the long, massive walls of the temple complex.

'The Aegyptians don't build small structures do they?' said Leander, staring.

Are the buildings throughout Aegyptos similar to these and those in Memphis? Homer scribbled.

'They are and we haven't seen the tombs of the pharaohs,' said Evan. 'Ingenious architects.'

How are they built? The size of the blocks must have taken a team of people to cut and move, wrote Homer.

'Ask Hektor, he's the engineer,' Evan said, avoiding the question.

Homer frowned, bent over his wax tablet and then thrust it into his face.

'Yes, well best you ask Hektor,' he repeated.

Homer stared at Evan who kept his eyes askance and focussed on piloting the boat. After a few minutes, Homer approached Hektor. He watched them for a few minutes. Homer's question had stumped him. It rang in his head just as a bell chimed the hour of the day. How did he know?

The barge glided into a berth and touched the pier with a mild bump. Phameas and Leander jumped onto the platform and tethered the boat to pylons. Once Phameas was happy the boat was secured, Leander helped the High Priestess disembark.

'Where to first?' he said, turning to Evan.

'The temple to pay a visit to a priest,' he said and crossed his fingers. 'Let's hope they'll have the information we're seeking.'

'Why did you do that?' Leander said tilting his head to the side, perplexed.

'It's for luck,' Evan said.

'Oh.' Leander's face brightened. He crossed his fingers. 'Well, then "fingers crossed".' He grinned.

Evan smiled and shook his head.

'Not everyone needs to come along,' the High Priestess said in a firm voice. 'Evandros and I will meet with the priest.'

Hektor glowered; Leander shrugged and nodded; Homer did not react but took in the awkward silence. Evan exchanged looks with Phameas and Dexion.

'The two of you should meet with the Harbour Master and find out how much it costs to stay here a few days,' Evan said. He made them practise asking in Egyptian and nodded in satisfaction when they could repeat it back. 'We'll need accommodation and food as well.'

'I do enjoy a challenge,' Leander said, rubbing his hands. Homer's eyes sparkled and pointed at himself and nodded.

'Got it?' said Evan.

Leander grinned. 'We'll be fine.'

I can always draw what we need, Homer scrawled, and smiled.

Evan chuckled. 'Too right.' He handed Leander money. 'That's it then. We should go.'

The High Priestess gave a slight nod, and the two departed.

CHAPTER FORTY-NINE

'This region has more trees and is greener than its southern counterparts,' the High Priestess said.

'The annual flooding helps nourish and provides fertile ground for plants to thrive during the summer,' Evan said. 'Look at the compound.' He pointed. 'The ground it's built on is lower than the river and the land outside is inundated, bringing rich fertile soil. You can tell by the lush growth of flowers, desert plants and trees.'

'And this inundation happens every year?'

'It does.'

'What if the river doesn't flood the lands?'

'I daresay there are years when it is less than usual but it always floods.'

Around the complex were clusters of houses, single storey and double. The homes closest to the temple grounds were bigger and grander with flourishing gardens. To the north, on higher ground, was the palace; the buildings rivalled the majesty and imposing temples housed within the religious precinct.

The streets were jam-packed with vendors and buyers. Young children ran, threading their way between slow moving pedestrians and donkeys pulling carts. The smell of animal dung and urine mixed with aromas of cooked food. Dust billowed around their feet as they weaved through the crowd. The locals stopped and stared at the newcomers, their stature drawing attention. Children came up and reached out to them. Evan smiled and greeted them. The children beamed and chatted, running alongside. He spoke with them until a few adults pulled them away. They continued onwards, and the local inhabitants ignored them, until they reached the entrance of the complex.

Eight soldiers stood outside, each armed with a bronze-tipped spear and holding a shield made from wood and ox-hide. One of the warriors had a short broad sword and wore a blue and white striped headdress. He stepped forward as they approached.

Evan bowed from the waist. 'Honoured warrior, we come seeking the wisdom of your priests. The High Priestess and I journeyed from Memphis where a priest of Ptah suggested we visit the mighty seat of pharaoh's power. We offer a gift to your gods in their honour and for their knowledge.'

The Egyptian studied them as if weighing their hearts before the gates of eternal life. 'I will present your request to the High Priest.' He turned on his heel, marched towards the entrance, and was swallowed by the obscurity of the doorway.

Evan clasped his hands behind his back and gazed up at the enigmatic faces of the statues. He flicked from one to the other trying to spot any disparities between them. It reminded him of the cartoons in magazines and newspapers where you have to pick out the differences. They were identical. Every detail from the pharaoh's crown to the toenails was exact. He wiped his brow with the back of his hand. Beads of sweat trickled from his temple and along the side of his face.

'We should have brought water,' he said, 'and hats. I didn't expect to be standing here this long.'

'If the priests were in a middle of a ritual the soldier had to wait until they finished,' the High Priestess said.

Evan wiped his sweaty hands on his tunic. 'I might go and ask one of the villagers for a container of water. We may be waiting a while longer and in this heat we need to keep hydrated.'

He turned to leave.

'Wait, I see the warrior returning.'

Evan looked back just as the Egyptian stepped out of the dim entrance.

'Follow me,' he said. The guard did a quick about turn and strode back. They hurried after him and as he neared the immobile and watchful soldiers he snapped out a few unintelligible words. Within seconds two warriors fell into step behind them. Cool air washed over them as they approached the shady interior of the gateway.

The main entry was flanked by towering pylons and decorated with painted reliefs of the pharaoh smiting his enemy. On either side, flagpoles jutted out from the wall, and the red pennants fluttered in the wind. The turrets were capped with cavetto cornices. They walked through the shaded gateway and emerged onto a flagstone path lined with sphinxes. Ahead was another set of pylons, bigger than the first set. In front sat two gigantic statues of a pharaoh and above their heads were four flagpoles, two on each massive tower that rose into the sky.

The silent marble sentries watched as they marched past and into the next doorway. A little beyond the entry stood the High Priest in the same regalia as his counterpart in Thebes. He bowed. Evan and the High Priestess returned the gesture. He then acknowledged the guard who nodded and left, leaving behind the two soldiers.

'It is unusual for foreigners to ask for permission to enter our temples and to request information,' he said. 'Then again times are changing. Not far from here is a city of foreigners to whom the great Pharaoh Amasis granted land and permission to trade.'

'We are privileged to be here, High Priest,' said Evan.

'What is it you wish to know?'

'A long time ago a land not far from here and its people were destroyed, forever obliterated from the world. I wondered if the noble priests of the past had heard of such a story.'

'Of course,' the High Priest said with a nod. 'Those who witnessed the anger of the great Amun-Re wrote of the event.'

'Written? May we see it?' Evan said.

'If you'll come this way,' he said and extended an arm. He led the way deeper into the building, wove through a room full of pillars and stopped by a wall facing west. 'This is the inscription of the event you described.'

'What does it say?' said the High Priestess, her eyes fixed on the hieroglyphs.

'Once there was a great and powerful empire, an island that ruled many islands, called Atlantis. It was renowned throughout the seas for its wealth, richness of land and for its people. There were jewellers, philosophers, physicians, engineers, pilots of the sea and Great Ocean, cultivators of land and animals. Women and men held equal status in every facet of life. The islands were connected by an ingenious design of bridges and canals, which allowed the citizens to move with ease from one land to another.'

The High Priest went on to describe the palace, the stadium and temples. So prodigious was the information, the High Priest even explained how each house had access to hot and cold water.

'Then in a single day and night, a violent volcanic eruption and earthquake rocked this kingdom. Floods never before seen swallowed the land and it disappeared into the depths of the sea. The sky swelled with black clouds which spread across many nations. The wrath of the gods was experienced here and beyond,' said the Egyptian. 'Our shores and river-mouth altered and rain, the colour of ebony, fell from the sky, blackening the earth.'

'How did you come to have this information?' the High Priestess said, face pale.

'The gods gifted us with the ability to write, and decreed what happens must be recorded. This,' he indicated with a hand, 'comes from a group of people who escaped, arrived on our shores and asked for refuge. Our people helped them fix the ships and provided water, food and clothing. Those too ill to travel stayed while the rest set sail and vanished into the horizon. What happened to them remains unknown.'

'Is there any reference to the Mother Goddess or sacred relics?' Evan said, pointing to the hieroglyphs.

'No,' he said.

Evan's shoulders slumped, and a flicker of disappointment flashed across the High Priestess' face.

'The text reveals where the people of the sea came from,' the High Priest added.

'It does? Where?' said Evan, face brightening.

The Egyptian pointed to a hieroglyph. 'An island called Keftiu.'

'Keftiu... why does that ring a bell?' Evan said. He looked at the High Priest. 'Where is the island?'

'It lies west of our great land, perhaps a four day voyage by ship,' said the High Priest.

'West... hmm...' Evan's forehead furrowed. He stared unseeingly past the High Priestess, as his mind conjured an image of the world. After a few moments he smiled and turned to her. 'I know where, and that's our next destination.' He bowed before the High Priest. 'Many thanks, you have been most helpful.' He gave the Egyptian a small pouch. 'We are grateful for your time.'

The High Priest gave a small nod and had the guards guide them back to the main gates of the temple complex.

'What is the island's name you recalled and how long will it take to get there?' said the High Priestess.

'It's called Krete and as the High Priest said, the journey is a short one,' he said.

The High Priestess' step faltered. Evan stopped, noting the surprised expression on her face.

'What is it?'

'Very few have been informed of the ancestral home. How is it you possess the knowledge?' she said.

'I read, it's what I do, remember? If you knew it was Krete, why didn't you say something? We didn't need to come here, and waste time asking questions when you had the answer all along!' Evan said, and his ice blue eyes darkened like a storm cloud.

'I disclose information at point of need and in our current circumstance, there is none,' she said.

'You are wrong,' he said. 'There is a possibility the relic is on Krete and if not, we could find clues to its whereabouts. Did you stop to consider that at all?'

'You're the scholar, why didn't you suggest going there first? You are the one who reads.' The High Priestess thrust her face up at his.

'Clever but still wide off the mark. The island is on the maps,' he said. The High Priestess shuddered as the shade of Evan's eyes became as fathomless as the night sky.

'What is going on here?'

Evan whirled around at the interruption. Leander and Homer glanced from one to the other in concern. He straightened and the High Priestess took a quick step back.

'The High Priestess is withholding information essential to finding the relic. If she hadn't been so secretive, we'd be much further ahead. Now if you will excuse me, I need to chat with the Harbour Master about buying passage on a ship.' He strode away, long quick strides that put distance between him and the three Atlanteans. Homer ran after him.

CHAPTER FIFTY

'How far is it to Krete?' Hektor approached Evan and Phameas, disrupting their conversation. 'We've been at sea for eight days. Should
it take this long?'

'There are a number of possible reasons for the delay,' said Evan,
glancing at Phameas. 'It could be the wind, the current or both.'

'The journey has been unaffected by calamity since we left Aegyptos. The winds are favourable and the weather fair,' Hektor said
in a flat tone. 'There must be something wrong.'

'We'll go and chat with the captain,' said Evan. He and Phameas
headed for the helm, passing the puffing and heaving oarsmen, their
bodies covered in sweat. The Harbour Master at Sais recommended
they go to Naukratis, a Hellenic settlement, to find a captain and
ship. The town, he had said, had a busy port and vessels capable of
sailing on the sea.

'Captain, may we take a few moments of your time?'

'Evandros, Phameas.' The captain gave them a cursory look and
returned his attention to the horizon. 'If you're here to ask what is
going on, the answer is I don't know. The first few days we were
sailing towards Krete and on the third day it changed. I corrected the

navigation, and it happened again. I altered the course each time but it switched back. I stopped adjusting the triangulation and now we are cruising much faster, faster than this ship has ever gone. It appears the will of the gods is at work.'

The hair on Evan's neck stood on end. 'Has this happened before?'

The captain shook his head.

'Where are we heading?'

'Towards Hellas.'

'Did you experience drastic navigational changes in your years as a sailor?' Evan said to Phameas when they moved away.

'No, but there were stories of ships and entire crews disappearing,' said Phameas. 'What do you think is going on?'

'There's something not right with what's happening and I don't like it.'

'What did the captain say?' Hektor said when they returned.

'You were right. The captain is concerned with the lack of control and new destination,' said Evan. Hektor folded his arms against his chest and nodded. Evan repeated the conversation they had with the captain. When he finished the unsettled silence of the small group spoke louder than a squawk of a flock of seagulls.

'What do you make of this change in course, High Priestess?' Hektor said.

'The captain is right. The gods decided our journey must continue within this land of Hellas. We will soon learn of the purpose for the new destination,' she said.

'I'm not sure that's it; this situation doesn't feel right,' said Evan shaking his head.

'Then why are we sailing in the opposite direction from our intended landing-place?' she said.

'I can't explain why but something isn't right. If the gods are redirecting our ship, why are they? They didn't offer any assistance in locating the first relic. We,' he pointed to Phameas, Dexion and himself, 'found where it was hidden. And didn't Poseidon say they cannot get involved as it might expedite their downfall? We're steered towards Hellas for a reason and my instinct is telling me there's something amiss here.'

Dexion moved closer to Evan. He glanced at him with a reassuring smile. The others fell silent, their faces drawn.

'Who do you believe altered our course?' said Leander, and his usual twinkling and smiling eyes glinted.

'Whoever it is, they are powerful and aren't restricted by the same conditions as the gods.'

'You're speaking of the ancient gods who ruled the Earth and Universe for many thousands of years,' said the High Priestess in whisper, her face paling. 'If they or even one escaped from the nether regions of Tartaros, then we are in the hands of a formidable immortal.'

What can we do? scribbled Homer.

'The Elder Gods are strong and can only be vanquished by the Younger Gods, as they did once before several millennia ago.'

'The Mother Goddess is one of the Elder Gods, isn't she?' said Evan.

'Yes, but she and the female Elder Gods did not take part in the war. For not standing against the Olympians, Divine Zeus did not incarcerate them. I must commune with our Mother and ask for her guidance,' said the High Priestess.

'While you're at it, ask whether she knows who might be behind this predicament,' Evan said.

'If she knows, she will reveal it in time,' the High Priestess said with a stiff face.

'We don't have the luxury of time,' he pointed out. 'Besides being annoying and arrogant, they withhold information. Not telling us what we need to know may put us in jeopardy.'

'Better to be forewarned and forearmed,' Leander said.

'You said it.' Evan nodded.

'What do you know regarding this land we are heading towards, Evandros?' Hektor said.

'Before the destruction, Atlantis controlled the Aegean Sea. The traders of Atlantis and the Hellenic people interacted, which led to many deals and collaboration. Then it changed. A war broke out between the people of Athens and Atlantis over the trading ports and the Atlanteans proved to be too strong.'

'So we can expect a hostile welcoming?' he said.

'I don't think they'd give a warm reception,' Evan said in a bleak tone. 'Phameas, in your travels did you meet Hellenes?'

'They're very good sailors and traders, and renowned for their fighting skills. Many kings from my homeland and elsewhere hire them as mercenaries. I've also heard they are loyal,' said Phameas.

'It will be a hostile greeting then,' said Leander.

'We will do our utmost to allay their fears and show we are not militant and no longer seek to dominate,' said the High Priestess.

'Let's hope they don't remember the terrible deeds of our ancestors,' Leander said.

This may be the reason we are heading for Hellas, Homer wrote.

'It makes sense,' said Evan. 'A great tactic to create pandemonium, confusion and terror.'

'To what end?' said the High Priestess. 'Why would an Elder God want to harm us or interfere?'

'Imagine being beaten and then humiliated to spend eternity in a hell-hole. Wouldn't you want vengeance? And there's something to gain from preventing us collecting the relics,' Evan said.

'Yes, you'd want retribution for what they did but what could they achieve from it? The gods are here to stay...' Hektor's voice trailed off.

'That's it! The motive for obstructing our movements,' said Evan slapping his hand against his thigh. 'Why didn't I think of it earlier!'

'Dear Mother Goddess!' said the High Priestess, alarmed. 'They mean to prevent us from finding the relics and allow the birth of a new god.'

'I'd bet my life that's the plan,' Evan said, clicking his fingers.

'What can we do to stop the Elder Gods from hindering our search?'

Find the sacred relics, scrawled Homer.

CHAPTER FIFTY-ONE

'By Poseidon, we made it!' the captain bellowed, the relief and joy in his voice unmistakeable. 'I've never been so glad to see land.'

Ahead was an island nestled in a bay, with the cliff-face running along its entire length. The bay had two entry points; a large channel at the southern end and a narrow pass at the northern tip.

'We've attracted attention,' said the captain pointing to a sleek ship sailing towards them. Homer and Evan stood shoulder to shoulder, their gazes following the fast moving ship as it glided closer. The captain ordered the crew to stop rowing and pull in their oars.

'Why are they intercepting us? Isn't there a port close by?' Evan said. He squinted and raised a hand against the glare of the sun on the water. 'Is that a war ship?'

'Kings want to protect their provinces and their fleets patrol the coasts, guard dogs of the sea, against enemy invasion and pirates,' said the captain.

Phameas, Dexion and the other Atlanteans gathered around Evan and Homer. They watched the two tiered war ship, with painted blue eyes on the prow, reduce speed and drift alongside. An armoured warrior stood on the bridge and stared at them through the thin vertical slits of his helmet, face hidden. Standing behind him in quiet formidable formation was a retinue of soldiers. The sun glinted off their burnished cuirasses and helmets, hands not far from their swords.

'Captain, what brings you to the waters of Pylos?' His voice was disembodied and threatening.

'I'm a trader from Naukratis, I have goods to sell and passengers who wish to disembark!'

'Who are these passengers?'

The captain pointed. 'These people.'

'Follow us,' the taciturn warrior ordered after a lengthy period of unspoken contemplation.

'Not trusting are they,' said Leander as the war ship pulled away and glided ahead.

'The sea is infested with pirates. They take any opportunity to raid trade ships and don't hesitate to kill everyone on board,' said the captain. 'They dishonour the code of decent seafarers.'

'Pirates? I'm not familiar with the term,' Leander said.

'Lawless sailors, who steal, rape and destroy the lives of honest and hardworking people,' Phameas said with venom. 'They are despicable and deserve to be condemned to death.'

'A good thing we didn't encounter any on our voyage,' said Leander, taken aback by Phameas' harsh response.

'A ship of pirates stopped us on our way to Kyrene,' Dexion said in a rush. 'It was exciting! Master Evandros saved me and killed lots of them. So did Phameas.' He then added in a more calm tone and a firm nod, 'But I wasn't scared, not one bit.'

What happened afterwards? Homer scribbled.

'The pirate captain ran away with the little crew he had left, the cowered dog, tail tucked between his legs,' said Evan with a grin. He and Phameas beamed at each other. The smile faded on seeing the disapproving expression on the High Priestess' face. 'In any case, those few marauders were lucky to escape with their lives. If we weren't on the ship I suspect Captain Banipal would have given chase.'

Phameas agreed. 'And as warning to every pirate thinking to waylay a ship, they'd be quartered and impaled on stakes.'

'Why bother attack a ship if it doesn't carry goods?' Hektor said.

'The vessel is valuable and so are people. They can be sold as slaves,' said Phameas.

'As I mentioned earlier, glad we didn't run into any pirates on this journey,' Leander said.

'Not sure our current situation is any better,' said Evan scrutinising the war ship that was a stone's throw in front of them.

Land came into view, buildings on top of the hill visible to the naked eye. The captain adjusted the rudder to match that of their escort.

'Isn't it better to sail into the other strait?' Hektor asked.

'Not unless you wish to swim the rest of the way,' the captain said. 'The currents are too dangerous and difficult to row in the narrow channel. We'd be dashed against the jagged rocks which lie just below the water's surface. This pass is calmer and easier to navigate.' He altered the course with a deft touch on the steering rudder. 'Now, make your way to the prow and prepare for landing.'

'Does that mean there's no port?' Evan said to Phameas as they led the group away from the stern.

'I assume so.'

The captain shouted at his crew to ready the ship for entering the pass. A handful of sailors loosened the sail to half-mast, and the vessel started to slow down straightaway. The rowers took over and the wooden hulk moved at a more controlled pace. The cliffs loomed and blotted out the sun as the ship entered the strait. Evan's warm skin tingled as the sunlight withdrew for a moment.

From the shape of the rugged precipices, Evan guessed the small island once joined the mainland. The captain ordered the rest of the mainsail dropped and fastened. The crew rowed into the bay. Straight ahead was a long stretch of beach.

'Brace for impact landing!' the captain hollered.

'Huh?' Hektor said, backing away from the railing. 'What does he mean?'

'Hold on tight! The ship is making a dry landing,' Phameas said, wrapping his arms around the wooden rail. Homer looked to Evan and Dexion who were gripping the rail and had a leg wrapped around a wooden post. He pulled the High Priestess towards him, put an arm around her and clamped his hands down on the beam on either side of her. Evan clutched tighter, and the sandy beach loomed closer. He closed his eyes and braced his body. He pitched forward, the railing hitting him in the stomach and winding him. Hektor cursed as the ship lurched, and fell backwards.

'Now I understand the purpose for the flat hull,' Leander said, getting to his feet and rubbing his backside.

'Is everyone all right?' Evan turned to the others. 'Dexion? Where's Dexion?' He scanned the deck behind and then peered over the side. 'Dexion!'

The boy was lying face first in the sand, the water lapping at his feet. Evan leapt over the railing and landed in shallow water. Water and sand sprayed his legs and Dexion. He turned him over and brushed away the dark locks of wet hair from his face. Dexion's face was colourless, white as the fluffiest clouds. Evan placed two fingers on his neck and felt the slow steady beat of his heart.

'Dexion! Can you hear me?' Dexion's eyelids snapped open. 'Thank goodness.'

He blinked, sucked in a rugged breath and moaned.

'Don't move.' Evan turned at the sound of splashing behind him. He saw Phameas wading towards them as fast as he could. 'He's wakened.'

'Is he injured?'

'I have to check.' Evan ran a hand along his limbs. 'Nothing is broken thank goodness.' He clicked his fingers in front of Dexion's face. 'He's responsive at least. Dexion, do you understand me?'

'Huh? Wha...?'

'Can you sit up?'

'I think so.' Dexion closed his eyes, pushed himself upright.

'Does it hurt anywhere?'

'No.' He looked up at Evan and then to Phameas who hovered wringing his hands.

'Do you think you can stand?'

Dexion nodded.

'I'll help you get to your feet.'

'Is that wise? He's fallen from a great height,' Phameas said.

'Best he moves around, otherwise he'll go into shock and that isn't good.'

Evan put his forearms under Dexion's armpits. 'Now when you are ready, stand and I will stand with you.'

Dexion nodded, bent his knees and drew them close, leaned forward and straightened. Evan moved with him.

'I'm fine now, you can let go,' said Dexion.

Evan let his arms fall away but stayed close. Dexion looked up where the Atlanteans, the captain and crew gathered. He smiled and waved at them. The sailors cheered, drawing startled looks from those on the war ship.

The warrior in charge and a small group of soldiers had disembarked and approached Evan, Phameas and Dexion. Leander and Homer watched on from their lofty position on the prow.

'What brings you to Pylos?' the warrior said. His face was obscured by the helmet, and his hazel eyes glinted from behind narrow slits.

'Pylos was not our intended destination. We were sailing for Krete,' said Evan.

'You are a long way from Krete,' he said. 'Did you get caught in a storm?'

'You should speak with the captain. He can best explain how we came here,' said Evan. He craned his head back and saw Leander, Homer and the High Priestess watching. 'Leander, could you get the captain? He needs to tell the guard how we arrived here!'

Leander nodded and retreated with haste.

Evan put a hand on Dexion's shoulder and drew him to his side. He took in the warrior's and the soldiers' apparel. Their polished helmets and cuirasses shimmered under the glare of the sun. The images he'd seen in books and on the internet didn't do justice to the armed men. Their demeanour and gleaming weapons were much more menacing.

'Where have you come from?' the warrior said in a clipped tone.

'Egypt,' said Evan.

'You are not Egyptian,' he said then glanced at Phameas and Dexion, 'nor are they.' He turned back to Evan. 'What business did you have in Egypt?'

'Recovery,' Evan said.

The warrior blinked.

Leander cupped his hands around his mouth and called out. 'Evandros, the captain is on his way!'

'Thanks, Leander.' He acknowledged him with a wave but did not take his gaze from the warrior's. Warm water lapped at their shins, the sand burying their feet. The sound of splashing and puffing came from the hull of the ship. The captain waded towards them, the lower half of his khiton wet and the top marked with splatters of water. He nodded at the warrior and stopped next to Phameas.

'Captain, can you enlighten the guard here as to how the ship's original destination altered,' said Evan.

'Yes, of course,' said the captain. He went on to describe the multiple navigational changes, the moderate sailing conditions and the new route set for Hellas.

'You believe the gods set this path?' the warrior said. Evan could imagine the look of incredulity on the man's face.

'Oh yes,' the captain said and nodded, his head bobbing up and down with vigour. 'I have no doubt the gods adjusted our journey's end.'

'Why would they want to do that?'

The captain shrugged. 'Who knows the minds of the gods? Why does Almighty Zeus make the sky rumble and the earth tremor?

Why does Divine Poseidon send storms to destroy ships? The immortals need not explain themselves to us.'

The soldier stared at them, and clenched and unclenched his jaw. 'I will inform the king. My warriors will remain here until I return.'

'Then you won't mind if my crew and passengers disembark,' the captain said. 'We've been on board longer than anticipated and need to set our feet on firm ground.'

'Fine,' he said and then added in a hostile tone, 'No one is to wander off.'

The captain rolled his eyes. 'Where shall we go?' He spread his arms.

A steep precipice and long stretch of beach surrounded the bay. The only possible means of escape was either by ship or the invisible path the soldiers defended by the command of their leader.

'Sometimes I wonder whether stupidity is bred or engrained in soldiers,' the captain said. He folded his arms and shook his head as the warrior trod the narrow track. 'We could be here a while. We might as well get supplies and eat.' He shouted for his bosun, gave instructions and ordered the crew to come ashore. The High Priestess sat in a makeshift harness and was lowered to the beach, followed by their possessions. While the ship's cook set to organising a meal, a few members of the crew set up a tent for the High Priestess. With little to do but wait, the men took the opportunity to relax and enjoy the early respite.

'What happens now?' Leander said. They were sitting with the High Priestess eating stew the men cooked from the stores on the ship.

'Who knows? It's anyone's guess,' Evan said, 'and it depends on how the king responds to our arrival.'

'What should we tell him if he asks where we come from and what we're doing?' Leander said, looking from Evan to the High Priestess.

'Given how the warrior reacted, an inhospitable reception is probable. And he doesn't know who you... we are,' said Evan. 'I suggest not mentioning Atlantis or what we're seeking.'

'We cannot lie as to who we are or why we are here,' said Hektor.

'I didn't say we lie,' Evan said in an even tone. 'If asked, avoid offering the real purpose of our presence.'

'I'm not sure that is the best approach,' said the High Priestess. 'There is nothing wrong with being truthful. The king may be an honourable person.'

'Just as the King of Kyrene showed his hospitality?' said Evan. 'Do as you must but keep in mind what I said.'

CHAPTER FIFTY-TWO

While they waited for the warrior to return, Evan, Phameas, Dexion and Homer frolicked in the water. Evan flipped Dexion into the air, and watched as he twisted and fell back into the crystal blue water. Dexion's carefree laughter echoed as he jumped onto Evan's back and flung his arms around his neck. Evan laughed, grabbed his arms and tossed him into the air. He landed with a splash next to Homer. Evan grinned as Homer took hold of Dexion's legs and pulled him backwards.

The space between Evan's shoulder blades prickled. He turned and noticed a figure standing on the periphery of the shoreline, watching them, a good way from where the others sat under the tent. Evan lifted a hand to shade his eyes. The person did not move and stared straight at him. A breeze swept at her dark long tresses and full-length khiton, and exposed her lily-white shoulders. He wondered who she was and from where she came. There was no one else on the beach when they arrived and nor did he spot anybody descend from the city. He patted his ears, making squelching noises with his wet fingers. The sound of his companions' laughter and chatter faded.

'From where do you hail?'

Evan blinked. 'Huh?'

'Don't you remember where you come from, Evandros?' He blushed at the mirth in her voice.

'I... ah... what? How do you know my name?' He took a step and stopped. 'What on earth? Where did she go?'

'I am right here.' Her husky voice and breath brushed at his ear. The sweet-smelling scent of lavender washed over him.

'Who are you?'

'I am Melaina,' the voice said, speaking in his other ear. 'What brings you to Pylos?'

Evan whipped his head to the left. 'What are you?'

'A friend or foe,' she said, the voice coming from his right. 'Which are you?'

'Neither,' he said. 'What of you Melaina, friend or foe?'

'That will depend on you,' she said, her soft lips grazing his ear. Evan's heart thumped in his chest, and he felt his ears and cheeks grow hot. 'Until the next time we meet.' The trail of her perfume grew fainter. The boisterous clamour of his friends' voices jarred him back to the present.

A pair of large hands fell on his shoulders and shoved him under the water. Evan pushed against the heavy weight and thrust the hands away. The three were laughing as he emerged, sputtering, but their chortles dwindled. The wrinkles on Homer's brow deepened, he grabbed Evan's arm and gestured he was sorry.

'It's fine Homer, I'm not upset at being dunked,' he said. 'It's just... I don't suppose you saw...'

'Saw what?' said Phameas.

Homer cocked his head to the side. Dexion gazed up at him.

'There was a woman standing over there.' He pointed. 'Did any of you even catch a glimpse of her?'

They shook their heads.

'She spoke to me. Did you hear her?'

Again they shook their heads.

Evan heaved a sigh.

'What did she say?' Phameas said.

'She asked where I was from, why we're here and whether I am a friend or foe.'

'Friend or foe? Why ask such a question?' Phameas looked from Evan to Homer then to Dexion.

'Why did she talk to me and just me?' Evan said with a shrug. 'The whole experience was strange. So you weren't aware I conversed with a stranger?'

'No.'

Homer pointed towards the beach where the others sat.

'You're suggesting I should tell the High Priestess?'

He nodded.

'Not sure she'd have any idea as to who it may be,' he said.

Homer gave him a gentle push and gestured him to go.

'Fine. I'll tell the High Priestess,' Evan said, turned up his nose and waded out of the water. 'But it will be a waste of time, she won't know who she is or why she visited,' he added, twisting his upper body to look back at his friends.

Homer raised his brows and pointed.

'I'm going!'

Evan pondered how he was going to raise the issue with the High Priestess. It was preposterous. No one with half a brain would believe him. He wouldn't. Then again, considering where he was it was possible she just might. He ran his fingers through the cool water and felt his feet sink into the sand, the fine granules pushing between his toes. He still had a hard time reconciling this place and time. He wanted to consider it was a fantastic dream. Yet after what he had seen, experienced and touched it was difficult to discount as a mere illusion.

Once out of the water, he walked over to his clothes, picked up the khiton and dried himself. He wrapped the coarse cloth around his waist and walked over to where the Atlanteans sat under the shade of the tent.

'May I speak with you?' he said, stopping in front of the High Priestess. She looked up at him, eyes searching, and nodded.

'Do you wish Leander and Hektor to leave?' she said.

The two men looked at him, Leander's face open and friendly; Hektor sullen and broody.

'They can stay,' Evan said. 'It may be something of concern or it's nothing.' He knelt, the sand crunching beneath his knees. The sun warmed his back as he stared at the High Priestess.

'What is it?' she asked, leaning forward, head tilted to the side.

He explained seeing the woman, described his encounter with her and their discussion.

'I swear she was here. She's as real as you and me and a person just doesn't disappear,' Evan added when he finished.

'She must be an immortal,' said Leander. 'They are the only ones who can do what you've mentioned.'

'Did she give you her name?' the High Priestess asked.

Evan nodded. 'Melaina.'

'She must be one of the lesser gods,' said Hektor with a sniff. 'She's not essential to our quest.'

'Yet here she appeared.' The High Priestess studied Evan. 'What we need to consider is why.'

'And what does she want with Evandros?' said Leander.

'Indeed. Why did she make contact with you and not one of us? What do you possess that we don't?'

Evan shrugged thrusting his palms outwards. 'Who knows? The question is, what do I do if she shows up again?'

'Ask what her purpose is and whether she intends to aid or hinder our progress.'

'If she is a goddess as suggested, I don't expect asking questions would be well received. Not from the experiences I've had,' he said.

The High Priestess sucked in her cheeks. 'Nevertheless we need to learn what her intentions are.'

'Fine, but don't say I didn't warn you.' He rocked back onto his feet.

'What has Dexion foreseen?' she said, stalling his movement.

Evan hesitated and looked at her. 'Nothing, not that he's said as much.'

'The actions of the gods are difficult to read,' said Dexion.

Evan spun around. The boy walked up and stood alongside him. His hair was plastered to his skull, rivulets of water dripping, and his attention fixed on the High Priestess. 'When they wish for me to witness what they are doing, they grant me visions. What I do picture is the past, present and future of people. This goddess wanted to make her presence known to Master Evandros.'

'To what end?' she asked him.

'That, I haven't identified,' he said. 'Though, I am certain she considers Master Evandros as a curiosity.'

'I've been called many things, but a curiosity is a first,' said Evan. 'You didn't mention any of this earlier when I asked,' he said to Dexion.

'I couldn't tell you because I can't. What I do have is a sense of her, nothing more. She and the immortals are difficult to read and it's only when they appear, I can determine their intentions.'

'She'll return and when she does, we'll learn what her plans are,' the High Priestess said. 'In the meantime we must discuss our next course of action when the warrior returns.'

'We first must find out which of the Elder Gods brought us here and why,' said Hektor. 'The dalliances of the local king are the least of our concern.'

'I agree,' Evan said. Hektor's eyes widened in surprise. 'Why redirect our ship to Hellas and to what end?'

'If their intention is to supplant the Olympian Gods, why send us here?' said Leander.

'It has to be connected to the relics,' said Evan.

'What do you mean?' said the High Priestess.

'He, or they, wants us to locate the objects. It's no different to the gods who need us to find them,' said Evan. 'They could save us time by doing this themselves.'

'Don't you have any respect for our divine parents?' said Hektor.

'It's a love-hate relationship, with more hate,' he said.

Homer hit him in the back of the head.

'Ouch! What was that for?' Evan said, and scowled up at his burly friend.

Homer shoved the tablet under his nose. *Speaking with such malice will get you into trouble with the gods and sent home. Is that what you want?*

'I wish,' he said under his breath.

The High Priestess overheard the whispered comment. She gazed at him with renewed interest.

Homer continued to glower at him.

'Fine!' Evan said throwing his arms up in the air. 'I, from here on, will refrain from speaking out of turn with regards to the gods.' He crossed his arms and bristled. 'Satisfied?'

For now, wrote Homer.

'Strangers.' They turned in unison. The warrior had returned and stood by the tent. 'The king wishes you to come to the palace.'

CHAPTER FIFTY-THREE

The High Priestess stood with the aid of Leander and Hektor. 'We shall collect our belongings and join you in a moment.'

The soldier bridled and took a step towards her. Leander and Hektor moved, shielding her.

'Our High Priestess said we'll be with you,' Leander said in a quiet, even tone.

'High Priestess?' The armed man's eyes wavered from Leander's hard face to Hektor's flintier one.

'Yes,' Leander said.

'No one mentioned she was a High Priestess,' the warrior said, fingers fiddling with the hilt of his sword.

'No one asked,' Hektor said.

They glowered at the warrior. Beads of sweat dotted his upper lip. 'The king doesn't appreciate to be kept waiting,' he said with a bark, turned on his heel and went to join his men at the base of the hill.

It took time to strike the tent, return the equipment to the captain and to collect their gear and weapons. When ready, they made their way to the waiting soldiers who flanked them without hesitation.

'Captain, should we disarm the men?' one of the hoplites asked.

The warrior took one look at Homer, Hektor, Leander and Evan. 'They are outnumbered and know how futile it is to cause trouble.'

The hoplite and his fellow foot soldiers did not flinch at their captain's answer. To Evan's ears, the response sounded lame. Although, given the way his companions carried their weapons, he'd err on the side of caution as well.

The well-armed warriors led them over the dunes and towards a track at the base of the hill. The path showed signs of regular use, the surrounding vegetation giving way to a hard, flattened surface wide enough to walk three abreast. Elm and ash trees spread across on either side but a glimpse between the bushes showed open spaces of cleared land. The climb up the hill was steady, the rise a gradual incline. As the trail levelled near the crest of the hilltop, the City of Pylos came into view. Children's voices and laughter filled the air as the large group approached the outer limits. A scattering of people wandered the street, crossing from one to the other in a casual stroll, immersed in conversation.

Evan turned his head from one side to the other, drinking in the architecture. The outlying houses were modest in style, made from stone foundations, sun-dried bricks with wooden roofs and a door that opened onto the street. The narrow cobblestoned streets forced them to walk close together and just about rub shoulders with the soldiers. Evan wanted to take in as much as he could of the city, his professional interest piqued by the design and layout. Distracted by the details, he just about twisted his ankle as his sandaled foot slipped on the smooth cobblestone and into a slight dip in the path.

He bumped into the warrior to his right. The word "sorry" died on his lips, seeing the man's crystallised glare. He bit his tongue, thinking it best to keep his mouth shut, and concentrated on walking.

The street wound in and out for a while before widening onto a bustling and clamorous marketplace. As the oddly assorted troupe marched past, people stopped and pointed, the expressions on their faces mixed with bewilderment, awe and fear.

'They don't get many newcomers here,' Leander said in a mild yet amused tone.

The children, more daring than the adults, drifted closer, but did not dare pass the line of soldiers. They ran alongside, and a few reached out to Dexion and spoke to him. He responded, evoking excited chatter.

There is something odd with this place, Homer scribbled and gestured at the gathering crowd. They observed the swarm of faces, the din growing. Words began to filter towards them.

'How tall are those men?'

'What's she doing not wearing a headscarf?'

'How dare she?'

'What woman travels alone with men?'

The soldiers raised their shields and formed a barrier between their charges and the disgruntled masses. Evan edged closer to the High Priestess and kept a keen watch on those nearest them. His fingers twitched, eager to grab hold of the sword, but he knew if he did, it may provoke the uptight crowd into a nasty reaction.

'Where are the women?' said Hektor, raising his voice.

'Women are not permitted to leave home unless they're accompanied by household slaves or a male family member,' said Evan. 'If they're poor then they have no choice.'

'Not allowed to leave home,' said Hektor, staring at Evan.

'What are you discussing?' The captain's words were sharp and terse.

'He asked the whereabouts of the town's women,' Evan said.

'What barbaric place do you hail from? Virtuous women do not venture into public places. Their duty is to look after the home and have our children. Decisions of the house, business and opinions of government are men's domain.' The captain sneered. 'Women seen outside the confines of their houses are either slaves or harlots and those whose honour is not esteemed.'

'What foolishness,' Leander said, his face clouding.

'We must not judge those who have different ideals,' said the High Priestess.

'Of course, High Priestess,' Leander said with a slight bow of his head.

The palace, located on top of the Akropolis, overlooked the city and was protected by a defensive wall. The soldiers steered them towards a ramp which hugged the hill, and up to the fortified citadel. At the end was the main entrance where four soldiers stood in pairs on either side of the gateway. More walked along the ramparts. They passed the impassive guards and were ushered into a dim passage. The walls graduated inwards and formed a peaked roof. They turned left and came onto an open-air courtyard. The pillars were painted red and trimmed in black. Behind the columns was a series of rooms festooned with many colours.

'Extraordinary,' Evan said in a breathless tone.

'Keep moving,' said the captain with a quick jerk of his head.

They entered the antechamber, where two soldiers pushed open large bronze doors. The warriors escorted them into the megaron under the watchful gaze of more armed men and to where the king waited, seated on a throne. On either side of him sat a group of men, each with a cup in hand, eyes unyielding, bearded faces chiselled and hard as marble statues.

Four wooden columns surrounded the circular hearth. At its centre was a brazier, logs burning, heat radiating, warming the chilly room. Wafts of smoke eddied from the hearth, escaped through the oculus and drifted into the blue sky. The walls of the room were painted in various scenes: exotic wild animals, hunting expeditions and warriors fighting. In contrast, the floor was inlaid with small tessera, tiny tiles, of colourful geometric shapes.

'King Mentor.' The captain bowed. 'These are the people who arrived on the ship. They claim the gods brought them here.'

The room grew quiet.

'Is this true?' the king said, a smirk playing on his face.

'We have no reason to lie,' said Hektor.

'You were heading for... Krete.' The king turned to his captain for confirmation. He nodded. The king continued, 'and behold you end up here, by the gods?'

'Yes,' Hektor said.

'To what purpose did they do that?'

'I don't know. Who knows why the gods do what they do.'

There was a murmur and nods from the nobles seated.

'From where have you come?'

'Aegyptos.'

'No, no, no, where do you hail from?' said the king.

'Atlantis.'

Evan shut his eyes and his head slumped, chin brushing his collarbone. The silence deepened. He pursed his lips and waited.

The king roared with laughter, and his companions joined him. The room resounded with guffaws and howls, bodies doubled over, while others slapped their knees.

'We are from Atlantis!' Hektor said, face turning to a mottled red.

The king laughed harder, and tears coursed down his face as he clutched his stomach. After a while, the king wiped his face, the smile as broad as the shield Evan carried.

'Now, really where is your home?'

'May I address you, King Mentor?' said the High Priestess.

The smile on the king's face faded, and he ignored the unhappy mumbles from his noble guests and nodded. 'Of course. What is your name?'

'Alexina. I am the High Priestess of the Mother Goddess.'

The men shut up straightaway and sat up, their attitude changed in an instant.

'I am not familiar with your goddess,' the king said.

'She is an ancient deity, going back to the birth of our world. Your forebears worshipped our goddess during the era of the Titans until Divine Zeus and his siblings cast them out.' She glanced at Hektor. 'My companion spoke the truth. We are from Atlantis, except for the boy and our Phoenician friend.'

'Can you prove you're Atlantean?'

She frowned. 'I don't understand the question, King Mentor.'

'There are stories of the great achievements of the people of Atlantis: tamers of wild animals, craftsmen of fine jewellery, gifted sailors, and able warriors.' He stared at Homer, Hektor, Leander and Evan for a moment before continuing. 'Your claim to be from Atlantis is questionable. Such a place never existed except in fables we tell our children. A tale of how not to behave and what happens when you act with hubris and against the gods. So if you are Atlanteans, present me with evidence.'

'Show him the maps, Evandros,' she said, keeping her attention on the king.

'Yes, High Priestess.' He pulled out parchments from his bag and unrolled one. 'May I approach, Your Majesty?' The king gave a nod. Evan brought the map to the king. It showed the geography of the island, the three concentric circles and the details with houses and ships in a harbour.

'This is the Temple of Poseidon next to the palace.' The High Priestess pointed to the Akropolis. 'The island has many forests, gardens, gymnasiums and an agora. While in Aegyptos, we visited one of the priests who showed us ancient texts. The transcripts explained how our home ceased to exist and spoke of survivors who asked for refuge from their king. Those unfit to travel stayed, and many left to head west to establish a new Atlantis.'

'West? There's nothing there except the Great Ocean,' the king said, sitting back, fingers drumming on his knee. He pointed at the map. 'Where is the temple for your goddess?'

'She doesn't require one. The earth is her temple,' she said. 'Our home is one of many islands to the west. We sailed the Great Ocean and passed through the Pillars of Herakles to come here.'

'What brings you to our lands?'

'That King Mentor is a matter for the gods,' she said.

'Still, what you've said doesn't prove who you are,' King Mentor said. 'What is your intention while here?'

'We've yet to learn why the gods sent us here,' the High Priestess said. 'As mentioned earlier, we planned to go to Krete. However despite the skills of the captain and his crew, they could not change the ship's destination. They tried many times without success.'

'I'm not convinced that the nature of your business is benevolent. Your lack of a valid explanation and a good reason why the men in your party carry weapons is suspect. The quality is superior and denotes wealth. Could you be mercenaries sent here to kill me and my people?'

The High Priestess recoiled. Evan saw her golden bronze skin lighten a few shades and her hands shake.

'King Mentor, the divine blacksmith Hephaistos made these weapons. They are gifts from Divine Zeus,' Leander said, stepping to the fore, 'given to us for our protection. We are not here to kill you or anyone else.'

'How many mercenaries have you known or seen carry weapons of this calibre?' said Evan.

'Hmm... not many,' the king admitted.

'Would you like a closer look?' Evan felt his companions' eyes boring into his back and heard their muted protests. 'You are welcome to hold my sword,' he said. He could visualise Hektor's choked response and the look on his face.

Evan pulled the sword from the scabbard, and the sound of metal ringing reverberated in the megaron. The king's guards stiffened, their hands clasped spears and they watched in tense silence as Evan flipped the sword, hilt towards the king. The king stood, his scrutiny intense as he regarded Evan and then reached out to take the sword. Evan let go. The king's jaw clenched. He spread his legs and clasped the sword with both hands. The tip hit the floor. His eyes flashed up at Evan who stood out of reach, hands sitting idle at his side. The king took in a deep breath, bent his knees and tried to lift the sword.

His arms shook as he raised it a foot from the ground. The point dropped to the tiled floor sending small sparks into the air.

'Eumenides! Get over here!' the king snapped.

The captain of the warriors who escorted the group into the city hurried to his liege's side.

'Yes my king?'

'Lift the sword.'

He gave a sharp nod and grabbed the sword. His eyes widened for a second. The captain gripped the hilt with two hands. The muscles in his forearms bulged, and the veins popped as he struggled to raise the sword. He began to breathe heavily, the length of the weapon shaking as it moved upwards. His face took on an unhealthy pallor, and he gritted his teeth as he laboured to lift the weapon.

'Enough!'

Evan took the sword from the warrior and slipped it back into the scabbard. 'Can you recommend a good hostel for us to stay, a place fitting for a High Priestess?' he said.

King Mentor's attention shifted from Evan to the others and back to him. 'You will stay here in the palace as guests.'

Evan smiled. 'Thank you King Mentor, but we are more than happy to stay in the city.'

'I will not hear of it. My servants will take care of your needs, and I'm sure you'd want to bathe after a lengthy sea voyage. The guards will escort you to your quarters.'

CHAPTER FIFTY-FOUR

The king's reluctant guests were herded and chaperoned to the west wing of the palace. The High Priestess was afterwards shepherded to a series of rooms where the women resided. True to the king's word, baths were drawn and their clothes collected to be washed. New clothes were left for them when they finished. Never alone, each had two attendants who assisted.

'Excuse me, I don't mean to be rude but I can do this myself. I don't need your help,' Evan said, backing away from the female servants holding tight to his loin-cloth. 'And I much prefer if you wait outside the room.'

The two young women shook their heads. 'If we leave you alone, we will get into trouble with the king,' one said.

Evan grimaced. 'Fine but turn and face the wall.'

The girls giggled but did as requested. A little while later, refreshed and clothed, Evan emerged from the bath. The two attendants tittered as they trailed behind him. He joined the others in the courtyard and when the two girls neared they beamed at him, eyes sparkling with mirth. Evan's face reddened, the girls gave him a toothy grin and continued on their way.

'What happened?' Phameas said, noticing the exchange.

'Nothing,' Evan said and turned his back on the giggling attendants.

'We were discussing how to deal with our current predicament,' said Leander. He looked at the soldiers posted by the gateway to the enclosure.

'This is no guest-friendship,' said Hektor, glowering. 'We are detained against our will.'

'At least the accommodation is comfortable,' Evan said.

Hektor's mouth pressed into a thin line, his eyes contracted and he was clearly on the verge of launching into a tirade.

'Wait,' said Evan, putting up a hand. 'I agree with you. Unlike your previous incarceration, this is different. I don't get a sense King Mentor means any harm, but I do believe he doesn't intend to allow us to leave, not anytime soon.'

'To what end?' said Leander.

'If you wanted to keep track of those you aren't sure of, what would you do?'

'Keep them close,' said Phameas, 'see what they do and with whom they interact.'

Evan nodded. 'That's what I'd do. The king is wary of us and this way he can at least control our whereabouts.'

'We must earn his trust,' said the High Priestess.

The men stood, bowed and made room for her to sit.

'How? How can we convince the king we aren't a threat?' said Leander.

'We're wasting time sitting here and talking when we should leave,' said Hektor. 'The gods have tasked us to find sacred relics of the Mother Goddess and their wishes supersede those of a king. I will not be dictated to or confined again. We should force our way out.'

'Hush Hektor,' said the High Priestess, taking hold of his hand. 'You did what you could; you are not to blame for the actions of another.'

Homer patted him on the shoulder.

'There was nothing we could have done,' Leander added.

'We should have fought back,' Hektor said, biting back.

'If we did, the achievements of our predecessors and efforts to live in peace would mean nothing,' the High Priestess said. 'We don't want to repeat the transgressions of the ancients.'

'I do prefer diplomatic resolutions and it's always better to talk it out,' Evan said. 'Though in certain circumstances, I'd rather take action rather than sit back if one needs to defend oneself. It's better than being pummelled to death. The king hasn't made any threats so we wait.'

'And what we do in the meantime? We don't have time to sit around and linger so the king can make up his mind,' Hektor said.

'I am sure we won't be here long,' he said.

'You!' They turned to see a soldier tramp across the paved yard, pointing.

'Me?' Evan stood up.

'The king wants to speak to you.'

'Perhaps the High Priestess should come.'

The warrior shook his head. 'Just you.'

'Right.'

He could feel the weight of the others' eyes on him. Their anxiety was palpable as he walked away with the soldier and tried to ignore his own growing disquiet.

The king was sitting alone when Evan and the guard entered the throne room. Extra logs added to the hearth filled the room with smoke. The king viewed their approach with keen interest, his hand clasping a golden double handled cup. He took a sip as they came to stand before him.

'How were the baths and rooms?'

'Excellent King Mentor, and comfortable, thank you.'

'What is your name?'

'Evan...dros.'

'Of Atlantis?' the king said with a sceptical arch of his brow.

'I am a citizen of the world,' said Evan.

The king blinked and his mouth twitched for a few seconds before he composed himself. 'If you are from Atlantis you won't mind answering a few questions.'

'I'll do my best.'

'Who is the King of Atlantis?'

Damn, thought Evan, Come on! Think back to those visions! 'You ought to speak with the High Priestess,' he said stalling for time. 'She is one of the Elders and knows the city's history better than I.'

The king dismissed his suggestion with a wave of a hand. 'I'd have to offer a gift to her goddess and to be honest she'd be too much of a distraction. I want to bed her, not talk to her. One fine-looking woman amongst you all... do you share her?'

'So we are clear King Mentor, she is an honoured Elder and my sister.'

The king's mouth formed an O and he avoided Evan's steady gaze. 'Yes... well... you haven't answered my question.'

'Atlantis is no longer ruled by kings. The Elders of the Senate set the laws and govern the city, after the High Council has made their deliberation.'

'Are the Elders nobles?'

'Two positions are hereditary: one held by the High Priest of Poseidon and the other by the High Priestess. The other two Elders are elected from the High Council and preside for a year.'

'What is the function of the High Council?'

'They speak for the people, air their concerns and confer over civic matters. Each citizen spends one year as a member of the High Council and makes sure the Elders do not abuse their power.'

'If you are indeed Atlanteans, why hasn't communication been made till now?'

'The ancient Atlanteans promised the gods there'd be no contact with the outside world, and in exchange they'd permit Atlantis to grow and flourish.'

'But here you stand.'

'Yes.'

'Why are you here and why now?'

'As the High Priestess mentioned, it's a directive from the gods.'

'That's all you're going to tell me?'

'It's not for me to divulge the nature of their business.'

'You're either being secretive on purpose or it's one great big lie,' said the king, brandishing his cup at Evan spilling the contents.

'I wish it were the latter,' said Evan, 'then what's going on makes sense.'

'Care to explain what you mean?' The king raised his cup to his lips and took a drink.

'I'm still trying to work it out myself.'

'Kings don't have the luxury of reflecting and deliberating. We make decisions and are done with it.'

'You are fortunate.'

'Still, what you have told me or the little you revealed doesn't convince me,' the king said with a glint in his eyes. 'According to legends, Atlanteans were great hunters. Tomorrow we hunt wild boar.' The king stood up. 'Tell your companions to be ready, we leave at sunrise.'

He nodded at the soldier by Evan's shoulder. The man thrust an arm out, hand closed in a fist. Bemused, Evan stepped around the hearth, the armed guard right by his side.

On his return, he found the others sitting in the same place where he left them. Phameas and Dexion met him halfway, questions flying at him with the precision of an archer hitting a target. Leander and Homer came up behind them adding to the confusion.

'Whoa! Let me speak!' They quietened. 'He wanted to know more regarding the political structure of Atlantis, and that's it. The king still doesn't accept the story is true but has invited us to go hunting with him in the morning.'

'He'll let us use our own weapons?' said Hektor.

'I am assuming so.' Evan shrugged.

'What is he after?' said the High Priestess.

'The truth.'

CHAPTER FIFTY-FIVE

The king and a small group of invited nobles led Evan and the others out of the palace grounds, and into the forest north of the city precinct. The king's guard trooped behind, a reminder of the tenuous pact between the new arrivals and the king's goodwill.

'Why are we hunting the boar?' Leander said.

'The beast is destroying crops and eating fodder for our farm animals. Besides it is a vicious creature and will rip your stomach out if you stand in its way,' the king said over his shoulder.

'Oh good, I do enjoy a challenge,' said Hektor. The king looked at him searching for a hint of mockery but saw Hektor was serious.

'There's nothing better than pursuing a crazed boar, well except for chasing a lion or an enraged woman.' The king laughed. 'My servants will track the boar and drive it our way. The man to kill it gets first servings at the banquet this evening.'

Four young boys, not much older than Dexion, ducked away from the large group. They ran into the forest, each following a different path.

'Evandros! Come and walk with me,' the king ordered.

He despatched a handful of soldiers into the forest. The early morning sun shone off their helmets and gave away their erratic movements as they tracked the path of the boys. The group continued along, ears pricked and alert, searching the bushes for signs of movement. Evan held the spear the king provided in a loose grip, thinking how surreal this was, half listening to the excited chatter of the king and the other men. The smell of pine and myrtle and the warm sun bearing down on his head reminded him of the verdant and leafy National Park back home. He visualised himself standing by the war memorial and looking out across the city split in two by a large river.

Homer poked him between his shoulders with the butt of his spear. Evan stumbled and turned, half annoyed at being disturbed from a pleasant memory.

'What?'

Homer put a hand to his ear. Shouts followed by loud grunting and snorting drew near. Evan tightened his hold on the spear, and his heart thudded against his ribcage. The king changed direction and aimed for the noise and then a black, bristled and tusk bearing boar charged. Everyone scattered like pins falling in a bowling alley. The wild pig huffed and stampeded through their midst.

'After the beast!' shouted the king as he brandished a sword and ran after the animal.

Evan gave chase, the wind in his face, the sound of his breathing loud to his ears as he gained on the king. His feet pounded the ground, and within seconds he outran and outdistanced the others. He was less than a metre from the boar and threw the spear. It arced through the air and pierced the hog in the shoulder. It squealed, skidded, and turned.

'Oh cripes.' Evan took a step back, panting from his sprint. A shiny long object whistled past him. He watched the sword flash through the air, flipping from end to end at the injured boar. It flew over its head. The wild pig hurtled straight for him.

'This is not good,' he said.

'Evandros!'

He jumped into the air, tucked his knees and the animal raced on underneath him. The boar snorted, confused, slowed and continued to rush through thick bushes, making its own path. Evan, both feet back on the ground, pivoted to see where it went. Adrenaline surged and blood pumped through his veins like a fast flowing river.

'Come on!' said Hektor, running past him. 'We must go after it. It's losing blood and won't last long!'

They chased the boar as it wove in and out of unseen paths. The spear had fallen. The constant thrashing through the brushes had knocked it free. Sometime later, the animal slowed to a walk. The wild pig wheezed and rasped, and lowered its head. Its legs trembled and then it collapsed. It grunted as it sensed their presence and tried to lift its head.

'It's your kill,' said Hektor, passing him the sword.

Evan looked from him to Homer. He'd never before killed an animal. Homer gave him an encouraging nod. Evan took the sword from Hektor, stepped over to the boar, and placed a hand on its head.

'I am sorry,' he whispered. He then plunged the sword between the shoulder-blades and into the heart. He wiped the blade clean on the animal's bristles. Homer joined him and placed a hand on his shoulder. Hektor stood with them and the three stared at the fallen boar. Evan's ears twitched at the rustle of leaves and branches. Their sombre solitude was broken by shouts and the thunder of feet.

'By Zeus, are you all right?' said Leander just as he, Phameas and Dexion broke into the clearing. Dexion walked over to Evan and took his hand. Evan gave him a small smile.

'I am fine,' he said.

'In the name of the gods, just cut through it!' the king roared, expletives spewing from his mouth. 'Useless! Good for nothing imbeciles! My daughters make far better men than you!'

The sound of wood splintered and the whistle of blades drew closer. A body appeared at the brand new path and behind, still sputtering, was the king, his face a blotchy red. He shoved the servant aside, and the man fell face first into the dirt. King Mentor drew in a deep breath, expression as black as turbulent clouds, and stepped into the small clearing. He stared at the dead animal.

'Who slew the boar?' he said, as if the recent outburst hadn't happened.

'Evandros.' Hektor then added, 'He hit it with the spear and the boar charged at him. He jumped over the animal in the manner of our bull leaping. We gave chase and here we stand.'

'Bull leaping?' said the king, his head swivelling from face to face.

'Yes, a sacred ritual to the god Poseidon which we've done since our youth,' said Leander.

The king sniffed. 'I've heard the story since a boy but never believed a person performed it. It is an impossible feat.'

'Not at all,' said Leander. 'I've done it at least seven times.'

'No fewer than six,' said Hektor, pointing at himself.

Homer held up both hands. The king gawped.

'I can't remember how many,' said Evan, his gaze sliding away from the king's.

'If true then you can execute this incredible feat for me and the people of Pylos,' said the king. 'I have the finest and most ferocious bulls in this entire region.'

'Homer is our Master of Animals. He'll need to check the bulls and choose the right one,' said Leander. 'You need a large square area, the ground covered with a large quantity of sand and no obstacles.'

'The agora is big enough and I'll have the slaves cart extra sand. As for the bull, my herdsman will go with your man,' King Mentor said, eyes gleaming.

'Once we have completed this task, we leave,' Hektor said.

The king considered Hektor for a few minutes. 'If none of you is impaled by the bull, then yes, you are free to leave. Though, the odds of surviving are slim. It will take a few days to prepare the marketplace but first, a feast to celebrate the day's successful slaughter of the boar.'

On the walk back to the palace, Evan tried to think of ways to get out of the bull leaping. He exploded into a tirade back in the room he shared with Phameas and Dexion.

'I've never leapt a bull, ever! This is suicide! At best I am injured, at worst gored to death!'

'Master Evandros, you have done this many, many times,' Dexion said.

'Not in recent times!'

'You've nothing to worry about,' Dexion said. 'It's in your blood.'

'Are you delusional? I prefer to fight pirates!'

'I'm glad I don't have to face a bull,' said Phameas.

'You know how it's done,' said Dexion.

'In theory yes, but in practice, it's a whole different ballgame!'

'You will make the jump and survive,' the boy said with certainty.

'I suppose you've already seen it,' said Evan in a resigned tone.

Dexion nodded.

'I sure hope you're right.'

'This evening's feast will make you forget about it,' he said.

'I doubt it.'

Dexion grinned from ear to ear.

CHAPTER FIFTY-SIX

The feast held in the megaron resonated with laughter and voices competing to be heard. The story of how Evan killed the boar was recounted many times and with each telling embellished as the raucous evening drew on. The logs in the hearth crackled, the smoke eddying towards the oculus in the ceiling. Serving girls carrying large bronze platters of roast boar and leavened bread entered the room.

The king offered Evan the first piece of the mouth-watering meat then King Mentor took a piece, followed by the rest of the partygoers. A young woman poured wine into Evan's cup and gave a coy smile as their eyes met. He smiled back, feeling relaxed. She leaned in and whispered into his ear, her warm breath sending tingles along his spine. A warm rush and a surge of longing spread throughout his body. It had been a while since he'd been with a woman and her tantalising offer stirred deep. He was about to get up when the king clapped his hands.

'Esteemed guests, it's time for entertainment.'

The gilded doors swung open and in strolled three musicians. One held a five stringed instrument; another had a double reed fluted pipe; and the third, a three stringed object. It had a long neck and tapered into an oval shaped base with a hole at its centre. It reminded Evan of an early version of a mandolin. The musicians sat on stools and began to play a spirited tune. Six dancing girls appeared from a side door. Their movements were energetic and sensuous as they kept time with the music.

Evan watched, entranced by the beauty of one of the dancers. Attired in a golden diaphanous khiton, she had the serving girl's proposition forgotten in an instant. He could not take his eyes off her. The gown accentuated her curvaceous body, a tantalising and athletic figure. Observing her dance around the hearth and across the room and back again in time with the music was erotic. The lights flickered, as if caught by a breeze. Evan hadn't realised he was holding his breath until the music stopped. The girl stood still, chest heaving, the fabric straining against her breasts. Her golden brown eyes met his. It was as if he were swept away into the depths of a spellbinding trance. Then there was an explosion of enthusiastic cheers and clapping.

'Aren't they talented?' said the king over the din.

'Ah... yes, quite gifted performers,' Evan said. He stared at the young dancer, who with skill and a winning smile avoided the fervent clutches of amorous men.

'Antheia is an exceptional dancer,' said the king as he glanced at Evan with a sly smile.

'Antheia... a beautiful name,' he said in a murmur.

The musicians launched into a slower and seductive piece. The six women moved with deliberate subtleness that made Evan perspire. He picked up the wine goblet and tossed back the contents.

The heat from the hearth and crude wine made his head swirl. He stood and knocked over the stool.

'Excuse me King Mentor; it's a bit too warm in here. I need fresh air to clear my head.'

'I hope you are not unwell,' the king said, eyes twinkling.

'No, no... the heat from the hearth is... overwhelming.'

The king nodded, but did not hide the smile on his face. 'Of course, take your time.'

Phameas and Homer looked at him and stood to follow but Dexion leaned over and spoke, and they sat back down. Evan walked around the hearth and headed for the exit. He hurried through the vestibule and out onto the portico where the fresh cool air hit him and chilled his clammy skin. He shut his eyes and took a deep breath. The night air was calming and dried the perspiration on his face.

The music filtered through faintly. Its evocative lure began to lose potency the longer he stayed outside. He stretched his neck from side to side and gave himself a pep talk, as a boxer did waiting in the ring for the bout to start. He was about to head back inside when he sensed another presence behind him. His heart quickened. Melaina's face came to mind. He spun on his heel and saw the young dancer standing under the moonlight. He couldn't take his eyes off her as she walked closer. The fragrance of roses and the musk of her body quickened his pulse.

He cleared his throat. 'Shouldn't you be inside dancing?'

'I am no longer needed.' With feather-like fingers, she ran a hand along his arm, and the touch made Evan catch his breath. She clasped her hands around his neck and pressed her body against his. She pulled his head towards hers, her fathomless eyes fixed on his. Her gaze flashed to his mouth and then her soft lips were against his.

He wrapped his arms around her slight, curvaceous body. Her tongue thrust into his mouth, her arms tightened at his neck and fingers clutched at his hair as the dance evoked a deep response. She broke away, gasping.

'Come.'

She took his hand and led him away from the megaron. She turned right, and with quick steps passed through doorways and passages until they came to a staircase. They climbed the staircase and entered one of the small rooms that ran along the length of the second floor. Against the wall under the small window was a bed and opposite was a table. The curtain swung back into place as Evan entered the room. She removed the pins at her shoulders and the gown slipped to the floor. Evan sucked in a breath.

She pulled him towards her. The rapturous expression on her face smouldered as she removed the belt at his waist and the pin at his shoulder. The khiton fell away. His skin tingled when her hands dropped to his waist, her touch light as she undid the loincloth. It joined the discarded khiton. Her eyes caressed the length of his body as Evan drank in the sight of her. A broad smile covered her face when her gaze fell below his waist. Just as her gaze fondled his body, so did her hands, then her mouth as she rained kisses all over. Her tongue left a hot trail from his chest and moved with determination downwards.

Evan threw his head back and moaned as she stroked him with gentle, yet practised hands, and then with urgency. Unable to contain himself, Evan picked her up, placed her on the bed and covered her body with his. The events of the day soon became a distant memory.

***

The sun's radiant beams streamed through the small window, the shaft of light striking Evan in the face. He turned his head away and moved. A soft warm feminine body curled up against him. Evan moved her arm and placed it by her side. He eased out of bed, picked up his clothes from the floor, threw on the khiton and left, leaving the dancer asleep sprawled on the bed. He approached the staircase and had his foot on the first step when he heard giggling and whispering. He turned. Two girls from the dance troupe peered from behind a curtain of the room next door, faces beaming. He smiled, saluted and left.

He whistled on his walk back to the quarters assigned to them by the king, and decided to stop by the baths for a wash. No one was around. He stripped and lowered himself into the warm water. The soothing temperature and tranquil surrounds were relaxing and before he knew it, he'd dozed off.

'Ahoy, Evandros! Did you have a late night or an early start?' said Phameas, splashing water at his face.

'Wha…' Evan bolted upright and stared at the amused faces of Dexion and Homer. He gave them a lopsided grin. 'Both.'

'Have you had breakfast?' said Phameas. 'Oh wait, you just did.'

Phameas roared with laughter at his own joke and Homer chortled in silence. Dexion smiled.

'Very funny,' said Evan rolling his eyes. 'Can you pass me that towel?'

'The king is asking after you,' Phameas said. Dexion handed him the towel.

'What? Why?'

'Who knows, maybe he's disappointed you didn't stay around for the night's entertainment.' Phameas' eyes twinkled.

'Ha ha, very funny.' Evan dried off and wrapped the towel around his waist.

'I hope you're not going to see the king in that,' said Phameas in mock horror. 'The girl might be more than pleased but I don't think it's fitting for a king.'

'Would you stop it,' Evan said, taking a playful swipe at his friend.

Phameas laughed and dodged the swing. 'Better go and see what he wants.'

The throne room did not bear any remnants of the previous night's festivities. Gone were the long couches, stools, small tables and fur-lined rugs that covered most of the tiled floor. Only the smouldering ashes in the hearth remained. The king was waiting, eyes gleaming.

'Evandros, of fabled Atlantis come, come.' He clicked his fingers, and an attendant scurried forward with a stool. The king beckoned Evan to sit.

'King Mentor.'

'Did you enjoy the night's performance?'

Evan gave a mental groan. Discretion is not a better part of valour in these times. 'I did.'

'And the girl, was she to your liking?'

He hesitated. He wasn't one for discussing his relationships, not with anyone.

'Perhaps a boy is more to your taste,' the king said, the smile fading.

'What? No!' Evan said, startled. 'I was trying to find a polite way to say thank you.'

The king stared at him and then laughed till tears came to his eyes. 'Well I am pleased,' he managed to say. 'She's my most skilled concubine.'

'I am grateful to you but in particular to Antheia,' said Evan with a straight face.

The king chuckled and shook his head. 'I have spoken to my chief herdsman and he'll take your man Homer to see my herd. He'll be waiting by the eastern gate. You and I will go to the agora and discuss what is needed to prepare for the bull leaping.'

'If you agree, my companions should come as well. The collective memories of many are better than one,' Evan said.

'If you believe that will help. My guards will come for you in the hour.'

CHAPTER FIFTY-SEVEN

The light of the oil lamp flickered as Evan sat at a small table sketching. While visiting the agora earlier that day with the king, he had spent time studying the various buildings and the plan of the city. He wanted to capture every detail and when he did get back home he would transcribe the experience. As a child and in particular as a teenager, he'd cursed having an eidetic memory. But when he went to university and began work, he grew to appreciate and enjoy the unique ability. The benefit of writing it now meant the task was less arduous and easy to recall. His hand flew, images and annotations filled many blank pages.

He sat back and smiled, satisfied with what he'd produced. With a small groan he stood and stretched, moved his head from side to side, the tightness in his shoulders lessening. He looked out the window. Nestled below, under the protective watch of the palace, was the lower city of Pylos. The full moon lit the empty streets and dark buildings. He yawned, and took a step to move away just as a figure emerged and stood at the entrance by the ramp. The hairs on his arms stood on end. The person stepped away, casting a long shadow, and wandered towards the slumbering city. Evan shrank back when the person stopped, turned and glanced up. The figure resumed walking, seeming to float as it moved away. Long hair flowed in the wake of the night air. Without thinking, he left the room.

Evan dashed down the stairs and raced across the moonlit path, out of the palace grounds, stirring the king's sleepy guards. He came to an intersection, looked left and right, his heart galloping like a racehorse. Which way? Without a second thought, he turned left, and hurried past silent buildings, his feet slapping against the flagstone paths. Then he caught sight of her, just before she vanished around the corner at the end of the cobbled street.

He sprinted down the lane, feet beating a rapid staccato on the stones. He stopped when he came to the end, puffing. It was empty. He lifted his nose and sniffed.

'I'd recognise that perfume anywhere,' he murmured and followed the scent. 'Now I'm a bloodhound,' he said with a derisive snort.

Evan entered a narrow avenue that led to an open space. Further on was a temple dedicated to the city's patron god, Zeus. 'Nice little fan base you've got going here Dad,' he said and walked along the promenade. Whoever it was did not come through here, he thought, and turned to face the sanctuary.

The moonlight cast an ethereal light over the building. Evan strolled along the sacred way, drawn by the architecture and sheer size. To enter the grounds, he passed through the propylaeum and came to a stop at the foot of the steps of the temple. He gazed up at the tympanum where sculpted life-size images of Zeus and the other gods featured. He took in the columns, the girth of the drums and the seamless fit. Curious, he placed a foot on the marble step. Then he caught a glimpse of movement. He wheeled around. Nothing was there except the votive column and its long silhouette. A familiar sound caught his attention. He moved towards it, the grass cool under his feet. The roar of crashing waves grew louder as he drew to the edge.

'It's beautiful, wild and dangerous.'

Evan turned his head and saw Melaina. She stood a few steps away, her gaze fixed on the inky sea. She tilted her head a little to the side and gave him a small smile.

'Are you here to see me?' he said.

She looked at him, amused. 'Aren't you one full of self-importance.'

'That's not what I meant,' Evan said, somewhat flustered. 'What... why are you here?'

'That woman you were with, what does she mean to you?' Her face was obscured by the darkness and her tone wooden.

'Huh? Woman?' Evan said, thrown by the sudden change in conversation. 'Oh...' Then came the realisation of whom she meant. 'A sweet girl but if you're asking if I have feelings for her, then no.' He peered at her. 'Why do you ask?'

Melaina swung away, her back to him, and lifted her face to the sky as if listening to someone.

'I must go.' She spun on her heels, hesitated and looked over her shoulder. 'You must go to Delphi.' On quick and light feet, she ran along the rear of the temple, slipped around the corner and out of sight.

Evan stood fixed to the spot, stunned by her sudden departure, and then sprang into action. 'Wait!' He reached the corner, but she'd gone. 'Why Delphi?' he shouted into the air. 'What will I find there?'

A gentle breeze swept by him.

'There you will find answers.' The fragrance of lavender wafted close. 'You must visit Pythia, the Oracle of Apollo. Go to her and ask your question.'

'Wait! Please!'

He heard her chuckle. 'Until next time.'

CHAPTER FIFTY-EIGHT

Melaina sat back and observed with a satisfied smile as Evan circled the temple a few times calling her name. She watched him give up and leave, but not before he took one last time to search the grounds. She sighed, her heart heavy, and gazed with longing at his strong lithe body and the grace with which he moved. Quick and volatile as molten liquid mercury she scowled, recalling how the mortal wench enticed and lured him to her bed. Her stomach clenched, she balled her hands, flung her arms out and stretched her fingers.

'Melaina! Desist!' A deep voice thundered.

Her outstretched taut hands began to shake.

'Now!'

Melaina let her arms drop to her side, bowed her head and turned.

'Daughter,' the voice commanded. When she looked up, Kronos stood before her, his power radiating like the flares on the sun. He looked at her, expression forbidding. 'What are you doing here? You will jeopardise everything if they find you. I have taken a great risk to remain anonymous and if they learn of my existence what I have planned is for nought.'

'You worry too much, Father. You should be worried about Eris, as she has the power to ruin your plans,' she said with a coy smile. She stole a quick peek at Evan as he arrived back on palace grounds.

'Do not concern yourself with Eris,' he said, noting her object of attention. 'You will stay away from Zeus' changeling.'

Melaina's gaze swung back to her father.

'He is to be left alone, he's mine to attend to when the time comes.'

'I can help,' she said.

'I do not want you meddling,' he said. 'There is something amiss with that mortal and Zeus is behind it.'

'Let me be of assistance,' she said laying a hand on his arm. 'Evandros is curious and finds me attractive. If I earn his trust, I will learn who he is, what his powers are and where to find Mother's possessions. Once that happens, you can conquer Zeus and the other immortals. After your success, you are free to place the one you have chosen to lead the humans and obey you as the one almighty god.'

The pupils in Kronos' eyes dilated and then constricted as he contemplated Melaina's proposition. He put a hand over hers.

'It may work,' he said and his grip tightened on hers. Melaina's heart quickened and her mouth went dry. She clenched her teeth as he continued to squeeze her hand, the colour turning an angry red. 'If it doesn't, you will reside in Tartaros for eternity.' He let go. Melaina blinked back tears. 'If you are caught by Zeus or by chance your plans are found out, you are on your own.'

In a blink he was gone.

Melaina sobbed and cradled her bruised hand. As much as she despised her father she feared him more. She shuddered. She didn't relish the thought of spending endless days and nights in Tartaros. The scheme had to work.

***

In the dark realm of Tartaros, Eris paced back and forth waiting for the return of the harpies. A little anxious and annoyed at their tardiness, she lashed out, kicking the hindquarters of Orthos, a two-headed dog. He snarled and snapped at her.

'Do shut up, you worthless cur.' She stomped up to the throne and plonked herself on the unyielding stone seat. 'What is taking them so long? They should be back by now.'

Orthos growled.

Eris threw her head back, laughing. 'You will kill the Atlanteans?' She laughed even harder, doubling over in pain. Orthos' red eyes glowed and he bared his fangs. 'Do you believe you stand a chance against the Atlanteans, when that useless Herakles incapacitated you with an arrow?' The scowl on her face deepened. 'No, I don't think so. I must find out more in regards to the birth of this new god. And of the one who intends to remove the Gods of Olympos from their lofty and comfortable home. It will not be easy to thwart Zeus and his family, yet this immortal has found a way.' She pondered for a while and then called for a stymphalian bird.

'Seek out this god, the one who has caused a stir amongst our dear Olympians, and learn of his plans. I don't care how or what you do, just bring me the information.' As the bird turned to leave, Eris added as an afterthought, 'Don't kill too many mortals.' The bird opened her beak, showing off pointed teeth.

Eris summoned the chimaera and sphinx.

'Go find the harpies and send them back to me then follow the Atlanteans. Discover as much as you can of where they are and why. In particular, I want as much information on this Evandros as you can find. He is the key and I need to understand why.' She reached out and touched the cheek of the sphinx. 'Be mindful of the gods, they may no longer roam the world of the mortals but are ever so possessive. They will not hesitate to kill. Now go.'

The Goddess of Discord watched with a wistful expression as the pair leapt into the air and flew upward. They spiralled into the dark neck of Tartaros and disappeared, the void swallowing them.

Orthos barked.

'Well, that is to be seen Orthos. We must not underestimate these Atlanteans. Even though they lived in isolation for over eight millennia that does not mean they haven't learnt new tricks. Remember, they were the greatest power of their time. Regardless of their isolation, one does not forget what it felt like to be supreme rulers. Even the mildest mannered human can change given the right motivation.'

CHAPTER FIFTY-NINE

Evan sat on the edge of the bed, foot tapping as he waited for Phameas and Dexion to wake. He drew in a deep breath and exhaled out loud. Phameas rolled onto his back, opened an eye, sighed and sat up.

'What is it?' he said, yawning.

'You are not going to believe who I ran into!' he said edging closer on the wooden frame of the bed.

'I have no clue. Tell me,' said Phameas rubbing his groomed beard.

Dexion mumbled and turned over to face the wall.

'Melaina.'

Phameas stopped what he was doing. 'What? Who? Say that again.'

'I met with Melaina last night.'

Dexion propped himself on an elbow and gaped at him.

'You didn't...' Phameas said with a wave of a hand.

'No! We just talked,' said Evan, affronted.

'Oh... what about?'

'She said we must go to Delphi and talk to Pythia.'

'What and who?'

'Pythia,' repeated Dexion. He bolted upright and got out of bed. 'The most powerful oracle in the world. Why did she tell you to visit her?'

'She didn't say, just that Pythia may well give us the answer we need.'

'You must tell the High Priestess,' said Phameas, thrusting the blanket off and getting out of bed. 'She'll want to hear of your meeting.'

'I'll go and get her,' said Dexion. He ran out the door leaving the two men alone.

'So you chatted,' Phameas said, eyebrow raised.

'Yes! Nothing else happened.'

'Oh well, there's always next time.'

'That's what she said.' Evan stared at Phameas, who grinned and patted him on the shoulder as he walked to the doorway.

'My boy is growing up.' Phameas gave a sniff, wiped a fake tear from his eye and exited the room.

Evan dropped his head and groaned. He heard Phameas' big belly laugh echo outside in the courtyard.

Everyone gathered by the citrus trees, the new blooms of which perfumed the air. Stone benches placed against the walls under the trees provided much needed shade from the mid-morning sun.

'Do you think it's a trap?' said Leander once Evan finished telling them of his bizarre meeting with Melaina.

'Of course! First our ship is redirected here by an elder god and now this goddess appears the instant we land. Nothing about this feels right,' said Hektor.

'I agree we need to be cautious. There is more going on than we first assumed,' the High Priestess said. 'I am concerned she has fixated on Evandros for these odd encounters. The question is why and what is her intent. Is she doing this of her own accord, or is she acting on behalf of another?' Her ice blue eyes serious as she turned to Evan. 'What impression did she give you?'

'I still think she is curious, trying to work me out. I must admit, this titbit of information has thrown me. It sounded genuine, like she wanted to help. Then the question regarding the girl came from nowhere.'

'She's jealous,' the High Priestess said.

'Well that's crazy. I met her once and then again last night. Why would she be jealous?'

'The gods and goddesses aren't bound to the Earth as we are. They come and go as they please, see and hear more than we can ever comprehend. It's possible she's been watching you for a while.' She paused. 'Have you, since the departure from Atlantis, noticed or suspected another presence?'

Evan opened his mouth to say no but changed his mind. 'There was an incident back at the port of Rusaddir. I thought there was someone following me but there wasn't. Then there's the time when we rescued you from the king of Kyrene. There's a temple built on the slopes and I swear I saw someone watching as we walked to the palace.'

'It was her.'

'Or it may have been this elder god,' Evan pointed out.

The High Priestess shook her head. 'No, she's been tracking you.'

'So what do we do? We can't stay here, it makes us targets,' Hektor said.

'We go to Delphi.'

'What?'

'It might be an ambush!'

Objections flew fast and became more heated. The High Priestess sat and waited until they ran out of excuses. She turned to Dexion.

'Do you sense any danger in going to Delphi?'

Dexion closed his eyes, face tilted skywards. He stood that way for ten minutes. When he opened his eyes, he said, 'Pythia is waiting for us. The message is genuine.'

'It's settled then, we are leaving,' the High Priestess said.

'The king is expecting us to perform the sacred bull leaping in a few days,' said Leander.

'I will meet with the king and explain we must go,' she said.

'I don't think the king will care too much as to why we have to leave. He's set on the idea of us jumping,' Leander said.

'I will help him understand how important it is we leave,' she said, standing. 'We are not here to perform tricks and satisfy the whims of a king.'

'About time!' said Hektor.

The High Priestess called one of the guards. 'Tell King Mentor I wish to speak with him.'

'I don't take orders from a woman,' he said.

Homer and Hektor stood, towering over the man. 'Show the respect our High Priestess deserves and go tell the king of her request,' Hektor said. Homer laid a heavy hand on the man's shoulder and squeezed. The warrior winced, his knees buckling. The other guards came rushing forward.

'You don't want to do anything stupid right now,' Leander said stepping forward to confront them. Evan, Phameas and Dexion moved with him.

'I will... go to... the king...' the warrior said, gasping.

Homer smiled and lifted his hand. The man took a swift step back and out of arm's reach.

'Best you leave now or one of my companions will go in your stead,' the High Priestess said.

The warrior whirled on his heel and left the courtyard. The remaining guards, spears clutched in hand, stood in a line and within launching distance.

'This may turn ugly,' Evan said in a soft voice.

'Quite,' Leander agreed.

'I am prepared to fight,' said Hektor drawing up next to Leander.

The warriors, in unison, took a step and lifted their lances.

'Let me pass.'

Evan glanced back at the High Priestess, noticed the look on her face and stepped aside. Her voice was soft as she moved towards the soldiers, the words rhythmic and repetitive. The courtyard grew brighter and brighter and soon a white light enveloped her. She raised her hands at the guards. A bolt of light struck their weapons and turned them into sand. Pools of fine granules lay at their feet, and the warriors stood stripped bare of their arms with their sweat stained tunics revealed. Their mouths gaped. With stunned expressions they looked at their empty hands and patted their chests where the gleaming bronze cuirass sat seconds ago. A few touched their heads as if expecting to touch helmets.

'What have you done to my men?' King Mentor thundered. A retinue of more soldiers accompanied him. He pushed through his disarmed guards just as a flash charged from the High Priestess' hands. The warriors cried out; the king turned and witnessed their weapons disintegrate. He turned back to the High Priestess, mouth ajar.

'We are leaving, King Mentor,' she said, still luminous. 'Our time together has come to an end. The gods have grown weary of your antics and if you prevent us they will show their displeasure.' She lifted her face to the sky. 'Yes, Mother? Of course, I shall tell the king.' She looked back at the king, who flinched. 'The queen is with child. She is carrying your son.'

'You tell lies! My wife is beyond her child bearing years!'

'Not so. She is in her prime. Our Mother wishes to give you a personal message.' The High Priestess strode towards the king and placed an incandescent hand on his forehead. King Mentor fell to his knees as the light blanketed his body. Everyone watched in breathless silence as the two radiant forms, one standing and the other kneeling, remained motionless. Minutes later, the light faded and the king was sobbing. The High Priestess moved her hand from his forehead to his bearded cheek. He looked up at her, eyes shining, tears running down the side of his face.

'A son? After all these years...'

'He will make you and your wife proud and be a good leader to his people,' the High Priestess said with a smile.

'The Mother Goddess blessed my wife and me with a long awaited son. I will build a temple in her honour and appoint priestesses to keep her shrine burning day and night,' he said, wiping the tears with a hand.

'Our Mother doesn't require a temple,' she said. 'She asks you plant a tree on the hilltop, declare it sacred to her and on your son's birth, bring him to be presented to her.'

The king nodded. 'I shall.' He rose to his feet. 'I will have the servants bring what you need for your passage to Delphi. My soldiers will escort you to the farthest reaches of our lands. I'll have my cartographer give you a map with the main roads to Parnassos Mountain.' He beckoned a few soldiers and as soon as he finished speaking, the men hastened away. He glanced back at the High Priestess. 'If at any time you need my help, do not hesitate to send a message and I will come.'

'Thank you King Mentor, your offer is most generous and if our need is such, we will be in touch.'

'When do you wish to depart?' he said.

'As soon as possible.'

He nodded. 'The quest you are on is of great importance and one you must succeed in completing. You will have my finest wagon and horse to carry provisions.'

'My thanks again, King Mentor,' she said.

'I will have the horse and cart ready within the hour by the entrance.'

'We'll pack and be there as soon as possible.'

The king bowed, and had a few of the soldiers stay behind to escort them to the main gate while the main cohort followed him. He barked out instructions, and in ones and twos, they ran to obey.

'I am glad the Mother Goddess was here,' said Leander. 'No doubt once she spoke to King Mentor, he could not deny her wishes.'

'Mother helped him be aware of our purpose and of his future,' the High Priestess said.

'I'll say,' said Evan. 'Whatever you did, the king is now our best friend.'

'I didn't do anything,' she said with a stiff lip. 'Mother prevailed on the king to envision a world with his progeny and legacy for years to come. She gave him what he'd desired.'

'She made his wife pregnant?' Evan said, alarmed.

'Mother provided the opportunity the king and queen did the rest.'

'She interfered,' he said with disapproval.

'Nonsense. Mother helps those who ask for her aid, nothing more.'

'Still, I don't think…'

'Evandros, don't question the actions of the Mother Goddess, she alone has the right to make such judgements. You should understand this. And given our circumstances, we needed her. Now, we pack and take our leave.'

The High Priestess swept past him and headed to her room. Hektor looked him up and down and stalked off. Leander gave him a puzzled look and took off after Hektor.

Homer slapped Evan across the back of the head and thrust forward his tablet. *What is wrong with you? You need to be more careful or do you want their suspicions confirmed?*

Evan stared at his scrawl. A feeling of dread crawled up his spine. 'They are suspicious of me? What do you know?'

Homer glowered at him, wiped the tablet clean and scribbled fast. *I know more than you realise about where you've been. If you want that part of your life to continue to be a secret, be smart about it. You are intelligent enough to keep the pretence going otherwise you jeopardise everything.*

Blood drained from Evan's face and his body chilled. 'How is it possible you have any knowledge of who I am and where I am from?'

Zeus is my father too. I am here to protect you.

'Holy shit! Were you sent away too? Why weren't you my brother there?'

No, Father wanted me to stay here, though he did bring me on a several occasions to observe you in your new surroundings. And he kept me informed for when the time came for you to return, I am here to help.

'The rotten scoundrel! The bastard played me.' Evan clenched his teeth.

If Father didn't send you away you'd have been killed and everything lost, Homer wrote. *It was the only way.*

'That's what he told you, right? Words he wanted you to hear and believe?'

Do you really think Father would go to the trouble of sending you to the remote distance in the future and bring you back now so you can be killed? Homer shook his head. *The knowledge and skills you acquired give us the best possibility to succeed. More than that, an opportunity to survive.*

'This is stupid. Why did he send me and not you?'

Father realised you'd adapt more easily and be more accepting of your situation.

Evan sat with a thump on the bench. 'This is too much. You tell me this is where I am from, yet it feels wrong. This is not my world.'

Homer sat next to him and put an arm around his shoulders. *It's a lot to grasp. The first time Father took me to check on you it was a shock seeing all those machines, the roads, buildings, and the people. I did wonder how you'd fare but like a dolphin swims in the ocean, you took to this new world and thrived.*

They fell silent and then Evan said, 'No wonder you were happy to see me and didn't worry about my strangeness.'

Homer smiled, a crooked lilt on his mouth.

'Do the others know you're my brother?'

He shook his head.

'Let's keep it to ourselves, at least for now,' said Evan. He looked over to Phameas and Dexion who'd stood by and watched the exchange. The perplexed expression on Phameas' face gave him pause. He stood up. Phameas stepped back.

'What do you mean this is not your world?' the Phoenician said.

'I'm a little confused about that myself,' Evan said, scratching his head. 'It's hard to explain, as I'm not sure I believe it.' He took a deep breath. 'This,' he said with a sweeping gesture, 'is not when I am from.'

'When?' said Phameas. He looked from Homer to Dexion. 'What is that supposed to mean? What's when?'

'Master Evandros has shades of the past, present and future,' said Dexion. 'Although this is his true home, he is unable to accept his fate.'

'Wait, wait... back on the ship, Evandros said something about the twenty-first century. Isn't that a place?'

Evan bowed his head, finding the stonework of the courtyard much more interesting than answering his friend's question.

'Not quite,' he said in a soft voice, 'it's the name given to a particular period. Do you remember my asking you what year it was?' Phameas nodded. 'I wanted to know how far back I'd been sent.'

'Sent? By who?'

'Zeus, my father, and Homer's as well. Only I didn't know we were brothers until just today.'

'Zeus?'

'He'd be the equivalent to your god Baal.'

Phameas' eyes widened. 'You're gods!' He began to stumble over his words. 'I knew it! I said it the first time I saw the weapons that you were a god.'

Evan shook his head. 'I'm not a god. How can I be? I'm stuck here. Phameas, I am still the same person you fished out of the sea. The one you taught Phoenician, how to row, who fought the pirates with you.'

'Why didn't you tell me the truth about where...*when*...you came from?'

'If I didn't believe it myself how can I convince you?'

'I might have believed it,' Phameas said. 'You should have trusted me.' Phameas looked like a wounded animal.

'I agree and I do,' said Evan.

Phameas stared at his feet. 'This future you're from, is it a hundred years or two from now?'

'No, about three thousand years give or take a century or two.'

Phameas' mouth fell open. 'Moloch!' He paled. 'I need to sit.' His knees began to tremble. Evan rushed to his side, grabbed his elbow and guided him to the bench.

'Put your head between your knees, it will help get the blood flowing and calm you down,' said Evan. He patted Phameas on the back. 'That's how I felt when Zeus brought me here and then I was furious.'

Phameas nodded, his head still lowered. 'I can understand why.' He raised his head and gazed at Evan with a solemn expression. 'It must be difficult, taken from your home and all that's familiar to you.'

'It hasn't been easy but you and Dexion have helped... much more than you realise.'

Phameas smiled at him. 'And will continue to do so.'

'Thank you my friend.' Evan turned to Dexion and Homer. 'I am grateful to each of you.'

As he went to his room to pack, his mind tunnelled deep into memories of the life he once lived, drawing a comparison with the ancient world he had been thrust into.

Would he find the last relic?

He thought it was probable.

Would he be able to return to his 21st century home?

He wasn't sure.

AUTHOR'S NOTE

For the name of characters and places, I have used the transliteration of their Greek names and not their Latin form. To understand these changes, the following modifications were adapted from Latin to pseudo-Greek:

AE=AI, C=K, OE=OI, U=OU, Y=U, -ER=-ROS, -UM=-ON, and -US=-OS.

For example: Achilles = Akhilleus, Medusa = Medousa, Hephaestus = Hephaistos, Hippolytus = Hippolytos

Please note: I am not expert in the Ancient Greek language but tried to honour the spelling.

In the case of Egyptian and Phoenician names and places I have used their proper form.

THE LABYRINTHINE JOURNEY
SERVANT OF THE GODS: BOOK 2

Follow Evan as he continues his odyssey as Servant of the Gods in *The Labyrinthine Journey*. The quest to locate the sacred object adds pressure to the uneasy alliance between Evan and the Atlanteans. His inability to accept the world he's in, and his constant battle with Zeus, both threaten to derail the expedition and his life.

Traversing the mountainous terrain of the Peloponnese and Corinthian Gulf to the centre of the spiritual world, Evan meets with Pythia, Oracle of Delphi. Her cryptic prophecy reveals much more than he expected; something that changes his concept of the ancient world and his former way of life.

To keep up-to-date with the latest news on the developments of the Servant of the Gods series visit:
http://www.luccav.com
and sign up for the FREE e-Bulletin
http://eepurl.com/bhESs1

411

ABOUT THE AUTHOR

Historical fiction fantasist Luciana Cavallaro, and a secondary teacher, meanders from contemporary life to the realms of mythology. Luciana has always been interested in Mythology and Ancient History but her passion wasn't realised until seeing the Colosseum and the Roman Forum. From then on, her inspiration to write Historical Fantasy was borne.

She is the author of 5 eBooks and 1 paperback and has spent many lessons promoting literature and the merits of ancient history.

Subscribe to her free short story at http://www.luccav.com.

Mythos | Publications

www.luccav.com

For more information, visit our website where you'll also find
exclusive discounts, competitions and giveaways.
Be sure to sign up to our monthly e-Bulletin to keep up to
date with our latest releases, news and upcoming events.